The Critics on Erica James

'There is humour and warmth in this engaging story of love's triumphs and disappointments, with two well-realised and intriguing subplots' *Woman & Home*

'Scandal, fury, accusations and revenge are all included in Erica James' compelling novel ... this story of village life in Cheshire is told with wit and humour' *Stirling Observer*

'Joanna Trollope fans, dismayed by the high gloom factor and complete absence of Agas in her latest books, will turn with relief to James' ... delightful novel about English village life ... a blend of emotion and wry social observation' *Daily Mail*

'An entertaining read with some wickedly well-painted cameo characters. It's a perfect read if you're in the mood for romance' *Prima*

'This is a really sparkling novel, full of drama and laughter'
Bookcase

'A bubbling, delightful comedy which is laced with a bittersweet tang ... a good story, always well observed, and full of wit. The characters walk out of the pages to greet you, and you know you are in good hands from the start – a very assured comedy' *Publishing News*

'Erica James is now a household name in the world of romantic novels' *Manchester Evening News*

'Erica James' sensitive story ... is as sparklingly fresh as dew on the village's surrounding meadows ... thoroughly enjoyable and fully deserving of a place in the crowded market of women's fiction' *Sunday Express*

'Wry humour and romance ... Erica James is a breath of fresh air' *Daily Mail*

'Another witty, sharply observed tale of the kind that we've come to expect from this author. James' readers won't be at all disappointed with this book' *Woman's Weekly*

Born in 1960, Erica James grew up in Hampshire. Since then she has lived in Oxford, Cheshire, Yorkshire and Belgium. After a series of diverse administrative jobs ranging from Oxford college to supplier of mining explosives, Erica decided that the best employer would be herself. There then followed several burning-the-midnight-oil years of cottage industry before she finally turned to an even harder life of toiling at the fictional coal-face of novel writing. She now lives in Cheshire with her two sons, Edward and Samuel. Her short stories have won prizes in various competitions, her first novel, *A Breath of Fresh Air*, was selected for the W H Smith's Fresh Talent promotion and *Airs & Graces* was shortlisted for the 1998 RNA Romantic Novel of the Year Award.

By the same author

A Breath of Fresh Air
Airs & Graces
A Sense of Belonging

Time For a Change

ERICA JAMES

ORION

An Orion Paperback
First published in Great Britain by Orion in 1997
This paperback edition published in 1997 by
Orion Books Ltd,
Orion House, 5 Upper St Martin's Lane,
London WC2H 9EA

Reissued 1999

A CIP catalogue record for this book
is available from the British Library.

Typeset by Selwood Systems, Midsomer Norton
Printed and bound in Great Britain by
Clays Ltd, St Ives plc

To Edward and Samuel
who said it would be all right

Thanks to everyone who helped me through *Time For A Change*. To Big G for making it happen. To Helena for the gossip and inspiration. To Maureen for the laughs and kind words of encouragement. To Miranda and Adrian for the quality bed and breakfast facilities. To John and Eirian for the long, long phone calls. To Jonathan and Victoria at Curtis Brown.

And lastly, but by no means least, thanks to Jane and Sarah at Orion who know how to make a girl feel great.

'Change is not made without inconvenience,
even from worse to better.'

Richard Hooker 1554–1600

'The mind is its own place, and in itself
Can make a heav'n of hell, a hell of heav'n.'

Paradise Lost
John Milton 1608–74

Chapter One

Hilary Parker was a Monday-morning kind of person, but there was something not quite right about this particular Monday morning.

Usually she liked nothing better than to answer Terry Wogan back while bustling about her large cluttered kitchen, organising breakfast with one hand and sorting out her daughter's lunch-box and her son's chaotically filled sports bag with the other. She believed in taking the start of any day firmly by the horns and meeting it head on. Today, though, Hilary had the uneasy feeling that something was wrong.

She popped a couple of tea-bags into the Welsh-dresser-shaped teapot and swept aside the thought that a potential disaster was hanging over her.

Breakfast dealt with, she watched David make his escape to his estate-agency office in the centre of the village and then she began the ritual of shouting at the children to make them get a move on while she filled the washing machine and added a few last-minute thoughts to her shopping list. Eventually, when Becky had found her gloves – not the plain blue hand-me-downs from Philip, but the cream pair with the fluffy bits at the wrists – they set off to wait for the bus to take Philip to his new school. One child down and one to go, Hilary took her seven-year-old daughter's hand and crossed the road to join the posse of frazzled mothers heading for the local primary school.

It wasn't until Hilary had reached home and drawn breath

as she stood over the washing machine waiting for it to finish its last spin cycle that she could no longer avoid the unconscious thought that was battling its way through the Monday-morning rush-hour traffic of her mind. Had she forgotten to do something?

She bent down to the machine and looked through the glass port-hole. She caught strobe-like flashes of Becky's pink pyjamas being chased by a pair of Philip's rugby shorts. The machine finally shuddered to a halt and she waited impatiently before the door-release button would work. She debated whether to go and clear the breakfast things from the kitchen table but the nagging worry wouldn't leave her. Was she supposed to have telephoned somebody? Was it some PTA matter? Georgia D'Arcy could be quite sharp if she felt people weren't pulling their weight.

She pressed the button and started hauling out the clothes. First came Philip's determined shorts, followed by a tangled ball of leggings, socks and pyjamas. She tugged hard at the bulky mound until it finally burst free – pulling washing out through that black rubber ring always reminded Hilary of childbirth, especially Philip's difficult breech birth.

No. It wasn't something she hadn't done. It was David. Something *he* had done.

She moved the basket of wet clothes to one side and refilled the machine, pushing David's work shirts into the gaping hole; something that never failed to give her pleasure. Ever since they had been married and she had washed and ironed David's shirts she had enjoyed the smell of maleness from his clothes. She picked up the last of the shirts, the one he had worn last night for a Rotary Club dinner.

Last night. That was it. David had been talking in his sleep.

Then suddenly there it was: the nagging subconscious knowledge that had been with her throughout the darkness of night to the break of day was finally free and she heard David's words as clearly as if he were crouched on the floor next to her and reciting them: '*Catherine ... Hilary must never find out ... she'd never forgive me ... the children.*'

She gasped and crushed the shirt to her face, but something hard in the folds of the fabric scraped against her cheek. She pulled out a small restaurant card together with a bill. The strip of paper had yesterday's date on it and showed it was a meal for two.

But David had said he was going to a specially arranged Rotary Club dinner ... '*Catherine ... Hilary must never find out.*'

Well, she had. She bloody well had!

Hilary turned the key in the ignition of her car. 'It can't be true, it just can't be. Not David!' She pressed hard on the accelerator and launched her Renault Clio out of the drive. She hurtled noisily down Acacia Lane, ignoring the look of outrage on the face of Iris Braithwaite, who was already hard at work sweeping the autumn leaves from the baize-green lawn of the White Cottage, and drove through the village, past the row of shops including David's black and white half-timbered office and reached the supermarket in less than ten minutes. She bolted into the first available space in the car park.

Inside the store and propped up by a trolley, Hilary gripped her shopping list. Fruit, vegetables, she muttered. Fruit, vegetables. How could he? How could he have an— She scrunched up her shopping list unable to utter, even in her head, the unthinkable. Anger and bewilderment threatened to overwhelm her and she made for the neatly constructed pyramids of fruit, which normally appealed to her sense of everything being well ordered and exactly placed. 'A home for everything,' she always told the children. David wasn't tidy, though. Ties strewn all over the bedroom, trousers left on the ... Her throat tightened and her legs went wobbly. She felt sick.

Concentrate, she told herself. The shopping. She ripped off a plastic bag and with shaking hands she picked an apple from the top of the pyramid of Granny Smiths. She carefully selected another three but as she reached for a fifth her hand knocked against the pile and she watched in helpless horror as she set off a shiny green avalanche; apples cascaded onto the floor, bumping against her legs as they fell.

'No!' she cried out. 'No. Stop it.' Tears streaming down her cheeks she fled, aware of people staring at her as she skittered up the next aisle. She raced alongside the shelves throwing things into the trolley: baked beans, sweetcorn, flour, rice.

Why had she come? What was she doing here in the supermarket? She had just discovered her husband was having an affair and she was doing the weekly shop. Was she mad?

On autopilot she reached the aisles of frozen food. Pizzas, garlic bread, peas. Stir-fry vegetables, where were they? It was Monday. She always did stir-fry vegetables for David on a Monday evening. She leaned over the freezer, pushing the packets of frozen broccoli and cauliflower aside in her determination to find what she was looking for. 'Where are they? They must be here.'

'Hilary?'

She jerked upright and found herself face to face with her neighbour Cindy Rogers, who together with her husband Derek ran In the Pink, the thriving health and beauty centre in Acacia Lane. As ever Cindy's hair and make-up were immaculate. Hilary felt Cindy's critical eyes sweep over her. 'Hello, Cindy,' she said. Her voice sounded breathless and overly cheery.

'You okay?'

'Of course I am ...' *Catherine ... Hilary must never find out ...* 'I'm fine, why wouldn't I be?'

Cindy was convinced Hilary looked far from well. It was obvious that the Princess of Hulme Welford – as Derek called

4

their neighbour – had been crying. She said nothing and reached into the freezer for a packet of peas. If Hilary was upset and didn't want to share it, then that was her business and Cindy certainly wasn't going to get involved in someone else's problems if she could help it.

'I'm fine, really,' Hilary repeated, 'just a bit of a cold, that's all. It's always the same – soon as the children go back to school after the summer holidays it's an endless stream of colds and runny noses' ... *she'd never forgive me* ... 'run down a bit I suppose if I'm honest.' The flow of words came to an end and she stood staring blankly at Cindy.

'How's David?' Cindy asked. It was all she could think of to say.

'David? Oh, he's fine. Busy, working all hours, you know what it's like.' He had, hadn't he? He'd been coming home later and later just recently. And there'd been all those phone calls in his study with the door shut. Oh, it was all so obvious! How could she have been so blind and not seen the signs? Her lip trembled.

Cindy didn't know what to do. She hated being confronted with emotion of any kind. She'd spent a lifetime keeping hers in check and she expected others to do the same. 'I must get a move on,' she said. 'I only slipped out for some—'

'Yes, of course, don't let me keep you, I know how busy you are.'

'I'll see you, then, Hilary. Why don't you call me some time? Treat yourself to a facial.' Heaven only knows she could do with it.

'Yes, perhaps I will.' What, at their prices? Hilary watched Cindy push her trolley further up the line of freezer compartments. But suddenly she felt frightened at being left alone. Cindy might be an ice maiden but her company right now seemed infinitely better than her own. 'Cindy,' she called out. 'I just wondered ...'

'Yes?'

Something in Cindy's manner was so cold, so matter-of-fact, it prompted a mirrored reaction from herself. 'I've just discovered David's having an affair,' she said. She saw Cindy's hand tighten on her trolley, her long pearly pink nails curling round the metal handle. 'I ... I don't know what to do,' she added, her voice now wavering and not at all stoic as she had intended.

'Come on,' Cindy said, 'I'll take you home.'

They abandoned their shopping, left Hilary's car in the car park and drove back to The Gables in Cindy's brand new Celica.

'I'm all right. Really I am,' Hilary said, sniffing loudly as they got out of the car.

'Don't be ridiculous,' Cindy threw at her. 'You feel awful. You feel like your world's just come to an end. I should know.' She glanced over the road towards In the Pink. 'Just remember who I'm married to.'

Cindy made Hilary sit in a chair next to the Aga. She filled the kettle and to her shame found herself cringing at the state of Hilary's kitchen. While her own kitchen was spotless and devoid of clutter, Hilary's worktops were lined with rows of brightly coloured tins, above which were intricately carved shelves weighed down with a hundred and one cookery books. Did anyone really cook that much? She herself ate little more than a lightly dressed salad each night. She reached out for one of the brightly coloured tins, hoping it contained coffee. It was tea and behind it was a faint tidemark of dust. She pulled a face, wondering how long it was since there had been the merest hint of Jif behind the tins. Weeks possibly. Months more like it. But whatever else had been going on at The Gables just recently it certainly wasn't any cleaning, not to her way of thinking anyway.

She poured out the tea into two mugs with pictures of huge pigs on tiny legs. 'Here you are,' she said to Hilary, who was now sitting at the kitchen table, her elbows resting amongst the breakfast things. There were toast crumbs and splashes of milk everywhere. A blob of orange marmalade was clinging to the side of the jar. Cindy had to fight the urge to gather up all the offending mess and put the kitchen straight. It would be a far easier task than trying to reassure Hilary that everything would be all right. In her experience, once a man had one affair it didn't stop there.

Hilary sniffed. Cindy glanced round the kitchen for a box of tissues. All she could see was some kitchen roll on one of those green cast-iron posts. She tore off a square and handed it to Hilary.

'Cindy, I'm so sorry to land you with all this ... I didn't mean for you to ...' She sniffed again.

Blow it, for goodness' sake, Cindy thought.

'Look,' Hilary said. She pushed a small piece of paper across the table towards Cindy.

Cindy read the restaurant bill. It was familiar enough. 'Could it have been an ordinary business dinner?' she responded. She had asked herself the same question twenty-two years ago, a year after her first wedding anniversary.

'No,' Hilary whispered. 'He told me he was going to a Rotary Club dinner. He lied to me, Cindy. He's been coming home so late these past few weeks, and he talked in his sleep last night. Her name's Catherine ... How could he, how—' She began to cry.

Cindy didn't want Hilary to cry but she had no idea how to stop her. She sipped her tea and tried hard not to think of the grotesque pig in her hand. Instead she thought of herself twenty-two years ago: first she had found a restaurant receipt, then a letter and then the phone calls had started. She had tried to ignore it, just as her mother had advised her. 'Let him get it out of his system. It'll blow over.' And it had. Until the next gust of wind had brought with it another black cloud almost a year later.

Another sniff from Hilary made Cindy put down her mug

with a bang. 'So what do you want to do, Hilary?'

'Do? What do you mean?'

'You either confront David with this,' she waved the small piece of paper in the air, 'and risk losing everything, or you pretend you never found it.'

'Pretend I never found it!' Hilary shouted, her bloodshot eyes wide in bewilderment. 'How can I do that? I mean, he's been ... he's been ...' Her voice trailed away.

Cindy leaned forward. 'It just happens in some marriages. Particularly in mine.'

'Oh, God, Cindy. I'm sorry. I've been so insensitive to you, haven't I?'

Cindy nearly smiled. She knew only too well that in the nineteen months they'd been living in the village of Hulme Welford it had become common knowledge what sort of a man Derek Rogers was. It was also generally accepted that Cindy knew exactly what was going on but chose to turn a blind eye to his infidelity and, more importantly, nobody spoke to her about it. Though recently she had become increasingly concerned about Derek's behaviour, but for the life of her she could not work out exactly what was wrong. It was odd that he had taken to reading all those strange books – that really was out of character. It was the first time she had known him to sit still long enough to get through anything more detailed than the front page of the *Daily Mail*. She was concerned that Derek was dissatisfied with his life. Perhaps even the affairs had begun to pall for him. So what was next?

'You have to decide what it is you want, Hilary,' she said at last. 'I presume you do love David.'

'How could you ask such a question?'

'I'm sorry, but it would make things easier if you didn't.'

'Don't you love Derek, then?' Hilary asked, hardly daring to ask Cindy such a personal question. Before today their conversations had always been impersonal and along the lines of 'Tea or coffee?' and now here they were discussing adultery and whether or not they loved their husbands.

'Goodness knows why, but yes, I do love Derek,' Cindy said simply. 'That's why I know it would be a lot easier if love didn't come into it. It's easier to be objective then.'

Hilary raised her tea to her lips. It was cold. She put it down. 'I can't believe we're sitting here and being so rational. I mean, aren't you at all shocked by what David's doing?'

'That's hardly the point, is it? The point is, what are *you* going to do?'

Hilary started to cry again. 'I don't know,' she squalled. 'I just don't know.'

'Do you want me to make a suggestion?'

'Please,' Hilary said, lifting her eyes from the screwed-up piece of kitchen roll in her hands. 'I need all the help I can get. I don't want to lose him, Cindy. He's the only man I've ever loved.'

'Right, then. The first thing is that you mustn't tell anyone. The fewer the people who know the better. From now on you've got to pretend, just as I said earlier, that you never found that receipt or heard David talking in his sleep. Hilary, you're going to have to fight for your husband.'

'Like you have for Derek?'

'Yes,' Cindy said grimly. 'Like I have for Derek.' She got up from her chair and took the mugs to the sink. 'By the way. Do you know who this Catherine might be?'

'Yes,' Hilary said softly. 'She's his new secretary.' Her body shook and she covered her face with her hands and sobbed.

Men, thought Cindy. Consistent if nothing else.

Chapter Two

'Okay, folks. Let's cut the waffle and get straight on. We've got a hell of a lot to cover tonight and I don't know about you but I'm knackered.'

Hilary saw the raised eyebrows along the front row of chairs which testified to the fact that this was not the usual way to open a St John's Infant and Junior School PTA meeting. There had been murmurs and more vocal expressions of dissent at the start of term when the outgoing chairwoman Patricia Longton had been replaced by Georgia D'Arcy, whose eager supporters were presently occupying the back row of seats in 2A's classroom, while Patricia and company were at the front where they felt they could be most intimidating. They had no idea what the members of the opposing camp were mouthing behind their backs.

Hilary did a quick head-count. Numbers were abnormally high. She suspected it had something to do with the free drinks on offer that evening – another change from the norm. She jotted the number down, disappointed that yet again she had been asked to remain as secretary – it was always the job nobody else wanted. She had hoped to step into Patricia's shoes herself but had withdrawn her name from the selection procedure when she found out she was up against the formidable Ms Georgia D'Arcy who had been well backed by the hairy-armpit brigade, as David called the more maverick and Bohemian inclined mothers of the school – 'Hippie by nature and hippy in size,' he would laugh.

'First on the agenda,' Georgia D'Arcy announced, 'is to

thank all those present and note those absent.' She gave a deep laugh, which belied her bone thin appearance and put paid to David's hip theory. 'Jobs will, of course, be allocated to those not here to defend themselves.' There was raucous laughter from the back row, while Patricia and Co., scandalised, exchanged sideways glances, uncrossed and recrossed their legs, knowing that this jibe was aimed at one of their number – Kate Hampton, the PTA treasurer.

Hilary wrote down 'thanks' and wished she was at home. She was exhausted. It had been a long day since her discovery that morning that David was having an affair. She hadn't eaten a thing, had felt too sick even to consider food. It was as though a pneumatic drill was at work inside her and one minute she was hot, the next cold.

Cindy had told her to expect this. 'You'll lose weight as well,' she had gone on to say. So that was the secret to Cindy's enviable sylph-like figure, Hilary had thought cynically. 'You must keep yourself busy,' Cindy had instructed, as they drove back to the supermarket to pick up her car. 'Or otherwise you'll find yourself thinking of *them*.'

'But what else can I think of?' Hilary had wailed in return.

'Your children, for a start.'

After Cindy had left her she had tried to keep herself busy. But it was hopeless. All she could think of was David's betrayal. So wantonly had he destroyed all that was important to her. She had tried to occupy herself by switching on the television but had ended up mindlessly channel-hopping between *The Rockford Files*, a programme on flamenco dancing, an old movie with Bette Davis and horse-racing from Newmarket until it was time to go and collect Becky. They had walked back from school and, turning into the tree-lined cul-de-sac of Acacia Lane, they had made slow progress as Becky kicked her way through the drifts of fallen leaves in the gutter. 'Ooh, what's this?' she had said, her voice ringing with seven-year-old delight as she bent down. It was a dead mouse. 'Why's it so flat?'

'Because it's dead.'

'Will I be flat like that when I'm dead?'

'No, dear,' Hilary said, taking hold of Becky's hand.

'But why—?'

'Because it's been run over lots of times,' Hilary answered, feeling a bit flat herself.

She had been looking forward to Becky's company, hoping that her daughter's usual demanding behaviour would occupy her. It hadn't. Instead she found she was irritated by Becky's incessant chatter.

'Are you listening to me, Mummy?' Becky had asked in the kitchen where they usually sat with a cup of tea and a biscuit discussing what kind of day Becky had been subjected to.

'Of course, darling,' Hilary had replied.

'Fibber.'

'I'm not lying.'

'Yes, you are. I can tell.'

'Well, what were you saying? Tell me again.'

Becky pouted. 'No.'

Hilary had wanted to cry then. Had wanted to put her arms around her small daughter and talk woman to woman with her. But she couldn't. She'd have to wait at least ten years before she could do that.

Philip's first words when they went to pick him up from school after his rugby practice were: 'You been crying, Mum?'

Strange that her eleven-year-old son should have noticed her red eyes and not Becky. But that was Becky all over.

Tea-time had passed without event, until David had telephoned. Philip took the call. 'Dad'll be late,' he had shouted from the hall. 'He's got an appointment to keep.'

She had cried again, upstairs and alone. Then she had phoned Cindy's daughter Tiffany to see if she could babysit that evening. 'Sorry it's such short notice, I just can't keep up with David,' she had said brightly to Tiffany when she arrived to take charge of the children ...

'I'd like that going on record.'

'Hilary, you are getting all this down, aren't you?'

Hilary lifted her head and wondered what on earth she was doing at a PTA meeting when her life was falling apart. 'Carry on as normal,' Cindy had told her. But not a word had she said about how one went about acting normally when all Hilary felt like doing was throwing herself on the floor and screaming like a baby.

'Hilary?' Georgia D'Arcy was frowning at her, one eyebrow quizzically arched beneath an urchin short fringe which had the colour and shine of a perfectly plump aubergine. Two fob-watch-sized ear-rings dangled either side of her sharp little face. She wore no make-up but her complexion was nut-brown, corroborating the fact that she worked outside each and every day. Since her husband Rory had left her two years ago the inhabitants of Hulme Welford had watched Georgia singlehandedly build up and run Hulme View Nursery on the edge of the village. She was not a woman who suffered fools and Hilary was a little in awe of her. 'I'm sorry,' Hilary said, 'what did you say?'

Georgia caught sight of Hilary's blank note-pad. She cleared her throat and waved to one of the mothers in the back row. 'Crack open those bottles of wine, will you, Cas, and pass some cups round while I have a chat with Hilary.'

Hilary heard muttering from the front row. 'Wine? We've never had wine before.'

'Right, chuck,' Georgia said, turning back to Hilary. 'What's up?'

Hilary's mouth opened but no words came out. She shut her mouth and tried hard to keep her lips from trembling.

'Come on, Hilary. I've watched you do this job standing on your head for the past three years. Granted I've seen you get flustered, but never incapable. Is it me? Can't you work with me? Because if so—'

'No. I mean, no, it's not that.'

Georgia smiled. 'Good. I know I put certain backs up, like

the frosty five there,' she inclined her head towards Patricia and company, 'but I'd hate to think I was that bloody obnoxious. I had hoped that you and I could get along. Perhaps some wine will help.' She got up from her chair and went across to where Cas Mitchell and Jo Shaughnessy were handing out plastic cups. Hilary noticed that the 'frosty five' were huddled together and guzzling their wine enthusiastically.

'Here,' Georgia said, coming back. 'Take a big mouthful. I'm not going to pry. It's none of my business what's given you a face like an empty coal scuttle, but I guarantee there's a man in there somewhere prodding you where it hurts.'

Hilary tried to protest but Georgia ignored her. 'Sod the lot of them, I say. If it'll help I'll take notes as we go along.' She drained her plastic cup, faced everyone and instantly called the meeting back to order.

Hilary felt herself relax for the first time that day. How good it was for somebody else to take charge. She had been grateful to Cindy earlier that morning for being there when she needed somebody in whom to confide, especially with her own experiences to tell, but she hadn't made Hilary feel any better. In fact, she had made her feel worse. Listening to Cindy had filled her with fear, as if all that lay in store for Hilary was a life stretching ahead as dauntingly as a life prison sentence. But Georgia was different. Somehow, in those few no-nonsense words Georgia had just uttered she had lifted some of the awful responsibility of the day off Hilary's shoulders. She felt enormously grateful to Georgia.

Chapter Three

Cindy came out of the *en suite* bathroom, a thick peach towel swathed around her slender body. She was surprised to see Derek sitting up in bed reading. He slapped the book shut when he saw she was there.

Just over an hour ago she had left him downstairs in the office. 'Paperwork,' he had said to her when she had looked in on him before coming upstairs for a bath.

'Everything's all right, isn't it?' she had asked. It was more by way of making conversation than worrying about the state of the business. All their married life Cindy had kept a firm hand and a weather eye on all the financial elements of the six salons they owned, as well as In the Pink. There was nothing that could get past her. But the persistent thought that had kept running through her mind these past few weeks was the possibility that Derek was sorting out their finances before leaving her. Since this morning when she had witnessed Hilary's shock she had felt it was an omen that she, too, was about to discover something unpleasant.

'Good book?' she asked, pulling a silk nightgown out of the stencilled chest of drawers by her side of the bed.

'Not bad,' he answered, his face noncommittal. He dropped the book face down onto the floor.

'You've been doing a lot of that lately,' Cindy said, her back to Derek. She let the towel fall away from her and slipped the nightgown over her head.

'A lot of what?'

She caught the defensiveness in his voice, and to avoid any

kind of confrontation that might lead to him declaring his hand, she said, 'Have you seen much of David recently?'

'Are you going to stand there all night giving me the third degree or are you getting in?' He pulled back her corner of the duvet and patted the bed.

She climbed in and sat stiffly beside him, taken aback by this simple act of courtesy ... Helping her into bed? What was it she had heard once? A man about to leave his wife behaves out of character, starts doing all he can to please her before dealing the final blow. Scared, she said, 'Well, have you?'

'Have I what?'

'Seen much of David recently.'

He shook his head. 'Same as usual, I suppose.' He took off his paper-thin wristwatch and gold bracelet and placed them by the bedside lamp. 'What's all this anyway? What's the sudden interest in David?'

'Oh, nothing,' Cindy said, turning out her light. She lay back and waited for Derek to do the same. She had the feeling, though, that he wasn't about to. She was right.

'Cindy?'

'I'm tired, Derek. Can it wait?'

'I'm tired as well.'

'Then switch off your light.'

'Not that kind of tired.'

She sat up. Well, if this was it, if he was about to tell her he wanted a divorce, she might just as well pay attention and listen to him.

'Are you happy, Cindy?'

'Happy?' This was new. He'd never asked her that before.

'Because,' Derek said, facing her, 'I'm not.' He smiled.

Oh, God. How could he? How could he smile like that? Was it supposed to soften the blow? She clenched her fists under the duvet and braced herself for what she had feared all her married life.

'I've been thinking about us.'

'Yes.'

16

'I think it's time for a change.' He kicked back the duvet and suddenly leapt to his feet. He pulled on his towelling robe and started to pace the bedroom floor, backwards and forwards at the end of the brass bed.

'What kind of change?' she asked.

'Life-enhancing!' he shouted, throwing his arms up in the air. He stared at her, wide-eyed. 'Tell me, Cindy, how long have we been in the beauty business?' He didn't wait for her reply. 'Too long is the answer.' He came round to her side of the bed and sat down. She moved her legs away from him.

He grabbed her hands and held them tightly. 'I've had this idea. I've been working on it for weeks now. I want to turn In the Pink into a sanctuary of spiritual exploration, where the hopeless can find hope, where ...' He looked about him as though seeking inspiration from the walls of their bedroom. 'Where the unsure can find themselves. And let's face it, there's plenty of people like that here in Hulme Welford. What do you think?'

'You're hurting my hands,' Cindy whispered.

'I'm sorry,' he said, letting go. 'Don't know my own strength. But what do you say to my idea?'

Cindy was speechless. She was so relieved that Derek wasn't about to leave her that she knew at that precise moment she would agree to anything he wanted to do. She hadn't been so relieved since the day just over a year ago when she had realised that Hilary's sister Charlotte Lawrence was in love with her tenant Alex Hamilton. Prior to that day she had been convinced that Charlotte would be yet another woman to come between Derek and herself. But it was clear to Cindy, as it was to everyone in the village, that Charlotte and Alex were very much in love, and even Derek himself had made it obvious that he was no longer interested and had backed off.

'I don't know what to think, Derek,' she said finally.

He kissed her, excitedly. 'That's the whole point. Too many

people out there don't know how or what to think. We're going to help change all that.'

'A sanctuary of what did you say?'

'We'll run courses on inner healing, assertiveness, there'll be journeys of self-discovery—'

'There won't be any chanting, will there?'

'Chanting?'

'I've seen things like that on the television. People sitting on cushions, their eyes rolling and rubbish coming out of their mouths. It's so embarrassing.'

He laughed. 'Cindy, Cindy, this is me, Derek. Would I be that stupid?' He mentally ruled out that particular course he'd been reading up on. 'Come on, I feel like celebrating. Let's go down and open a bottle.' He kissed her again and ran his hand the length of her arm. 'Then we'll come back up and I'll take you on a journey of self-discovery.'

'I haven't said yes yet,' Cindy said, getting out of bed.

'You will, though. I just know it.'

Cindy had a feeling he was right.

Chapter Four

Becky looked pleased with herself, which Hilary knew meant one thing and one thing only: Becky had got one over her brother. For most of her young daughter's life Hilary had generally taken her side in any sibling fracas, but more recently her loyalty had been pushed to its limits and Philip had started to gain more of her respect and sympathy.

She handed Becky the packet of breakfast cereal and scanned her daughter's face for any tell-tale signs of guilt. She found none, only a look of undisguised glee.

She lifted the kettle from the Aga and made the tea, setting the pot down on the table. She then switched on the radio. 'Are we downhearted?' asked Terry Wogan from beside the bread bin. Yesterday the self-effacing Irishman had posed the same question and she had smiled back at him. Today she had nothing to smile about. She *was* downhearted.

When she had got home last night after the PTA meeting she had gone straight upstairs, calling to David in the sitting room that she had a headache and was going to bed.

She had pretended to be asleep when he had joined her. She had lain silently beside him, her body tense with fear and anger, trying hard not to think of him as he lay on the other side of the bed; a chasm of duplicity between them. And as the night hours had slowly passed she had punished herself again and again wondering how many times David had done *it* with *her*? And was *it* better with Catherine? Of course it was, she had told herself angrily while tiptoeing to the toilet at three in the morning, why else would he be having an affair? Illicit sex early in the evening was always more fun than a tired ten-minute domestic session slotted in between Jeremy Paxman's *Newsnight* and setting the alarm clock.

Eventually, worn down by such torturous thoughts, she had given up the fight and had slept, but now it was breakfast time and any minute David would be out of the shower and downstairs. How would she cope? She would have to look at him, speak, even. She could avoid him no longer. There could be no escape.

'Mummy?'

'Mm . . .'

'What do you get if you hang—?'

'Please, Becky, not now.' Hilary could hear footsteps on the stairs. She pushed four slices of bread into the toaster.

'Daddy, what do you get if you hang Pamela Anderson upside down?'

'Shut up, Becky,' Philip said, coming into the kitchen behind his father. He knew he shouldn't have told his sister that joke. She was always getting him into trouble with her big mouth. 'Mum, these pants you got me, they're too small.'

Hilary looked at Philip. She could see David out of the corner of her eye. He was pouring himself a mug of tea. 'I only bought them at the start of term,' she said. 'They can't be too small.'

'Well, they are,' Philip said sullenly. He sat down. Hilary noticed him wriggling. She noticed too that David seemed to be moving uncomfortably in his chair. He looked shifty. Guilty. How long had he been doing that?

'Any toast?' he asked, barely lifting his eyes from the level of his mug.

'Coming,' she replied. She filled the toast rack and sat down.

'Flora?'

She looked up at David and moved towards the fridge. 'Flora,' she repeated slowly, taking off the lid and dropping the plastic tub onto the table. The china and cutlery rattled and a small yellow dollop of sunflower spread leapt out of the carton and landed on David's forehead. For a few moments nobody spoke, then Becky's shrill laughter, accompanied by the eight o'clock pips on the radio, filled the kitchen. Hilary didn't know what to do. The atmosphere was awful. She watched David take out his handkerchief from his trouser pocket and wipe his forehead. He didn't look at her and he wasn't smiling. 'Here,' she said, offering him the dishcloth. 'Wipe up your tea.' Then, sensing Philip wriggling next to her, she vented her anger on him. 'For goodness' sake, keep still!' she shouted.

Philip sprang from his seat. 'I can't,' he shouted back. 'It's these pants. I told you, they're too small.'

'And I told you they can't be.'

'Mummy's right,' Becky said slyly, her mouth a dark cavernous hole of Coco Pops. She started to laugh again and getting up from her chair she began pirouetting about the kitchen. 'Itchy bum, itchy bum!' she chanted delightedly.

Hilary looked from Philip to Becky. 'What have you done?' she demanded.

Philip's face darkened and he rushed from the room. 'Itchy bum!' Becky yelled one more time after him.

'Becky!'

Becky came to a balletic stop, her feet in a perfect first position. She looked like a penguin. 'I put itching powder in his pants,' she confessed with a giggle. Her words were said with immense pride and satisfaction. She looked like a smug penguin now.

For the first time ever, Hilary slapped her daughter, hard, on the legs and then she too left the kitchen.

Hilary couldn't bear to see the expression of humiliation on Philip's face as he climbed onto the school bus. His sister's antics would be with him for the rest of the day, a day that Hilary knew would be bad enough for him anyway. The transition from the village primary to senior school had not been an easy one for him. He had won a scholarship to the same school Tiffany attended and which her brother Barry had recently left with his string of grade A A-levels. He was now studying medicine at Leeds, and while Derek was vocally proud of his son, Cindy was more reluctant to sing his praises. It never ceased to amaze Hilary that Derek and Cindy could have produced two such unlikely children – Tiffany, possibly every mother's nightmare and Barry, every mother's dream son-in-law. On the other hand, she herself had produced Becky.

'Come on, Mummy. We'll be late. I want to get to school before Sarah Jenkins today.'

There was no contrition in Becky. No sense of remorse for what she had done to her brother. Not even any hurt pride or anger for having had her legs smacked. Life was just one series of practical jokes as far as Becky was concerned. It made Hilary even angrier, this blatant cavalier attitude to life that Becky had. It made her want to lash out at her daughter. Life wasn't one big bloody joke. Life was hard, tough, and just now hers was tumbling down around her. She stuffed her fists inside her coat pocket. She had always prided herself that while most of her friends gaily slapped their children for their wrong-doings, she had not. 'A mother who resorts to violence has lost the respect of her children and the right to their love,' she had said, on so many occasions. She could remember telling her own mother this after she had caught Louise smacking Becky for smashing a small china dog in her antique shop. Her mother had responded with, 'Don't you know anything, Hilary? You slap the respect into them.' And now here she was, twice in one day wanting to unleash an extraordinary amount of violence on her young daughter. She knew, though, that it had nothing to do with disciplining Becky and all to do with her anger and frustration at what David was doing to her and what he was apparently prepared to keep on doing.

They walked away from the bus stop and crossed the road towards the church. At the school gate Becky skipped away, leaving Hilary standing empty-handed. She felt relieved, rid of Becky and the threat of causing her any real physical harm. She turned to hurry off, not wanting to get caught by Patricia or any of the other mothers and be sucked into the early-morning school-gate gossiping session.

'Hilary, I was hoping I'd catch you.' It was Georgia D'Arcy striding purposefully behind her. She was wearing a mustard-coloured beret pulled down over her head and a bulky scarf wrapped loosely around her thin neck. She wore no coat, despite the sharp October wind that morning, just a striped woollen jumper and a pair of khaki dungarees.

'I'm sorry,' Hilary said automatically, 'I haven't had a chance to write up the minutes yet.'

'To hell with those. The meeting was only last night.'

Only last night. It felt an age away.

'Why don't you come for lunch? I usually break about twelve thirty. The nursery's as dead as the grave then.'

'Oh, I couldn't. I've got—'

'Suit yourself,' Georgia said, already moving towards her mud-splattered Jeep. She looked back over her shoulder. 'But if you change your mind, you know where I am.'

While Hilary cleared up the debris of breakfast she had the strongest of desires to smash everything within sight. She was shocked. She was not a violent woman, not one of those drama queens given over to fits of plate-smashing pique. But now she crashed and slammed her way about the kitchen until at last everything was put away. Then she found one of David's whisky tumblers in the sink. He usually had a glass of whisky when he came in from work each evening and never once did he wash the glass or put it in the dishwasher, he just dumped it in the sink each night. She picked it up and turned it round in her hand. She wanted to smash the glass, wanted the satisfaction of throwing it hard against the wall. But she thought of the shards all over the kitchen and knew she couldn't do it. How about outside? Against the garage wall, perhaps? No. There would still be all that mess to clear up afterwards; slivers of lethal glass everywhere. Surely there had to be some way of satisfying her craving to destroy something of David's that wouldn't involve her in clearing up any mess.

Yes, of course there was. She laughed. My God! She could laugh at a time like this. Was she going completely round the bend? She opened the glass display cupboard above the worktop at the far end of the kitchen. There were twelve tumblers in it, all expensive cut glass, which David's mother had given him over the years. In the drawer below Hilary found a plastic carrier bag and started filling it.

She drove to the local council tip, negotiating the bumps and bends in the road with infinite care – she didn't want to waste her precious cargo and be cheated out of her moment of revenge.

She drew up alongside one of the huge metal containers and put on her sunglasses from the glove compartment. On the back seat she saw one of Philip's old Manchester City caps. She grabbed it and forced it on her head.

She carried the glass-filled bag under one arm and made her way up the metal steps to the container. After a quick surreptitious glance to check that she was completely alone, she pulled one of the tumblers out of the bag and threw it. It was a lousy shot. A timorous effort that had the glass landing comfortably on a discarded piece of Axminster. It hadn't even broken. She felt no satisfaction. She picked out another tumbler and this time extended her arm for greater leverage. The tumbler crashed noisily against the sides of the container and Hilary felt the smash deep inside her. Thoughts of a broken heart flickered through her mind, but she dispelled this poetic image instantly by reaching into the bag for another glass. She threw it, followed by a fourth and a fifth. She was well into her stride now, remembering how at school she had been rather good at rounders; the best fielder, she had been called, noted for the quality of her over-arm throw; she had even won a small medal. 'Bastard!' she shouted, as the sixth glass shot into the air.

'Deceitful bastard!' she hurled after the seventh.

'Having fun?'

Shocked, she spun round and nearly toppled off the narrow gangplank and into the container. A strong arm caught her and held her firmly. 'Steady on. You don't look ready for the rubbish heap yet.'

'Somebody obviously thinks I am,' she muttered, without looking up. She clutched the half-empty bag to her, rigid with embarrassment and the realisation that she had been so engrossed in exacting what now seemed her petty revenge on David that she had been oblivious to everything around her, even the sound of an approaching car.

She moved to get past the man but found his hand was still on her arm. She slowly lifted her head, mortified that he must have heard all the terrible expletives she'd just uttered.

He released her and bent down to a cardboard box of junk at his feet and because there wasn't room on the gangplank for Hilary to squeeze past she was forced to stay where she was. She watched him drop his box into the container. A gust of wind snatched at a small wodge of photographs and they flew up into the air then fluttered momentarily in the breeze before settling like butterflies on an old mattress, its springs bursting through the stained and ripped fabric.

'No point in hanging onto the past,' he said, as though addressing the mattress. 'It only makes us cling onto what we once thought was important.' He turned and gave her an uncomfortably direct stare.

Hilary was glad of the sunglasses she was wearing, but not of the hat – it probably made her look like an eccentric old bat.

'Go on, then, throw the rest of them away, don't mind me.'

She suddenly remembered the bag in her hands. 'I don't need to,' she said, knowing that her voice didn't ring true.

'Perhaps you should, though.' And without another word he left her and walked back to where his car was parked just behind hers.

She watched him go. His hair was dark and slightly curly, streaked with grey and much too long, she decided. His plum-coloured jacket and black polo-neck struck her as being of good quality and quite fashionable but his moss green trousers were rumpled and baggy with creases at the knees. He looked vaguely arty or perhaps academic, or how those types were so often portrayed on the telly.

He drove away leaving her alone with her bag of whisky tumblers. She tried throwing the eighth glass, but she felt no anger, no excitement at what she was doing. She had run out of adrenaline and the moment had passed. She dropped the carrier bag on top of the mattress displacing the rubbish the man had just left behind him. A wedding photograph showed itself fleetingly before it coyly slipped under cover beneath an unwanted pushchair.

Hilary got into her car and drove home, disappointed and annoyed that the interfering man with his direct stare and untidy trousers had spoilt things for her.

Chapter Five

'Good God, Hilary, you look awful!'

'And what, in the name of all that is wonderful, is that disgusting smell?'

Hilary looked first at her mother then at Iris Braithwaite, whose nose was twitching like that of a cartoon mouse catching a whiff of cheese on the air. 'Must be *eau de* tip,' Hilary said, surprising herself with the unexpected sharpness of her wit. She tried to squeeze past Iris and her mother who was scrutinising her so intently that she was inadvertently blocking the path of a man behind her, pinning him against the racks of greeting cards with her shopping basket.

'Oh-the-what?' Iris demanded, her nose still taking in the air.

'I think my daughter was trying, in her oh-so-clever way, to tell us she's just been to the council tip,' Louise Archer said, shifting her basket from one hand to the other. Seizing his moment, the man behind her made his escape.

'Never go there myself,' Iris said. 'I have a perfectly good working compost heap at the end of my garden. Grass cuttings in one, peelings in another and leaves ... Hold it right there, young man.'

The escapee froze, his hand hovering over the door handle.

'It's you, isn't it?'

He looked at Iris. 'Sorry?'

'Dog mess. Check your shoes, young man, and watch where you're walking in future.'

He fled.

'Now, as I was saying, I always put my leaves in a separate area. Laurel leaves never rot down. Remember that.'

Oh, shove your leaves, Louise thought, as Iris moved away. I want to know why Hilary's looking as threadbare as an old rug. 'Join you for lunch, Hilary?' she said, curious rather than concerned, because nothing ever went wrong in her younger daughter's life. She watched Hilary straightening the magazines; a crooked *Bella* here and a slipped *Hello!* there. You always were a fidgety little madam, Louise reflected. 'Lunch, then – what do you say?'

'*Orgasms for the Woman in a Hurry*', Hilary read to herself from the cover of *Cosmopolitan* as she jerked it upright, trying hard to concentrate on anything but her mother. She couldn't bear the thought of Louise knowing that she had failed in her marriage. Oh, God. It was such basic stuff. She was ashamed that she had failed to please her man. She pulled out the magazine and pretended to flick through it, while all the time thinking of a way in which she could avoid having lunch with her mother and end up spilling the beans.

'Hilary, in my opinion if you haven't learned about multiple orgasms by now it's much too late. Now do you or do you not want me to join you for lunch?'

'Multiple what?' exploded Iris Braithwaite, from the revolving rack of tights.

'Multiple orgasms, Mrs Braithwaite,' called out Ted the Toup helpfully from behind his counter. His hands covered in newspaper print, he was putting the finishing touches to his display of confectionery.

Iris gripped the ends of her headscarf as though protecting herself from a high wind. 'All I came in for was a pair of tights. I did not think I would be subjected to the smell and language of the gutter.' She slapped a packet of tights on the counter.

Ted the Toup's face cracked into a nicotine-tinted smile. 'Three pounds fifty, love.'

'Don't you love me anything, you charlatan!' Iris roared. 'Three pounds fifty, indeed. Last week I only paid—'

'Ah, well, these ones you've picked out are special, like.'

'I should say they are at that price. Explain yourself.'

Ted leaned forward, his patched elbows resting on the counter. 'Peephole gusset,' he said confidentially.

Iris gasped and shrank back from Ted's leering face.

He picked up the packet of tights and began reading from the label, curling his tongue round the words as though giving them extra meaning, '"Glamorous and fashionably hygienic, to leave you cool and sensual—"'

'Stop!'

'You haven't heard the best bit. It says here—'

'Outrageous,' fired back Iris, breathless with shock. 'Absolutely outrageous.' She turned on her heel and pushed past Hilary and Louise. She gave Ted one last look of disgust before slamming the shop door behind her.

'What about you, ladies?' Ted tried gamely.

'Not now, Ted,' Louise said, amused. She had other fish to fry. She took Hilary by the arm and led her outside.

In the chill, leaf-swirling wind Hilary felt like a small child who had just been dragged out of a sweetshop before having the chance to spend her pocket money. She said, 'But I didn't get my magazine, Mother.'

'Never mind your magazine, Hilary. Just what the heck is going on? You look dreadful. Come on, out with it.' Stern words had always worked with Hilary when she was little; they would have her trembling into submission in no time at all.

'Why aren't you at your shop, Mother?'

Louise frowned, annoyed that she didn't seem to be getting through to Hilary. Normally her daughter was a giver of information, painfully honest and unable to avoid answering a direct question, and here she was parrying with all the ease of a well-seasoned, tabloid-hounded politician. 'It's Tuesday, Hilary,' she said. 'I never open the shop on a Tuesday. It's my day off, you know that. Would you like to join me for lunch?'

'Lunch?' Hilary tried to appear thoughtful, as though giving the invitation all her consideration. Inside she was panicking. If her mother got her round the lunch table she would never be able to withstand her lightbulb-in-the-eye interrogation tactics. 'Oh, yes,' she suddenly said, inspiration dawning.

'Krakatoa erupts,' Louise said scornfully. 'I'm getting through at last. Shall I come to you, or shall—'

'Sorry,' Hilary said, sounding as genuine as she could, 'but I'm having lunch with Georgia D'Arcy.' She edged towards the door of the newsagent. 'I really must get her a box of chocolates.' And before her mother could say another word she shot back inside the shop.

Louise was put out. She decided to pay a call on her elder daughter, Charlotte, to see if she knew what was going on. She wheeled her bicycle along the pavement, passing the row of shops until she came to the end of the road where the expensive kitchen and bathroom shop had been in business, selling Jacuzzi baths and rainforest-free mahogany units at vastly over-inflated prices – until last winter, that was, when the market for conscience-clear goods at unrealistic prices had slipped down the plug-hole, as David had joked when he'd put the leasehold of the premises on the market. 'It's impossible to be truly environmentally friendly and make money,' he'd said. A few days later they had all been surprised when Charlotte had pulled out her cheque book and announced she would like to take on the lease and run her own business again. 'Another attempt at turning back the clock, Charlotte?' Louise had said to her daughter.

Charlotte had had her own shop years ago, before her marriage to Peter. As sons-in-law went Peter hadn't been a bad effort; not the worst but certainly not the best. Louise herself didn't like men who had too high an opinion of themselves and Peter had definitely thought a little too well of himself for her liking, though since his death she was conscious that he had gone up in her estimation. Death did that, she supposed, softened and smoothed the bits that had previously irritated and snagged on one's nerves.

She propped her bicycle against the plate-glass window of Charlotte's shop and thought of Alex, who was shaping up into a much better proposition. She opened the door.

'Hello, Mother.'

'Surprised you've not got yourself one of those twee tinkly little bells for the door.'

'What, and go completely round the bend?' Charlotte replied, wanting to add, *like you*.

'Of course, you wouldn't catch me dead with one,' Louise continued, coming further into the shop. 'I've come in for some of those dried flowers,' she said, deciding to take the devious route for what she really wanted, 'the dusky pink ones that look like they were used in Miss Havisham's wedding bouquet.'

'Sorry, I've sold out of those. And, anyway, I told you last week I wasn't going to let you have any more, not after Mrs Braithwaite told me you were selling them on at double the price.'

Louise smiled. 'That's the antique trade for you.' She rested her heavy basket on the corner of the stripped pine table which Charlotte used as a counter. She watched her daughter arranging some large china ducks, their long necks straining over the wooden shelf, black beady eyes staring dumbly at the floor. She was reminded of Hilary's expression just now at Ted the Toup's.

'Anything else I can help you with, Mother?'

Louise wasn't going to be rushed. 'Set a date for the wedding yet?' She knew that would annoy Charlotte and set up a suitable smoke-screen for the real question she wanted to ask. If Charlotte did know what was wrong with her sister and was under orders to keep quiet, Louise knew it would be a waste of time coming out directly with 'What do you know about Hilary?' Charlotte would only dig in her heels and refuse to tell her. Her elder daughter had always played it close to the chest and it had irritated the hell out of her.

Charlotte swung round. 'No, not yet, but I'll stick an invitation in the post for you, just as soon as we know ourselves.'

'You've lost one husband, Charlotte, you don't want to let Alex slip through your hands. Husbands aren't like buses, they don't come along in threes.'

Charlotte returned her attention to the necky ducks. 'If he's that slippery a customer, I'm not so sure he's worth keeping.'

'And if you're going to bore me with your enigmatic routine, Charlotte, I'll be off.' She picked up her shopping basket and said casually, 'Seen much of Hilary recently?'

'No. Why?'

Louise decided to offer a snippet of information. 'I've just seen her in Ted's. She really doesn't look at all well.'

Charlotte was suspicious. Her mother rarely noticed what was wrong with anyone, and if she did, she never commented on it. 'Perhaps she's got a cold. You know what a terror Becky is for bringing germs home from school.'

Louise knew only too well what a terror her granddaughter was, and not just where germs were concerned. She said goodbye and left.

Charlotte stood in the window and watched her mother cycle across the main road, past the church and towards Pippin Rise, the new development which had been built almost on the doorstep of her parents' black and white thatched cottage.

Even when Louise had disappeared out of sight, Charlotte remained where she was. Why had her mother asked about Hilary? And why did she have to keep bringing up the subject of marriage? That was the third time in as many weeks. It really was none of her business, but all the same, she hugged the thought to herself that only that morning before she'd left to open up the shop she and Alex had been discussing what they were going to do.

He had been Charlotte's tenant, and technically he still was, but now he used the granny annexe of Ivy Cottage solely as his office. Since last Christmas when he had moved in with her, Charlotte had lost count of the number of times he had proposed. He had been so patient, never once giving her an ultimatum, and not once had he made her feel guilty for her indecision. But last week she had finally said yes to the idea of marriage. He had been delighted, had wanted to rush her down to St John's there and then. 'No!' she had cried, as he'd swung her round.

'Now don't give me any of that,' he'd shouted. 'You can't change your mind. I clearly heard you say yes.'

'I mean yes, I'll marry you, but no, not straight away. Let me get used to the idea.'

He had bought her a ring the very next day. It was beautiful and, looking at it now on her finger, she felt so sure she was doing the right thing. Her hesitation in marrying Alex was nothing to do with him, but all to do with herself. The latter years of her seven-year marriage to Peter had had a disastrous effect on her self-confidence, and the circumstances surrounding his sudden death in a car crash had compounded her already low sense of self-worth to the extent of making her think she wasn't capable of making a relationship work.

A cold draught blew in at her feet through the badly fitting door and she moved over to the counter where Mabel, her West Highland White terrier, was curled up in her basket in front of a small fan heater which was gently humming to itself. She smiled, reminded of Alex. He had been humming this morning in the shower and she had thrown a wet sponge at him for his choice of song – 'I'm Getting Married in the Morning'.

'Don't waste your breath,' she had said, laughing at him, loving him for his ability always to make her feel *something*. But to surprise him, just as she was leaving the house she had promised she would make up her mind by that evening as to when they would get married. He had telephoned her three times already that morning. She shook her head and suddenly thought how happy it would make not just herself but her sister to see her and Alex married. How busily Hilary had schemed all last summer to get the pair of them together but, then, she always had been such a shocking schemer.

Charlotte's thoughts strayed from her sister to their mother. It was so unlike Louise to notice anything amiss with either Hilary or herself, and yet she had been very specific: 'She really doesn't look at all well.'

Charlotte bent down to a box under the pine table and opened it up. It was full of the dusky pink roses Louise had asked for. She filled a large wicker basket with them and decided to call in at The Gables on her way home later that afternoon.

Chapter Six

Hilary parked in the gravelled area alongside a row of large greenhouses; they were constructed of plastic sheeting and as she got out of her car a gust of wind rippled their sagging sides, making them flap and snap like sails in a boatyard.

She was nervous. It had been all very well using Georgia D'Arcy as an excuse for avoiding her mother but the trouble was, as she'd known the moment she'd uttered the words, she was then committed to following through. She had never been able to lie to her mother and, having told Louise she was seeing Georgia, there was nothing else for it but to do exactly that or the inevitable would happen – her mother would find out she had lied.

She had fibbed once to her mother when she was ten years old. It had been her birthday, and while Louise had been busy in the kitchen preparing for the party and putting the finishing touches to her birthday cake Hilary had been in the sitting room, playing with one of her presents, a plastic dolls' house, which for months she had longed for and had been promised. She had been delighted with the gift, so much so that she had hopped and skipped around it. But disaster had struck. She had slipped and kicked it with her black patent-leather party shoe. Quick as a flash she had carried the dolls' house to her mother in the kitchen and said – with real tears welling up in her eyes – 'Mummy, look, there's a crack in one of the walls. It must have been like this when you bought it.' The next day, she and the dolls' house were taken to the toy shop in Macclesfield where Louise had made the purchase. Hilary had stood there, mortified, in front of the little bald man who, from behind his counter, was being pebble-dashed with a vitriolic attack on shoddy shop practice. When the man tried to defend himself, Louise, with a curious smile on her lips, had said very quietly, 'On one side of this counter stands a liar.' Unable to cope with ten-year-old guilt and feeling sorry for the poor pink-headed man, Hilary had piped up with, 'It's me. I'm the liar.'

In the car going home she had cried and her mother had said, 'I knew all along you were lying, Hilary. I hope I've taught you a valuable lesson today. Lies always have reper-cussions.'

She glanced at her watch, it was just before twelve thirty. Probably Georgia wouldn't be over at her bungalow yet. Through the smeared window of a small battered caravan beneath an oak tree Hilary saw Georgia's bereted head bobbing to and fro as she talked into a mobile phone. When Georgia caught sight of Hilary she beckoned her over.

It was three years now since Georgia and Rory had moved into the village with their young daughter Chloe. Shortly before this Rory had lost his job with a local pharmaceutical company and had decided to use his redundancy money to start up his own landscaping business, but within a short space of time things started going wrong and gossip began flying round Hulme Welford. The most credible rumour Hilary heard was that Rory had started to drink more than was good for him and the offers of work had dwindled away to nothing. Not long after this Georgia had thrown out her husband and instigated divorce proceedings. Rory had been a good-looking man, full of bonhomie, and had been generally well liked in the village, so not surprisingly Georgia was cast as the villain of the piece. 'A woman should stand by her man,' was the commonly shared view and voiced principally by Patricia Longton. And Georgia had not. She had kicked a man when he was down.

Before yesterday Hilary would have agreed with these smug sentiments. But now she wasn't so sure. Based on what she had unearthed in her own marriage in the past twenty-four hours, what did any of them know of Georgia's and what had gone on before? How easily they had taken sides, because they had all been fortunate enough to have the safety net of a trouble-free marriage.

But that had all changed now.

She remembered how David had come home one evening and said, 'Poor old Rory's ended up with nothing and that hard piece of an ex-wife of his has just been into the office today and bought a two-acre parcel of land up at Hulme View.' Even Hilary had known that Rory had ended up with a whole load more than nothing – namely, most of their savings, what was left of them. In order to buy the land for the nursery Georgia had sold the house, which she'd been awarded as part of her settlement, and she and Chloe had lived in a draughty old caravan while she got the nursery business up and running, working and saving like mad to have a small bungalow built for the two of them.

'Come in,' Georgia mouthed as Hilary peered into the caravan. She stood awkwardly amongst the piles of paperwork, seed catalogues and ripped-open bags of potting compost and bone meal. Georgia pointed to a bench seat and after Hilary had brushed off a sprinkling of white powder, which she then identified as mildew, she sat down and tried her best to pretend she wasn't listening to Georgia's one-sided conversation.

'I don't give a damn about your mother's plastic hip. I ordered that forest bark two months ago ... Well, don't complain to me. I didn't vote this bloody government in ... I'll expect you tomorrow, or I'll come over and do your mother's hip for her.

'Hi,' Georgia said, facing Hilary and slipping the phone into the pocket on the front of her dungarees. 'Come on, let's go over to the house. It's freezing in here.'

Hilary was glad to get out of the caravan. The confined space, together with its damp coldness, was having a depressing effect on her. How on earth had Georgia and Chloe stuck living in it? She followed Georgia down the rusting metal steps, across the gravel car park to a muddy path that led to the recently built bungalow, which in Hilary's mind sparkled like an oasis in this jumbled mess of dirt and toil. She imagined the house to be warm, clean and inviting.

Georgia unlocked the front door and kicked off her mud-caked boots. 'I didn't think you'd come,' she said. 'Throw your coat over the back of that chair and come on through to the kitchen.'

Hilary's oasis image was fast disappearing as she watched Georgia washing her hands at the sink amongst an enormous pile of dirty pots and pans. The kitchen was almost as untidy as the caravan, but at least it was warm and there was the tantalising smell of garlic and herbs, which certainly had the edge on bone meal.

'I'm not going to apologise for the state of the place,' Georgia said, as she bent down to open the oven. 'I know it's a mess, but Chloe comes first, the nursery next and the dust and mess a poor last.'

'It's not a mess at all,' Hilary said, politely turning away from the sight of Georgia's and Chloe's underwear drying on the radiator. To her shame she found herself thinking how much more acceptable washing was hanging from the ceiling on one of those smart Edwardian clothes-dryers.

'That's a load of crap, Hilary, and you know it.' Georgia slammed the oven door shut. 'Now what have you got there?'

Hilary looked down at her hands, suddenly remembering what she was holding. 'They're for you. Chocolates. I thought you'd like them.' She offered them to Georgia and found herself holding her breath. *Déjà vu*. She breathed out. No, it wasn't *déjà vu* at all. It was the past, something that had happened a long time ago, when she had moved on to grammar school, joining Charlotte who was already there in her third year. In her first term she had developed a monumental crush on a girl in the fifth form and after days of plucking up courage she had approached Naomi Scott with a box of chocolates that had cost her several weeks' pocket money. 'I thought you'd like them,' she had said. Naomi, beautiful as well as clever, had taken the box and walked away without even thanking her. Later that day Hilary heard Naomi laughing about her with her friends. She had cried that night in bed, trying to come to terms with her first lesson in rejection.

And now something very real and intense inside her was making her hope that Georgia might be her friend, that she wouldn't reject her.

'How bloody daft and lovely of you,' Georgia said, taking the box and placing it beside a pile of ironing. 'I can't remember the last time anyone gave me chocolates.'

Lunch was better than Hilary had expected. She hadn't thought a radical like Georgia would be able to do anything creative in the kitchen. She didn't know which most surprised her, that there was meat on the table and not beans and pulses, or that she had actually managed to eat any of it. It was her first meal since yesterday morning.

'We must leave enough for Chloe's tea,' Georgia instructed, scooping out a second portion for Hilary, 'or I'll be in the doghouse for days.'

Hilary could think of nothing more unlikely.

'So, Hilary, what gives in Acacia Lane?'

'Gives?'

Georgia smiled. 'What's going on at The Gables that's made you take up a wild invitation for lunch with a heretic like me?' Georgia watched Hilary closely as she finished chewing what was in her mouth. She was aware she had just put Hilary on the spot, and even more aware that she was making her guest nervous. She was often told she made people feel uncomfortable. It was her honesty, she supposed.

People didn't usually appreciate such directness. But life was too short to waste time beating about the bush.

'Nothing,' Hilary said at last. 'Why ever would you think there was?'

'In my experience, there's always something going on at home. When there isn't, that's the time to worry.'

Hilary felt torn. Something made her want to confide in Georgia, but Cindy's words telling her to keep quiet were rattling around inside her head. 'How long is it since you've been on your own?' she asked, already knowing the answer, but finding herself wanting to hear it from Georgia herself.

So that's it, thought Georgia. Our old friend matrimonial trouble giving Hilary grief. Wasn't it always?

'Two marvellous years,' she answered, resting her elbows on the table and her chin on her roughened and scratched knuckles. A moment passed, then she threw back her head and laughed, her long ear-rings dancing against her slender neck. 'Okay, then, I admit it. One exhausting year preceded by one year of sheer hell.'

'Why did—?'

'Why did I throw him out? Is that what you want to know?'

Hilary nodded and lowered her eyes, unable to meet Georgia's gaze.

'Ever since Rory had been made redundant he'd been knocking about with another woman. Coming here to Hulme Welford was supposed to have been a new start but I soon found out that he was still seeing her. And why did our marriage go wrong in the first place, is probably your next question. The answer to that is easy. Like so many men, Rory couldn't handle the dent that redundancy had made in his self-esteem. And yeah, sure, I'm fully aware that Rory is by no means the first man to seek out somebody else to bolster up his deflated ego.'

'So where is he now?'

'God knows. We've not seen hide nor hair of him for over

six months. But Chloe and I are just fine without him. At least now I don't have to spend half my time mothering an overgrown schoolkid who still needs to be told what a good boy he is. Men just never grow out of needing a mother figure to tell little Johnny, or little Rory ...' she hesitated before adding one other name '... or little David, what a good boy he is. When they come home from work, their briefcases bulging with the flimsy achievements of the day, they're only after one thing, and that's to be told what clever boys they are. Do you see what I mean?'

'I think so, but—'

'It's all sick. If they think they're not getting enough praise at home they simply look elsewhere.'

'Why did you mention David's name just now?' Hilary said quietly. 'He isn't like that.'

'You sure?'

Hilary thought for a moment. She tried to think of an average evening spent at The Gables: David would come home from work, pour himself a glass of whisky and stand in front of the Aga – getting in her way – and proceed to tell her about the latest house he'd sold or been offered to sell. And she, while getting the supper ready and supervising Philip's homework, would nod and say things like, 'That's nice, dear.' She swallowed hard. Maybe Georgia was right: perhaps David had simply found somebody who would listen more attentively; somebody who would ask all the pertinent questions that she was too tired or bored even to consider.

She put down her knife and fork and looked up at Georgia. For a split second Cindy's words from yesterday went quiet inside her head and she seized her opportunity, wanting Georgia to know ... wanting Georgia to help her. 'David's having an affair,' she heard herself say. 'Oh, God. This is like something out of a Joanna Trollope novel.'

'Get out of here. This is an Aga-free zone, I'll have you know.'

'Please don't joke with me,' Hilary said, her stomach

beginning to churn, her throat tightening with the effort of holding back the tears.

'I'm sorry. So what are we going to do about it?'

'*We?*'

'Good grief, Hilary. You don't think I'm going to let you go through this alone, do you? Hey, come on. Don't go all trembly on me.'

'I can't help it,' Hilary whispered, tears filling her eyes and trickling down her pale cheeks. 'I can't help it. You're so much nicer than Naomi Scott.'

Georgia didn't have a clue what Hilary was talking about, but she got up from her chair and went to her. She knelt down and put her arms round Hilary's shaking shoulders.

The comfort of Georgia's slight body against her own made Hilary lean into her and she cried all the more.

Chapter Seven

'So, Dad, let me get this straight. You want to give up the world of curling tongs and mud packs for the world of emotional cripples looking up their bums?' Tiffany let out a loud laugh. 'This I have to see!'

Derek looked across the office desk at his seventeen-year-old daughter. He had just told Tiffany about his plans for changing In the Pink into a centre of self-discovery and he knew, as any parent knows, that his teenage daughter was probably his biggest critic. Part of him, the old Derek, wanted to shout at Tiffany for her insolence and tell her not to be so bloody rude, but the new Derek was struggling to remain a paragon of selfless patience and understanding. There was no room for outbursts of indignation and anger in the new world he wanted to create. 'Prejudice against any new idea does, of course, betray an underlying sense of inadequacy and inferiority,' he said smoothly, pleased with himself for being able to quote so easily from the book he'd been reading earlier in the salon while Mrs Jeffs was at the back wash.

Tiffany laughed again. 'Muffin 'ell, Dad. What's got into you? You've not been the same since Barry had his born-again experience.'

Derek shuffled some papers in front of him. He kept his eyes down, finding Tiffany's words uncomfortably near the truth, but he'd be damned if he ever let on. All that talk from Bas of a living Christ had brought him up short and left him feeling embarrassed but strangely curious. Sure, it was all gobbledegook, but for the life of him he couldn't work out how a smart bloke like Bas could get caught up in it. But that wasn't really what had got to him. What had was Bas being flown home from Romania with meningitis. That was when things had got to him. He'd always kept his distance with Bas because secretly he'd been afraid of him. Bas was so effortlessly more intelligent than he was, but seeing his son helpless in that hospital bed, not knowing whether he was going to live or die, had made him feel so useless, had made him face up to how badly he'd let his son down. That was the moment when something – something he didn't really understand – had touched him on the shoulder and said, 'Get a grip, Derek old mate. There's more to life than touching up Mrs Jeffs' roots every three weeks.'

But it wasn't until he'd been listening to some of his customers discussing how they had to get home early that afternoon because they wanted to catch the latest daytime discussion show on the telly that an inkling of an idea had begun to take root in his mind.

The following day he'd set the video to record the programme and later that night, when both Cindy and Tiffany were asleep in bed, he'd secretly watched a dozen or so Americans laying out their neuroses in front of a live audience along with countless numbers of viewers. An expert in an absurd waistcoat with an equally absurd name – Dr L. S. Nutter III – was there on hand to help these troubled people work through their phobias and self-doubts. He'd been gobsmacked. It was incredible. And rewinding the tape he'd watched the bit again where a grossly overweight man had stood up and said, 'Help me! I'm terrified of my left hand.' He had gone on to explain in detail that ever since the age of thirteen he'd been unable to bring himself to use it. Dr L. S. Nutter III had suggested that the man was, in fact, lying and that what he was really saying was, 'Hey, look at me, I'm into self-abuse and what about it?' The fat man had leapt out of his chair and grabbed Nutter by the throat, but the doctor, cool as you like, had merely said, 'The truth has cured you. You see that hand you're about to hit me with? It's your left one!' The fat man had broken down and cried like a baby and the audience had gone wild, clapping and stamping their feet. They'd witnessed not only real live drama but a miracle. It was heady stuff.

'Just wait till I tell Barry.'

Derek dropped the papers he'd been shifting around on the desk. 'No. I'd rather you didn't.'

Tiffany stared at him, her eyes dark and critical – a reflection of her mother's. He had a pretty good idea what she was thinking and he didn't want to hear it. He got up from his chair and went over to the filing cabinet behind the desk. He opened one of the drawers. 'I want to be the one to tell Bas,' he said casually, his back to Tiffany.

'Suit yourself.'

He heard her open the door and when he turned round she was gone. Well, that wasn't so bad, he told himself.

'Classic mid-life crisis behaviour, I reckon,' Tiffany said, her head suddenly appearing round the door. She was grinning at him.

'Out!' he shouted.

Damn silly thing to say. Of course he wasn't going through a mid-life crisis. Good God, anyone would think he was behaving like those stressed-out executives you read about, who for no apparent reason give up their smart company cars and take to growing turnips in Wales. He wasn't like that. All he was doing was reviewing the schedule. It was time for a change. Surely that wasn't such a big deal. And there were market trends to take into account. It didn't pay to play the same game for too long, not when there were so many other opportunities out there to grab hold of.

There was still the question as to how he was going to tell Bas. The last thing he wanted was Tiffany running off to the phone and smirking into it that their father was going doo-lally. He hoped Bas would be pleased, even proud of him. It was important to him now that he had his son's approval.

45

'Life. Bloody old life,' he said out loud. 'What's a simple guy supposed to make of it?'

Tiffany gave a quick knock on the conservatory door. There was no response so she knocked again. She hoped Charlotte and Alex were in. She liked coming next door to Ivy Cottage where she was never treated as an awkward teenager. Instead Charlotte and Alex treated her as an awkward adult. She often came round to them when she wanted to get away from In the Pink – at least here she could escape the sight of all those gullible over-dressed women pandering to their vanity. Sad. Woefully sad the whole lot of them. Didn't they know that there were millions starving all over the world while they tried to sweat a few pounds off their wobbly bums and chins? Disgusting.

She knocked at the door again then turned the handle. 'Charlotte,' she called out. 'It's me, Tiffany.'

'Hello, you Tiffany,' said Alex, from the kitchen. 'Charlotte's upstairs having a bath. Anything I can help you with?'

Tiffany rolled her eyes and pouted. 'I need some help with my biology homework,' she said, sounding and wiggling her hips like Marilyn Monroe. It was a ritual she and Alex went through occasionally – she parodying the dumb blonde and he the lecherous older man.

'Ah-ah! And would I be right in thinking it was to do with the reproductive organs?'

She rolled her eyes again. 'You've found me out. How about we try psychology, then?'

Alex sidled up to Tiffany. 'Miss Vogers,' he said, 'I know your problems only too vell. You are mad for zee right man in your life. Am I correct?'

'Oh, oh,' squeaked Tiffany, sounding more like Betty Boop. 'Take me, Doctor, take—'

'Just watch yourself, Dr Kildare!'

It was Charlotte, standing in the doorway wearing Alex's bathrobe and a towel round her head. She was smiling.

'Honestly, I leave you to tidy up the kitchen and then find you seducing our next-door neighbour's daughter. Is it your age? Or am I making your tea too strong?'

Alex put his arm round Charlotte and kissed her.

Tiffany coughed loudly. 'If you could stop thinking about sex for a few moments, you two, I've got some news.'

Alex could feel the warmth of Charlotte's naked body through the towelling robe and suddenly sex was very much on his mind. 'Well, don't let us keep you, Tiffany,' he said.

'Don't be so rude,' Charlotte said, pushing him away.

'That's all right. I've heard about men like him. Anyway, do you want to hear my news, or what? Dad's having a mid-life crisis. The full works. He's chucking in exploiting women under the guise of health and beauty and setting himself up as a manager of some kind of therapy clinic. Never mind In the Pink, this'll be In the Stink if you ask me.'

'You mean no more Don Juan of the curlers?' Alex laughed.

'No more Lothario wielding his scissors?' Charlotte said, amazed.

'He's not been the same since Barry was ill. I've seen him mooching about the salon. He's obviously bored with the whole scene.'

'Perhaps he thinks he'll make more money out of therapy. Your dad's no fool.'

'You could be right, Charlotte,' Tiffany said. 'On the other hand, maybe he's worked out he can get to women more successfully by curing their emotional problems.'

'Talking of which,' Alex said, 'time you were going. I want to talk to my future wife about her emotional problems.'

'Future wife, eh? When, how and why?'

'That's what I want to talk to her about, little Miss Nosy Parker. So on your way.'

'I'm going, I'm going,' Tiffany said good-humouredly. 'I'm due at Hilary's in a few minutes to babysit.'

As Tiffany closed the door behind her, Charlotte frowned.

'Oh no you don't,' Alex said. 'Don't go pretending you're suddenly ill in an attempt to get out of our conversation.' He picked her up and carried her through to the sitting room where earlier he'd lit a fire. Mabel was stretched out in front of it on the rug. He set Charlotte down on the sofa and knelt beside her.

'What a suspicious nature you have, Alex. As a matter of fact I've just remembered I was supposed to go and see Hilary myself.'

'Hilary can wait. I can't.'

She raised an eyebrow and reached out to him.

'No,' he said firmly. 'I'm withholding my body until you've given me a date, time and place.'

She laughed. 'Ssh, you're embarrassing Mabel.'

He kissed her, then stood up. 'I'll get you a glass of wine, then I'll have your answer.'

When he came back into the room, Charlotte was sitting in front of the log fire; she'd removed the towel from her head and was running a hand through her long dark hair. She looked up as he stood over her.

'What do you think about Christmas?' she said.

'I rather thought we'd have it here again, like last year.' He put another log on the fire and nudged it into place with his foot.

'I didn't mean that.'

'You mean . . .'

'Christmas Eve falls on a Saturday this year. I've phoned Malcolm and he says he can fit us in. What do you think?'

'I think I've just stopped withholding my body.'

'Où est Paul?'

How should I know? Hilary thought angrily to herself. Carry on as normal had been Cindy's advice and, God help her, she was doing her best. Tuesday night was David's squash night and her French evening class at Becky's school,

48

and unbelievably, here she was – but was David really playing squash?

'Hilary, où est Paul?'

She looked down at her textbook and studied the drawings. 'Il est encore au lit,' she answered. Typical. Half past eleven in the morning and the stupid man was still in bed.

'Pourquoi?'

The classroom door opened.

'Bonsoir! Sorry I'm late.'

Everyone looked up, including Martina their French teacher. 'Hello,' she said, from the desk on which she was perched and uncrossing her legs. 'Are you sure you've got the right room?'

'I hope so. French, intermediate? My name's Nick Bradshaw. I should be on your list.'

While Martina flicked through the names on her register, Hilary bent her head and tried to sink as low as she could into the small primary-school chair. Her only hope was that he wouldn't recognise her without her sunglasses and ridiculous hat.

'You *are* late, aren't you?' Martina said, looking up from her file.

'About three weeks late, I make it.'

She laughed. 'Find a seat and we'll chat at the end of the session. If you sit at the back with Hilary you can partner her in the conversational work in a moment. Hilary, would you mind sharing your book?'

Hilary mumbled a yes and without looking up she slid it across the small desk.

'D'accord. Paul, il est encore au lit. Pourquoi? Patricia?'

'Parce qu'il est fatigué.' Hilary heard Patricia's reply, quick as a flash.

'Hi,' Nick Bradshaw said, squeezing himself into the chair next to her.

She managed a nod.

'Et Maman, où est-ce qu'elle est?'

'Where all good mothers are,' Nick Bradshaw whispered, 'at the tip throwing away expensive cut glass.'

Hilary froze. Out of the corner of her eye she could see he was smiling at her. He was making fun of her.

At the front of the classroom Martina closed her textbook. 'Okay,' she said, 'conversation work now. Pair off and choose one of the following subjects.' She started writing on the blackboard: Shopping, Gardening or Discussing a Book or a Film.

'What shall we pick?'

'You choose,' Hilary murmured, her head still bent over the textbook.

'How about some small-talk instead?'

Oh, please, the smaller the better. 'Oui,' she said.

He laughed. 'Très bien. Bonsoir, je m'appelle Nick.'

At last she looked him full in the face and flinched slightly under the same direct stare he'd offered her at the tip. He seemed older than she'd remembered him; somewhere in his early forties. His face had that rumpled kind of look that she supposed some women found attractive. She decided it matched his trousers – a quick glance downwards told her he was wearing the same pair as this morning. When she didn't say anything, he said, 'Hilary *qui*?'

'Hilary Parker,' she said reluctantly.

'Et qui est le bâtard?'

Who is the bastard? Oh my God! He *had* heard her this morning. She turned away, the colour instantly draining from her face.

'Votre mari peut-être?'

What was he, some kind of mind-reader? 'My husband? Of course not,' she said loudly.

'En français, Hilary.'

'I'm sorry, Martina,' Hilary said, suddenly gathering up her book and getting to her feet. 'I'm not feeling well. I'd better get off home.'

'Okay, everyone. Time's up anyway. Now remember,

there's no lesson next week, it's half-term break, so that means you have two weeks in which to do your homework. I want you to prepare a talk on your last holiday. Hilary, you do look rather pale, do you want me to give you a lift home?'

'No. I'll be fine once I'm outside. It must be the heating in here.' She struggled into her coat.

'What, no hat?'

Hilary flashed an angry look at Nick. 'Why don't you mind your own business?' she said. Then, astonished at what she'd just said, she hurried out of the classroom. But Patricia was there, barring her way at the door.

'Martina's right, Hilary, you do look pale. You do know there's diarrhoea doing the rounds at school, don't you?'

'Then you'd best get out of my way,' Hilary snapped.

Outside in the corridor as she hurried past the frieze of autumn artwork displayed on the walls, Hilary wondered what was happening to her. She was never bad-tempered with other people. Patience was her middle name and here she was sounding off at anyone who spoke to her. Bloody David! It was all his fault. Because he had changed, she was changing. She didn't like it. She wanted him to be the same old David and her to be the same old Hilary.

She scurried across the floodlit playground and paused at the school gate to catch her breath. How long was she supposed to keep this charade going? How had Cindy managed it all these years? From behind her she heard the sound of footsteps.

'I'm sorry about that, back there,' a voice called out. And before she was able to push open the gate Nick Bradshaw was next to her standing in the light cast from the street-lamp above them. 'I have a habit of wading in, I can't be bothered with mincing about. Getting to the nub of things is what I like to do, it's what I'm paid to do.'

'I'm sorry too,' she responded, deciding that David wouldn't change her completely. She would still remember her manners. 'I shouldn't have bitten your head off like that.'

'I probably deserved it. Fancy a drink?'

The rest of the group were now coming towards them across the Tarmac. Hilary could see Patricia walking alongside Martina. Bet she was teacher's pet at school, she thought. 'A drink?' she repeated, suddenly registering what this practically unknown man had asked her. How ridiculous. She was a married woman, a mother of two young children being asked out for a drink! The very idea.

'From the look on your face I'll take that as a no.'

'I really must be going,' she said, flustered. 'I've a babysitter waiting, PTA minutes to type up and—'

'And a husband.' He smiled. 'No worries. I'll see you in two weeks.' He held the gate for her. 'Don't forget your homework.'

Chapter Eight

When Hilary let herself in there was no sign of David, or of the children. Tiffany was lying on the sofa reading a book. She moved her long legs and made room for Hilary.

'I hope that's homework,' Hilary said, betraying her years as a teacher. She knew that Tiffany's mock exams were fast approaching, and although it was obvious that Tiffany was a bright and able student, she was also aware how easy it was for her to get sidetracked. In the short time that the Rogers family had been living in Acacia Lane Hilary had not only witnessed Tiffany trying to come through her adolescence by battling with her parents over her individuality – whether it was dressing herself from top to toe in black or dyeing her hair bright pink – she had also watched her go through her vegetarian phase, her custodians-of-the-earth phase and more recently her singlehanded attempt at shaming the residents of Hulme Welford into donating money for the homeless by sitting in a cardboard box outside Ted the Toup's shop one wet Saturday afternoon. Cindy and Derek had been away that particular weekend, had been blissfully ignorant of Tiffany's plan and had missed the sight of their daughter drenched and shivering, her hand outstretched, and the opportunity to try to stop her. But Hilary suspected that even if they had known about the collapsible cardboard box Tiffany had stashed away under her bed, Cindy and Derek would have been powerless to prevent their daughter's protest – like herself, they must have long since arrived at the unpalatable truth that there was nothing they could do to dissuade their youngest child from pursuing her chosen line of action.

'Background reading for Jane Austen,' Tiffany replied, waving the cover of *Emma* in front of Hilary. 'Bit of a spoilt madam, isn't she? Always poking her nose into everybody else's business and all the time she hasn't got a clue what's going on right under her own smug nose.'

'I think you'll find things change for her later,' Hilary said thoughtfully, struggling to recall her own A-level studies.

'Yea, well, she deserves the fall that's coming to her, if you ask me.'

'Children okay?' Hilary asked, suddenly feeling uncomfortable with the conversation.

'Philip was his usual quiet self and Becky got worked up over something and nothing.'

'Mm ...' Hilary said, distracted. Her mind was still on *Emma*. At the door she paid Tiffany and said goodbye, then went back into the sitting room where she looked along the shelves of the bookcase to the right of the fireplace. There, on the highest shelf, she found what she was looking for. She blew away the dust and opened the book at chapter one.

Emma Woodhouse, handsome, clever, and rich, with a comfortable home and happy disposition, seemed to unite some of the best blessings of existence, and had lived nearly twenty-one years in the world with very little to distress or vex her.

Apart from the age and perhaps the *handsome* and *clever* references it could be herself. Hadn't she always thought she'd lived a charmed life with David? All these years she had been so complacently happy with her lot ... and now there was the risk that she was about to lose everything.

She put the book back in its place on the top shelf then caught her reflection in the mirror above the fireplace. She looked tired, dull even, but surely not so awful that David had stopped loving her? When had it all gone wrong? She thought back over the past year or so, searching her mind for some tell-tale sign that would explain David's indifference to her. She could find none, but she could hear Charlotte's voice telling her how bossy she was. And, yes, deep down she knew her sister was right, but that wasn't such a crime, it was just her way, and anyway everybody had their little foibles. But Charlotte had also implied that she had a habit of interfering and David himself had accused her of the same thing last year. 'Stop meddling in other people's lives,' he'd said, 'especially your sister's.' She had been stung by his words – after all, she'd only been helping Charlotte to get over Peter's death by nudging her in Alex's direction. What harm had she done? And were these crimes justification for a husband to cause untold harm to his family by having an affair? Tiffany had just condemned *Emma* by saying she deserved the fall that was coming to her – would people say that about herself, she wondered.

The phone rang.

'It's me.'

'Where are you?'

'Still at the squash club.'

Hilary pushed the receiver closer to her ear, trying to make out the sound of squash balls being whacked against a wall – she wanted to believe David, truly she did.

'I'll be a bit later than usual. There's a free court so I'm having another game ... Hilary, you still there?'

She slammed down the phone and was still crying when she heard somebody at the front door.

'Cindy!' She had never known Cindy to go calling, not even during the day, let alone at night.

'When Tiffany came home, I thought I'd see how you were.'

'As you can see, not very well,' Hilary answered, making no attempt to wipe away her tears.

'Would you rather I left you alone?' Cindy said awkwardly.

'No, no. Please come in, I was just going to make myself a drink.'

Cindy followed Hilary into the kitchen and while Hilary made some coffee, she took off her coat and started to clear away what was obviously the remains of tea. 'You should get Tiffany to tidy up for you while she babysits,' she said.

'I couldn't do that,' Hilary snivelled, 'she's got her homework to do.' She blew her nose, loudly and messily, knowing she looked awful; she always did whenever she cried. At the first sign of a tear her eyes would swell and redden, almost to the same shade as the rubber gloves Cindy was now pulling on. What on earth was Cindy doing? She sensed Cindy didn't approve of tears, which made her want to cry even more. Disapproval was almost as bad as rejection.

As she watched Cindy wring out the dishcloth she realised that the other woman made her feel ashamed and inadequate. Georgia hadn't made her feel like that. Georgia had been warm and comforting, which had surprised Hilary. She hadn't expected kindness from such a tough woman.

Cindy had now moved on to wiping the work surfaces. Hilary felt a stab of anger towards this woman who was so calm, so cool, and who had probably never cried in her life. 'Cindy,' she said, trying to sound assertive, 'you don't have to do that. Come and have your coffee.'

'It's no trouble,' Cindy answered, moving back to the sink and spraying some Mr Muscle behind the mixer taps. She rubbed hard then, satisfied that the worst of the tears were over, she peeled off the gloves, sat opposite Hilary and thought, Thank God I never fell apart like this. She felt proud of herself that during all the years of putting up with Derek's dalliances she had held herself together as well as their family.

She had called on Hilary to see how she was and to escape Derek's endless talk of his latest brainchild. She was finding it hard to be as motivated as he was about the whole idea, but in a funny kind of way it pleased her to see Derek so enthusiastic about something. Just after Barry's confirmation last summer Derek had seemed more content than she'd ever known him, but more recently he had become distant and distracted. She hoped that the transformation of their business would be the answer to whatever had been causing him to wander listlessly about the salon. Perhaps, finally, he was about to find his true vocation. It might even stop him from straying, give him a sense of fulfilment. She was beginning to sound like him now, as though quoting from one of his wretched books.

A sniff from the other side of the table reminded her of Hilary.

'I don't think I can carry on much longer pretending nothing's happened,' Hilary said flatly.

'Why don't you come over to me tomorrow and I'll give you a facial?'

'Georgia D'Arcy says I should confront David.' She paused. 'Actually, Georgia said I should confront the sodding bastard.' She gave a queer little laugh. 'I don't normally go in for profanity, but since yesterday I seem to have done little else.'

Cindy examined one of her long, varnished nails. It was chipped. She must have knocked it just now. She said coolly, 'Well, Georgia D'Arcy would say that, wouldn't she?'

Hilary looked up sharply. 'What do you mean?'

'And just where did it get her when she confronted her husband? Living in a caravan and working all hours just to scratch a living together. Is that what you want, Hilary?' She cast her eyes round the cluttered but comfortable Aga-warmed kitchen. 'You'd lose all this. You know that, don't you?'

Hilary began to cry again. 'She doesn't live in a caravan any more and at least she has her dignity.'

'And I haven't?' suggested Cindy.

'I . . . I didn't say that. All I meant was—'

'I know what you meant, Hilary, but are you strong enough to do what Georgia did?'

'Georgia says that a woman is like a tea-bag and it's only when she's in hot water that she knows how strong she is.'

Cindy's usually brittle features softened. 'I like that,' she said, smiling.

'I don't think I have the same kind of strength you have, Cindy. I'm not at all stoic like you.'

Stoic? Strength? Cindy had never thought of it like that. She had merely taken it for granted that she would hold things together.

Hilary sniffed. 'Georgia says—'

Cindy raised her hand. 'Okay. I think I've heard enough from Ms D'Arcy. As far as I can see, you've a choice to make, Hilary. Either you play it my way and hope David tires of this one-off thing—'

'If it is a one-off—'

'Or you confront him and risk losing your husband because you've forced him into making the wrong choice. It's up to you.'

Not long after Cindy had left, Hilary went upstairs to check on the children. She stood in Philip's bedroom at the end of his bed. She watched him turn over in his sleep. He was restless, the duvet tossed aside, his pillow hanging over the edge of the bed. She moved forward and stooped to rearrange the duvet, remembering how when Philip had been a baby she would put him in his cot on his side at bedtime and in the morning he'd be in exactly the same position – the sheets barely wrinkled, the blanket undisturbed. So when had he changed? And when had he started biting his fingernails, she wondered, catching sight of one of his hands in the strip of light from the landing as it streaked through the doorway and across his bed? Poor Philip, she suddenly thought, what was troubling him?

And how on earth could she confront David when it might threaten her children's security?

Chapter Nine

It was Saturday morning when Charlotte remembered she still hadn't called on her sister to see how she was. But as she unlocked the door of her shop she decided that if anything had been seriously wrong, Hilary would have come to see her.

Not so long ago Hilary had practically been a permanent resident at Ivy Cottage, continually popping over the road with some spurious reason for visiting when all the time she had been checking up on Charlotte and Alex.

Their relationship had been what Charlotte had supposed was a fairly typical one between sisters. As children they had been the best of friends one moment and sworn enemies the next. Best friends had consisted of sleeping together in the same bedroom, playing T. Rex records until gone midnight and then tuning in to Radio Luxembourg. Enemies had consisted of Charlotte defacing one of Hilary's treasured David Cassidy posters and Hilary jamming her up against the wall and beating her about the head with the lid of a biscuit tin. Thinking about it, it was the only time Charlotte could recall her sister losing control. On the whole, and especially so nowadays, Hilary had always been a control freak; worrying and herding those around her like the most persistent of sheepdogs.

There had, of course, been the one-way rivalry between them. Hilary had desperately wanted to be the older sister and had fought sneakily as well as blatantly to usurp Charlotte's role; a role for which Charlotte had never given tuppence. She knew that, after Peter's death, Hilary had relished her role as sister of mercy to the rescue and had played the part with supreme heavy-handedness.

Charlotte opened the small safe at the back of the shop and then put the float into the till. At nine o'clock she switched on the lights and waited for her first customer of the day, knowing that trade wouldn't really get going until gone nine thirty, and now that the weather was turning nasty perhaps it would be even later. She was enjoying running her own business again, even if her mother had greeted her decision to take on the lease with her usual scorn. 'Just don't be muscling in on my patch,' Louise had said. 'Only room for one antique shop in the village.' Charlotte knew that her mother was as mad as hell that by somebody else's bad luck she had acquired one of the largest shops in the village with its spacious double frontage – Louise had only the one cramped window. Dad had been great and helped her and Alex redecorate the place after Jim Lloyd had cleared the last of his bathroom fittings from the shop.

She had decided against going back into clothes retailing, which she had done in London, all those years ago, before Peter had forced her to sell up and move abroad. What Hulme Welford needed, she had concluded, was a shop selling quality gifts, along with a cheaper line in Third-World goods for the caring nineties consumer.

Filling a basket with a new batch of friendship bands – ready for the pocket-money spenders – Charlotte thought of the look that she would put on Hilary's face when she told her she and Alex had at last fixed a date for the wedding. The only downside was that Hilary might dive in, take over and organise a monumental bunfight. The last thing Charlotte wanted was her sister hijacking her wedding.

The shop door opened and Charlotte lifted her head to greet her first customer. It was Hilary with the niece from hell, Becky. 'Hello,' Charlotte said, trying to keep the shock out of her voice. Her sister looked dreadful. She was so pale.

'Hello, Auntie Charlotte,' piped up Becky, making a bee-line for the shelves of china candlesticks.

Charlotte watched Becky start to move the expensive pieces of Italian chinaware as though she were playing chess, while at the same time she was conscious of Hilary drifting towards the counter, her hands playing nervously over the pile of paper bags next to the till.

'You're out and about early,' Charlotte said, troubled that for the first time in her life she was experiencing the sensation of feeling sorry for her sister.

'I'm selling tickets for the school firework party. Do you want some for you and Alex?' Hilary replied, without looking at Charlotte. Her voice was flat and mechanical, and unmistakably wrong to Charlotte's well-trained ear. Even though Hilary believed herself the most circumspect woman alive, Charlotte knew otherwise. Her sister had never been able to hide anything – secrets had always burst out of her with rocket-like propulsion and her face was as easy to read as a book.

'I'll get my bag,' Charlotte said.

When she returned from the small back office, she found her sister looking at a handmade Advent calendar. Charlotte noticed that Hilary's hands were shaking. 'What is it, Hilary?'

Without turning round, Hilary said, 'I was just thinking of Christmases when we were little. It was always Dad who made it happen, wasn't it? I'd never thought of that before.'

'Dad did the presents, but it was you who made everything else happen, bossing everybody about like a good 'un.'

'I wasn't that bossy,' Hilary retaliated.

Charlotte frowned. Hilary, bossy – the two were synonymous, everybody knew that. 'How much are the tickets?' she asked, moving onto safer ground.

'Two pounds fifty each. There's a free drink thrown in.'

A sudden crash from Becky made them both turn.

'I haven't broken anything,' Becky said brightly.

'For heaven's sake,' shouted Hilary, 'can't you be more careful?'

Charlotte was taken aback. She'd never heard Hilary admonish her daughter like this before. It had always been Charlotte's privately held opinion that if Hilary had been firmer with Becky from the word go, she wouldn't be such a pain now. 'Hilary,' Charlotte said, quietly, 'what's up?'

Hilary glanced away, but not before Charlotte had seen her lips trembling and her eyes filling with tears.

'Has something happened?'

Hilary shook her head.

'Please, Hilary. If I can help.' She placed a tentative hand on her sister's arm. 'What is it?'

'I'm not supposed to tell anyone,' Hilary blurted out. It sounded ridiculous.

'For God's sake, why?'

'I ...' Hilary finally met her sister's gaze and disintegrated beneath it. 'It's David ...' She looked over to where Becky was still playing chess. 'An affair,' she whispered, 'he's having an affair.'

'No! Not David, I don't believe it.'

The door flew open, followed by a dramatic blast of wind which brought with it a flurry of leaves and Iris Braithwaite.

'Mrs Lawrence, a word, if you please.'

'Can it wait, Mrs Braithwaite?' Charlotte asked, her eyes never once leaving her sister's face.

Iris rattled the door shut and approached Charlotte and Hilary. She had with her a pen on a long piece of string attached to a black clipboard. 'I'm on a mission of merchandise cleansing,' she boomed, 'so no, it cannot wait. And waiting, I might say, Mrs Lawrence, is the very kind of attitude that has got us where we are. The day has come—'

'Mrs Braithwaite—'

'I haven't finished, Mrs Lawrence. The day has come for us to rid Hulme Welford of everything unsavoury and of an ambiguous nature.' Her eyes swept accusingly round the shelves of Charlotte's shop.

'What on earth are you talking about, Mrs Braithwaite?' Charlotte asked.

'A smut-free zone is what I'm talking about and I'm not at all sure I like your tone of—'

'A what zone?' Hilary interrupted, speaking for the first time.

Iris approached the counter and banged down her clipboard. She gave Charlotte a handwritten poster. 'Make Hulme Welford a Smut-free Zone' it declared in large letters. 'In the window, if you please, Mrs Lawrence, and if you'd like to sign my petition I'll be on my way. You too, Mrs Parker.'

Charlotte read aloud from the piece of paper: ' "I the undersigned agree to the closure of Ted Cooper's newsagent's and will not tolerate the selling of undesirable items in any other retail establishment in Hulme Welford." '

'Undesirable items?' Charlotte repeated.

'Pornographic!' exclaimed Iris, so vigorously that her brown cowpat of a hat with a little stalk sticking up from it nearly slipped off her head.

'But he's always sold smutty magazines.'

'I'm not referring to those.' Iris shuddered. 'It's pornographic items of clothing he's moved on to. He'll be turning the premises into a sex shop next. Hulme Welford will soon become the Soho of the North if we don't stop him.'

Charlotte wanted to laugh, but Iris's highly censorious manner was verging on the manic and it was possible that an unchecked snigger might tip the old woman over the edge.

'What exactly is Ted selling?' she asked patiently.

'Tights with . . . tights without a . . .' Iris cleared her throat and began again. 'No gusset,' she hissed. ' "Peephole", he called them.'

'Peep-bo!' sang out Becky, her head appearing over the top of a display rack of cotton throw-overs. 'What's a sex shop?'

*

It was complete chaos. They would never be ready in time, and just how on earth had she let Derek talk her into this?

Cindy looked at what, until a few days ago, had been the reception desk in the foyer – it was now pushed against the door waiting to be thrown away. According to Derek they weren't going to have a desk. Apparently such a solid block would act as both a mental and physical barrier, making a them-and-us situation. 'We are to meld as one,' he had explained last night, while watching Cindy stack the dishwasher after she'd got back from seeing Hilary. Tiffany had walked in at that point looking for food and had muttered something about melding her father together.

'And what exactly are we calling ourselves?' Cindy had asked.

'Don't tempt me,' Tiffany had sniggered, her head inside the fridge.

Derek had looked pleased with himself. 'All in the Mind. What do you reckon?'

'I should think it bloody well is all in your mind!' Tiffany had shrieked, her raucous laughter telling Derek exactly what she thought. Cindy had wanted to laugh, too, but had refrained from joining in with her daughter's ridicule.

Cindy was struck now as she had been last night that this was a new and strange phenomenon – Tiffany and herself in agreement. For years it had been open warfare between the two and over the slightest of issues, mainly her daughter's appearance. But recently the friction had eased. It was as if all Tiffany's energy was being channelled into the superhuman feat of her becoming a woman, leaving her little or no strength to be so antagonistic – though there had been that recent incident with the cardboard box outside Ted Cooper's.

Earlier in the year, she and Derek had breathed a sigh of relief when Tiffany had at last thrown away her wrung-out dishcloth look in favour of the more stylish and flattering clothes she spent her Saturday afternoons unearthing in the charity shops in Congleton. She still wore predominantly black but gone were the heavy eye make-up and dyed black hair: instead she'd let her own sandy colour grow through and had actually allowed her father to restyle it, asking him to cut ten inches off the length, keeping it bulky on the top but graduated into the nape of her neck. It made her look older but at the same time more vulnerable.

Tiffany's appearance might have softened over the last year but Cindy knew, better than anyone, that her tongue had not. That was still as sharp as ever, but instead of being directed at her, it was now aimed mostly at Derek.

Funny thing was, Derek seemed reluctant or perhaps unable to fight back with his daughter. Was this because he no longer saw Tiffany as a child, but more as a woman? Derek had never been able to resist the charm of any woman, no matter what kind of charm she exuded. In many ways Tiffany was just as much a challenge to win over as any of his past conquests. It was also true that since Barry had gone to university the atmosphere in the house had changed. Derek as the sole man was up against two women, who were showing all the signs of joining forces.

Cindy smiled to herself as she heard the sound of a radio playing loudly from somewhere in the salon. Bob Dylan was singing 'The Times They Are A-Changin''. And weren't they just?

She looked out of the large window onto the front garden and the parking area filled with builders' and decorators' vans. At the end of the drive two men were hard at work removing the old In the Pink sign and replacing it with a new one. She supposed that it was only a matter of time before the colour of the house was changed. Cindy had been well aware that when the first coat of pink paint had been brushed onto the walls there had been shock waves of disapproval in the village. She had asked Derek to show restraint but he had ignored her. 'Cindy,' he'd said, 'this is to be the pinnacle of our career in the health and beauty industry, we've got to go for it.'

So, Cindy thought wryly, as she watched the two men at the end of the drive, if the pinnacle of their career was in the process of being dismantled, what was next? Her life before had been predictably unsure, but she had successfully walked the tightrope of their precarious marriage in the knowledge that beneath her was the safety of the business. It had been the one certainty in her life and had provided the reassurance – the only tangible reassurance – upon which she had been able to rely. But what was she sure of now? What was her role to be at All in the Mind? Not so long ago, Tiffany, in one of her bitchier pre-menstrual moods, had described her as being good only for plucking and pruning. Had her daughter been right? After all, she was no counsellor, no mind-bender, as Tiffany described the people who were going to be taking the places of Tracy and Lorraine, along with all the other members of staff who had grumbled to hell and back at being made redundant. Their grievances had soon been mollified by the generous financial packages Cindy had offered.

Last night she had asked Derek what her role was to be. Plumping up the cushion in his armchair he had said, 'We'll all find our own niche, given time.'

'Niche?' she had repeated. 'I'm not sure I want a niche, Derek. I want something I know I can do. Something real.'

He'd smiled. 'Finding our own personal niche is the challenge we're all seeking in this life.'

She'd switched on the television at that point and settled down to watch a videoed episode of *Coronation Street* – something she could understand. Her husband was now communicating in a language she didn't recognise, but at least the goings-on of the Street were familiar territory.

'Cindy! There you are, I've been looking all over for you. I'd like you to meet Rosie Williams. She's to be our marriage guidance expert.'

A bit late for that, thought Cindy, as she turned round to face a statuesque young woman at Derek's side. She took in the soft brown eyes flecked with green, the smart suit and the long, long legs encased in the sheerest of tights. One hand held a briefcase and the other was extended towards her.

'Your husband has just confirmed my position.'

'Has he, indeed?' Cindy was nettled, not just by this woman with her smooth poise and well educated voice but by Derek. 'I had no idea he was interviewing this morning. I thought *we* were doing that *together*, this afternoon.'

Derek laughed awkwardly and Rosie raised a surprisingly large hand in the air. 'And there we have it,' she said, in a tone of voice that smacked of teacher-knows-best. 'Communication. That's the name of the game, isn't it? It's the basis of every sound, rock-solid marriage.' She put down her case and drew a square in the air with her two forefingers. 'See?' she said. 'The lines meet head on. There are no crossed wires.'

'That's the stuff,' Derek said enthusiastically.

God help us, thought Cindy.

'I'll see you to your car,' Derek said, filling in Cindy's obvious silence. He steered Rosie Williams towards the door. 'Mind how you go, don't want you breaking your neck on all this rubbish before you've even started work with us.' He picked his way over a large blue tool-box and a coil of electric cable with a drill attached at one end.

'Nothing is rubbish,' Rosie said meaningfully. 'Everything and everyone has a purpose. Thrilled to have met you, Cindy. Byee.'

'Goodbye, Miss Williams, or is it Mrs?' Cindy asked, her voice just as meaningful.

'Oh, definitely Miss.'

Perfectly qualified, then, to guide others through the misfortunes of marriage. Cindy watched their first recruit follow Derek out of the door and down the steps to the parking area. 'Late twenties perhaps, and about as many brain cells,' she muttered. She turned away and tried hard not to think of leopards and spots.

Chapter Ten

Thank God, Hilary thought from her front pew.

Thank God it wasn't her turn on the Sunday School rota. And thank God Malcolm Jackson was a devil for rambling sermons and she could sit here in peace for a whole hour and thirty minutes. No Becky – she was tormenting some other unfortunate volunteer. And no Philip either – he was playing in a school rugby match with David standing on the touchline ... Please, God, let David freeze to death.

She could hardly believe it was a whole week since she'd discovered David's affair and it was a reflection on her own life that up until now she'd had no idea what despair and misery were really about. How glib adultery was made to look on television. How poignant it was in novels, and how glamorously sensational in the tabloids. Never was it portrayed as it was. It was terrifying. Terrifying and bewildering, so much so you could barely eat, sleep or even think properly.

Yesterday Charlotte had suggested she go to the doctor. 'You're obviously worn out, Hilary,' she'd said, when Iris Braithwaite had finally left them in the shop. 'Are you eating? And what about sleep?'

Sleeping and eating were the least of her concerns right now. Coping was uppermost in her mind and it seemed to her that that alone was taking up all her energy. David, blast him, had even had the nerve to say, 'What's wrong, Hilary? You don't look right.' She had nearly confronted him then, had so very nearly thrown the whole damn thing at him and shouted, 'Of course I'm not looking right, and is it any wonder knowing that your every spare moment is spent with that ...?' But she hadn't. She had kept quiet and carried on ironing his shirt, banging the iron down on the cuff, wishing his arm was still in it.

And each day it took all her powers of self-restraint not to march straight into David's office in the village and have it out with that wretched Catherine. How could she do it? How could one woman treat another so badly? It was beyond her. A part of her didn't want to confront Catherine. It was almost as though her subconscious was saying, 'If you leave well alone, then it's more likely that none of this is really happening.'

Like Cindy, Charlotte had urged her not to have it out with Catherine. 'You're blameless in all of this, Hilary,' she had said. 'Keep it that way. If you see her you'll lose your temper. Just don't do anything you'll regret. Would you like Alex to talk to David?'

'No!'

'But he might be able to get David to see what he's doing, what he's risking.'

'I don't want David to find out that I know—'

'Why in heaven's name not?'

'Oh, Charlotte, you just don't understand. Just think yourself lucky that Peter died.'

Their conversation had ended at that point with a sudden rush of customers coming into the shop and Hilary and Becky setting off for home.

Now, in St John's, Hilary felt appalled at what she'd said to her sister: ... *think yourself lucky that Peter died*. What a dreadful thing to say. She tried to concentrate on the sound of Malcolm Jackson's voice telling her, along with all the other sinners assembled in St John's that morning, that she was saved, and wasn't that wonderful.

But all Hilary could think of was how wonderful it would be to be saved from having to go back to The Gables when this service came to an end, and how wonderful it would be to be saved from pretending that everything was fine. Everything was not fine. Far from it. David, her husband, a man whom she had trusted with her life all their marriage, had betrayed her in the worst possible way, and what, she demanded, looking up at the stained-glass window above the altar, was God doing about it? Never mind all this stuff about saving sinners. How about some old-fashioned retribution? In her opinion a dose of Old Testament wrath was called for. A thunderbolt or two wouldn't go amiss, especially in the direction of the trollop who had thrown herself at David.

Aware that all behind her were now on their feet, hymn books open, Hilary stood up. Still thinking of this other woman in David's life she clenched her hymn book as though she were grasping Catherine bloody Renshaw around the neck while she sang with the rest of the congregation, ' "Your hands swift to welcome, your arms to embrace." '

As usual coffee was being served at the back of the church by Iris Braithwaite along with Mrs Bradley and Mrs Haslip. Alex nudged Charlotte. 'There go the Golden Girls,' he whispered.

'Why don't you make Mrs Bradley's day by chatting her up over the coffee urn?' Charlotte replied. 'You love it when she goes all breathless over you.'

'I'd rather you were breathless—'

'That's as may be but I need a word with Hilary.'

Charlotte found Hilary at the foot of the altar, not deep in supplication, as her position suggested, but fiddling with the large arrangement of autumn flowers. Since yesterday morning Charlotte hadn't had an opportunity to talk to Hilary about what she'd told her in the shop – after all, she could hardly have gone over to The Gables with David there. She still couldn't come to terms with what her brother-in-law was up to. She bent down and touched her sister lightly on the shoulder. Hilary almost leapt in response, pushing Charlotte up against the altar and sending the eucharistic tackle crashing.

'Charlotte! I'm so sorry, I had no idea you were there.' Hilary was flustered.

Charlotte tidied up the mess and led her sister to a pew.

'Please don't be nice to me,' Hilary suddenly said. 'I ... I really couldn't bear that.'

'Okay,' Charlotte agreed, remembering how difficult she had found coping with sympathy offered to her after Peter's death. 'I'll do my normal horrid-sister routine, shall I?' She was conscious that, whether Hilary liked it or not, she was going to have to let her, Charlotte, be the older sister for once.

Hilary sniffed. 'All right,' she said, staring straight ahead of her, her hands twisting the stalk of a dying chrysanthemum she had just pulled out of the altar flowers. She suddenly faced Charlotte. 'You haven't told anyone, have you?'

Charlotte shook her head. 'Nobody.'

'What about Alex?'

'Hilary, you made me promise not to tell anyone. Now stop worrying about that and tell me when you found out about David.'

'On Monday.'

All that time ago and her sister hadn't come to her. 'How? How did you find out?'

Hilary told her.

'But are you sure? I mean—'

'Good God, Charlotte, of course I'm sure. You always did treat me like a fool. I never could—'

'Shut up, Hilary,' Charlotte said sternly. 'This is no time for one of our squabbles.'

'I wasn't squabbling, I was merely—'

'Never mind that. What are you going to do?'

'Cindy says I should pretend it isn't happening and Georgia D'Arcy says I should confront David.'

'Who else knows about this?' Charlotte asked, surprised at how hurt she felt that Hilary hadn't come to her for help. But then she herself, when her own marriage had been falling apart, hadn't turned to her sister or any member of her family for advice and support. Even now Hilary had no idea that she had asked Peter for a divorce the morning he had died.

'Nobody else,' Hilary replied, 'just Cindy and Georgia.'

'So you've told me what they think you should do, but not what you want to do.'

'It's obvious, isn't it? I've got to try and ignore what's happening.'

After a moment's quiet Charlotte said, 'If it's worth anything I agree with Georgia. Until you and David talk this through you're not going to be able to—'

'But don't you see? I could risk losing him if I do that.'

'You risk losing him anyway,' Charlotte said softly.

Hilary swallowed. 'There's less danger this way.'

'But, Hilary, you never could keep a secret, or lie convincingly. You've got to say something to David, or you'll end up making yourself ill.'

'I've got Philip and Becky to think of, they need their father. I'll do it for them.'

'And you truly believe staying silent will—'

'It's worked for Cindy. Why not for me?'

Charlotte covered her sister's hands. Poor Hilary. Poor Hilary trying to be so brave. 'Because you're not Cindy and you're not used to living with all this bloody chaos.'

'Auntie Charlotte, that's not nice,' Becky said, squeezing into the pew. 'Jesus won't have you in heaven if you go round saying bloody all the time. Ooh!' she squeaked, and quickly slapped a hand over her mouth. 'Now Jesus won't want me to sit by his throne either.' Her eyes swivelled in their sockets as though expecting to see the Messiah himself lurking behind one of the pillars.

Charlotte watched Hilary hug her daughter to her. What

a mess indeed, she thought, raising her eyes to the vaulted ceiling above. Sorry, Jesus, but throne or no throne, it's a bloody fine old mess down here.

Chapter Eleven

Monday morning, the first day of half-term. David had already left for work, the children were downstairs, plugged into the cartoons so thoughtfully programmed for the school holidays, and Hilary was in the shower. She was crying and washing away David's semen. How could he have made love to her? How could she have let him?

The questions had ricocheted around inside her head all night. She had no answer for why David should want to have sex with her, when he was obviously satisfying himself elsewhere, but she knew well enough why she had offered herself to him. It was all part of the charade: letting him, encouraging him even to make love with her might make everything all right. Allowing him to join their bodies as one would perhaps magically hold their marriage together – might even make him give Catherine up. In the moment he had reached out to Hilary in bed last night she had known that her decision to follow Cindy's example was the right one. She would do exactly as Cindy had done all these years. It was a small sacrifice to ensure their family stayed together.

She turned off the shower and reached for a towel. She wrapped it round her and walked over to the basin. Wiping the steam away from the mirror she looked at her wet face. Tears or shower water? Who would know? Who would even care? She felt herself succumbing to that one single emotion she despised in others – self-pity. She had never once pitied herself and something deep within her was telling her to pull herself together. 'Right,' she said aloud, 'you may cry in the shower, but nowhere else. You are going to be strong. You are going to smarten yourself up and show David you're worth a hundred Catherines – bet she can't make flapjacks like you!' She gave a brave little laugh, but immediately felt the onset of tears again. She quickly leapt back into the shower so as not to break her first resolve of the day.

At half past ten Hilary left Philip in charge of Becky while they watched a video and she went across the road to see Cindy. Cindy, Hilary had decided, was going to be instrumental in her plan to win back her husband.

She stood for a moment at the end of the drive of In the Pink, except it wasn't any more. Gone was the puce board and in its place was a discreet dark blue sign with stylish Gothic letters in gold: All in the Mind, it read. How long had that been there? Was she in such a state that she'd lost touch with what was going on around her? She walked past the caravan of builders' and decorators' vehicles and found the front door wide open. Loud music, accompanied by the sound of an electric drill, blasted out at her, along with the smell of paint. A man in overalls with a woolly hat pulled down over his head was kneeling on the floor painting a skirting board.

'They're busy,' he shouted at her, pausing briefly with his paintbrush, 'interviewing.'

'Oh,' Hilary said, her disappointment obvious.

''Bout another ten minutes, I should think. They said they'd be free at quarter to.'

'I'll wait, then,' she said, knowing that if she went back to The Gables now, she might never pluck up the courage to come back to see Cindy.

'Suit yourself. There's a chair in one of them back rooms.'

She picked her way carefully over the dust sheets, minding the haphazardly placed tools and off-cuts of wood. The hair salon had undergone a dramatic change. The back washes and mirrors had all gone, so had the chairs and shiny floor. Now all there was was a large empty room with an oatmeal-coloured carpet, the smell of which testified to it being new and only recently laid. Behind the door was a small stool and on this was a stack of glossy pamphlets. Hilary helped herself to one. On the front cover was a picture of Derek and Cindy with the words All in the Mind emblazoned above them. She turned the first page and started to read about Derek and Cindy's new venture:

Join us at our sanctuary of inner spiritual exploration and hope. Come on a voyage of discovery to experience your hidden depths. Let us help you to find the real you so that you can reach your full potential. Marital problems a speciality at All in the Mind.

In the background all went quiet as the sound of the drill stopped. 'Brew up,' shouted a man's voice. Then Hilary heard Derek. She replaced the pamphlet on top of the pile and went out to the reception area.

'Hello, Hilary,' said Derek, 'you anxious to get your name down for one of our classes? Positive thinking, assertiveness or how to pep up your marriage? Take your pick.'

'Goodness. What would I want with all that?' Hilary said, her cheeks reddening. 'I've only come over to see Cindy.'

'She'll be out in a moment. She's just showing one of our new members of staff round the place.' He looked about him. 'What do you reckon, then? Bit of a change, isn't it? Might even put sleepy old Hulme Welford on the map.'

'Lovely,' she responded, trying her best to sound enthusiastic.

'Marriage will be the thing, mark my words,' Derek continued, rubbing his hands together. 'Always marital problems going on, especially in a place like this.'

'Really,' Hilary said quietly. 'What makes you think that?'

He grinned and slipped his arm round Hilary's waist. 'Now I know what you're thinking. That's rich coming from old Derek, but believe me, I'm a reformed character. I—'

'And what could that possibly mean, I wonder?'

'Ah, Cindy my pet,' Derek said, swinging round to face his wife.

Hilary tried to manoeuvre herself away from Derek's arm, but he didn't seem at all inclined to let her go. At Cindy's side stood someone she recognised only too well. Nick Bradshaw. He smiled at her and she wished even more that Derek would remove his arm.

'What do you make of the set-up, Nick?' asked Derek. 'Glad to be in on the ground floor, I should think.'

'I'm impressed. You've thought it all out very well.' His words were aimed at Derek but his eyes were on Hilary. She felt uncomfortable beneath his now familiar gaze and wanted very much to wriggle out of Derek's grasp and away from this man's direct way of looking at her.

'Sorry,' Derek said suddenly. 'Forgetting my manners. Let me introduce Hilary Parker, she lives over the road and is one of our most industrious neighbours, organises us all like you'd never believe.'

'We've met already ...'

Oh, please don't mention the tip, thought Hilary, not that.

'... at, of all places, the local tip,' Nick said, with a light, easy laugh.

Derek gave Hilary a squeeze with his arm. 'Well, you are a dark horse, Hilary,' he said, 'but I can think of more salubrious venues for a secret assignation.'

'Don't judge everyone by your own standards, Derek,' Cindy said coolly.

'I was only throwing away some rubbish, that was all,' Hilary said, flustered.

'Aha,' Derek said, remembering Rosie's words of a few days ago. 'There's no such thing as rubbish. Everything and everyone has a purpose.'

Cindy shook her head and Nick Bradshaw gave his new employer a polite smile.

'Nick's going to be head of stress and positive thinking here at All in the Mind,' Derek went on. 'Perhaps you should book your David in for a course. He's looking a bit frazzled these days. Been burning the candle at both ends, has he?'

'Derek!' snapped Cindy. 'I'm sure that what David is or is not doing is none of our concern. Mr Bradshaw, I'll show you out. Hilary, I presume it was me you wanted to see. I'll be back in a few minutes. Derek, go and put the kettle on.'

'Ja, mein Kapitän!' Derek said, letting go of Hilary and clicking his heels together.

Chapter Twelve

It was nearly half past three when Neville Archer remembered he hadn't been out to the shops. He threw a last handful of leaves onto the bonfire, picked up his rake and lumbered up the path to the back porch of the black and white timbered cottage.

He slipped off his gardening boots and padded through to the kitchen where he'd left his shoes over an hour ago. From the window he could see a thin trail of smoke threading its way upwards in the still, damp afternoon air. He knew he shouldn't leave the bonfire unattended but Louise would play up worse than a child if she came back from the shop and found no supper to eat, which right now far outweighed the potential risk of their thatch catching fire. But gradually the thought of explaining the remains of their burnt-out cottage to Louise took root in his mind and had him reaching under the sink for a plastic bucket. He carried it, slopping, down the garden path and doused the fire.

Back inside he grabbed his keys from the hook above the boiler, put on his overcoat and banged the front door shut after him. He left his Volvo in the car park behind the doctors' surgery, where he hoped that neither his wife nor Hilary would catch sight of it. 'Not too old to learn to ride a bike,' Louise would, no doubt, jibe at him for his laziness. He crossed the road and delved in his coat pocket for his shopping list. He tutted. He'd left it behind on the kitchen table. With a surge of regret he remembered how easy and straightforward his days as a GP had been – diagnosing and prescribing had been simplicity itself compared to the haphazard way he led his life now.

Now that he had been retired for some time the tasks of cooking and shopping had fallen into his lap. Not that he minded. But Louise seemed to take great delight in making things more complicated than they needed to be. Instead of writing a clear and easy-to-read message on the wipe-board on the kitchen wall as a reminder of something they had run out of, she would leave him cryptic notes lying about the house, yellow rectangles of paper with messages such as, 'We need some cuts grease to the squeak' – that was washing-up liquid – and 'some squeezably soft', toilet paper.

She was going through a phase of avid television viewing and she plundered the adverts each evening not only for new slogans to add to her collection of obscure names for household products, but for new and faster ways of eating. No longer was she obsessed with trimming him down to what she felt was a better weight. Now she had a thing about convenience foods. 'That looks easy enough,' she'd say, in response to a parsley-garnished meal-for-two emerging from a gleaming microwave. 'Even you could manage that, Neville.'

In defiance he'd taken to watching a cookery programme just before the lunch-time news. Last week he'd jotted down the recipe and served up beef and orange stir-fry for supper the following evening. He had thought it a culinary triumph and later that night had caught Louise hunting in the kitchen bin for the packaging.

Today on the television that nice blonde girl with the lisp had been making carrot soup. It had looked easy enough to him, just a matter of putting all the ingredients into a blender and Bob's your uncle – if only he could remember all the ingredients.

There was nobody in the grocer's when he pushed open the door. Joan Carter, whom he'd diagnosed three years ago as having angina, served him.

'Carrot soup? Well, you'll be wanting some carrots, then, won't you?' she said, putting some muddy ones onto the scales. 'A couple of pounds should do it.'

'I need an onion as well.'

'Spanish or home-grown?'

'You've got me there,' Neville said, trying to remember what the girl with the lisp had said above the noise of the blender.

'I've no truck with all this Euro nonsense,' Joan said. 'Have home-grown. How about some coriander?'

'Curry what?'

'Coriander. It's a herb. Here.' She handed him a bunch. 'You chop it up and sprinkle it over the food. It's all the rage, but give it a while and we'll soon be back to parsley. Probably them that knows best will find coriander's bad for you and say it's poisonous.'

Neville thought of Louise and nearly asked for two bunches.

Outside on the street again, he walked along the row of shops until he came to Charlotte's. She was busy stacking a set of shelves with Christmas ornaments. It didn't feel two minutes since Charlotte had stood on a chair helping him to decorate the Christmas tree each year; he passing the glass ornaments up to her while she, with infinite care, placed things in order of colour and size. 'No, not there,' she would say to herself, 'that bauble needs more space.'

'Hello, Dad,' she said, turning round to face him, 'and, yes, before you say anything I know I'm early with the decorations, but what the heck? Can you pass me that box from the counter?'

He handed it to her. 'I can't stop for long. I just thought I'd call in to see how you are.'

'I'm fine.'

'And Alex?'

Charlotte smiled. 'He's fine as well. How about you?'

'Fine.'

'Good,' Charlotte said mischievously, 'it's good that we're all fine.'

Neville picked up one of the large glass ornaments and turned it round in his hand. He could see his face looking back at him, all bulging eyes and bulbous nose. 'Any sign of ... well, you know?'

'Oh, Dad. Stop beating about the bush. Come right out and ask me.'

'Ask you what?' Neville said, putting the ornament back on the shelf.

'When Alex and I are getting married.'

Neville looked away, embarrassed. 'I'm not being nosy, Charlotte.'

She gave him a hug and breathed in the smoky smell of burning leaves from his clothes. 'I know you're not and as a matter of fact I'd like you to do something for me. Are you free on Christmas Eve?'

'I should think so. You know me, more time on my hands than I know what to do with.'

'Well, put it in your diary. You're coming on a walk with me.'

'I am? Not some ghastly rambling event, is it? That's more your mother's line of country.'

'Up the aisle of St John's. Let's see if we can get it right this time, shall we?'

Neville looked affectionately at his favourite daughter. Last year Charlotte had told him the truth about her marriage to Peter. At first he had been shocked, not so much because Charlotte's life with Peter had worked out the way it had but for the pain she had gone through alone after Peter's death – until, that was, Alex had come on the scene.

'I've a feeling Alex will make you a good husband,' he said simply. 'Peter was all right, but he wasn't really ...'

'He just wasn't the right man for me, Dad.'

'And you're absolutely sure Alex is?'

'I'm as sure as I can be.'

'Shall I tell you mother you've set a date?'

'Why not? She'll have to be told sooner or later.'

'You'll be making Hilary's day. She's convinced it's down to her that the two of you got together. Flushed with this victory under her belt, who knows who else will come in for her Cupid's arrow?'

Poor Hilary, thought Charlotte. The last thing she needed to think about at the moment was a wedding, never mind Cupid's arrow. She was wondering whether she ought to say anything to her father when the door opened and in walked David's secretary, Catherine Renshaw.

Too thin, was the first thought that came into Charlotte's head. Too thin, with much too much of the little-girl-lost look about her.

David's previous secretary had left to have a baby last year and Catherine had been the replacement. Then, a little over five months ago, David had reported to them all one night over dinner at The Gables that Catherine had been in tears in the office that day. 'That wretch of a husband has simply upped sticks and walked out. What kind of a man does that? Of course I've said I'll help all I can. Probably a pay rise would be a good idea.'

A pity David couldn't have stuck with just adding a few extra pounds to his secretary's salary, Charlotte thought angrily, watching Catherine in her smart woollen jacket move about the shop. She came to a stop at the shelf of silver frames and took off her leather gloves. Must have been a damn good pay rise, Charlotte thought bitterly, thinking how simple it was for a man like David to fall so helplessly for the oldest trick in the book, that of providing his strong manly shoulder to the tearful woman who seemingly has no one else to turn to.

'I'd better be off,' Neville said. 'I'm making carrot soup for your mother's tea.'

'Lucky old Mum,' Charlotte said, opening the door for her father.

She returned to displaying and pricing yet more Christmas decorations, while all the time keeping a watchful eye on her only customer. She felt fiercely protective towards her sister and wanted very much to lay into this smart piece of work who was doing her best to destroy another person's life.

'Do you have this in a smaller size?'

What, to match your brain? 'No, that's the smallest I have.' Charlotte kept her eyes on the frame in Catherine Renshaw's hands, not trusting herself to look her in the eye without revealing her anger. She was only too thankful that although this woman worked for her brother-in-law, there had been no previous social contact between them in the village, so no bright chit-chat was expected of her. She could remain aloof and sacrifice a sale if need be.

'Oh, that's a real shame. I suppose I could always have this one and put a mount in.'

'You could,' Charlotte replied airily.

'Except I don't really like mounted photographs.'

And I don't like you, so why don't you push off and leave my brother-in-law alone? 'Not working today?'

'Yes, but I've just slipped out. It's so quiet at the moment. No one likes to put their house on the market at this time of the year.'

'That's funny. David seems to have been pretty busy just recently. Hilary was only telling me the other day how he's always so late coming home these days.' She gave Catherine a long, hard stare, deciding to make her understand that nobody messed with the Archer sisters.

'I don't think I'll bother today.'

'Bother?'

'With the frame. I think I'll sleep on it.'

'Okay.' And make sure it's alone!

Chapter Thirteen

'What do you think?'

Cindy didn't answer. All her working life she'd been asked to transform women into something they weren't meant to be. She had lost count of how many women had asked her to turn them into the Princess of Wales – with or without the marriage problems. Years ago, of course, there had been a run on young girls wanting the Kylie Minogue or Madonna look, but the older women usually went for television presenters. Jill Dando was popular at the moment with the every-hair-in-place look, along with that wine expert now turned antiques buff. Judy Finnigan and Anne Diamond continued to have a steady following for the stay-at-home-mum look, but Gaby Roslin and Anthea Turner, with the more tousled appearance, were definitely number one for the wannabes.

'Well?'

'Hilary, are you sure this is a good idea?'

'I wouldn't be here if I didn't think it was,' Hilary answered with more assurance than she felt. She'd have preferred to be at home in the kitchen baking parkin and wrapping potatoes in foil ready for tonight's PTA bonfire party as in previous years, not sitting here in Cindy's pristine bathroom. It had seemed such a good idea on Monday when she'd called in and asked Cindy to do her hair later in the week for her – but, then, she hadn't let on to what she had in mind.

Cindy looked again at the picture Hilary had given her. It

was a cutting from the *Radio Times* and Anthea Turner stared back, eyes twinkling, mouth grinning, skin perfection itself. Cindy gave Hilary's face in the mirror a professional appraisal: eyes red, mouth sloping, complexion mottled. She would have to lie, she decided, like she had to all those other women. So why, then, was she hesitating? Because ... because Hilary was depending on her. Poor Hilary was hoping that this was all it would take to save her marriage. And it wasn't the first time she'd been asked to perform this miracle.

'Wouldn't you rather stick to your own hair colour?' Cindy suggested. 'This will be such a dramatic change.'

'I want it just like that,' Hilary replied, pointing at the picture in Cindy's hand. Her voice was raised and bordering on the petulant. 'I want my hair and make-up exactly like that. David likes Anthea Turner. He never used to miss her on a Saturday night. He once said he'd rather win a night out with Anthea than the lottery.' Hilary almost snatched the piece of paper out of Cindy's hands. She looked at it closely. When she'd been younger she'd always had her hair lightened, but since she'd had the children she hadn't bothered. At odd times over the years David had hinted at her having her hair like she'd worn it when they'd first met. 'Why?' she'd once asked him. 'Don't you like me as I am now?'

'Please, Cindy,' she said, 'can't we try it? What have I got to lose? It shouldn't be that difficult. After all, she's about my age, isn't she?'

True, thought Cindy, but sadly that's the only similarity. 'I'm sorry, Hilary, but I'm not a miracle worker.'

'Then I'm sorry to have taken up so much of your time,' Hilary said, getting up from the chair and mustering what little dignity she had left.

Years of professionalism hit Cindy smack in the face – she'd never yet lost a customer. 'I'm sorry, Hilary. I didn't mean that the way it sounded. Sit down and I'll explain.'

Under the slight persuasive pressure of Cindy's hands on her shoulders, Hilary sat down.

'I was going to say that I'm not a miracle worker in as much as I can't turn you into a replica of Anthea Turner. Your bone structure's completely different for a start and your hair—'

'How about as near as you can?'

Cindy smiled. 'So long as you accept the limitations I'm working with.'

Hilary nodded.

'Okay. Let's get started. It's going to take a few hours. I'll do the cut first, then put the highlights through and after I've blow-dried your hair and done your make-up we're going into Manchester.'

'Manchester?'

'Clothes, Hilary. We're going shopping.'

'But I can't, the children—'

'Tiffany won't mind babysitting for a few more hours. She needs the money.'

Manchester was busier than they had expected and when they had managed to find a space on the third level of the multi-storey car park Hilary and Cindy joined the warm buzz of shoppers inside Kendal's.

'These are much too expensive,' Hilary protested, after Cindy had guided her towards an area of spaciously displayed suits and separates. 'I can't possibly afford these prices.'

'It's your marriage we're trying to save, not your money,' Cindy said impatiently.

'But you know how stingy David is. He's only one step away from recycling the toilet paper. It won't just be my marriage I'm trying to save when he sees the bank statement, it'll be my neck. Can't we go downstairs? The clothes are cheaper – I mean, more reasonable – there.'

Resigned, Cindy headed towards the escalator. Hilary

followed quickly behind and they climbed aboard. Half-way down Hilary caught sight of herself in the mirror that lined the wall to her right. She felt a slight quickening in her stomach at the thought of surprising David when he came home from work that night. She felt so sure that her new hairstyle and make-over would bring him to his senses, would make him appreciate what he already had.

When Cindy had turned the chair round and Hilary had seen her hair for the first time, several shades lighter than her own natural mouse, it had been a shock. It certainly was a startling transformation, that and the effect of Cindy's cleverly applied make-up techniques. The initial shock now dealt with, Hilary was delighted with her new look and she smiled back at her reflection, confident that she had found the answer. *She would have her man.*

They stepped off the escalator and made for the racks of colour co-ordinated clothes. Hilary's eyes lit up at the sight of a display of red polo-neck sweaters. On the front of each jumper was a Scottie dog wearing a large tartan bow.

'No!' Cindy said adamantly.

'What do you mean?' Hilary said, already searching the rail for a size twelve.

'Tat!'

Hilary looked hurt. 'But they're so cute.'

'Look, Hilary. Cute is not going to woo David away from what's keeping him late at the office.'

'But I've always worn—'

'They're awful and I'm not letting you buy one. Not after all the trouble I've gone to. Believe me, Anthea wouldn't be seen dead in one. Now come on.'

Hilary raised her eyebrows. She'd had no idea Cindy could be like this – and Charlotte thought *she* was bossy!

An hour and a half later Cindy sank gratefully into a chair in the Venetian Restaurant on the fourth floor of the department store. She slipped her heels out of her shoes and moved her feet around, easing away the strain of supervising

Hilary's new wardrobe. She poured out two cups of tea and saw Hilary coming towards her, squeezing her way through the crowded restaurant. She looked hot and flustered, her hair showing signs of beginning to flop. More mousse needed, Cindy told herself. She would have to tell Hilary.

'Sorry I've been so long. The queue for the loo was horrendous. I thought I'd never get in.' She plonked herself down and stowed all her carrier bags on a ledge behind her. 'Oh, lovely, a cup of tea.'

'I got you a cake as well.' Cindy pushed the plate towards Hilary.

Hilary was touched. 'Thank you,' she said. 'And thanks also for, well, you know ... I'm sure it's going to work.' She looked at Cindy expectantly, hoping for her agreement.

Cindy didn't say anything. She opened her napkin and placed it on her lap. She knew the words Hilary wanted to hear – *Don't worry, this will put an end to David's adultery* – but she couldn't say them. She sipped her tea, feeling surprisingly sorry for Hilary and remembering how years ago when she had stumbled on Derek's second affair she had confided in Angela, her closest friend. Angela had been so helpful, had let Cindy cry on her shoulder and had even said all the right things, that everything would be all right. A week later she had discovered that it was Angela with whom Derek was sleeping. She had never trusted another woman since, which was, perhaps, why she had relied so heavily on the potential Tiffany had offered. She had hoped that Tiffany would become the close female confidante that she had so badly needed, someone who would never betray her. Poor Tiffany, Cindy thought, no wonder she had bucked from such an early age at her attempts to make her an ally. She had probably felt used and put upon.

But, now, here she was, helping another woman to cope with her husband's adultery. Why? What did she feel towards Hilary, with whom she had nothing in common, other than their unfaithful husbands?

Cindy's silence was making Hilary feel uncomfortable. She could sense some of her new-found hope slipping away from her. 'Cindy, you don't think I look like mutton dressed ...?'

Cindy placed her cup on the saucer and, meeting Hilary's anxious eyes, it came to her that it wasn't just pity she felt towards Hilary, she actually quite liked her. Since living in Hulme Welford she had viewed Hilary as nothing more than a neighbour – a rather interfering neighbour at times – but more importantly she had seen her as safe, someone who wouldn't interest Derek and pose a threat. Now she saw her not only as neutral territory but as someone she could trust. Suddenly she wanted Hilary to be able to trust her.

'I'm not going to lie to you,' Cindy said, 'but I really do believe that what you've done today will make you feel better about yourself. It'll give you more confidence, which in my opinion is the most important aspect of trying out a new image.'

'You're right,' Hilary said, stirring her tea thoughtfully. 'You're absolutely right. And I'm going to go home and show David that I'm the best thing since sliced bread.' She took a long sip of her tea, then said, 'Cindy, can I say something?'

'Go on,' Cindy said warily.

'Since you've lived in the village you've always kept yourself to yourself and I think that's a waste, because until today I hadn't appreciated what a strong and considerate person you are. You don't mind me saying that, do you?'

Cindy slipped her shoes back onto her feet. For the first time since Angela's betrayal, she had allowed herself to make a friend. 'No,' she said quietly, 'I don't mind at all.'

Hilary sensed Cindy wasn't going to say any more on the subject and because she never felt comfortable with pregnant pauses in conversations she said the first thing that came into her head. 'That Nick Bradshaw character you've just taken on, what's he like?'

'That remains to be seen,' Cindy answered, forever cautious. 'He's certainly got all the right credentials and at least he . . .' Her voice trailed away.

'At least he's what?' Hilary asked, curious.

'I was going to say at least he's a man and not another woman roaming around the place.'

'Oh,' Hilary said, disappointed. For some reason she had hoped Cindy was going to embark on some long, elaborate story about this man, who from nowhere had suddenly appeared in Hulme Welford. 'Is he married?' she found herself asking.

'Has been, I think.'

Come on, Hilary thought, what kind of an interview session was it? 'How old is he and where does he live, in Hulme Welford?'

'Forty-four, I think, and not in the village, though off-hand I can't remember exactly where. Why all the questions?'

'No reason,' Hilary answered, annoyed with herself for having even thought of the wretched man. But then he had, in fact, provided her with a few short moments during which she had thought of something other than the pain David was inflicting on her. Maybe he wasn't all bad.

Chapter Fourteen

'Bloody hell!' David stood in the kitchen doorway, his brief-case in one hand, the evening paper in the other, his mouth wide open. 'What have you done?'

'Don't you like it?' Hilary asked, as she passed him a glass of whisky and offered him a smile, both of which she'd prepared in advance.

'It's ... so different.' He took a gulp of whisky and continued to stare.

'Cindy did it for me. I fancied a change,' Hilary said, as casually as she could manage. Earlier, in the bedroom, she had stood in front of the mirror and practised what she was going to say to David. *I fancied a change* was supposed to have been accompanied by a sultry stare and a nonchalant flick of her hair while leaning back against the worktop, a vision of sexual enticement. But, from the way David was staring at her, she had the feeling that she looked about as alluring as one of those models from a fifties knitting pattern.

'You remind me of someone,' David said, putting down his briefcase and loosening his tie.

Self-conscious, Hilary turned her back on him and straightened the tea towel on the Aga rail.

'Damned if I can think who.'

'But you like it, don't you?' Oh, God, she was almost pleading with him. It wasn't supposed to have been like this at all. Why couldn't she be more confident?

'Hope Cindy gave you a bargain rate.'

Hilary whipped the towel off the rail and twisted it in her

hands. 'No, she didn't,' she almost shouted, turning round and facing him. 'Cindy did it for free, if you must know, as a friend.'

David smiled. 'Clever old you. What do the children think?'

Bugger the children! Hilary wanted to scream, I haven't gone to all this trouble to please Philip and Becky. When she'd arrived home from Manchester their reaction had been predictably derisive, with Becky shouting out the most painful comments. 'Mum looks like that woman on the telly.'

'Which one?' Hilary had asked hopefully.

'That one in the film we saw. Mrs Doubtfire!' She had then collapsed in exaggerated laughter on the floor in Philip's bedroom.

Philip had been comparatively less hurtful in his condemnation. 'It makes you look . . . well . . . kind of too young.'

'Too young?' she had repeated. 'What's wrong with that?'

Barely taking his eyes off the computer screen, he had gone on to say, 'Well, you're old, Mum, aren't you? And now you don't look right. You look wrong. I can't explain it any better.'

Tiffany had been sweet, though, but then Hilary had just been handing over her babysitting money. 'You look great,' she had said, eyeing Hilary up and down, taking in the new clothes Cindy had insisted she change into before dropping her off at The Gables. 'You've got less of the Marks and Spencer about you now.'

Under David's critical eye Hilary could feel her cheeks reddening despite the foundation and blusher Cindy had applied. 'Becky laughed, if you must know,' she said.

David gave a loud snort of appreciative laughter.

Hilary glared at him, knowing that all the anger she had been working so hard to keep in check since she had discovered David's unfaithfulness was no longer in check. She took the glass from David's hand and tipped the last quarter of an inch of whisky over his head, then calmly handed it back to him.

'What the hell—?'

'Yes, David,' she said, over her shoulder, as she walked away from him. 'What the hell indeed?'

'The flames of hell will be hotter still for some of those in this village,' declared Iris Braithwaite, as she and Charlotte backed away from the twenty-foot-high bonfire – all that was left of poor old Guy Fawkes was a pair of charred safety shoes, which were more than living up to the manufacturer's claims.

In the darkness and flickering orange light Iris's face had taken on the guise of a luminous Hallowe'en pumpkin. She looked dangerously menacing and, assuming that the older woman was referring to Charlotte and Alex's impure state, Charlotte prepared herself for the onslaught of a homily on the avoidance of sin. Instead, and above the crackle of burning garden refuse and wooden pallets, Iris hissed just two words, 'Ted Cooper.'

Charlotte relaxed and unclenched her gloved hands. At least she was off the hook. 'Ted Cooper?' she asked innocently. 'What's he been up to?'

'Been up to?' repeated Iris. 'Been up to, Mrs Lawrence? The man's a monster. A sexual fiend, peddling . . .' She paused for breath.

'Peddling what, Mrs Braithwaite?' Charlotte said, hoping the laughter rising within her could be staved off just a few minutes longer.

Iris fixed her with a long, hard stare. 'I notice you did not put my poster in your window as I asked.'

Charlotte stamped her feet on the iron hard ground; her face was hot and flushed from the heat of the bonfire, but her feet were frozen. 'I can't see what Ted's done wrong,' she said. 'You can buy those sorts of tights in most department stores. They're quite respectable, in fact women who suffer from thrush wear—'

'I'll thank you not to go into details, Mrs Lawrence. But I

take it, then, that you have not been in for a newspaper today?'

'No. No, I haven't.'

'I suggest you get down from your high and mighty position on the fence, Mrs Lawrence, and see for yourself what's going on here in Hulme Welford. It's quite apparent that Ted Cooper is not going to stop at the one lewd item of merchandise in his shop. He's added to his stock and it's the fault of people like you who don't care a fig. I hope your conscience allows you to enjoy yourself here tonight. Good night.'

Charlotte watched Iris Braithwaite disappear into the crowd. Added to his stock, she reflected. What on earth had Ted the Toup placed on his shelves that was giving Iris such apoplexy?

From the other side of the bonfire she saw Derek Rogers in a smart blue and cream skiing jacket and matching band round his head. He was waving to her through the smoke and flames. She waved back and he started making his way through the throng of over-excited children waving sparklers in the air and overwrought parents trying to prevent a replay of last night's television programme, 999.

Derek would be bound to know of any dodgy goings-on in the village, Charlotte decided. After all, he had been the main perpetrator of most things newsworthy since his arrival in Acacia Lane.

'Charlotte, where's that man of yours?' Derek greeted her, kissing her on the cheek. 'Abandoned you already, has he?'

'He's gone for some mulled wine.'

'Now, what's this I hear about you finally succumbing to his charms? I hope I'm invited. I'd love to be the one at the back of St John's with a just cause or impediment.'

'Well, you've certainly got an impediment,' Charlotte said, with a laugh.

'Oh, Charlotte, how did I ever let you slip through my fingers?'

'Derek,' Charlotte said firmly, 'I was never even there in your hands.'

He grinned. 'I distinctly recall a moment when I had you up against the kitchen sink in what the romantic novelist would describe as a passionate embrace.'

'Rubbish. You kissed me and tried to stick your hand down my blouse, in what a pubescent *Just Seventeen* reader would describe as a grope.'

'Yeah, well, call it what you want, but the old Derek Rogers School of Charm never fails. I still got you to kiss me.' And, as though to prove his point, he leaned into her and kissed her on the lips.

'Having trouble with your balance?' asked Alex, coming up behind Derek. 'Or are you still testing the water?' He handed Charlotte a polystyrene cup of mulled wine and placed a proprietorial arm around her shoulder. 'Oh and, Derek, if you're going to make a habit of kissing Charlotte, perhaps you could go easy on the aftershave. Less obvious that way.'

'Hey, you've got me all wrong,' Derek said, putting up his hands in a gesture of innocence. 'I was merely congratulating Charlotte on her good fortune. The best man obviously won.'

'Oh, shut up, Derek,' Charlotte laughed, 'and tell us how All in the Mind is shaping up.'

For a few minutes Derek had wandered back into the territory of his old self. He hastily switched to the new-style Derek – this New Man thing was going to be harder work than he'd supposed. 'We open next week,' he said, adopting what was fast becoming his welcome-to-the-fold voice. ' "Spiritual Journey" is fully booked. So is "Reaching Your Full Potential".'

'How about the marriage seminars you were advertising in the *Chronicle* this week?' asked Alex. 'Many takers?'

'Little disappointing there. I feel people are reluctant to step forward to the altar on that particular subject. They're frightened to admit to problems going on in the jolly-rogering department. So often marital problems are caused by sexual inadequacy and people just don't want to admit to it. But you, Alex, you wouldn't have any qualms about coming to our "Screw Your Inhibitions to the Bedpost" seminars if you weren't all that our lovely Charlotte was in need of, would you now?'

Alex smiled. 'Maybe people just can't equate All in the Mind with the man who probably thinks *The Man Who Mistook His Wife For a Hat* is a Les Dawson joke book.'

Charlotte gave Alex a dig in the ribs, but Derek looked at him as if he'd just flown in from Mars.

'Ever thought of some kind of therapy, Alex? Perhaps you should book in to see our Nick Bradshaw. He's head of stress and would be great at getting to the bottom of all your funny little quirks. He's here tonight as my guest with Rosie Williams. I'll introduce you. He'll have you sorted out in no time.'

'If Alex has got any funny little quirks, I'll be the one to minister to him.' Charlotte laughed, then changed the subject. 'Tell me what you know about Ted the Toup. What's he doing to give Iris such palpitations?'

'Come off it! The Pope would give old Ma Braithwaite palpitations, never mind Ted's range of intimate items of clothing.'

'His what?'

Derek gave Charlotte a wink. 'Best get yourself down there and order your trousseau. You might even pick up a little something in the way of posing accessories for your man here.'

'For goodness' sake, talk sense. What exactly is he selling?'

'It's perfectly harmless stuff, just a little erotica to pick up with your daily tabloid – you know the kind of thing.'

Charlotte and Alex waited expectantly. 'Come on then, what?' Alex said at last.

'Well, he's moved up the body, doing a line in lingerie. Basic kind of things, mostly cheap imports from the sweatshops of our Far Eastern friends – nothing that I would buy for Cindy, of course.'

'But why?'

'Cindy prefers pure silk, not—'

'No,' Charlotte said, exasperated. 'Why's Ted doing this?'

'You can't knock a man for extending his business, Charlotte.'

'Cods!' she retorted. 'Why smutty underwear? Why not birdseed?'

'Obvious, I suppose,' Alex said. 'After Mrs Braithwaite's petition he's coming back guns blazing.'

Charlotte shook her head and, as the first of the rockets was let off on the far side of the school playing field, she thought of the fireworks about to explode in the village, and of Iris Braithwaite putting on her boxing gloves for possibly the fight of her life.

As the fireworks exploded high above her head, Hilary caught sight of David and Catherine Renshaw standing together. Catherine's face was turned upwards, her lips parted in the obligatory *aah* position as diamonds of white magnesium light speckled the windless night sky forming, for a few magical seconds, a perfectly shaped dandelion.

Hilary's first thought was to run; to run all the way back to the safety of The Gables. Her second inclination was to ram the hot dog in her hand down that *aah*-shaped mouth.

She did neither, hearing the sound of her name spoken at her side.

'*Bonsoir*, Hilary.' It was Nick Renshaw. 'Go easy on that hot dog – you're squeezing the life out of it.'

Hilary grimaced at the sight of mustard and ketchup oozing all over her hands. The twisted bread roll and sausage looked disgusting. She threw it on the grass.

'Here.' Nick offered her a tissue from his coat pocket.

'Thank you,' she mumbled.

'I nearly didn't recognise you.'

She looked puzzled.

'Your hair. You've changed the colour and the style. It looks good.'

She turned away self-consciously.

'Ah,' he said.

'What do you mean, *ah*?' she said, meeting his gaze.

'You've forgotten how to receive a compliment, haven't you? Especially from a man you hardly know, whose motives could be considered at best dubious and at worst manipulative.'

'Good Lord. How ridiculous.'

Overhead another firework illuminated the smoke-filled sky and Nick's face suddenly seemed much too close. She took a small step away from him.

'Do I make you feel uneasy, Hilary?'

'You say the most absurd things. Or is that what you're paid to do?'

He laughed. 'More or less, but if it makes people understand that bit more about themselves then I can justify it. That throttled frankfurter, anyone I know?'

Hilary caught her breath. 'I shouldn't think so. And, anyway, why should it be *anyone*?'

'Just wondered whether it had anything to do with those glasses you were smashing the other day and the rich vocabulary you were trying out.'

Hilary had had enough. Everything was going wrong. Her new image had done nothing to bring David to his senses, in fact almost the reverse. On the way here he'd even questioned her on how much money she'd spent in Manchester with Cindy and then he'd gone on to ask her where she'd put his special whisky tumblers – without looking at him she'd made up some stupid story about having an accident when cleaning out the cupboard – and now here he was enjoying the fireworks with his mistress. And here she was, stuck with this wretched man and his smart-alec questions, poking his nose in where it just wasn't wanted. 'Why can't you mind your own business?' she responded hotly.

'Ouch!' Nick said. 'That's the second time you've said that. But well done. Keep going and I might eventually get the message that you don't like me.'

Hilary turned her back on him and watched Patricia Longton's husband light the fuse for the mounted display of fireworks. The first to go was a Catherine wheel. In the hushed, expectant silence Hilary suddenly laughed.

'Want to share the joke?' Nick whispered in her ear.

'Definitely not,' she said, trying to stifle yet more laughter at the image so clearly forming in her mind's eye – that of David's mistress impaled on a spike and spinning round and round before being tossed into orbit, never to be seen again.

'Enjoying yourself, Hilary?'

'David!' She decided to test him. 'Where have you been?'

'Just over there.' He pointed to where Catherine was talking to someone Hilary didn't recognise. 'I'm surprised you didn't see me.'

How brazen he was!

'I'm afraid I'm probably to blame,' Nick said, 'I've been talking too much.'

'This is Nick Bradshaw, David. He's starting at All in the Mind next week.'

David gave a short, loud laugh. 'You need your own head tested getting in with Derek on this latest harebrained scheme of his.'

'David!'

'It's all a load of tosh, isn't it?' David carried on, ignoring Hilary's admonishment. 'Just another way to exploit bored housewives. I guarantee you won't find any decent hard-working bloke skulking there on a couch having his innermost thoughts paraded in front of him. What do you call it? Ah, yes, getting in touch with oneself.'

'That's quite a commonly held view. But usually voiced by

those with something to hide. Tell me, David, what are you most afraid of?'

'What's this? A free therapy session?' David said aggressively. 'I'm not that stupid. Next you'll be pulling out the ink blots and trying to draw out the feminine side of me.'

'David, stop being so rude.'

A firework screeched overhead, zigzagging its way high into the sky. In the sudden burst of silvery light Hilary saw both men clearly illuminated in front of her. In David's face she was struck by the hardness of his features, lips tightly drawn in a rigid line, which seemed to her in that moment to betray his dislike of their marriage. If there had been any trace of doubt in her mind that David was innocent of the crime he had allegedly committed, his face now confirmed his guilt. She felt sick, consumed with pain, as if her insides had just been ripped out. She turned to Nick and in his face saw all that she so badly wanted to see in David's face – warmth and understanding, kindness and humour. It was all there . . . *but in the wrong man.*

'I apologise for my apparent rudeness, which my wife has been only too quick to point out,' David said stiffly, when the sky darkened once more. 'I just wanted you to know that you're banging on the wrong door as far as I'm concerned.'

'You're probably right,' Nick said lightly. 'But at some time in our lives we all need a guiding hand. When we're up against the wall there's no better time to explore the dark nooks and crannies of our minds.'

'And what's that supposed to mean? Are you trying to tell me—'

'All I'm saying is that by having the opportunity to examine ourselves we can so often change our attitude or improve on our situation, not just for the benefit of ourselves but more importantly for those around us.'

'Mm . . .' David said. 'I suppose there could be an element of truth in what you say.' He turned to Hilary. 'You've got no complaints with me, though, have you?'

Hilary wanted to pick up the squashed hot dog from the grass beneath her feet and shove it down David's throat. No complaints! Not much she hadn't. She was only having to share her husband with another woman. 'Well, David, there are times when I feel you could—'

'There you are!' David rounded on Nick. 'You see what you've done. You've filled her head with silly nonsense about me not making the grade in some way.'

'And is that what you're afraid of, David?' Nick said quietly. 'Not making the grade?'

For a moment David seemed unable to speak. His anger was almost palpable. Then, as though fighting the urge to take Nick by the throat, he said, 'That's a load of crap. And if you want somebody to analyse try Hilary. Ask her why the new hairdo and why earlier this evening she poured whisky over me.' He walked away, his shoulders hunched, his hands thrust deep inside his coat pockets.

Hilary gasped.

'Interesting man, your husband.'

'Oh, shut up, can't you!'

Chapter Fifteen

'Bloody marvellous!' Georgia shouted at the top of her voice as she threw down the *Chronicle* on top of the paperwork spread over the small table in the caravan. Gordon, who was leaning on a broom outside, gave her a quizzical look. She went to the door and called him over. 'Come and see this.'

Gordon left his broom propped against a greenhouse, grateful for the opportunity to get out of the cold for a few minutes. He pulled off his gloves and climbed into the caravan. 'What's up? Not that git of an ex-husband of yours making a nuisance of himself again, is it?'

Georgia shook her head. Ever since she'd taken Gordon on as her right-hand boot – as he described himself – he had referred to Rory in this way, which was how he also referred to his previous employer. Several years ago, and at the age of sixty, local cutbacks in the National Health Service had forced him out of his post as a hospital porter. Then, having watched the work going on over the road from his cottage, he had called in one morning to ask Georgia if there were any jobs going. At first she'd turned him down for the simple reason that she didn't have the money to pay any wages. But within four months she was knocking on his door in a position to offer him part-time work. 'It's not much,' she'd told him.

'He'll take it,' his wife Winnie had said. 'I want him out from under my feet. He's always talking through Jimmy Young's programme on the radio. It's the medical bits he hates, embarrasses him summat rotten. If he starts giving you any nonsense just start talking prostate trouble. Lord knows how he lasted all those years in the hospital.'

Georgia had taken an instant liking to Winnie – who turned out to be a willing babysitter for Chloe – and Gordon, who more than proved his worth around the nursery.

She showed him the paper. He let out a long whistle. 'Skin and hair'll soon be flying, then, won't it?'

A black and white picture of fury stared back at them from the front page. Iris Braithwaite was photographed outside Ted the Toup's and the headline read, 'Hulme Welford's very own Mary Whitehouse'. The journalist had then gone on to report on Mrs Braithwaite's campaign to clean up the village of Hulme Welford. 'We must all fight this evil sin and do our public duty,' she was quoted as saying. The paper's editor had added to the article by inviting readers to write in with their comments on the debate 'To Censor or Not to Censor' – a debate which no doubt he clearly hoped would run and run and increase his circulation figures.

'I've said it once and I'll say it again,' Georgia said. 'It's bloody marvellous. Good for old Ma Braithwaite.'

'That's as may be,' Gordon said, pulling on his gloves to go back out into the cold. 'But, like as not, she'll bring trouble on herself and others.'

'How very profound of you, Gordon. You been listening to *Thought for the Day* again?'

From the doorway of the caravan she watched Gordon pick up his broom and start sweeping the leaves covering the path leading to one of the greenhouses. The newspaper was still in her hands and, catching sight of Mrs Braithwaite again, she made up her mind to go and see her.

'Gordon,' she called out, 'I'm going early to pick up Chloe, there's something I need to do. Hold the fort, will you?'

Georgia parked outside the White Cottage in Acacia Lane and as she walked up the garden path she tried hard not to be too disdainful of the overly ordered front garden. There was not a stray leaf in sight, not an overlooked bedding plant left there by chance from the summer. All was crisp and dreadfully bare.

She banged the brass knocker, loudly and eagerly: she had much to say to Mrs Braithwaite. She knew that most people in the village were scared of her, intimidated by her over-bearing manner. Georgia had always privately admired the way she handled herself. Before she'd encountered the older woman she had never come across anyone more single-minded than herself – a criticism Rory had levelled at her on more than one occasion.

But she was used to criticism, having put up with a bellyful since she'd got rid of Rory and his endless stream of excuses. She knew only too well what people like Patricia Longton had to say about her: What kind of a woman kicks out her daughter's father? She could have retaliated with the truth – which was, quite simply, that Rory couldn't be trusted to part his own hair, never mind run a business – but she'd chosen instead to thumb her nose at anyone who dared to point the finger of accusation in her direction. She knew, though, that despite themselves people had come to respect her for having got the nursery up and running. Where Rory had failed, she had succeeded. In her opinion people generally preferred success stories to depressing tales of failure.

She rapped the door knocker again.

'Whoever it is out there, kindly show some manners and have the goodness to wait a few moments.'

Georgia smiled and listened to the lock being turned.

'Oh, it's you, Mrs D'Arcy,' Iris said, surprised. 'What can I do for you?'

'It's *Ms* D'Arcy,' Georgia said firmly. 'I've come to see you about Ted Cooper.' Georgia felt the older woman's suspicious eyes weighing her up. She decided to take the initiative. 'May I come in?'

Iris pursed her lips at such forwardness. 'I'm a busy woman, Mrs D'Arcy.' She began to nudge the door closed.

'And so am I,' Georgia parried. 'I don't have much free

time but I've come especially to see you.'

The older woman seemed to consider this for a few seconds before saying, 'I can spare you a few minutes, no more,' holding the door fully open, and grudgingly allowing Georgia over the threshold. But almost immediately she shouted, 'Boots! Off with those muddy boots, if you please. I've had this carpet twenty-two years and I'm not about to have it ruined.'

She left Georgia to take off the offending articles and went through to the kitchen. 'I presume you do drink tea, Mrs D'Arcy,' she called out, 'or is that too conventional for you?'

'Tea will be fine and it's Ms D'Arcy. I was Mrs Maddox, but now that I'm divorced I've reverted back to my maiden name, okay? Perhaps Georgia would be easier for you to remember?'

Iris's head appeared abruptly at the kitchen door. 'Are you trying to imply I'm not capable of remembering a simple thing like a name? I'm not senile, young lady, if that's what you think.'

'Not at all, Mrs Braithwaite,' Georgia said, amused.

'Then I suggest you sit down in the sitting room and I'll join you there in a moment.'

Georgia went where she was told but prowled round the tidy room. It was almost as bare and clinical as the front garden, devoid of all the personal mementoes that usually cluttered up one's life. The thought occurred to Georgia that maybe this was deliberate. Perhaps Mrs Braithwaite didn't want the waters of the present muddied with reminders of the past because, as Georgia herself had come to know, retrospection of any kind led only to regret.

She sat in a high-backed winged chair and warmed her feet by the coal fire. It was two thirty on a Tuesday afternoon and here she was, lazing in an armchair feeling absurdly decadent, as if she was bunking off school. She almost wanted to laugh, but then her mood changed and she found herself feeling sorry for herself, that such a simple thing was now a complete luxury to her. She sat up straight and snatched her feet away from the fireside. Self-pity was such a wasted emotion and she couldn't afford to waste anything.

'I dare say you could manage a slice of Genoa cake,' Iris said, coming in with a tea-tray complete with a paper doily. 'You look like you could do with feeding up.'

'Please don't go spoiling me,' Georgia said briskly. A little too briskly. Iris's eyes shot up from the tea-tray.

'I've never spoilt anyone in my life,' she said firmly, handing Georgia a cup and saucer. 'I was merely making an observation,' she continued. 'In my opinion you look no more than two-penn'orth of copper. You clearly work too hard and give yourself little or no time at all in which to eat. Though I dare say you would disagree with me and tell me to mind my own business.' She passed a large slice of cake to Georgia, along with a napkin, and in a less strident tone added, 'It can't be easy for you, though, doing all that you do, alone.'

'Thank you,' Georgia muttered awkwardly. This was an area of her life on which she preferred not to dwell. There was nothing, absolutely nothing, to be gained in self-pitying explorations of the soul. If she did that she might lose the motivation to get out of bed in the morning. As it was, it was struggle enough summoning up the energy to face each day.

'So, what is it you want to discuss with me?' Iris asked, filling in the silence. 'I suppose you've come here to tell me not to be such a stupid interfering old woman. Is that it?'

'Quite the reverse, Mrs Braithwaite,' Georgia said, glad to be moving the conversation onto less personal ground. 'I've come to congratulate you and to offer my services.'

It was Iris's turn to be taken aback. 'You want to offer your help in ridding Hulme Welford of the likes of Ted Cooper? Go on.'

Georgia leaned forward in her seat. 'Yes,' she said, nodding, her long ear-rings swinging precariously 'There's 'no room for disgusting old men like him in this world.'

'How right you are Mrs ... Ms D'Arcy. And how refreshing to hear such a plainly spoken view on this contemptible issue. I had thought that people like yourself were full of rampant liberalism, promoting the ethos that anything goes.'

'I believe in absolute equality, Mrs Braithwaite, which means the exploitation of women has to be stopped. Do you see what I mean?'

'Good Lord, young lady. Please don't lecture me.'

'I'm sorry,' Georgia said, biting into her slice of cake. When she'd finished her mouthful she said, 'So what's the next step in your campaign?'

'I'm hoping that this newspaper article will shame the grubby little man into disbanding his ghastly scheme.'

Georgia shook her head, her ear-rings swinging again. 'No chance!' she said, with such vehemence that Iris clattered her cup on its saucer. 'I don't believe that will happen. The newspaper story will just antagonise the man. We're going to have to come up with further retaliation. We've got to produce a barrage of disapproval at what he's doing.'

'You've obviously given this some thought. And just what do you have in mind exactly?'

A slow smile spread over Georgia's face. 'Another cup of tea, Mrs Braithwaite, and I'll gladly tell you.'

Iris filled Georgia's cup, but when she handed it back Georgia nearly dropped the green Beryl-ware china as she heard the unexpected words, 'Perhaps you'd like to call me Iris.'

The three thirty school-gate gathering was buzzing with the news.

Patricia Longton pulled Hilary into the fold with evangelical zeal. 'I'm thinking of putting an opposing petition together,' she said. 'It's all perfectly innocent what Ted's selling. You'll sign of course, won't you, Hilary?'

Hilary shivered inside her coat and wondered why Patricia

never did up the zip on her smelly old waxed jacket.

'I'm sure we can rely on Hilary's support,' Kate Hampton chimed in. 'After all, she's always been one of the girls.'

'*Les girls*, that's us.' Patricia laughed.

Hilary didn't feel at all one of the girls, not after Patricia's comments this morning at the gate. She'd spent a good fifteen minutes tearing apart the organisation of the school bonfire party. 'Fancy not having enough hot dogs,' she'd opened up with. 'Not a hint of a relish to be had and as for having sparklers for all the children, well, let's just say it was a miracle we didn't have any serious casualties. *She* won't last long, take my word for it. And you know what people are saying about *her*, don't you?'

Out of habit Hilary had given the necessary tilt of the head thereby giving Patricia the green light to continue with her axegrinding.

'They say that Rory had other women because ...' here Patricia had paused for dramatic emphasis, turning her head from left to right, 'because she's a lesbian. I should keep your distance, if I were you. Just think what David would say if there were rumours that you, well, you know what I mean. People might not want to buy their home from a man whose wife ... I'm sure I don't have to spell it out for you, Hilary.'

It was all right, of course, for an estate agent to be bonking his secretary, Hilary had muttered all the way home, after managing to escape Patricia's vile tongue, but heaven forbid that his wife should have a friendship with another woman whose sexuality was in question. And how dare Patricia say such awful things about Georgia, especially when Georgia had been so kind to her? Stupid, smug Patricia was probably just jealous that she had found a new friend.

'French class tonight, Hilary,' Patricia said, bringing Hilary back to that afternoon's gossip session. 'Done your homework?'

Damn! She hadn't. 'Plenty of time yet,' she said airily.

'Hope you're not going to keep that nice Nick Bradshaw

all to yourself this evening. I'd rather like to do some conversational work with him myself.' She gave Kate Hampton a wink.

'You're welcome to him,' Hilary replied.

'A lover's tiff already?' Kate chirped. 'How much to keep it quiet from David?'

Oh, the irony, thought Hilary. With relief she saw Patricia's infamously uncontrollable sons coming across the playground.

'See you all,' Patricia called as she led away the two small boys, who lagged behind her throwing leaves at the passing cars.

Kate Hampton's pony-mad daughter Victoria was next to appear in the throng of children, and when she left Hilary felt herself relax. *Les girls*, indeed. *Les bitches*, more like it. And to think she used to consider them friends.

'Hello, Hilary.'

'Georgia,' Hilary said brightly.

'I don't know what I've done to deserve a smile like that, but thanks all the same.'

'Would you like to come back for a cup of tea and some cake?' Hilary asked, not sure whether she was responding to Georgia's undernourished appearance – she was wrapped in a duffel coat and looking even more urchin-like today – or more to spite Patricia.

'Must be my lucky day for tea and cake. Are you sure? Don't you have Philip to pick up?'

'He's got a play rehearsal tonight. I don't have to collect him until six.'

'Okay, then, but only for a short while. I've left Gordon in charge. And I ought to warn you about Chloe. No time, here she comes.'

A girl in a bulky duffel coat not much smaller than Georgia's was striding across the playground. And, also like Georgia, her hair was cut short framing a small pixie face. All that was missing to complete the similarity was a pair of dangling ear-rings.

In the distance was Becky, skipping happily along in a world of her own, her plaited hair bouncing on her shoulders, her pink lunch-box swinging in her hand.

'Okay, chuck?' Georgia said to her daughter.

'Another day of the same old female repression,' Chloe announced mournfully. 'Mrs Arnold is insisting I play Mary in the nativity play. I told her I wanted to be Joseph, that I know my way round a hammer and saw better than a baby's bum.'

Georgia smiled. 'Hilary's invited us for a cup of tea, that all right with you?'

'Fine.'

'Mummy, Mummy! Guess what?' Becky said breathlessly as she joined them. 'I'm going to be an angel in the nativity play. You'll need to get me loads of tinsel for my halo and wings, some white tights and a huge white sheet.'

Chloe gave a contemptuous grunt.

Hilary set the tea-things on the pine table in the kitchen. She was fussing, she knew, over-compensating for ten-year-old Chloe's disapproval of everything Becky said and did. But Becky couldn't help being a typical girl, it was just the way she was. She had always wanted long hair and to play with dolls.

'You've had your hair done,' Georgia said, helping to pass plates of cake around the table.

Hilary sensed yet more disapproval. 'I fancied something different,' she said defensively, convinced that Georgia had guessed at the reason behind the sudden change in her appearance. 'Do you want Ribena or orange squash, Chloe?'

Chloe pulled a face. 'I'd prefer tea, please. Black, no sugar.'

Becky was impressed. She sometimes had tea but it was always milky with a tiny bit of sugar, if she was lucky. Black without sugar was dead grown-up. 'I'll have the same,' she said, looking at her mother.

Eyebrows raised, Hilary fetched two more mugs and exchanged a knowing look with Georgia.

When tea was over Chloe reluctantly agreed to go upstairs to see Becky's bedroom.

'Poor Chloe,' Hilary said, after the girls had left the kitchen, 'she's so very grown-up and modern, Becky's the complete opposite.'

'No worries. Chloe will soon have her whipped into shape. Now tell me about this new look of yours. Has it worked?'

Embarrassed, Hilary started to clear away the mugs and plates.

'Leave all that,' Georgia said, sharply. 'Sit down, stop fidgeting and talk to me. Did the rat even notice the trouble you'd gone to?'

'Oh, he noticed all right,' Hilary said. She slipped into her chair. 'I think for the first time in his life he was stuck for words.' She chewed on her lower lip. 'Then he laughed ... Oh, Georgia, he laughed at me. He's probably been having a good laugh with her as well.'

'Best not think of that,' Georgia said softly.

'I only did it because I know how much he likes Anthea Turner on the telly. It's pathetic, isn't it? I got Cindy to do it for me ... She didn't want to, but I made her do it, so that I ...'

'So that you could please David?'

'Yes.'

Georgia leaned back in her chair and shook her head. 'Believe me, it doesn't work. I tried it for years with Rory. Whatever you offer to some men, it's just not enough.'

Neither spoke for a few minutes, the ticking of the clock above the Aga the only sound between the two women, that and the occasional thud from Becky's room above them.

At last Hilary looked up. She was shocked to find Georgia staring straight at her, as if she had been doing so for some time. Something in her face reminded Hilary of being back at school with Naomi Scott. How she had wanted Naomi to look at her in the way Georgia—

Suddenly she recalled Patricia's whispered words at the school gate: '*They say she's a . . .*'

Hilary swallowed hard, horrified. What was she doing? What kind of situation was developing between her and Georgia?

'Poor you,' she heard Georgia say. Then a hand reached out across the table towards her.

Panic-stricken she leapt to her feet. 'I've got to prepare the vegetables for supper,' she squeaked. 'And then I'll have to collect Philip.'

Georgia frowned. 'I thought you said he didn't finish until six. It's not even half past four.'

'I lied . . . I mean I forgot the play rehearsal isn't tonight, it's tomorrow.' She started clattering the plates into a pile and making for the dishwasher. 'I'm like that these days. Forget things all the time, must be hormones or something. Senile, even. Yes, that's it. I'm probably going senile. Not at all the kind of person you'd like as a friend.'

Georgia laughed and got up from her chair. She walked towards Hilary, her hands outstretched.

Oh my God, Hilary thought. She's going to kiss me. Help! Somebody help me.

Help came at once in the form of two loud rings on the doorbell.

Chapter Sixteen

Never in all her life had Hilary been so pleased to see a man. And Nick Bradshaw, all six foot of him, corduroys and plum-coloured wool jacket and scarf tied loosely round his neck standing on the doorstep, was a gift from heaven.

'Come in, come in,' she said, pulling him over the threshold. 'Tea! I'm sure you'd love a cup, wouldn't you?'

Nick was bemused. He had called on the off-chance of apologising to Hilary for what he'd said to David at the bonfire party last week and had expected little more than a frosty welcome. 'Thank you,' he said, 'so long as you're sure it's no trouble.'

'No trouble at all,' Hilary burbled, leading the way to the kitchen.

'I thought you were in a hurry to collect Philip?' Georgia said coldly, staring straight at Hilary. She was leaning against the Aga, her legs crossed at the ankles and her arms folded over her small breasts.

Nick looked from one woman to the other. He sensed he had come in on the middle of something. He also sensed hostility emanating from the woman by the Aga. 'Hi,' he said, offering a smile and a handshake. Just as he had expected, both were treated to a dismissive shrug by a pair of fragile-looking shoulders.

'I'll be off, then,' Georgia said, picking up her duffel coat from the back of a chair. 'I'll call Chloe down while you see to your *guest*.'

'Don't go,' Hilary said.

Alert to the falseness in Hilary's voice, Nick watched her closely. Relief was written all over her face. Intrigued, he turned to the other woman. 'Please don't leave on my account.'

'I wouldn't do anything on your account,' came the quick-fire put-down.

He listened to the politely said goodbyes in the hall and the sound of the front door shutting.

'Sorry about that,' Hilary said, coming back into the kitchen. 'Georgia's on the PTA with me. I barely know her, really, in fact I'd go so far as to say—'

'It's okay, you don't have to explain your friends to me. I was over the road with Derek and Cindy and thought I'd call by to apologise for the other night.'

'Oh,' she said, surprised.

'Any chance of that cup of tea?' He removed his scarf and took Georgia's place against the Aga. 'Or was that just a ruse to get rid of your unwanted visitor?'

Hilary was beginning to feel tired of having to keep up with so many different conversations. Her life never used to be like this. The most taxing word game she'd ever played before was second-guessing Becky. Fed up, she filled the kettle.

'I'm sorry I pushed your husband the way I did. Some might say I was behaving in an unprofessional manner, but I'm afraid I don't go in for the conventional tried and tested views a lot of the time. Do you forgive me?'

'If it makes you feel better, yes,' she answered wearily, staring out at the back garden. It was dark outside and something must have set off the security light: the lawn and flower-beds were brilliantly illuminated – she could see a cat disappearing into the laurel bushes at the far end of the garden.

'I would rather it made you feel better.'

'Sorry?'

'You look tired, Hilary.'

'I am,' she said flatly. She made him a mug of tea and wondered why she felt so uncomfortable when he called her by her name.

'Do you think your husband will accept my apology?'

Hilary thought how defensively aggressive David had suddenly become and of his many prejudices; his condemnation of the two and a half million unemployed in the country, his dislike of change and his reluctance to part with any money, and now his obvious cynicism towards the world of therapy, something she'd been unaware of until now. 'I shouldn't think so for one minute,' she said.

When Nick didn't say anything but watched her over the top of his mug, she felt even more uncomfortable and compelled to say something herself. 'Do you counsel people on their marriages?'

'I have done in the past,' he said slowly, 'but that won't be what I'll be doing at All in the Mind.'

'But you could offer help, for instance, to a friend of mine who was having difficulties?' What on earth was she doing? Of course he'd see through what she was saying. Why couldn't she just shut up, let him drink his tea then get him out of the house?

'I'd like to think that if anyone needed advice they would feel able to ask me straight out for help. You included, Hilary.'

There he went again. Why did he have to keep calling her by her name? She decided not to say anything further. She'd let him do all the talking.

'Are you and David—'

The door opened and banged noisily against a cupboard. Becky appeared with her arms full of Barbie dolls and accessories. 'Chloe says I must chuck these out. Oh, who are you?' She gave Nick an accusing stare.

'Oh, he's just a man,' Hilary said quickly, grateful for once for her daughter's habit of barging into conversations.

Becky gave a shrill laugh and squeezed her eyes tightly

shut. She looked constipated, but Hilary knew better: some newly learned piece of knowledge was about to be given an airing.

'Chloe says that when God made man she was only joking.'

It was pitch black and Philip was alone. All the others had gone, picked up by their mothers or fathers. He peered into the darkness of the badly lit school driveway, hoping to see his mother's Renault Clio. Some of the mothers drove to school in sports cars, most drove estates or Shoguns. It would be nice if Mum had a flashier car. In the mornings he came to school by bus, which was okay, but because there were so many activities to do after school it usually meant that he was picked up by Mum in the afternoon.

Most of his friends from junior school had gone on to the High, but he'd won a scholarship to the same school that Tiffany went to. He could remember the look on his dad's face when the letter had come in the post. Yeah, that had been great. He and Mum had bought him a computer for doing so well in his exam. It was hard being at St Hugh's, though, more difficult than he'd thought it was going to be. Some of the masters seemed to enjoy making him get upset when he couldn't do the work. He cringed at how he'd wet himself on his first day. Bloody-hell! Eleven years old and he'd wet himself. Bloody, bloody hell!

He looked at his watch. Where was she? He hoped she was okay. He'd heard her crying last week and just the other day. Why? What did she have to be sad about?

Batesy said his mother was like that last year. But, then, she'd had something to cry about. Batesy's dad had left home last year just before Christmas; brought them all presents, Batesy said, then disappeared off with another woman on Boxing Day.

Philip chewed what was left of his bitten thumbnail. His dad wasn't going to leave, so Mum wouldn't be crying for that reason, would she? Stuff Batesy! Batesy's dad probably left home because Batesy was such an idiot. He wasn't an idiot, he'd won a scholarship. So that was okay then.

But where was Mum?

'Still here, Philip?'

'Yes, sir.'

'Why don't you come into the warm and wait?'

'I'm all right, sir. I'm sure my mother will be here soon.'

'Suit yourself.'

He watched Mr Wells, the Latin master, disappear into the school building. Mr Wells was okay. He was one of the nicer teachers. It was Mr Wells who had caught those boys the other day. Tiffany had warned him that there were bullies in the school. She'd even said that she'd sort them out if he needed help. Flipping heck, no girl was ever going to sort out his problems. Anyway, if those boys tried it on again, he'd be ready for them.

He looked at his watch. In the distance he heard the sound of a car and saw two headlights coming towards him. He held his breath. Please let it be Mum. The car drew level and he caught sight of Becky sticking her tongue out at him. He let out his breath in one long deep sigh.

'How are you getting on with *Emma*?' Hilary asked Tiffany, watching her drop her large bag of schoolwork onto the floor in the sitting room.

'That geek Mr Elton has just tried it on with her. He's really got the hots for her, hasn't he? Serves her right, if you ask me. I can't understand what George Knightley sees in Emma – you'd think he could do better for himself.'

'Well, I'd better leave you to it,' Hilary said, gathering up her own schoolwork. 'Becky's in her room having a sort-out and Philip's on his computer. I've left some cake for you and there's plenty of biscuits in the cupboard.'

'Thanks, have fun with your French.'

Hilary banged the door shut after her and turned up her

coat against the wind as she walked the short distance to school. Have fun, Tiffany had said. How could she? Not only was that wretched Nick Bradshaw going to be there but she hadn't done her homework. A sudden gust of wind cut through her coat and she shivered. And on top of that Patricia would be gloating like mad that she'd done hers.

The day had rushed past her in such a flurry of activity that she'd barely had time to think of David. Even when he'd got in from work she'd been so preoccupied thinking about Georgia and Nick that she hadn't thought twice about what David may nor may not have been up to at the office, or, indeed, whether he would be going anywhere near the squash club that evening. Thinking about it now, he had seemed distracted at the supper table and hadn't even said anything when the children had started bickering. Philip had started to tell one of his jokes and Becky had looked him in the eye and said, 'You're just a boy.'

"Course I am. So?' he had answered.

'My new friend Chloe says that boys don't grow as fast as girls, so you know what that means, don't you? It means I'm probably more intelligent than you.'

'Let's see you get a scholarship, then!'

Even when Becky had flounced out of the kitchen with her nose high in the air like Miss Piggy and had then bumped into the door and started wailing like a siren, David had seemed oblivious to it all and had got up from the table saying he'd better hurry or he'd be late for his game of squash.

It started to rain just as Hilary crossed the main road opposite St John's. She quickened her pace and shuddered as a drop of water trickled down her neck. By the time she reached the school gate the rain had turned to hail. She bolted across the playground, head down, at the same time trying to shelter her textbook by tucking it close to her chest. At the main entrance door she stepped inside and gasped for air, shaking her wet and bedraggled hair. As she walked along the echoing corridor she could hear Martina's voice giving out instructions for the lesson.

Damn! She was late.

Then behind her she heard the sound of the door crashing shut, followed by hurried footsteps.

'Glad I'm not the only one who's late.'

Without turning round she knew who it was. Subconsciously she slowed her step. Some mad part of her wanted to be able to enter the classroom with Nick – That'd show Patricia, she thought.

Nick held the door open for her and she went in. 'Hello, Martina,' she said brightly, 'sorry I'm late.'

'Me too,' Nick said.

'Make them stand in the corner,' Patricia said, 'but not together.'

'Shame,' laughed Nick, making his way to the back of the classroom where he'd sat previously. Hilary immediately started for a free chair next to an elderly woman who had never once, in Hilary's knowledge, opened her mouth during any of the lessons.

'Hilary, would you mind sharing with Nick again?' Martina asked. 'I haven't managed to get a book for him yet. We're on page thirty-one: "Dans la Chambre à Coucher".'

Hilary heard a snigger from the front row – Patricia. Reluctantly she sat next to Nick.

'Sorry to get you lumbered with me again,' he said. Then, in a quieter voice, he added, 'Thanks for the tea earlier, by the way.'

After Becky had made her dramatic entrance into the kitchen, Hilary had been surprised at how Nick had treated Becky. He'd bent down to her and thoughtfully examined one of the Barbie dolls destined for the bin. He'd shaken his head and tutted loudly. 'Dolls, instruments of oppression without a doubt. I'd get rid of the whole lot of them if I were you.' Then he'd stood up and, with his back to Becky, he'd winked at Hilary and smiled. 'Time I was going. Looks like you've a revolution on your hands, I'll leave you to it.'

'Hilary. Qu'est-ce qu'il y a dans l'armoire?'

Hilary studied the picture. *Armoire*. What on earth was an *armoire*? 'Um ... *le lit*?' she said hopefully.

Patricia laughed. 'It'd be a pretty big wardrobe!'

'Quelle chatte!' Nick whispered at Hilary's side. 'Me-ow!'

'Non, Hilary, le lit est sur le plancher. Qu'est-ce qu'il y a dans l'armoire?'

Hilary hesitated. What was the wretched word for clothes?

'Vêtements,' whispered Nick.

'I knew that,' she hissed at him. 'I don't need any help. Vêtements,' she said out loud.

'Bien, et maintenant vos devoirs. Patricia?'

'Oui, Martina. Mes vacances en Florida.'

Hilary closed her eyes and groaned quietly to herself. She'd heard it all before at the school gate. Patricia and family at Manchester airport. Patricia and family miraculously upgraded. Patricia and family at Kennedy Space Center. Patricia and family at Universal Studios. She felt a nudge at her elbow and opened her eyes to see a scrap of paper on the desk in front of her. On it was written, *You thinking what I'm thinking?*

She nearly laughed – nearly risked one of Patricia's disapproving looks. She turned the piece of paper over and wrote, *I doubt it.*

He passed her another note: *Do you think you could chance just one drink with me when we've finished here tonight?*

Certainly not. I'm married! she scribbled in large letters.

'Does that mean you never get thirsty?' he whispered.

She laughed. Patricia huffed in her direction. 'Quand nous sommes arrivés ...' she repeated for Hilary's benefit.

Good grief, thought Hilary, we haven't even got to the bit where the hotel porter got the brand-new Samsonite luggage mixed up with some inferior cases.

At this rate maybe she'd need a drink by the end of the class.

Chapter Seventeen

'Come on, stop fussing. They'll be fine.'

Hilary heard David leave the room and go downstairs. She thought how easy it was for men to switch off their emotions, even when it came to their children.

Very carefully, Hilary sat on the edge of Becky's bed – she was fast asleep and looking her most benign. Hilary kissed her lightly on the cheek and breathed in the smell of her newly washed hair. It made her want to take off her coat and nestle down beside Becky. She didn't want to go out. She didn't want an evening with David, pretending to all those at Derek and Cindy's launch party that their life was just fine. Her life was far from fine and she felt like shouting it out to everyone that night that David was an adulterous, selfish swine.

She kissed Becky once more as if for luck, then went across the landing to Philip's room where she could hear the low throb-throb of Oasis's latest CD. Philip was bent over his desk staring at a book.

'How's the homework going?' she asked.

'The Crusades,' he answered, without looking up. 'It says here they boiled babies alive and then ate them. You don't suppose we could do the same with Becky, do you?'

'Philip!'

'Only joking.'

'And I only came in to say goodbye. You're sure you'll be all right?'

'I'll be fine, Mum, honestly.'

'I'll keep popping back every thirty minutes.'

'You're only going over the road. I'll be okay.'

'You won't go watching anything unsuitable on the television, will you?'

'Mum!'

She gave him a quick kiss on the top of his head, so quick he didn't have time to duck out of the way.

Philip waited for the sound of the front door to shut. Then, reaching across his desk, he parted the bedroom curtains with the end of his pencil and peered through the inch gap. He watched his parents cross the road but flicked away his pencil when he saw his mother glance back up at the house. Had she seen him? He hoped not. He didn't want her thinking he was scared of being on his own.

He wasn't scared.

Like he wasn't scared of those idiots in the changing rooms at school. Batesy was pathetic to have given in to them. He shouldn't have done that, not when they'd promised each other they'd stick together.

He chewed his little finger and returned his attention to the gruesome pictures of severed heads and blood-tipped spears in his history book, convinced that what the Crusaders had experienced was nothing compared to what he was going through.

When at last there was nothing left of his finger-nail he slapped the book shut, threw himself on his bed and buried his head under the pillow to block out the thought of Batesy's betrayal and how alone he felt.

It was almost freezing, just as the weather forecast had predicted, and their breath formed gauzy clouds in the still night air. Alex wrapped his arm round Charlotte. 'Shall we make a run for it?' he asked, as they set off down the drive of Ivy Cottage.

'What, in these heels?'

'Well, I'm not carrying you. I'm saving all my energy for

the honeymoon. There are certain obligations a man's got to fulfil on his wedding night.'

Charlotte laughed. 'You've still not told me where we're going.'

'And nor shall I.'

As they turned into Derek and Cindy's drive Charlotte stopped and faced Alex. 'What, not even if ...' She buried her face in his neck and whispered in his ear. He laughed out loud and kissed her.

'Well really!' reprimanded Iris Braithwaite, appearing from nowhere in the darkness with a puff of dragon-like steam coming out of her mouth.

Ignoring the ticking off and taking in Iris's voluminous fur coat Alex said, 'You're looking very fetching tonight, Mrs Braithwaite.'

'Don't waste your flattery on me, young man. Save it for Mrs Lawrence. It might help you to get her to the altar quicker.'

'Hadn't you heard, Mrs Braithwaite? We've already set a date for the wedding,' Charlotte said, as they fell in step up the floodlit driveway of All in the Mind.

Iris gave her a reproachful glance. 'Yes, I had heard talk, but not having seen hide nor hair of an invitation I dismissed it as nothing more than idle gossip.'

'Alex, you surely didn't forget Mrs Braithwaite's invitation?'

'Silly me,' he said, squeezing Charlotte's hand. 'I must say, I'm surprised to see you here tonight,' he said to Iris. 'You're not exactly one of Derek's greatest fans, are you?'

'I'm here in an official capacity. In a small community such as ours it pays to keep one's finger on the pulse.' And coming to Derek and Cindy's front door she raised her hand and gave the bell a long, hard prod.

Tiffany greeted them.

'Love the dress,' Charlotte said, kissing Tiffany. 'Very vampish.'

Tiffany smiled, one hand fiddling with a wispy tendril of hair hanging in front of her right ear and the other playing with a black velvet choker at her throat.

'You'll catch your death of cold, young lady,' declared Iris, casting a disapproving eye over Tiffany's *décolletage*. It was encouragement enough for Tiffany to lower both her hands and push out her chest.

'Attagirl,' whispered Alex, coming forward to kiss her. 'Take no notice, you look great – especially without the Doc Martens.'

'I'm into glamour these days,' she purred provocatively, and kicked him with an elegant black suede shoe with a three-inch heel. 'Give me your coats and I'll throw them on the bed upstairs.'

'You'll do no such thing with mine,' Iris said. 'I've had this coat since nineteen fifty-seven.'

'Too late to give it back to the poor animal who lost it in the first place, then.'

'I beg your pardon, young lady. I'll have it—'

'Stuffed?' said Tiffany, under her breath.

'Hung up, if you don't mind.'

'Go through and help yourselves to a drink,' Tiffany said to Charlotte and Alex. 'Barry's here somewhere. He's come home for the weekend specially for Dad's big night.'

The sitting room was packed and guests had spilled out into the conservatory. Both rooms were decorated with navy blue and gold swags with matching balloons with the words All in the Mind printed on them. Music was playing but was only just discernible above the noisy hubbub of voices.

'There's Dad,' Charlotte said straight away, seeing her father standing alone. He was giving all his interest to a large ornately framed photographic portrait of the Rogers family. She and Alex grabbed a couple of glasses of champagne from a passing waiter and headed over towards Neville.

'Charlotte. You've rescued me at last. What took you so

long? I've been waiting ages for you. You know how I hate parties.'

'I'm partly to blame,' Alex said. 'Mrs Braithwaite caught us kissing.'

'Not enough of it going on, in my opinion.' Neville laughed.

'Not enough of what going on?'

'Kissing,' Charlotte said with a wink, making room for Derek to join them. He was dressed in cream trousers with a dark navy-blue T-shirt with the words All in the Mind scrolled across his chest in gold letters.

'You really must stop all this sexual harassment, Charlotte. After all, I am a married man.'

'And since when has that ever stopped you?' Cindy said, coming over with a tray of bite-sized vol-au-vents. She, too, was wearing cream trousers and a top just like Derek's.

'So how are all the alterations going?' Alex asked.

'Fine, just fine,' Derek answered. 'The only job pending is to repaint the outside of the house. I know you'll all be disappointed, but I'm afraid it's time to say goodbye to Windolene Cottage. Anyway, how do you like the T-shirts? Good bit of advertising, eh? I'm thinking of selling them to the punters ... I mean, clients.'

'I feel like having one with Losing my Mind on it,' Cindy muttered.

'Hey! I like that.' Derek laughed. 'Catchy slogan, "Losing your mind? Then come to All in the Mind". You're a genius, Cindy. Perhaps we could get it put to music and have it as a jingle on local radio.'

Cindy groaned – he was probably serious.

'Well, I think we ought to drink to your new venture,' Charlotte said, raising her glass. 'To All in the Mind. May it be all in the bank as well.'

'Oh, Charlotte,' Derek said, shaking his head. 'No, no, no. This isn't about making money. This is a window of opportunity to save lost souls.'

'I thought that was my department,' Malcolm Jackson called over, from where he was talking to Louise.

Derek grinned. 'The ones we can't help I promise to send on to you.'

'Very generous of you,' Malcolm said. 'Any chance of a repeat performance of Barry's confirmation party tonight? Music's a bit on the dull side so far.'

Cindy looked away guiltily. As a precautionary measure she had hidden some of Derek's favourite CDs, knowing what the outcome of the evening would be if he and Malcolm got together over Meatloaf's *Bat Out of Hell*. She had never forgotten the sight of Derek and Barry singing together at his confirmation party over a year ago. She had been moved to tears that it had taken eighteen years for father and son to reach a point where they could enjoy each other's company.

'Hey up, Cindy's off in a dream,' Derek quipped.

'I'm sorry,' she said quickly, 'I was thinking of Barry.'

'Where is he?' Charlotte asked. 'Tiffany said he was home for the weekend.'

'He was just finishing off some work the last time I saw him,' Cindy answered.

'Nothing changes, then,' Alex said.

'*Au contraire*,' Derek said enigmatically. He pointed to his chest. '*Au contraire*.'

Hilary wanted to go home. She'd had enough of listening to David talking about the state of the property market. But, most of all, she'd had enough of watching David lie his great big fat head off. He was a liar, a cheat, a betrayer of trust, a complete and utter double-crosser – all the right credentials, some might say, for a good estate agent.

Disconsolately she wandered away from David, who didn't even notice she'd gone – he merely closed up the gap she'd created by moving one step to the right within the circle and waving his arms about more expansively as he spoke.

'You look glum.'

Automatically she forced a smile to her lips, even before she'd registered who was talking to her. It was Nick Bradshaw and, like Derek and Cindy, he was wearing one of the specially designed T-shirts. She decided, though, that she liked him better in a polo-neck sweater and jacket.

'How did you enjoy hearing about Florida in such detail the other night?' she asked, finding herself slipping into conversation with him more easily than she had previously.

'I feel like I've been there,' he answered.

'Me too. Many times.'

'Tell me, Hilary, you were almost tempted, weren't you, to have a drink with me after the class?'

How arrogant of him. 'Not for a single moment,' she replied.

As she'd walked home afterwards she'd asked herself the question over and over again: Why not? Why not go to the pub with him for a drink? If he'd been a woman she wouldn't have thought twice about going home to David and saying she'd been for a drink with one of the girls from the group.

'I wouldn't have tried anything, if that's what you were worried about.'

'Well, of course, you wouldn't,' she said quickly, 'I know that.'

He stared at her. 'Why?'

'Why what?'

He smiled. 'Why are you so sure I wouldn't make a pass at you?'

'Because ... because you just wouldn't, not with somebody like me. Men make passes at women like my sister Charlotte. Look, there she is, over by the fireplace talking to Derek, and that's Alex next to her. They're getting married next month.'

'She's an attractive woman,' Nick said, glancing across the room. He turned his attention back to Hilary. 'And would I be right in thinking that you're the younger sister?'

Hilary frowned. 'Yes, but what's that got to do with anything?'

'Quite a lot I should think. When was the last time you read *The Ugly Duckling* to Becky?'

She opened her mouth to reply, then snapped it shut.

'Think about it, Hilary.'

'Stop teasing me,' she said, in a small voice.

'I'm not, I assure you.'

A loud laugh coming from David made Hilary frown again. Anger flared within her.

'Your husband's enjoying himself tonight,' Nick said, watching her closely.

'And why shouldn't he?' she said crossly.

'More to the point, why aren't you?'

'Says who?'

'Hilary, how long do you think you can live like this?'

She stared at him, suddenly scared. 'Like what?' she asked, hesitantly.

'Pretending. Pretending that whatever it is in your life causing you pain isn't happening.'

'Heavens, Mr Bradshaw. Whatever makes you say something as ridiculous as that?'

'Don't Mr Bradshaw me, Hilary. Just stop lying, not only to other people but to yourself. Face up to what David is doing to you.'

Hilary felt sick. The noise of so many voices, together with the sound of the Gypsy Kings, began to pound inside her head. In front of her Nick's face filled her vision and she swayed slightly. She felt his hand on her arm. She jerked away. 'I need to check on my children,' she said, pushing past him.

When she was outside she breathed in deeply, wanting the icy air to cut through her, wanting everything that was hurting inside her to be cut clean away.

'You okay?'

Damn. It was him. 'Yes,' she lied, and started to walk away from the house. But she heard his footsteps coming up behind her. She had no idea what to say, so she said nothing and let him follow her across the road to The Gables.

The children were both fast asleep and when she came downstairs she found Nick in the kitchen. He handed her a glass of water. She took it gratefully and sat down. 'Must have been all that champagne,' she said, avoiding his eyes. 'It suddenly made me feel sick.'

'How long has this been going on?'

She gripped the glass in her hands, unable to speak.

He sat down opposite her. 'Hilary, I'm pushing you, I know. Something tells me that things are not right between you and David and it won't be long before everyone else starts noticing it. And what will you do then?'

She ignored his question.

'Look,' he carried on, 'people don't have to go around in pain, and that includes you. If you had a broken arm and I was a doctor you'd let me help you, wouldn't you?'

She nodded.

'You've potentially got a broken marriage on your hands, so why not let me help you?'

'I have nothing of the sort,' she said adamantly. Broken marriage – how awful that sounded, how statistical! 'And how dare you suggest David doesn't love me? Why on earth wouldn't he? Now please—'

'I didn't say that, Hilary.'

'Oh, stop it, stop it! You're too clever for me. You're trying to trip me up. All these ghastly word games I keep getting caught up in. If you want to help, just leave me alone and stop trying to make me say things I don't mean.'

A few minutes later she heard the front door close quietly.

'Oh, come off it. What harm is he doing?'

'Muffin 'ell, Dad! You've got to be joking.' Tiffany looked

around the group for support. Charlotte was the first to speak.

'Tiffany's right,' she said. 'Ted's gone too far.'

Derek laughed. 'Didn't have you down as a prude, Charlotte.'

'Far from it,' added David, tottering towards Charlotte.

She pushed him away in disgust, thinking how pathetic he was at that moment, her drunk, adulterous brother-in-law.

'And you, Mr Hamilton,' Iris said, poking Alex's shoulder with her finger. 'Where do you stand on this issue? Should we, in your opinion, be subjected to this filth Mr Cooper seems intent on peddling right here under our noses?'

Alex took a long, deliberate sip of his wine. 'No,' he said at last, 'no, I don't believe we should, I think—'

'Thank you, Mr Hamilton,' Iris said, pleased, and turning her attention to Derek, she said, 'I think you'll find yourself outnumbered, Mr Rogers.'

'How about we widen the net?' Derek said.

'Certainly,' Iris replied, sure of her ground.

Derek went out to the conservatory and asked Nick and Rosie to join them.

'Now, Nick,' he said genially, his hand on Nick's shoulder, 'you're a man of the world, liberal and broad-minded, wouldn't you say?'

'I'd like to think so, yes.'

'Now I know you don't live here in Hulme Welford, but I'm sure you're aware of some ill-feeling in the village regarding our local newsagent selling something a little more exotic than the usual newspapers and sweets.' He gave his nose a tap and added, 'And I'm not talking mangoes, Nick.'

Nick ran his hand over his chin and looked at the expectant faces all around him. 'All things considered, I don't think it's appropriate for a village newsagent to be selling the things Ted Cooper is.' Then, shrugging his shoulders, he went on, 'Call me old-fashioned, but if I wanted to go and buy some seductive lingerie for a special person, then I'd rather go to a shop which specialises in such things, not a paper shop run by a man who doesn't know a camisole top from a filter-tip cigarette.'

'I've heard all I need to hear,' Iris announced, allowing herself a small triumphant smile. 'I congratulate you, Mr Rogers, on your choice of personnel. Mr Bradshaw has a refined quality about him which I admire and I would strongly recommend you to take note of it.' She acknowledged Nick with a nod, then turned away and went in search of something to eat.

'Hear, hear!' laughed Tiffany. She was delighted with Nick's response to her father and offered Nick one of her most beguiling smiles. Charlotte nudged Alex and whispered, 'I think you've just been usurped.'

'I don't agree with you, Nick,' Rosie Williams said serenely, her long fingers steepled together in front of her, just below her nose, as though deep in an act of worship. 'What are you all afraid of?' she asked, facing them all, one by one. 'Why are you so hung up about sex, because that's what this is about, isn't it?'

'I agree,' said Derek. 'Our old friend sex, once again, pulling back its foreskin and penetrating the bashful.' Everyone cringed at this graphic metaphor, but undeterred, Derek carried on. 'Sex,' he said loudly, 'the Englishman's—'

'Achilles' heel?' suggested Rosie, helpfully.

'Cock-up!' finished Derek.

They laughed but all fell silent when Iris rejoined the group with a plate of food. In the ensuing quiet a voice said, 'Hilary likes underwear.'

Surprised, they all looked at David, who seemed to stagger under the sudden focus of attention.

'She's got drawers full of the stuff. She thinks I don't know. She buys it and then hides it. What do you make of that?' His eyes swept round the hushed and embarrassed group. When he saw Nick Bradshaw he repeated the question. 'What do you make of that, then?'

'I think you've had too much to drink,' Nick said politely.

'No, I haven't,' David answered, his voice slightly raised. 'Now answer my question, Mr Damn-Know-It-All-Psycho ... Psycho-bloody-Expert.'

'Come on, David,' Charlotte urged. 'Leave it be and go home before you make a fool of yourself.'

He shrugged her hand away from his arm and moved nearer to Nick.

Derek tried to intervene. 'Let me get you another drink, old mate. Come out to the kitchen.'

'Another drink, I should think *not*!' declared Iris. 'He should be horsewhipped for his appalling behaviour, besmirching his wife's good name in public.'

'I want an answer,' David demanded, continuing to hold his ground.

'Okay,' Nick said calmly. 'Perhaps your wife feels the need to fill a void created by someone she loves.' He met David's angry gaze and didn't flinch, not until David landed a fist in his jaw and sent him sprawling across the room.

Chapter Eighteen

Hilary gave the visiting curate from Knutsford a cursory glance then ran her tongue over the top row of her teeth. She had been up early this morning after waking from one of her recurring dreams – the teeth dream. Ever since she'd sat her O-level exams and in subsequent periods of stress she'd had the same dream of her teeth crumbling and falling out. Apparently it was a sure sign of anxiety.

Last night she hadn't bothered going back to the party after Nick had left The Gables, and, convinced that David wouldn't even miss her, she had gone upstairs to bed. He'd come home just over an hour later and when he'd flopped onto the bed fully dressed she had pretended to be asleep. He had fallen into a heavy stupor almost immediately, leaving her wide awake and thinking what nonsense the phrase 'no peace for the wicked' was.

She had left him half an hour ago, still asleep but now under the duvet. The children had been in one of their lazy moods and, feeling the need to be alone, she had willingly left them with a video to watch and made her escape to St John's.

'And now let us confess our sins to Almighty God,' the visiting curate said, his arms outstretched and his voice resonating with a touch too much of the dramatics. Hilary lowered her head along with the rest of the congregation. But I haven't sinned, she thought, lifting her head. I haven't done anything wrong. It's David who's sinning like mad. Indignation bit deep as she stared at the robed man in front of her. How dare this silly young curate with his newly acquired theological-school piety tell her how bad she was. If he wanted a real sinner he should go and knock David up and make him confess. Why was it always the innocent who were called to ask for forgiveness?

To the right of the curate in the choir stalls, Hilary noticed Iris Braithwaite. She had one beady eye open and it was directed at Hilary. Hilary bent her head and snapped her own eyes shut, blocking out that dreadful face; not so much the beady eye but the shocking and improbable smile the woman had just given her – shocking because Hilary recognised it as a smile of sympathy. Did it mean ... that Mrs Braithwaite knew about David's affair?

Had Charlotte told her? Surely not. Cindy, then? Even more unlikely. Perhaps David and Catherine had been seen together and the pot of gossip was already beginning to bubble.

Oh, God! she started to pray, don't let everyone start talking about me. I'm sorry if I've ever gossiped in the past. Sorry that I might have said the odd unkind word about anyone. I'll never do it again. Just please don't let people talk about me – give them somebody else to gossip about.

Audience participation had never gone down well at St John's and this morning was no exception. The inexperienced curate had now taken up residence in the pulpit and was on to his sermon, and it was falling flat. Hilary felt almost sorry for the man. Perhaps over in Knutsford this kind of thing went down well, but here in Hulme Welford they didn't take kindly to being asked daft questions. One or two rebel members of the congregation were deliberately calling out the wrong answers. What awful stories would go back to Knutsford, she wondered. That they were all as thick as two short planks in Hulme Welford? Undaunted, he continued to take them by the hand through Isaiah's condemnation of sin, fully determined to get his message across.

'Would anyone care to share with us,' the curate offered

up, his eyes scanning the congregation, 'what they think the great prophet would have said if he had been approached by one of his contemporaries and asked, "What's the matter, Isaiah?"'

'That's obvious,' somebody called out from the back.

The curate's relief was obvious too, that somebody was actually listening to him. 'Yes?' he said eagerly.

'He'd say, one eye's higher than the other! Boom, boom!'

Guffaws of laughter reverberated around the church and even the young man in the pulpit had the grace to concede a small smile. If he had started out that morning believing himself to be of the Laurence Olivier school of liturgy he was now heading for the club circuit, where he'd be lucky to finish his act.

But, true to his profession, he carried on valiantly. 'Don't think for one moment that I'm scaremongering,' he said, beginning to raise his voice and alerting everyone to the fact that that was exactly his intention, 'but there's real evil going on out there. We live in a fallen world. Society is falling apart. Businesses are falling apart. Marriages are—'

Stop! Hilary wanted to shout back. Stop it. I don't want to hear any of this. Don't you understand, you silly fool of a man, we don't want to hear this kind of thing. Hulme Welford's a nice place in which to live. We lead nice, comfortable lives where not very much happens. We don't want people like you coming here and telling us how awful the rest of the world is. Leave us alone. I want to be happy. I don't want to be miserable and dream of my teeth falling out.

'I sense real pain here in this church,' the curate said, theatrically, at the same time pointing his finger round the congregation.

'Yes, and I'm looking at it right now,' someone muttered behind Hilary.

Over coffee it seemed that part of Hilary's prayers had been answered. Almost everybody was talking about the sermon they'd just been forced to endure and agreeing that Malcolm Jackson had had no business going away to visit his elderly mother in Lincolnshire without checking the suitability of his locum.

Reluctant to go home, Hilary busied herself with collecting stray pew bibles.

'There you are, Hilary,' her mother said, handing her a bible. 'Wasn't that just the most banal sermon you've ever heard? How's David after last night?'

'What do you mean?' Hilary said warily.

Louise smiled. 'Exactly what I said.'

'He was asleep when I left him.'

'I bet he was. Sleeping it off, more like it.'

'Are you trying to tell me something, Mother?'

'I hope you gave him hell and didn't fuss over him with any sympathy.'

'Sympathy?' she repeated. 'Whatever for?' There were times when Hilary felt sure that Louise lived in a different world.

'Come on, Hilary, loyalty only needs to go so far. It's very admirable that you should want to stand by your husband, especially after the things he said about you, but so many people heard and saw what he did last night that you're going to have to face up to what happened.'

'Mother, I have no idea what you're talking about. I left the party early. Just what did David—'

'Don't start bleating, Hilary,' Louise said, deciding that her daughter really didn't have a clue what she was referring to. 'David hit somebody last night. To the ground, in fact.'

'I don't believe you,' Hilary said, astonished.

'Close your mouth, Hilary, or we'll all fall in. If you don't believe me, ask your sister. She'll tell you exactly what we all saw with our very own eyes. David punched a man to the floor, right there in front of everyone.'

'Who?'

'That new fellow, just started at Derek and Cindy's—'

'Nick Bradshaw?'

'Yes. That's right. You know him, then?'

Something in Louise's voice made Hilary feel guilty. Ridiculous. She had nothing to feel guilty about. 'He's in my French class,' she said. 'But why did David hit him?'

'I rather think David had enjoyed too much of Derek and Cindy's champagne and started talking. Well, more like shooting his mouth off, really. You know the way he is when he's had too much to drink.'

'Can you get to the point, Mother?'

'Okay, seeing as you've asked. But I'm warning you, you won't like it. David said something about you of rather an intimate nature and then asked Nick whatever-his-name-is to comment. He wouldn't – obviously more of a gentleman than your David – and that seemed to make David fly off the handle and he forced Nick to answer his question. When Nick did, David punched him in the face.' Louise laughed. 'You've got to hand it to Derek. Whenever he's at a party something always happens. Remember at your welcome home party for Charlotte and how drunk—'

'What did he say?' Hilary demanded, more concerned with what David had said about her than her mother's admiration for Derek's effect on any social gathering.

'What? When Nick was lying on the floor?'

'No. About me?'

Louise tried her best to keep a straight face. 'Something about you having a penchant for drawers full of lingerie.'

Hilary's face coloured. How could he! 'So what did Nick say that made David hit him?'

'David wanted this penchant of yours psychoanalysed by Nick. He refused at first. Then, when pushed, and you know how pushy David can be at the end of a good evening, he said that maybe you were filling a void created by someone you loved.'

'What rubbish!'

'If you say so, Hilary. By the way, is it possible David's

suffering from some sort of stress? It might explain his bizarre behaviour. Maybe you should book him into All in the Mind. Leave that little thought with you. Must dash. See you.'

Stress! What a joke, thought Hilary, watching her mother hurry away to shake hands with the curate.

'Mother looks as if she'd like to take him by the scruff of the neck, doesn't she?'

'Charlotte!' Hilary exclaimed, seeing her sister at her side. 'Don't say anything to me, just take me back to Ivy Cottage, please. I don't want to go home today. I've had enough.'

Outside St John's the cold air hit them full in the face and, buttoning their coats, Charlotte, Alex and Hilary walked in silence down the gravel path, through the lychgate and out onto the main road. There they caught up with Iris Braithwaite, who was staring straight ahead of her and clutching her handbag as though it were a shield.

Charlotte followed her gaze. 'What on earth's going on?'

The main street of the village was lined on both sides with cars parked bumper to bumper, and outside Ted the Toup's was a queue of men waiting to go in.

'Armageddon,' replied Iris, her face like thunder. 'I warned you.'

They crossed the road, Iris leading the way. She accosted a youth just getting out of a rust-pocked Ford Fiesta. He wore a cap back to front and a thick unbuttoned check shirt over a T-shirt with the words *Stay Cool* written on it. He gave Iris a scornful look and said, 'You'll catch myxomatosis in that fur coat.'

'I beg—'

'Forget it,' he answered, and sauntered away to join the queue outside Ted's.

Hilary and Alex went over and peered inside the shop. It was full and Ted was up to his armpits in red and black lace. Hilary thought of what her mother had just told her and turned away.

'Come on, Mrs Braithwaite,' Charlotte said, when Alex and Hilary came back. 'Let's go home.'

'Outrageous. Outrageous. I shall personally see that that disgusting Ted Cooper is hounded out of the village.'

They left Iris marching up her own drive and walked on to Ivy Cottage, where they were greeted by Mabel as Charlotte let them in through the conservatory.

'Go into the sitting room, Hilary,' Charlotte said. 'We banked the fire up before we went out and it should be nice and warm in there for you.'

When they were alone Alex turned to Charlotte. 'What's wrong with Hilary?' he whispered. 'She's not herself at all.'

'It's nothing,' she said, remembering her promise to Hilary.

'Charlotte?'

Oh, what was the point? The way things were going it wouldn't be long before others found out what was happening. And who knows, Alex might be able to help.

'It's David,' she replied. 'He's having an affair with his secretary.'

'Bloody hell! Since when?'

'I haven't a clue,' she said, shaking her head. 'And I doubt whether Hilary has either. So far David doesn't know that Hilary has sussed him. She thinks if she stays quiet she'll ride out the storm while David comes to his senses and gets over his mid-life crisis, or whatever it is that makes a man jeopardise everything he once held precious.'

'But that takes all the coolness and determination of . . .'

'Of somebody like Cindy,' Charlotte said, reaching into the fridge for a bottle of wine. 'That's why Hilary's in the mess she is. She's too impulsive to play the hard, confident wife willing to preserve her marriage.' She took three glasses from the cupboard and handed Alex the bottle of wine. 'Come on,' she said, 'I'm going to get my sister to loosen up and then hopefully talk some sense into her.'

'What about David? Won't he wonder where Hilary is?'

'Stuff David! Let him wonder.'

Chapter Nineteen

As Georgia drove along Acacia Lane she thought how it was that a good cause never failed to bond a group of people together, even the most diverse characters. In her experience it was usually a transient yoke of loyalty but one that was guaranteed to bring out the gung-ho spirit in all concerned.

'You sure we've got enough stuff?'

'Plenty,' Georgia answered, looking at Tiffany in the mirror. Next to Tiffany was Chloe, her small face hidden by a balaclava and on whose lap was a large cardboard box with the lid firmly down. Georgia hadn't questioned her daughter on the contents of the box as they'd rushed out of the house after Iris's call, but she'd noticed when locking the back door that the cat-litter tray was suspiciously empty. Tiffany's box, on the other hand, had a far less sinister look about it and contained an innocent collection of hair products.

In the front passenger seat, as rigid as a corpse, and about as white, was Iris Braithwaite, nursing a box of the remains of a Chinese takeaway from Georgia and Chloe's supper last night, half a dozen eggs, some overripe tomatoes along with what Iris had personally contributed, a quantity of rotting vegetable peelings. It was to be real chemical warfare.

They hadn't had much time to put together their weapons – Iris had only called her fifteen minutes ago.

'Ms D'Arcy,' she'd commanded down the phone, 'I would greatly value your assistance. Now!'

Chloe had jumped at the chance to join in with the action.

'Time to nuke the oppressors!' she'd shouted, climbing into the Jeep. They'd left Gordon holding the fort with a bemused look on his face.

It was while they were parked outside Iris's house that Tiffany had appeared. Tiffany had babysat once or twice for Georgia on the few occasions Winnie had been busy and, seeing her coming out of the drive of All in the Mind, Chloe had leaned out of the window and waved to her, shouting, 'We're going to have some fun down at Ted the Toup's. Want to come?'

They turned right at the end of Acacia Lane and drove along the main street of the village. Georgia could see a small line of parked cars and a tall thin man standing outside the newsagent's. She felt a rush of adrenaline.

'There's one!' shrieked Chloe. 'Open the sun roof, Mum, quick.'

Georgia slid back the glass panel. 'Ready everybody?' she said, smiling. 'How about you, Iris?'

'Ready,' the older woman replied. 'Let's not defer a moment longer.'

Both Tiffany and Chloe were already preparing to take aim, and as Georgia slowed the Jeep, the first dollop of grey, clinging ammunition was fired through the air. It caught a man full in the face just as he was coming out of the shop. His stunned pebble-dashed expression was only clearly revealed when he wiped away the sticky stones. He looked upwards, as if expecting to see a bird of enormous proportions flying overhead. The tall thin man next to him started to laugh until he caught a chest-load of shrapnel. In disbelief he, too, lifted his head skywards.

Chloe squealed excitedly, exposing her ten-year-old self in a rare moment of giddy delight.

'Talk about thick,' Tiffany shouted, aiming a plastic bottle of shampoo and firing out globs of orange gunk. Even she was surprised at what an effective cannon she had in her hands. She squeezed again on the bottle and a large jelly-like blob landed exquisitely on the crown of a bald-headed victim also standing in the doorway of the shop.

Seeing that Ted's customers had now found the source of the missiles, Georgia pushed her foot down hard on the accelerator and sped off to the other end of the village. They hovered outside Patricia Longton's double-fronted cottage.

'Close that box, Chloe!' shouted Georgia. 'The smell's disgusting.'

'An inspired idea, though,' Iris said in congratulation, turning round to Chloe, whose eyes were shining brilliantly through the holes in her balaclava.

'It's your turn now, Mrs Braithwaite,' Chloe said. 'You'll get them from your side of the car as we go past.'

'Ready for round two?' asked Georgia, revving the engine.

'Drive on,' instructed Iris, pulling on a pair of rubber gloves and delving into the box on her lap.

Still dusting themselves down, the three men didn't hear the sound of the approaching Jeep, not until it was once again alongside them, broadside fashion, with what looked like Queen Boadicea leaning out of the passenger window firing off a round of beansprouts and chewed spare ribs. Slimy, curled-up potato peelings that had taken on the appearance of slugs followed, hotly pursued by eggs which Tiffany hurled, yelling, 'Surface-to-air missiles.'

'Myxomatosis, indeed,' Iris called, taking aim with a tomato.

Georgia reckoned that the onslaught had by now girded the collective loins of their victims, so she pressed on the accelerator pedal again, but the engine stalled. 'Shit!' She turned the key. Nothing. She caught the expression on Iris's face beside her and the sound of angry voices from the pavement. She tried the key again, promising the Jeep unswerving loyalty in the future if only it would start. It did, and as the engine roared into life, she gripped the steering wheel and pushed her foot to the floor. They rocketed away, just as the group of men began to move towards them.

Georgia gave them a glance in her mirror and grinned at the sight of the man – the one who had been the first on the receiving end of the ballistic cat litter – losing his balance on the mucus-like mixture of shampoo and raw eggs. She watched him land on his backside with a bump.

The bald man with the skullcap of protein-enriched shampoo was now also sporting a medal of beansprouts on his right shoulder. He threw his hands in the air. 'Sodding hell! I only came here for a present for my wife.' Bewildered, he wiped away the beansprouts and wandered back to the safety of his car. He'd stick to catalogues in the future, he decided, less bother that way.

At the nursery, Georgia brought the Jeep to an exhilarating halt, sending up a cloud of dust behind them.

'Mission accomplished,' she said, snatching on the hand-brake.

'I'll say it is,' agreed Tiffany, grinning broadly and pulling off one of her father's skiing hats.

'Iris?' Georgia asked cautiously. 'You okay?'

The older woman was staring straight ahead through the windscreen. She was motionless and still bearing the same cadaverous pallor she had worn earlier. The only colour in her face came from her eyes, which were as dark and as shiny as those of a bird.

'Iris?'

She turned to face Georgia. 'I heard you the first time,' she said, carefully peeling off her rubber gloves as though they were expensive kid leather.

'I need to wash my hands,' Chloe said, opening the door and getting out.

'I bet you do,' Georgia said, cuffing her daughter lightly round the ears. 'Take Mrs Braithwaite and Tiffany over to the house while I check that Gordon's okay. I'll be with you in a minute.'

Chloe led the way, and once she'd washed her hands, she went outside leaving Tiffany and Iris alone.

Tiffany threw herself onto the sofa and fiddled with the fringe of the throw-over on it. She watched Iris Braithwaite, who was standing perfectly still at the window, and began to wonder how she had ended up spending part of her Sunday afternoon lobbing rubbish out of a sun-roof with, of all people, old Ma Braithwaite. She herself was a known trouble-maker in the village, but what the hell would people start saying about Mrs Braithwaite when they found out that she had been part of the attack on Ted the Toup's shop?

'Gordon seems to have managed pretty well without me,' Georgia said, joining them. 'Won't you sit down, Iris?'

Iris threw a disdainful look at the only free chair with its threadbare arms and collection of brightly coloured cushions. She remained standing. She was still deathly pale.

'You okay?' Georgia asked, concerned. Since her after-noon-tea session with Iris some days ago she had surprised herself at how often she had thought of her, surprised, too, that she found herself caring about Iris. Sure, she was nosy, bossy, interfering and as dogmatic as hell, but the old girl had spirit in spades, which was more than you could say for most of the people in Hulme Welford. It amused her to know that she felt a curious sense of empathy with Iris. She hadn't yet worked out why. 'No regrets, I hope?'

The loose skin under Iris's chin wobbled, reminding Georgia of a turkey, and suddenly laughter filled the room. 'Good Lord, why on earth would I regret anything? I've just had the time of my life!'

'I wondered if you thought we'd gone too far,' Georgia replied, relieved. How could she have doubted Iris's nerve?

'Too far? We've barely begun. Our cause has a long way to go yet, young lady, if we're to beat our old enemy Beel-zebub. St Paul himself told Timothy that they had to fight the good fight.'

'Good for you,' Georgia said, not sure that she wanted the

likes of St Paul brought into it – he'd had some pretty weird ideas about the role of women. 'I can see you would have been one of the first to have been tied to the railings.'

'That's as may be, but I certainly would not have been so stupid as to throw myself under a galloping horse.'

'I wouldn't half mind pushing Ted the Toup under one, though,' Tiffany said, with a giggle.

Ted pulled at the blind on the shop door. He was knackered, like he'd just been knocked flat and run over by a steamroller. The shop had never been so busy. Stroke of luck, that publicity in the paper – it had attracted no end of people. A shame he hadn't had enough stock. Thongs were obviously the thing and he'd looked bloody stupid turning all those customers away empty-handed.

And as for that trouble outside, well, he knew who was behind that. Stupid old woman. Just what was wrong in selling some saucy kit anyway? Plenty of the usual customers had been in and made a few purchases during the week, like that Mr Longton. He'd come in yesterday to pay his paper bill and had left with a nice pair of knickers for his wife.

Providing a service, that was what he was doing.

He opened the till and began to count that day's takings.

Chapter Twenty

Charlotte was surprised at the depth of contempt she felt for David as he stood at the door. She had always got on well with her brother-in-law. In fact, there had been times in the past when they had turned to each other for help, especially when Hilary had what David would call 'one on her'.

'I'm sorry,' she said, standing two steps higher than David, her arms folded in front of her – an assertiveness technique Peter had learned on one of his many management courses and had come home and tried on her. 'Hilary's lying down. She's probably asleep by now.'

'But why?'

'I told you, she's got a headache.'

'Yes, but why here? Why didn't she come home and go to bed?'

Charlotte gave an exaggerated roll of her eyes. 'Come off it, David. You know jolly well you and the children wouldn't have given her a moment's peace. As soon as she'd walked through the door it would have been, "What time's lunch?" "Where are my football boots?"'

'Odd,' he grunted. 'Bloody odd I call it when a wife doesn't come home from church and goes to bed in another person's house. How do I know she's even here? She's been acting pretty strangely these past few weeks.'

Charlotte tried to lighten the mood with a laugh. 'So I'm just another person, am I?'

He scraped at some loose paint on the door frame with his fingernail. 'I should have known you moving back here would mean trouble.'

Again she laughed. 'You know what sisters are like.' She started to close the door. 'I'll let her home when I'm convinced she's fully rested. In the meantime, why not make some lunch for you and the children? I expect they're hungry by now.' She closed the door and listened to the sound of David's angry footsteps fading away.

'Was he very annoyed?' Hilary asked, when Charlotte returned to the sitting room.

'Not really, just confused. I told him to go home and make some lunch.'

'Talking of which,' Alex said, 'I'll do us some omelettes, shall I?'

'I couldn't eat a thing,' Hilary said morosely, staring into the fire.

'Nonsense,' Charlotte threw back, knowing at once how like her sister she was sounding – not the poor confused version sitting before her now but the strident, bossy Hilary, who had always turned any monumental crisis into an everyday occurrence with a hearty let's-roll-up-our-sleeves attitude. She would have been great in the war.

Alex laid a gentle hand on Hilary's arm. 'You'll feel better for some food inside you.'

They watched him leave the room. With tears in her eyes, Hilary said, 'You *will* marry him, won't you, Charlotte?'

Charlotte came and sat on the floor in front of Hilary's chair. 'Of course I will. You know as well as I do, the wheels are already in motion for our big day.'

'But you might get cold feet between now and then.'

Charlotte thought back to her wedding day with Peter, remembering how she had stood at the altar fighting against the nagging doubt that she shouldn't have been there. She shook her head. 'No cold feet this time.'

Hilary lifted her eyes. 'This time,' she repeated. 'What do you mean?'

'Oh, Hilary, it's a long story, and one I'll save for another day. Talk to me about David.'

'How's the dress coming on?'

Charlotte could have shouted at her sister for her persistent prevarication, but she knew it would get her nowhere. Right now, bullying was not the answer. She would have to cajole her. She reached for the bottle of wine and refilled Hilary's glass, inwardly cringing at the thought of Becky following her up the aisle on Christmas Eve. She must have been mad to have given in to her niece's pleading a few weeks ago. 'I've never been asked to be a bridesmaid before,' she'd said, 'please let me do it.' I'm not surprised, Charlotte had wanted to say. Who, in their right mind, would want to court disaster in such a deliberate fashion on such an important day? Goodness knows why, but she had finally said yes.

'It was good of Dad to suggest having the reception at their place,' Hilary said. 'I had no idea he was becoming such an expert in the kitchen.'

Charlotte frowned. And that was another act of reckless foolishness on her part. Who knows what on earth they'd get to eat? Dad might have developed a new hobby out of watching cookery programmes on the telly, but doing the buffet for her wedding reception was surely way beyond his capabilities. She suddenly smiled to herself – he'd never yet let her down, had he?

'David's not much cop in the kitchen,' Hilary said quietly. In the background they could hear Alex whistling to himself as he prepared their lunch. 'In fact, I don't think he's much cop at anything any more.'

'Oh, Hilary. This is all such a mess. What can we do to help you?'

'We?' Hilary repeated.

'I . . . I told Alex just now when we were in the kitchen,' Charlotte confessed.

Hilary covered her face with her hands. She started to sob. 'Not *another* person who knows what a failure I am. I can't bear it. Oh, Charlotte, how could you?'

Charlotte let her sister cry.

'How could you? How could you?' Hilary repeated over and over, rocking herself backwards and forwards in the armchair. 'I don't want anyone to know. I feel so disloyal towards David. It's as though I'm telling tales out of school.'

'And where's David's loyalty in all of this?' Alex asked, coming back into the room with a large tray.

Charlotte stood up and took one of the plates and handed it to Hilary. 'Alex is right,' she said. 'Why should you be so hung up on being loyal when David clearly doesn't give a damn?'

Hilary gave a loud sniff and looked down at the omelette on her lap. She should have been at home cooking roast pork, roast potatoes, sage and onion stuffing, apple sauce, parsnip chips – David always had to have parsnips – she shouldn't be here at all. What were they doing over the road? How were they managing without her? Just what kind of a mother was she to let her family go without their Sunday lunch? And who was Charlotte to say whether David gave a damn or not? 'He does love me,' she said defiantly. 'I know he does.'

'You may well be right,' Alex said, sitting down next to Charlotte on the sofa, 'but the problem still remains. How are you going to cope with David loving you and perhaps thinking he loves another?'

She prodded uninterestedly at her omelette. 'I don't know, but if Cindy's managed it all her marriage, then so can I.'

'But you're not Cindy,' Charlotte said.

'Then maybe I should become more like her.'

'That,' Alex said softly, 'would be a great shame. For what would happen to the real Hilary?'

'Is he always like this?' Hilary asked Charlotte.

Her sister smiled. 'From the moment I met him. Don't you remember him bullying me round your dinner table that night?'

Hilary managed a smile, remembering vividly the time to which her sister was referring. 'I was so very proud and sure of myself that night ... Now look at me.'

'You like to be in control, Hilary, don't you?' Alex said, unexpectedly.

'Yes,' she answered, not looking at him. 'I like to know what's happening, when and how. There's nothing wrong in that, is there?'

'Not at all. So, who at the moment would you say is in control? You or David?'

Hilary pushed her untouched meal away from her. She reached for the box of tissues. 'I ... I don't know. And I don't know why that question should upset me so much.'

I do, thought Charlotte. All those years in her own empty marriage with Peter she had kidded herself that she was in control of her life. She had convinced herself that as long as she was in charge she could control the amount of pain she was experiencing. But it was all a lie. Peter had been the one in charge of her emotions. She had been at his mercy, waiting for him to pull on the strings of her heart – today would be an okay day, or today would be a day of despair. She had even stopped trusting her own judgement because she'd been so busy trying to control her surroundings in the belief that that would prevent anything from hurting her. She had lived like that for too long – lying to Peter, but worst of all, lying to herself. Just as Hilary was now doing and was prepared to go on doing for as long as it would take. 'Answer Alex's question, Hilary,' she said. 'Think hard and answer truthfully. Which one of you is in control?'

Hilary shook her head. 'David,' she said. 'Bloody David is and I hate him for it.' She bit her lip. 'No!' she cried out. 'I don't hate him. I love him. I do honestly. Oh, God, I sound quite mad.'

'Not mad,' Alex said, 'but hurt and confused.'

In the silence that followed, Charlotte got up and threw another log on the fire. The light outside was already fading. She switched on the lamps, casting the room in a gentle roseate glow, then drew the curtains.

Hilary watched her sister moving about. She felt like a young, cosseted child, sitting here in Charlotte's warm and comfortable sitting room. Compared to The Gables it was a sanctuary of peace and quiet. Lucky Charlotte, she thought with envy, conscious that, for the first time in her married life, she wanted something her sister had.

Ever since she'd met David her world had revolved around his and while Charlotte had bounced from one precarious relationship to another, in her late teens and early twenties, she and David had lived in each other's pockets, planning with meticulous care each stage of their lives – careers, marriage and children. Everything had been so straight-forward, so well controlled . . . until now. The rigid timetable that had given her such security and comfort had suddenly been taken away from her, and in contrast it was Charlotte who was now cocooned by love and the stability of a settled existence.

That's what I want, she whined to herself, in the voice Becky usually used when she wanted something her brother had.

Just after six o'clock there was a knock at the back door. It was Philip.

'I'm afraid your mum's still asleep,' Charlotte said, quite truthfully, for Hilary was indeed now asleep by the fire.

'Oh,' he said, disappointed.

'Did your father send you over?' she asked suspiciously.

Philip shook his head.

Charlotte was no expert when it came to children, but this one looked upset. 'You okay?'

He wobbled his head in no particular direction.

She wasn't sure how to proceed with her unsmiling nephew – a nephew with whom she had never really had much contact. And now here he was in her kitchen, a picture of misery. What was she to do? 'How's school?' she tried.

'Okay.' Philip knew the score. All grown-ups asked about school.

'Made many friends?'

'A few. There's Batesy. He's okay …' But he didn't want to think of Batesy. 'Is Mum all right?'

'She's fine. She's just worn out,' Charlotte replied, genuinely surprised at the concern in Philip's voice. It showed in his eyes as well. 'She'll be home soon. Don't worry.'

He shrugged and turned away, his head bent and his feet dragging disconsolately.

Charlotte watched him go out into the dark. Poor Philip, she thought. She had never seen a more miserable-looking child.

Chapter Twenty-one

Cindy missed the smell of In the Pink – shampoo and hair spray in the salon, water-treatment chemicals in the Jacuzzi, the combination of perspiration and deodorant in the gym, even the smell of towels in the tumble-dryer.

All in the Mind smelled of new carpets and barely dry paint, with the occasional waft of essential oils. Cindy had insisted they kept on their aromatherapist, and with Hazel now reinstalled in her newly decorated room, the familiar smell of lavender oil and rosemary acted as a welcome balm against the insanity of Derek's latest idea on this their opening day.

So far they had got off to a good start. The classes were fully booked, just as Derek had predicted. Even when Cindy had helped to fill out the booking forms for people to sign up for their chosen seminars she had refused to believe that All in the Mind could possibly work – now, of course, she consoled herself with the thought that it couldn't possibly last.

For the life of her she couldn't understand what made anyone want to sit in a room full of strangers and bare their souls. Why couldn't they simply learn to keep their mouths shut and be quiet about their problems? Constantly talking about the problem served no purpose, in her opinion. Worse still, she had come across those who had merely exploited the role of a counsellor and got their wrong-doings sanctioned by continuous rationalisation of their appalling behaviour.

Just as well she'd never found the need to go running off

to some counsellor every time Derek had hurt her. If she'd done that she wouldn't have had time in her life to do anything else. Though what any counsellor would make of Derek was anybody's guess.

Sitting in the office, she started writing out a cheque for the exorbitant decorator's bill. She slipped the cheque into an envelope and sealed it up, then drummed her long fingernails on the desk and sighed.

She was bored. In the days of In the Pink her time had been crammed with appointments with her regular customers. Now she had nothing to do. So much for finding a niche, as Derek had claimed she would.

She got up from the desk and opened the door on to the corridor. All was quiet. Not a sound of a hair-dryer or the local radio station, not even the whirr of the washing machine. The place felt dead. She breathed in deeply, catching the smell of gloss paint. It reminded her of she and Derek decorating their first salon. It was over in Northwich, a tiny box of a place squeezed in between a down-at-heel ironmonger's and a flower shop – Derek had always been next door buying her flowers from the old woman, who he had said looked like the flower-seller in Trumpton. Their first day, all those years ago, had given them both such a thrill. Derek, with his Kevin Keegan hairstyle, had rushed about the salon chatting up the clients, seeking customer loyalty, while she, too, had enjoyed herself, achieving her ambition of running her own business. But she had been happy enough just seeing Derek so pleased with life.

So why wasn't she happy today, then? It was obvious to everyone that Derek was over the moon with their new venture, as Tiffany had pointed out at breakfast before she'd set off for school. 'Dad looks like he's died and gone to heaven,' she'd said.

'A man needs to be fulfilled to really know himself in order to be happy,' he'd said, his mouth poised over a croissant.

Typically Tiffany had laughed at her father and taken the

croissant from his hand. But not so typically she'd squeezed Cindy's arm and said, 'Best of luck, I think you're going to need it.'

Cindy went back into the office. It wasn't luck she needed, it was something to do. And what was frightening her most was that she suspected she was no longer required. Had Derek done this deliberately? Had he planned to squeeze her out of the business . . . and his life?

She went over to the bookcase beside the filing cabinet and idly read some of the titles of Derek's recently purchased books – *The Search for Self-Awareness*, *Journey into the Unknown* and lastly *Are You in Control?*. She picked this one off the shelf and started to flick through it.

'Hope you don't mind, Nick, old mate,' Derek said, coming into the largest of the seminar rooms. 'Just thought I'd sit in at the back and see how it all hangs together.'

The group of women looked up eagerly. They had been sufficiently encouraged with Nick to think the two-day course their managing director had sent them on wasn't going to be a total waste of time, and now they had the added bonus of a Phil Collins lookalike.

'I don't normally allow onlookers,' Nick said firmly. He was sitting in a chair in the gap of the horseshoe of occupied chairs around him, one leg crossed over the other, his hands clasped behind his head – he knew better than anyone how important body language was, and watching Derek stroll to the back of the room he could see quite plainly that his employer gave off an undisguised air of confidence.

'Shan't make a noise,' Derek said, smiling round at the group. 'Forget I ever came in.'

'We'd rather not,' one of the women said provocatively, and then laughed coarsely. Her personnel department colleagues joined in with her and instantly the atmosphere of the room turned into a girls' night out.

Derek smiled back at the ringleader, enjoying being the

focus of attention at the same time as wanting to get his hands on her hair and tone down all those over-bleached highlights – he realised too late that he should have been looking for the woman within.

'So,' Nick said loudly, leaning forward and clapping his hands together sharply. Instantly the group was back with him. 'Reaching your full potential is what we're about this afternoon, as indeed we will be tomorrow. What I hope to show you is the unlearning of unconscious responses which you learned as children. By unlocking this particular door you'll discover just how much potential there is deep inside each and every one of you. This will be the first step to freeing yourselves of the mental as well as the physical stress we are all likely to experience at various stages in not only our working life but our private life. Everyone with me so far?'

The woman with the highlights looked over to Derek. 'Certainly am,' she said.

The phrase 'money for old rope' was dangerously close to the tip of Derek's tongue as he left Nick to wind up his mid-afternoon session, but the new Derek made him swallow this unworthy thought clean away.

He pushed open the office door, hoping to find Cindy, but there was no sign of her. He felt disappointed. He wanted to talk to her about how well the day was going. This therapy game was going to be easier than he'd thought. All those years he'd been messing about with the outside of people's heads when all the time the inside was a whole lot more straightforward. Why he hadn't cottoned on to the therapy industry before he didn't know.

He sat back in his chair and put his feet up on the desk. He had Bas to thank for this, of course. Good old Bas. A rush of fatherly pride crept over him. God, he was proud of Bas. Medical school. Just think of it, a son of his a doctor one day, maybe even a surgeon. And wasn't he practically in the medical world himself now? He smiled. No more feeling inferior to his son. Those days were gone. At last he was on an equal footing with Bas.

He looked at the diary planner on the wall and saw that Rosie was about to start her six-week seminar on 'Marriage, Sex and Happiness – They Needn't Be Incompatible'. He decided to go and have a nosy.

Rosie welcomed him with a broad smile, unlike Nick, Derek reflected. 'Mind if I sit in on this?' he asked.

'No free-wheelers,' she answered, crisply.

Derek wondered if she was as brusque in bed. 'Now, darling,' he mimicked in his head, 'left a bit ... right a bit ... Here, let me do it!'

'Mr Rogers?'

'Sorry,' he said. Not only was Rosie looking at him but so were her clients – a lacklustre group of two couples. 'Miles away,' he apologised again.

'If you stay, Mr Rogers, you'll have to join in with the session.'

'Oh ... perhaps not, then.' He moved towards the door.

'Not frightened, are you?'

He recognised the challenge in her voice. 'Group sex? Nothing like it!' he shot back, and promptly sat next to a poker-thin woman in a flowery pinafore dress with eyes like gobstoppers. Her husband, the other side of her, was a Mr Comb-Over wearing a jumper that was home-made and looked far too small – to the point of asphyxiation. The old Derek thought they would both be better off for a damn good shop in Wilmslow to smarten themselves up and if that failed they should shoot each other and put everyone else out of their misery at having to look at them. But the new Derek considered how many sessions of positive stroking it would take to lick them into shape and give them both a new lease of life.

'Can we get on?' asked a large burly woman with nipples protruding like shuttlecocks through her turtle-neck sweater – she had more facial hair than Derek had ever seen in his entire career. 'Take the Braun to her!' Derek wanted to shout across the room. 'Somebody hold her down and I'll do it.' He tried hard to see her as a whole and complete person but all he could think of were those two enormous nipples and a beard which would have given ZZ Top a scare. 'We've already lost five minutes,' she continued, 'and I've come here expecting value for money because, since poor Alan's depression, we don't get out much.'

I'd have depression if Cindy had whiskers like that, thought Derek, contemplating *poor Alan* beside the incredible bearded woman. *Poor Alan* was wearing what looked suspiciously like Crimplene trousers, which were hitched up almost to his knees as he sat, straight-backed and embarrassed, trying to lose himself in the mind-bending business of pushing back his cuticles.

'Marriage,' struck up Rosie, her hands steepled in front of her, 'designed in heaven but lived out in hell. Does that mean anything to anyone?'

Nobody spoke, but the man in Crimplene hitched up his trousers a notch.

Tiffany saw Nick before he saw her. She flicked her hair back from her face, except for one tendril which she twisted round her finger. Despite the cold wind she unbuttoned her school-regulation duffel coat and walked nonchalantly up the drive. 'Hi,' she said, as he opened his car door.

'Hello,' he called back. 'Good day at school?'

She tried to think of something clever to say. 'It's a means to an end,' she said, with a long, bored sigh.

Nick smiled. She reminded him of his youngest daughter, who had recently left home to go off to university – all that reluctant enthusiasm for life stored up in such a delightful package.

'So how was your first day?' she asked, coming round to his side of the car and leaning against it.

'Your father's pleased with the way it went.'

Tiffany flicked at her hair. 'You mean nobody accused him of being a bungling quack?'

'No,' Nick answered, with a laugh.

'What about a bonehead? Somebody must have said that?'

He shook his head.

'A bogus—'

'Now why exactly would you think anyone would want to say those things about your father?'

'Because he is all those things! Therapy indeed!' She suddenly saw her mistake. 'I mean, he doesn't know the first thing about what makes people tick.' She tilted her head and smiled. 'But I'm sure you know what you're doing.'

'Quick on your feet, aren't you, Tiffany?' he said good humouredly.

Glad to have recovered the situation so easily, but cross with herself for having wasted valuable talking time discussing her father, she said, 'How's your jaw?'

'Not a mark on me,' he answered, giving his chin a rub.

'Do you always go around making such provocative comments?'

He laughed. 'It never fails to invoke the right response.'

'And getting David Parker to thump you, was what you wanted?'

'Ah. As you said a few moments ago, it was a means to an end.' He threw his briefcase onto the back seat of his car and stooped to get inside.

'I'll see you, then,' Tiffany said.

He heard the expectant tone in her voice. 'I should think so,' he replied, putting the key in the ignition.

As he indicated to turn left at the end of the drive – conscious that Tiffany was still watching him – he saw Hilary's car coming towards him. He flashed his lights at her in the dark, she came alongside him, and as they both wound down their windows he heard her young daughter say clearly, 'Here's Mummy's boyfriend,' followed by a loud ssh.

'How's things?' he asked.

Awful, Hilary wanted to say, I've had about as much as I can take. But instead she said, 'Busy. I've got a hundred and one things to start doing for the PTA Christmas Fayre.'

He looked thoughtfully at her. It never ceased to amaze him how adept human beings were at pretending.

'I heard about you and David . . .' she started to say.

But sensing that she didn't want to say anything more with the children in the car he shook his head and said, 'No worries. He's obviously got a lot on his mind at the moment.' He saw her grip the steering wheel, her knuckles turn white and, reaching inside his jacket pocket, he took out a card with his name and telephone number on it. He handed it to her. 'Ring me if you need to.'

'I'm never going to get married,' Becky declared, when Nick had driven off.

'Why's that, dear?' Hilary asked, as she parked outside The Gables. She brushed away an unchecked tear rolling down her cheek.

'I'm going to live on the moon with lots of other women and we'll talk about important things like making the men stay at home to look after the babies. Chloe says that way there won't be any wars because the men will all be too busy and exhausted to fight one another.'

'It's a commune, you idiot,' Philip said scornfully.

'Okay, then, a commune. But, Mummy, do you think Daddy's busy enough?'

Nick stopped his car one more time on Acacia Lane or, rather, Iris Braithwaite brought him to an abrupt halt by staging what looked like a stick-up in the dark alongside the entrance to the White Cottage. He quickly wound down his window. 'What's the problem?' he called out.

She lowered her arms and came round to his side of the

car. 'I wonder, Mr Bradshaw, if you could possibly help me.'

'Of course. What can I do? You've not locked yourself out, have you?'

'I may be many things, Mr Bradshaw, but careless is not one of them. Now if you'd just wait there for a few moments, I've got something which I'd like you to deliver to a friend for me. Not being able to drive can be such a nuisance at times.'

Nick watched Iris march back up her driveway and disappear into her cottage. Within seconds she reappeared carrying two large biscuit tins.

'I'm so pleased to have caught you,' she said, passing him the tins through the car window and offering him a smile. 'I had meant to call round and see you during the day at All in the Mind, but then who knows what I may have burst in on. So very kind of you to do this for me. I knew you were a decent and honourable man when I met you at the Rogers's party and you showed yourself to be a willing supporter of my campaign here in Hulme Welford. I'm most grateful to you. Good night.'

'But, Mrs Braithwaite,' Nick replied, nonplussed, 'where exactly am I taking these?'

She let out an unexpected laugh. 'Oh, didn't I say? I am sorry. If you could just see your way to dropping them off at Ms D'Arcy's. I believe you live only a short distance from her.'

'Do I?'

'She runs Hulme View Nursery, just off—'

He nodded. 'Yes, I know where it is. I had no idea it was her place and, to be honest, I'm not so sure she'll be all that delighted at seeing me.'

'Nonsense, Mr Bradshaw. She must get very lonely stuck out there with only her young daughter. She'll enjoy your company. Now hurry along, I've kept you long enough. Tell Ms D'Arcy those scones are best eaten tonight but the cake will last a few days.'

*

Driving out of the village Nick smiled to himself. He had the distinct feeling he was being manipulated. But from what he knew of Iris Braithwaite and from what Derek had told him of the woman, she was the last person in the world to try her hand at matchmaking. More likely she possessed a perverse sense of humour.

The main entrance to Hulme View Nursery was barred by a large, padlocked metal gate and Nick was forced to leave his car on the road and walk across the gravel car park, which he entered through a small wooden gate hanging off its hinges. His shoes crunched noisily in the dark and twice he nearly stumbled into the bushes, tripping over goodness knows what.

'Hell!' He righted himself a third time, only just managing to keep a hold of Iris's tins. He pushed on a few more steps, finding himself on what he hoped was a path. A security light flashed in his eyes, momentarily blinding him, then ahead of him a door opened spilling out yet more light from a small squat building.

'I can't afford double glazing or a time-share ... Oh, it's *you*, what do you want?'

'Mrs Braithwaite asked me to drop these off for you,' he answered, when he reached Georgia D'Arcy, who was leaning against the door frame.

She looked at him suspiciously, then at the tins in his hands. 'What's in them?'

'Testicles. Mashed up and trodden underfoot.'

She tried hard not to smile. 'Are you trying to tell me something?'

'No, I'm simply the errand boy trying to make a delivery.' He pushed the tins at her. 'And I've been told to tell you to eat the cake tonight and ... No, wait a minute, that's not right. You've to eat the scones tonight and keep the cake.'

Georgia laughed. 'The sly old bird.'

'Sorry?'

'Don't worry about it. And don't worry about me being

polite and asking you in and you having to put up with thirty minutes of deadly conversation.'

'I wouldn't dream of putting you to all that trouble,' he answered smoothly, already turning to go. 'Good night.'

'Who was that, Mum?' asked Chloe, as she came out of the bathroom and into the hall.

Georgia closed the front door. 'Just somebody Mrs Braithwaite conned into acting as a delivery boy.' She opened one of the tins and smiled. 'Silly old woman thinks I don't eat enough.'

Chloe picked out a scone. 'Mmm, yum. Have we got any jam?'

'Not sure. Have a look while I ring and thank her.'

Georgia left Chloe rummaging in the kitchen cupboards and went into the sitting room to look for the telephone book. She then picked up her mobile phone.

'Iris?'

'This is Mrs Braithwaite speaking.'

'It's Georgia, just ringing to say—'

'Ah, so Mr Bradshaw found you all right. He's a pleasant enough man, wouldn't you say?'

So she was right.

As improbable an idea as it was, Georgia was left in no doubt that it wasn't just her weight that Iris was concerned about. So why not tell her to mind her own business? Iris had no right to go poking her nose into her life. She was fine just as she was. The last thing she needed right now was a stupid man mucking up her life again.

'Ms D'Arcy, are you still there, I was just saying what a pleasant—'

'I heard you, Iris, and I wish you'd stop ...'

'Yes?'

'I wish you'd stop ...' She took a deep breath. 'You really must stop calling me Ms D'Arcy all the time. I told you before, call me Georgia, okay?'

Soft! She was going bloody soft in the head! Heaven help her.

Chapter Twenty-two

'Dinner?' repeated David. He lowered his *National Geographic* magazine. 'Why?'

'Does there have to be a why?' asked Hilary. 'I thought it would be nice to eat out tomorrow night. We haven't for ages.'

'I suppose so, if you really want to.'

'I do,' Hilary said firmly. The book she'd got out of the library said it was essential to keep a marriage alive by finding time to be alone with one's partner – *just the two of you*, the author of the book had stressed, *to enable each to focus on the other.*

It was a week now since Derek and Cindy's party, and while David had played down the Nick Bradshaw incident, laughing it off by attributing his loss of temper to high spirits and a misunderstanding between him and Nick, Hilary was aware that others were not so keen to accept this explanation.

At the school gate Patricia had given Hilary one of her notorious reassuring squeezes of the arm. 'Is he under a lot of pressure, your David? He's not being violent at home, is he?'

And as if it wasn't bad enough knowing that everybody knew that David had punched someone to the ground there was the small matter of his having made it public knowledge that she ... that she liked to buy underwear and save it for a special occasion. It was only an innocent treat she allowed herself now and again and David had somehow managed to turn it into something vulgar and shamefully sordid. She hadn't had the nerve to confront him over it, for fear of her anger and humiliation being unleashed at what he'd done, which would quite likely lead to her revealing that she knew about his affair.

But at least the Ted the Toup fracas of last Sunday afternoon had taken the heat off her and provided a diversion for the likes of Patricia. A picture in the *Chronicle* of Ted, standing outside his shop with the caption 'Ted Terrorised by Tomato-throwing Tearaways', had gone a long way to fuel the argument in the village as to whether Ted Cooper was right in what he was doing. There was no disagreement as to who was responsible for the attack, though. It was generally accepted that Georgia D'Arcy and her Jeep had been involved, but as to her accomplices, no one could come up with any names.

'She was outside my house for a bit,' Patricia had told Hilary, again at the school gate. 'I saw her face quite clearly, but the others were dressed up like bandits. Probably a load of her *friends*. They do things like that, you know. I'm just so grateful we haven't got any trees in the village that need knocking down or she and her friends would be up them like a shot! But I'm sure that on my evidence alone Ted Cooper could prosecute. Only I won't say anything, because what would happen to poor little Chloe if her mother went to prison?'

It seemed strange to Hilary that the whole point of what Georgia had done, if indeed Georgia had been responsible for taking up a stance against Ted the Toup, was being lost. The actual protest was being buried beneath the trivia of whether or not the protesters had any right to do what they had done.

Personally Hilary thought Ted deserved what he got, but David had read the local paper on Wednesday evening and said, 'They want a damn good sorting out!'

'I suppose you mean by having a decent man in their lives?' she had thrown back at him.

He hadn't caught the irony in her voice. 'Yes,' he'd said, 'I suppose I do mean that. After all, look at you, Hilary. You don't go around indiscriminately throwing eggs and tomatoes at strange men, do you? And why not? Because you've always had me in your life.'

'I think they were most discriminate,' she'd replied in a low voice, appalled at David's arrogance. 'But haven't you forgotten how I poured whisky over you a couple of weeks ago, or doesn't that count?'

His answer had been lost in the kerfuffle of Becky crashing into the kitchen with yet more toys destined for the dustbin.

'I think it would be a good idea for us to go out,' Hilary pursued, as she watched David pick up the remote control for the television.

'Okay,' he said, tuning into Trevor McDonald and *News at Ten*. 'How about we go to Tony Farrand's place over at Knutsford? The children like it there.'

'The children?' Hilary repeated, crestfallen. 'I thought we'd go alone.'

'No. Let's take them – that way we don't have to bother with a babysitter.'

No, we don't, thought Hilary. And you can hide behind Philip and Becky all evening and not speak to me. She got up from the sofa and went out to the kitchen where she had a pile of ironing to get through. She switched on the iron and picked up one of Philip's school shirts from the wicker laundry basket. The phone rang. She waited for David to answer it. After six rings she went through to the hall herself.

'Hello, is that Hilary – Hilary Archer as was?'

'Yes,' she answered, cautiously.

'Hi, this is Lesley Blake, or you might remember me more as Skinny Lesley or Lesley the Rake. I found your parents in the phone book, gave them a ring just now and your mother gave me your number.'

The voice at the other end of the phone rattled on while Hilary collected her thoughts. Lesley Blake, she said to herself several times before she heard the words *school reunion* mentioned.

'I thought it was time for a reunion,' Skinny Lesley was saying, 'especially when I heard how poor old Richard was killed in that plane crash in Scotland. Definitely time to gather everyone together before any more of us snuff it. I've had such a job tracking everyone down. You'll come, won't you?'

Hilary gripped the receiver in her hand. A school reunion was the last thing she needed right now. All those clever people brought together to outdo one another and what did she have to boast? A failing marriage. That was all. 'It's lovely to hear from you,' she said briskly, trying to imagine Skinny Lesley as an adult, 'but no, I shan't be able to make it. I'm so busy these days.'

'But I haven't even told you when it is.'

'Oh.'

'You always did jump to conclusions, Hilary. Remember how you caught me at school with my hands full of Wagon Wheels and you thought I'd stolen them from the tuck shop and reported me?' Skinny Lesley laughed.

Hilary squeezed her eyes shut. 'When is the reunion?' she asked politely.

'The eighth of December. Say you'll come. Everyone else will be there. Even Johnboy Malone has said he'll turn up. You'll never guess who he married. That stuck-up Naomi Scott! Can you believe it? And he was so sweet on you, Hilary.'

No. Hilary couldn't believe it. And neither could she believe this conversation.

'I'll send you a letter with all the details of the hows, whys and whens. I shan't ask you now what you've been up to these past eighteen years, you can tell me on the eighth. See you.'

The phone clicked and Hilary went back to the kitchen to stand over the ironing board and Philip's school shirt.

Skinny Lesley, Johnboy Malone and Naomi Scott all appeared in front of her. She slammed the iron down on top of them.

Star Struck was packed. It always was, and not just because the restaurant had such a good reputation for its menu. It was also renowned for its entertaining owner, Tony Farrand, who behaved like an eccentric showman – because that was what he was or, at least, what he had once been back in the seventies when, for a few short years, he had been very much the current flavour and had hosted not only his own comedy show, but *Star Struck*, a celebrity-quiz panel show. His act had been ostentatious and exuberant and had gone down well in the glittering seventies but the eighties audience had required something a little more succinct and sophisticated. His popularity had waned and brought him to the north-west of England, where house prices were lower than in the south and his style could be put to good use in the restaurant trade.

When he greeted Hilary and David at the door he was dressed in a flamboyant suit that had more than a touch of the Liberaces about it. Sparkling like a Christmas tree, he took Becky by the hand and led them to a central aisle table. He offered her a kiss and Hilary was amused to see how readily Becky accepted this, for all her recently acquired feminist tendencies. Philip was given a cigar, which was immediately snatched away, and when Tony blew into it a daisy popped out of the end.

Next Tony kissed Hilary's hand but thumbed his nose at David. Watch yourself, Hilary thought, as she sat down, or he might punch you in the face.

Menus were handed round the table, along with a bottle of Calpol for the children. 'Oh, so you're not ill?' he said, seeing the bemused look on Becky's face. 'Okay, then, I'll bring you something else.' He returned with two glasses of lemonade and said, 'These are on the house ... my house.

You're paying my mortgage!' He laughed and left them alone.

Hilary suddenly felt scared. Having Tony around had offered her a kind of protection. In his crazy way he made life seem sane and infinitely more bearable. She peeped over the top of her menu at David and caught him pushing back the cuff on his jacket to look at his watch.

'In a hurry?' she asked.

He ignored her, or perhaps he hadn't heard her above the loud music – she still wanted to give him the benefit of the doubt.

Next to David Becky was crumbling a breadstick into her mouth, while Philip was swinging on the back two legs of his chair, reading his menu.

'What do you fancy?' she asked him.

'The ravioli with ricotta cheese, please,' he answered, tossing the menu onto the table and bringing his chair down with a sudden bump.

'Not the Bolognese? You usually have that when we come here,' Hilary said.

'I had it at school for lunch yesterday.'

'How is school?' David asked, finally joining in with the conversation.

Philip looked at his father. 'I hate it!' he wanted to shout at him. 'And it's all your bloody fault I'm there!' It was true, it had been Dad who'd suggested he sat the scholarship exam and Dad who'd promised him a computer if he passed. Well, he had passed and he had got a computer but he was getting hell kicked out of him into the bargain. He reached under the table and rubbed his bruised shin. Yesterday he'd been pushed over. Then he'd had his briefcase taken and his work thrown around the classroom and all because he wouldn't give in and hand over any money. But at least Batesy had helped to pick everything up. 'Just do as they say and they'll leave you alone. It's easier that way,' he'd whispered. The hell he would!

'It's okay,' Philip said at last.

'What about Latin and classical studies? You didn't think you'd enjoy those, did you?'

Philip stared at his father again and shrugged his shoulders. 'It's not so bad. Yesterday was a bit tedious – we were learning about love.'

'Yuck,' Becky said, pulling a face. Hilary reached for a packet of breadsticks and started fumbling with the wrapper.

'Oh, yes,' David said. 'And what earth-shattering conclusions did you learned youngsters reach? Not to have anything to do with it, I expect.' He gave a short laugh which, to Hilary's ears, sounded pompous. Had he always laughed like that? Did other people find him pompous?

Philip ignored his father's question. 'There are three types of love,' he said, '*eros*, *agape* and one other that I can't remember. Sir says that *eros* is the kind of love that makes you do stupid things like Romeo and Juliet did, and *agape* is the unconditional love, which according to sir goes on for ever. How do you love Mum, Dad, in the *eros* way or *agape*?'

David shifted awkwardly in his chair. 'The most I learned in Latin at school about love was *amo*, *amas*, *amat*, never mind all this guppy stuff.'

'*Agape*,' Philip corrected.

'I want a pizza,' Becky announced, banging her menu down on the table and knocking over a tiny vase with its single red carnation. Water flooded across the paper tablecloth.

'Ah!' shouted Tony, appearing from nowhere to mop up the damage. 'An extra ten pounds on the bill. That was holy water I brought back from the Vatican after cooking dinner for the *Papa*. You don't believe me, eh? I'll ring him up and ask him to tell you it's the truth.' He grabbed a large pepper-mill from a passing waiter. 'Hello,' he said, talking into it as though it was a telephone. 'Hey, Papa, you tell the girl here about the holy water.' He passed the pepper-mill to Becky, who slowly raised it to her left ear but when she saw the look on Philip's face she flung it back at Tony.

'Silly man,' she said, embarrassed.

He took their order and, once again, Hilary felt the strain of being left to their own devices.

'I want the loo,' Becky said loudly above the sound of Wet Wet Wet – her boredom threshold nearing zero.

'You only want to play with the soap dispenser,' Philip accused her.

'I do not. I'm bursting and I'll prove it if—'

'Hurry up and go,' interrupted Hilary, who knew better than anyone to call her daughter's bluff.

'I'll go as well,' Philip said.

Just you and me, then, David, Hilary thought, watching David's turned-away face as Becky and Philip left the table. Speak to me! Say something nice. Give me some hope ... just a hint of hope that you do still love me.

He said nothing to her unspoken questions and his silence made her want to run away and cry. She felt unimaginably sorry for herself and blew her nose in an effort to hold back the tears. Oh, God, don't let me fall apart now, not in front of all these people. 'I think I'd better go and check on Becky,' she said, getting to her feet and stumbling away.

She met Philip and Becky coming down the narrow staircase on their way back to their table. Inside the ladies' there was soap everywhere. Without thinking she started to clear up the washbasins, throwing paper towels – which she suspected Becky had been using as water bombs – into the bin.

While Wet Wet Wet sang 'Put the Light On' through the restaurant sound system she tried to stem the flow of tears threatening to stream down her cheeks. Why doesn't he love me? she asked herself, looking in the mirror as she wiped away yet more soap. What's wrong with me? Why am I not enough for him? Nick obviously thinks I'm all right.

Horrified, she stared at her reflection in the mirror. Where had that thought come from? And why had Nick Bradshaw appeared in her life the moment she had discovered David's unfaithfulness? Thoughts of guardian angels crept into her mind. Had he come into her life to help her? *Ring me if you need to.* His echoing words seemed to join forces with those of Marti Pellow. '... put a little light in her darkest day ... ring me.'

Her meal was waiting for her when she got back to the table.

'We didn't wait,' David said, forking up a pasta bow and staring at a young waitress with a skirt no bigger than a napkin at the top of her long, slender legs.

When had he started doing that, Hilary wondered. He never used to eye up other women, let alone a girl young enough to be his daughter. So when had he got so bored with her and changed? Or was it she who had changed? Had he always been like this and she was only now waking up to him and his irritating habits?

'I need the loo again,' Becky said, having picked over her pizza and lined the edge of her plate with little bits of onion.

Oh, if life was as easy as playing around with a soap dispenser every time you got bored, thought Hilary, watching Becky disappear once more.

Playing around – she glanced across the table to David. He met her stare.

'You're not eating,' he said, pointing with his knife at her untouched plate.

'I'm not hungry,' she said faintly.

He rolled his eyes. 'A waste of an evening and more money down the drain!'

'More money?' she repeated. 'What do you mean?'

'New hairdo, new clothes, a meal out, and all for what, I ask you?'

That was it! He'd gone too far now. Her mind was made up.

Ring me if you need to.

She would! She would ring Nick. That would show David!

'Does that mean another lemonade's out of the question?' Philip asked, awkwardly.

'You'd better ask Scrooge here,' Hilary replied, unable to keep the anger and sarcasm out of her voice. Obviously running a mistress as well as a family was proving a more expensive proposition for David than he had thought.

Chapter Twenty-three

Hilary was up before anyone else. It was still pitch black outside and in the light cast from a couple of underlighters in the Aga alcove she stirred a pot of porridge.

She hadn't eaten a thing at the restaurant last night and had woken up at five o'clock almost sick with hunger. Knowing that she couldn't lie there a moment longer next to David's restless body, tossing and turning, she'd come downstairs in search of something to eat.

As she stirred the bubbling pan she found the smell of warm milk comforting and reassuring. In those first few days after finding out about David and Catherine she had cooked mechanically and without enjoyment. It had all taken too much effort. Then last week she had thrown herself into spending hours filling the freezer and cake tins with what she had felt sure would lure David back to the safety of The Gables, tempting him with his favourite Delia Smith sticky toffee puddings and gingerbread. She had done it because she recalled that earlier in the year David had said that Catherine was a lousy cook. At the time it had never occurred to Hilary to ask him how he knew this. Had she simply told him in the office one day or had he discovered for himself that she was disastrous in the kitchen but dynamite in bed?

Now, though, as she scooped out some porridge into a bowl she didn't give a fig about finding the way back to David's heart through his stomach. She made herself a pot of tea, opened the fridge for a bottle of milk and found a half-empty pot of double cream. She poured it over the bowl and then added a sprinkling of brown sugar, followed by some more and then a dollop of honey. She contemplated some maple syrup, but decided against it. That was going too far.

To hell with that, she thought, this was no time for propriety. She squeezed the plastic bottle over the bowl and it fired off a loud raspberry.

And with years of everything-in-moderation out of the window, Hilary raised the first wicked spoonful to her lips and wondered if this was how Eve had felt. Had she got up early one morning and wandered into the garden and done the unthinkable because Adam had pushed her beyond what she could bear – just as David was doing with her? She swallowed another spoonful of porridge and pushed this thought aside, preferring instead to equate herself with Goldilocks – Goldilocks hadn't meant any harm, had she? She helped herself to some more cream and thought of her resolution, made last night at the restaurant – the moment when she had decided to take control.

As she'd lain awake in the early hours listening to David's unsteady breathing and occasional bursts of muttered words in his sleep she had thought not just of Nick Bradshaw but of Johnboy Malone.

Skinny Lesley had been right: Johnboy had been sweet on her all those years ago. And at teacher-training there had been that rugby player with arms like bolsters who had always been knocking on her door wanting to have coffee with her – much to David's annoyance. She had been attractive once, hadn't she? So when had that all changed? When had she become so sexless? Was it during pregnancy? Or had it happened during those matter-of-fact years of leaky breasts, disgusting nappies, prize-winning moments of potty training and heroic sleepless nights? She had no idea. She got up from the table, went over to the dishwasher and placed her empty bowl on the top rack. In pursuit of yet more self-indulgence she opened one of the high cupboards where she kept a secret supply of goodies – deliberately stored there out of Becky's reach. She pulled down a packet of chocolate biscuits, sat at the table again and started flicking through her latest copy of *Hello!* Chocolate and the rich and famous with their beautiful designer homes and clothes – was there ever a better combination for inspiring and encouraging a search for something more exciting in one's own drab life?

When she had finished reading about the latest society goings-on in London she moved on to *Cheshire Life* and this month's feature article on the north-west's most wealthy and eligible men. 'Thirty-nine and how many millions?' she said out loud, looking at a photo of the handsome owner of a well-known chain of sportswear shops. She wondered whether the magazine would ever do an article on Derek and Cindy's latest enterprise. In her mind's eye she pictured the two of them smiling into the camera lens and appearing, to all intents and purposes, the perfect couple, with their long marriage and business partnership behind them and their new venture launching them into the future.

How many lies did they all cover up? Was everyone out there pretending to live lives that in truth they found unbearable at times? Was the answer simply to make the best of a bad job and get what satisfaction one could?

She picked up another chocolate biscuit and chewed it thoughtfully.

'Nick?' she whispered into the phone five minutes later.

'Yes ... Hilary?'

'I'm sorry it's so early, but you said if I needed help you'd—'

'I can be ready in ten minutes. Where do you want to meet?'

'I don't know,' she said, suddenly unsure.

'Come here, then, and we'll talk. That is what you want, isn't it, Hilary?'

She nodded dumbly into the phone and listened to him giving her directions to where he lived.

'Who were you on the phone to?' David asked, when she went upstairs to get dressed and found him awake in bed.

'Georgia D'Arcy,' she lied.

'What on earth do you want with that man-hater at this time of day?' He yawned.

'PTA stuff,' she answered, from the depths of the wardrobe. 'I need to go through a few of the arrangements for the end-of-term Christmas Fayre. I'm going to see her now.'

'What, this early? And, anyway, won't she be sharpening her claws in that nursery of hers?'

'She's capable of doing more than one thing at a time. Perhaps you could haul yourself out of bed and take the children to church this morning.'

David groaned. 'God won't miss them just one Sunday.'

'They missed last week so they really should go today,' she said, wanting her children to be in the safe hands of God for the next few hours. She selected one of the outfits Cindy had helped her buy in Manchester and sped off to the bathroom to get dressed. The thought of dressing for duplicity in front of David was too much. She slipped into the softly pleated trousers Cindy had chosen in preference to the crisp navy ones she had wanted, then pulled the pale pink angora sweater over her head. She brushed her hair away from her face and tried to apply some make-up. She managed some blusher and lipstick but her hands were trembling so much she had to give up on the mascara. She didn't look at all like Anthea Turner any more but she gave herself six out of ten for effort.

She closed the front door, climbed into her car and reversed out of the drive. She didn't look back at the house for fear of catching sight of the children peering out of a window at her. This, she told herself sternly, had nothing to do with the children. This was between her and David.

At the end of Acacia Lane she stopped the car and reached into her handbag for her small bottle of Anaïs Anaïs. She sprayed her neck and wrists liberally, then had to wind down the window for air. She coughed and spluttered, trying to catch her breath, and nearly jumped out of her skin at the sound of tapping and Iris Braithwaite's face appearing through the open window.

'You're surely not driving to early-morning communion, Mrs Parker.'

'Heavens, no,' squeaked Hilary.

'So where are you off to at this time of day, and all dressed up?'

Only Mrs Braithwaite could be so direct. Nerves and guilt rendered Hilary's reply almost inaudible.

'I beg your pardon, Mrs Parker.'

'PTA ... Georgia D'Arcy,' she managed more intelligibly.

Mrs Braithwaite's powdery face broke into an unexpected smile. 'Hulme Welford would be a far better place if we had more people like that young woman living here. And how's that ill-mannered husband of yours? Brawling in public and over what, one asks oneself? Where was his sense of decency and respect when he took it upon himself to besmirch your name?'

'I really must be getting on,' Hilary said boldly, and, ignoring the other woman's questions, she pressed lightly on the accelerator pedal and tweaked the engine.

As she turned the corner onto the main street of the village Hilary had the uncomfortable feeling that Mrs Braithwaite was still standing in the middle of Acacia Lane staring suspiciously after her and putting two and two together. The older woman's appearance had acted like a spectre at the feast, intruding in an area where Hilary wanted no reminders of everyday life. As she drove out of the village she struggled to reinstate the picture of the world she had created in her mind while reading about the Earl of Whatsit and his beautiful new girlfriend on holiday in the Maldives.

Nick's house was not far from Philip's new school, and as the fields and recently cut hedges of the familiar lanes slipped by she watched the sky on the horizon release its hold on the last remnants of night, finally giving way to morning strands of pink and gentian blue.

She saw the sign for the trout farm Nick had described and slowed down to third gear on the bend in the road as he'd instructed. His small end-of-terrace cottage was set back from the road and a plume of smoke was rising from the chimney. She felt her body go taut with nervous expectation.

She parked the car on the verge, switched off the engine, gathered up her bag, locked the car door and breathed in deeply. High up in the oak trees she heard the loud cawing of crows – or were they rooks? Dear God! She could think of things like that when she was about to embark on ... She cleared her throat, tucked her bag under her arm and went up to the door, which was at the side of the cottage. It opened before she had even raised her hand to the knocker.

'I've made us some coffee,' he said, as she stepped inside. He took her coat and hung it on the back of the kitchen door alongside an overcoat she recognised from bonfire night. 'Have you eaten?'

She nodded and looked awkwardly about the tiny kitchen; there was an empty wine bottle on the floor along with a brown carrier bag of foil cartons with the remains of some pilau rice clinging to the edges. 'You're not very tidy, are you?'

He passed her a mug of coffee. 'And you're making small-talk.'

She turned away and stared out of the leaded window which overlooked the road. She wondered if anyone would recognise her car.

'We all do it,' he said.

'Do what?' she said, facing him again.

'Avoid saying what we really want to say. Come through

to the other room. It's just as untidy but at least it's warm. I lit a fire as soon as I put the phone down.'

'I'm sorry to have put you to all this trouble. Oh,' she said, standing in the middle of the sitting room, 'you're right, this is as untidy.'

He laughed, gathered up a pile of books and files from an armchair by the fire, and flung the heap onto the floor where another stack of books teetered with intent. 'I'm disappointing you, aren't I?'

'How long have you lived here?' she asked, sitting cautiously in the chair he'd cleared. She half expected it to collapse beneath her. The fabric was wearing through on the arms and she played with a loose thread that stood proud from a faded dianthus.

'About three years. And if you want a life résumé before you're going to talk properly to me I'll give it to you.'

'I didn't mean to sound—'

'Relax and listen for a change. I get the impression you don't do a lot of listening, Hilary. You make a lot of assumptions, don't you?'

She said nothing. It wasn't turning out exactly how she'd imagined it would. Surely this wasn't how the Earl had wooed the lovely Annabel.

'I'm forty-eight years old. I used to be a lecturer in organisational behaviour, then when my second marriage hit the skids five years ago I took a long hard look at myself and found I didn't much like what was there. I decided to make the switch from always talking to occasionally listening, which is what I want to do with you.' He moved away from his position by the fire and sat in the chair opposite her. 'Are you ready to talk to me now?'

Would tears work? she thought. If she started to cry, would he take her in his arms and ...?

'David doesn't love me,' she said. 'He barely looks at me these days, let alone talks to me. He's ... he's having an affair and I feel ...'

She heard him move towards her, then felt his hand on hers.

'You feel hurt,' he said, taking her untouched mug of coffee away from her. 'You feel betrayed and rejected. You feel spread all over the floor and about as worthless as you can get ... and you want someone to put you back together again and make everything better.'

'Yes,' she whispered. Now hurry up and kiss me.

He did.

Chapter Twenty-four

Nick was surprisingly gentle with her, unlike David who had always treated her as though she were a rag doll. 'Don't push me about,' she had told him on their second date, when he had pressed her against the door of her room in the college hall of residence.

As Nick tilted his head to one side she wondered if she was going about things the right way – it was so long ago since she'd been in this situation. Would it be better if she was to open her mouth wider? And what about her hands? Should she be doing something with them?

One of Nick's hands was stroking the nape of her neck. She felt wobbly inside and even more conscious of his lips, so warm and soft against her own.

Just as she closed her eyes Nick pulled away. 'Tell me, Hilary,' he said, 'has that made you feel better? Did it stop you thinking of David for a few moments?'

'Yes,' she lied, 'completely.'

He gazed at her steadily and she sat waiting for him to say or do something else – she wanted him to stroke her neck again. He stood up abruptly and went and stood by the mantelpiece in front of the fire.

'It's only a short-term answer, Hilary,' he said firmly, his arms crossed in front of him. Suddenly he looked like a stern headmaster. 'And how about the guilt? Could you cope with that?'

Kiss me again and I'll see, she wanted to say flippantly, high on the thrill of having kissed another man – she had actually kissed another man! 'David's managing pretty well,' she said.

'But is he? He's obviously under an enormous strain at the moment, living his double life. How much longer do you think he can go on as he is?'

'Why is everyone so concerned about the strain David's under? What about the strain he's put on my life? This is no picnic for me I can assure you.'

He smiled, and came and sat next to her again. 'I know,' he said gently, no longer a stern headmaster. 'But having an affair with the first available man is not the answer.'

'So why did you kiss me?' she asked. 'Were you making fun of me?'

'I kissed you because I knew that was what you wanted.'

'I . . . I didn't,' she stammered.

'And I wanted to prove to you that it's not the answer. Tell me, Hilary, has your marriage made you happy?'

'I—'

'Or have you assumed you were happy – have marriage, have happiness? Can you remember the last time you were heart-stoppingly tickled pink with the love you feel towards David?'

She lowered her eyes and fiddled with her sapphire engagement ring. 'It's not like that,' she said at last. 'You just muddle along. Nobody can be expected to dance around the supermarket on a Monday morning in a state of euphoria after more than a decade of marriage. Life simply has a habit of getting in the way.'

'What a sad world we live in where our expectations become so dulled by routine. Hilary, when will you, and everyone like you, understand that this is not a dress rehearsal? This is it. You have to live life to the full.'

'I suppose that's what David's doing,' she said in a small voice, pulling absentmindedly at the thread on the arm of the chair.

'It could be. Though ask yourself this. Does he seem

happier because of what he's doing?'

Hilary thought of David's miserable face, his thin lips drawn in a tight line and his apparent ambivalence to their life together. 'No,' she said, 'he doesn't look like a man who's enjoying himself.'

'Because he's feeling guilty. He knows what he's doing is going to hurt you and the children, if he's found out. Like so many seeking a quick fix he's not thought this through. He should have looked carefully at his life to find the reason he felt the urge to stray.'

'Perhaps it's all my fault. Maybe because of the way I am I've made him have an affair. If I had been more—'

'It's a possibility. But in reality quite often it's not what's happening around the home that causes a partner to be unfaithful. I'm not making excuses or trying to justify what David's done but I guarantee that the reason for his infidelity lies deep within his own make-up, not yours. As Thoreau said, "The mass of men lead quiet lives of desperation." '

Hilary looked up sharply. 'Why's it always the men having such a hard time?'

He smiled. 'Don't take things so literally. And, as I just said, I'm not making excuses for David but what I am trying to say is that we all react to a given situation and our response determines the consequences.' He stared hard at her. 'David chose to have an affair ... just as you chose to come here today.'

She turned away.

'Did you really expect me to whisk you upstairs and bed you?'

She continued to stare into the fire, watching the flames lick at the loose bark on a log in the grate. 'You make it sound so sordid.'

He laughed lightly. 'The state of my sheets, it would have been.'

She tried to laugh as well but it came out more like a whimper. 'I've made a complete fool of myself, haven't I?'

'Not at all. You've done what so many people do in your situation.'

'Predictable as well as foolish. I'm sorry to be so boring.'

'Stop giving yourself such a hard time, Hilary. You're an attractive, intelligent woman with everything going for you—'

'Please, don't say any more or you'll start me crying.'

He put his arm round her shoulders and kissed her forehead. 'Go ahead. Feel free. But go easy on that armchair or it'll be shredded by the time you leave.'

She looked down at the thread of cotton in her fingers: it was twice its original length and there was now a hole in the middle of the dianthus. 'I'm sorry—'

'Would you stop apologising and listen to what else I've got to say? You've got some very difficult decisions ahead of you and only you can make them. You can talk it through with me, if you like, or any amount of your friends and family, but ultimately you're the one who is going to have to live with whatever is decided, so it's only right it should be you who reaches a decision. Remember, nothing is by chance. We each make a choice to determine our future. And the priority in your immediate future is telling David that you know about his affair. When are you going to tell him?'

'Not yet. Not with my sister's wedding and Christmas coming up so soon. I'll talk to him in the New Year.'

'And will you be ready for his response if he says he wants to leave you?'

'I feel like he's left me already. At least then the awful pretending will be over.'

On her way home Hilary called at Hulme View Nursery, so at least her alibi would have some weight should David have any suspicions that she hadn't been telling the truth. She hadn't seen Georgia since that dreadful scene in the kitchen when she'd invited her back for tea and Nick had turned up unexpectedly. How horribly complicated her life had become. Would it ever be the way it used to be?

The nursery was busy with Sunday browsers selecting trays of winter-flowering pansies and heathers. Hilary found Georgia pushing a large muddy trolley of potted five-foot-high conifers.

'Hello, stranger,' Georgia said, coming to a stop. She started to unload the trolley. 'I'd ask you to help,' she said, as she lifted the first of the tall conifers, 'only you're done up like a lardy cake. I suppose you've been to church, have you?'

Hilary nodded.

'I didn't think the devout still thought God loved them more when they were decked out in their finery.'

'They don't!' Hilary retorted. Dear God, she was fed up with all these sharp-witted people around her.

'I'm sorry,' Georgia said, settling the conifer next to a row of small laurel bushes. 'That was rude of me. The unconverted don't have the right to knock the few who do believe. What can I do you for?'

Hilary hesitated. She was doing a lot of that, these days. She never used to. She'd always known exactly what she wanted to do and say. 'PTA,' she blurted out. 'I thought we could go through some of the Christmas Fayre arrangements.'

Georgia frowned. She reached for another conifer but then changed her mind. She pushed back the sleeve of her donkey jacket. A quarter to eleven. She returned her attention to Hilary. 'Have I got this right? I'm making the assumption that you've been to church this morning and that you've left early to come here and talk to me about the fayre. How am I doing?'

Hilary looked awkwardly at her feet. 'It just crossed my mind—'

'To dip out of the Eucharist and dash along here. Well, that seems eminently feasible. I wish all the members of the PTA were as diligent as you. Just fancy, there you were, down on your knees, and suddenly you thought of me, or perhaps it was the hand of God intervening, "P-T-A," his sepulchral voice boomed through the vaulted ceiling.'

'Hardly anybody gets down on their knees at St John's,' Hilary said, petulantly.

'You speak for yourself,' Georgia said, struggling with another conifer. 'I'm frequently on mine.'

Hilary felt tired and out of her depth.

Georgia looked at Hilary's miserable and confused face. 'Oh, shit,' she said, 'I'm sorry. I'm premenstrual and feeling as bloated as the *Hindenburg* and about as volatile. Forgive me?'

Hilary nodded. 'And I'm sorry I lied to you.'

Georgia smiled. 'You mean, no PTA talk? You do surprise me. Come on, let's go over to the caravan and you can tell me what you've really come for.'

'But what about your customers?'

'Gordon's here today. He's taking care of them, leaving me to clear a space ready for the order of rooted Christmas trees coming in tomorrow.'

'I don't want to keep you from your work, I can easily—'

'Give it a rest, Hilary.'

The caravan felt only marginally warmer than it was outside. Georgia switched on a small heater, which whirred noisily. 'Fancy a coffee? I've got some in a Thermos here.'

Hilary shook her head.

'Suit yourself,' Georgia poured some for herself. She cradled her half-mittened fingers around the plastic cup. 'So what's been going on at The Gables since I saw you last? Which reminds me, you were acting very strangely that day. I could have sworn you were suddenly frightened of me.'

Hilary picked up a packet of lupin seeds and tipped it upside down. She listened to the seeds trickling from one end to the other.

Georgia laughed. 'And if I didn't know better I'd say that witch Patricia Longton put some silly idea into your head.'

'Goodness, of course not,' Hilary said, too quickly.

'Stupid bitch has always thought I was gay ever since I kicked Rory out. Well, to put the record straight, I'm not. Look at me when I'm talking to you, Hilary. I'm not some sex-starved lesbian about to take advantage of a vulnerable woman. Okay?'

'Okay,' Hilary repeated quickly. Heavens, what a morning it was turning into!

'Not that there's anything wrong in being gay, some of my closest friends are. But that's beside the point. Get on and tell me what you came here for.'

Hilary had had no intention of telling Georgia about Nick Bradshaw when she'd driven through the nursery gates, but now that their friendship was back on a more reassuring level she decided she wanted to confide in her. She explained about wanting to use Georgia as an alibi and why, then went on to tell her partly what had happened at Nick's.

'Bloody hell, Hilary! You mean you let that wily bastard get his tongue down your throat?'

Hilary frowned. 'I only let him kiss me,' she said defensively.

'Crap! *You* kissed him.'

The two women looked at each other in silence. Hilary was disappointed. She had made Georgia angry and she didn't want that. Then she saw her friend's face soften with a smile. 'Well, you've learned two important things this morning, Hilary. One is that you don't have to worry about me leaping on you and the other is that you've proved to yourself that if you wanted to dip your toes into the shark-infested waters of catching yourself a man, you could. So where exactly does that leave you?'

'Lord only knows. Probably going clean round the bend.'

Chapter Twenty-five

She was mad. Stark raving bonkers mad. She looked again at the clock on the dashboard. Five to eight – nearly half an hour late. What had made her agree to Skinny Lesley's invitation? Worse still, what had actually made her stick to it when she could have so easily backed out at the last minute claiming a headache? Nobody would have been the wiser.

It had been Charlotte who had insisted she go. 'It'll be a laugh, Hilary,' she'd said that afternoon at the shop.

'And how would you know?' she had thrown back at her sister. 'You've never been to one of these dos.'

'Only because nobody's bothered to go to the trouble to organise one for my year.'

'Well, I wish Skinny Lesley hadn't bothered. What on earth am I supposed to say to all those people I haven't seen for nearly twenty years?'

'I'm sure you'll think of something,' Charlotte had said, adding, 'strange, isn't it, that we haven't seen much of anyone from our schooldays?'

As Hilary flicked her headlights to full beam on the unlit stretch of dual carriageway she wondered about what her sister had said. Charlotte was right, it was strange. Their old school wasn't exactly a million miles from Hulme Welford but it was in a different county, chosen specifically by their mother for its vigorous hard-work ethic and long hours – it had been the only day school within a twenty-mile radius that had insisted on compulsory Saturday-morning attendance, something that had fitted in perfectly with Louise's work commitments at her antique shop and their father's surgery hours and house calls in the village.

But, then, perhaps it wasn't so much the geography of the school's location that had meant there had been no contact between the classmates once they'd left. Maybe it was simply that most people had moved away at the first possible opportunity and that it was only she who had unimaginatively moved back after going away to teacher-training. After a moment's reflection, she consoled herself with the thought that, years later, Charlotte was equally dull.

She turned left at the roundabout and there it was. School. Not that there was anything about the Victorian Gothic edifice in front of her that filled her with dread: she had enjoyed the period in her life that the building represented. School had been fun. All that structure and work to get on with, it had suited her just fine. But what *did* fill her with dread was facing everybody tonight, and them all guessing, one by one, that her marriage was on the rocks.

The car park – which had once been the netball courts – was almost full of sleekly moulded cars: Mercedes, BMWs, Audis, Volvos, a couple of Jaguars and every conceivable variety of four-wheel-drive vehicle, shining examples of success and affluence. Hadn't they all done well? she thought cynically.

She parked her Clio alongside a smart little midnight blue BMW Coupé. She had planned to drive David's Volvo, but only that afternoon he'd booked it in for a service. The garage had telephoned later, saying they'd found a fault on one of the wheel-bearings and that it would be at least Tuesday before they'd be able to fix it. So much for turning up in style.

She pulled on the handbrake, released her seat-belt and jerked the mirror towards her to examine her make-up. She bared her teeth, checking for any wayward smears of lipstick.

The main entrance door was decorated with a couple of balloons, one of which was already showing signs of deflating and wrinkling – not unlike herself, Hilary thought, as she pushed against the glass-panelled door. The foyer was empty, save for a massive Christmas tree covered with art-department-generated decorations and flickering lights. The door to the main hall, which had been used for gym and morning assemblies, was wide open and through it she could see a crowd of animated faces. Automatically she put on her best smile, hoping it would conceal the look of failure on her own face.

'Not so fast. You need a badge before you can go a step further.'

Standing to attention behind a table and holding a clipboard and a pen was ... Skinny Lesley?

'Hilary, it's you!' whooped an amazingly large Skinny Lesley.

'Lesley!'

'You look great, Hilary, and you've not changed a bit.'

'Neither have you.'

'Oh, come on! I've put on four stone since those days – gained one for each child I've produced and one for luck.' She let out a loud laugh and smacked a name badge on Hilary's shoulder. Hilary staggered slightly under the force of Skinny Lesley's hand. 'Now the procedure is this. First question is, do you still live in the area, followed by, are you married and how many children have you got? Bar's over there in the corner. I'll catch up with you later when I'm off duty.'

Hilary turned from Skinny Lesley's bristling efficiency and straight away saw Carrie Maxwell standing alone, an empty wine-glass in her hand – heavens, she'd been a terror with a hockey-stick in her hands. She went over to her. 'Hello, Carrie.'

'Hilary!' Carrie's delight was obvious. 'Just look at you! Apart from the colour of your hair, you're exactly the same.'

'Except I don't wear tank tops any more,' Hilary said, with a smile, finding some of her nervousness beginning to slip away.

'My eldest daughter does, though. You should see her, flares and platforms, the whole performance all over again.'

Hilary laughed and took a quick glance round the hall. 'Isn't this whole thing bizarre? How many have you stayed in touch with?'

'Nobody. I moved away after A-levels and never came back. I live in Kent now.'

'Married?' Hilary ventured.

'Hell, no! The rat deserted years ago.'

'Oh, I'm sorry.'

'And you?'

'Hilary Archer! I don't believe it!'

They both turned to see Johnboy Malone advancing towards them. 'I don't believe it!' he repeated, *à la* Victor Meldrew – he even had the same cropped thinning hair.

'Hello, Johnboy,' Hilary said, quietly.

'No, no, no. That won't do at all. You've got to get into the part, Hilary. The men slap and punch one another and you girls are supposed to throw your heads back and squeal loudly with your arms either side of you waving like a mad thing. Here, hold my glass and I'll show you.'

'You're such an exhibitionist, John,' came a deep, sexy voice from behind him. It was Naomi Scott.

Hilary gulped unthinkingly from Johnboy's wine-glass – Naomi Scott, dark-haired, dark-eyed and looking as fabulous as a model, dressed in an Audrey Hepburn tailored black suit with a small shiny handbag, no bigger than a handkerchief, hanging from her wrist. She was utterly gorgeous – and didn't she know it? Hilary watched, fascinated, as Naomi placed a hand of red-painted nails on Johnboy's shoulder.

'Introduce me,' Naomi purred in Johnboy's ear, then, looking at Hilary and Carrie beneath her long lashes, she said, 'I shouldn't really even be here, not being in your year group, but John never goes anywhere without me, these days.'

'I vaguely remember you,' Hilary said crisply. She was furious that this smouldering beauty couldn't even remember who she was. 'You're four years older than the rest of us, aren't you?' she carried on and, fired up with resentment, she pointed to the name badge on her left shoulder and added, 'You must have forgotten your glasses.'

'I'm dying for a drink,' Naomi said uninterestedly, after giving Hilary a vacant stare. She unwrapped herself from Johnboy and walked away.

'I don't remember you being such a tiger, Hilary,' Johnboy said, with a laugh. 'How about a kiss for old times' sake?' He leaned towards her and kissed her cheek. 'Can I have my glass back now?'

Hilary handed it to him. She suddenly felt very bold. There had been more than a hint of malice in the words she had just spoken to Naomi Scott and she knew that not only had she meant every ounce of it but that the poignant humiliation she had recently recalled over that wretched box of chocolates and what she had once felt for Naomi Scott had magically vanished.

'I'll get you a glass of wine while I leave Johnboy to chat you up like in the old days,' Carrie said, already moving off.

'You look well,' Hilary said awkwardly, when they were alone and she had the opportunity to take in Johnboy's expensive wool blazer and silk tie.

'Thank you. Though I can't say that stockbroking has done anything for my hair.' He ran his hand through what little he had. 'I like your hair short, by the way. You always wore it long, though I don't remember you being so fair.'

She smiled self-consciously. 'A bottle job.'

'Aha. To cover up the grey?'

'Certainly not!'

'Naomi does it all the time. But she'd bloody kill me if she knew I'd told you.'

Hilary wanted to hug Johnboy. What other spectres from

her past would he put to rest for her tonight, she wondered.

'So how about you, Hilary? What have you been up to since 'seventy-eight?'

'Nothing very exciting, I'm afraid. Teaching, marriage and children.'

'I always had you down as a career girl. When the rest of us were larking about you were there handing in the longest essays known to mankind. I dread to think how many times you saved my skin by letting me read through your work so that I could at least have a clue what the teachers were expecting me to write about. God, but you were sweet.'

'How long have you been married to Naomi?' Hilary asked, revelling in Johnboy's flattery. He hadn't changed.

'Only a year.'

'Is that all?'

'I kept putting marriage off then, purely by chance, along came Naomi. We met on a skiing holiday last year in Wengen.'

Hilary was just imagining the beautiful Naomi on skis – as quick and as sleek as a snake – when Johnboy said, 'We're not suited, I know it. I can see it in people's eyes every time they look at us. I'm her third husband.'

Hilary gawped. 'Third?' she murmured. She felt extraordinarily sorry for Johnboy. And was there nobody here tonight who had experienced a normal happy marriage?

'What's your husband like, Hilary?'

'He's an estate agent—'

Johnboy threw back his head and laughed. 'Are you telling me he's a dishonest, underhanded so-and-so?'

Hilary bit her lip, then remembered her lipstick.

But Johnboy had caught the change of expression on her face. 'I'm sorry,' he said. 'In poor taste, I assume.'

She didn't know what to say but was glad to see Carrie coming towards them with two glasses of wine.

'Sorry I've been so long, I've been talking to Craig Montana – just discovered he only lives a short distance away from me. Not married either.' She handed Hilary her glass. 'Mind if I get back to him?'

They watched Carrie disappear.

'Children?'

Hilary turned back to Johnboy. 'Sorry?'

'You said you had children. How many?'

'Two. Philip and Becky.'

'That's nice. And is Becky like her mother?'

'Lord, I hope not. Or, rather, I hope no one thinks she takes after me. She can be very difficult at times.'

'Substitute challenging for difficult,' Johnboy said, quietly. He leaned into Hilary. 'That's what I say to myself about Naomi at times.'

'I hope you're not trying out the my-wife-doesn't-under-stand-me routine,' Hilary said with a giggle, enjoying the close proximity of Johnboy and the expensive smell of him.

'As if I would,' he said, with a twinkle in his eye. 'But, then, you always were an expert at keeping me at arm's length.'

Hilary blushed. Right now she'd switch that particular skill for any other, given the opportunity. 'Where are you living?'

'Haslemere. Bloody great barn of a place and nothing to fill it.'

For the first time in their conversation Hilary sensed traces of anger in Johnboy's words, or was it regret?

'Kids,' he said flatly. 'I love 'em, but can't have any.'

'You could adopt,' Hilary said, beginning to feel uncomfortable with the way the conversation was going. Should they be talking about such personal things? Wasn't this whole evening supposed to be superficial and on the level of merely comparing notes on what they had all achieved?

'Can you see Naomi with her hands anywhere near a nappy?'

'She might if given the chance,' Hilary said brightly.

'She only married me because she knew I wouldn't be able

to get her pregnant and spoil that lovely body of hers.'

'I'm sure she didn't.'

He shook his head. 'You really haven't changed, have you, Hilary? You always did look on the bright side of things and see life through rose-tinted spectacles. What a wonderful way to be.'

The party broke up just after eleven. A few were heading off into town to a club but after Hilary had said her goodbyes she drove home, pondering on the evening. What had threatened to be a nightmare had actually turned out to be an enjoyable evening out. It had been fun catching up with all those people she hadn't thought of in years. What had surprised her most was that there had been no one-upmanship. Life had dealt each one of them a hand of cards which they had simply got on and played. It didn't seem to matter whether they had achieved incredible wealth, notoriety, or had been made redundant, got married or divorced, had children or not, they were simply living their lives as best they could – failure didn't come into it. What was it Johnboy had said when they'd been looking at the school photographs together? 'We're all monumental successes just to have got this far.'

He was right. And had he been right when he'd suggested it was time for her to start thinking about herself, now that the children were both at school? 'Go back to teaching,' he'd said, 'if that's what you're good at.'

Half an hour later, and still reflecting on the evening, it struck Hilary with force, as she drove along the main street of the village, that from now on David's affair was not going to make a failure of her. No longer would she allow her breaking heart to make her think her life was completely worthless. Skinny Lesley, Carrie Maxwell and Johnboy – especially Johnboy – had unwittingly helped her to see things more clearly.

She turned into Acacia Lane and, as the street-light on the

corner lit up the interior of the car, she caught sight of her handbag on the passenger seat. She smiled as she thought of Johnboy's business card tucked inside her purse. He had insisted they exchange addresses. 'We must stay in touch,' he'd said. 'Who knows what might happen to us from this night on?'

'Who knows indeed?' Hilary said out loud, as she looked thoughtfully up at The Gables.

Chapter Twenty-six

It was less than a week until Christmas and Hilary was rolling out a ragged oval of pastry to the sound of Johnny Mathis singing 'When a Child is Born'. For the first time ever, she was way behind with her festive preparations: the marzipan wasn't on the cake, the crackers weren't bought and she hadn't given a thought to the brandy butter.

She sprinkled more flour onto the worktop, glad at least that she'd ordered all the cards and wrapping-paper through one of those charity catalogues at school and that the children's presents were carefully hidden at the top of the airing cupboard – they'd been there since before ... before she'd found out about David.

She'd lost count of how many weeks it was since her life had undergone such a dramatic change, but somewhere along the line, during the time that autumn had given way to winter, the impossible had happened: she had become accustomed to this new way of life. Only yesterday one of those current flavour-of the-month clerics on the radio had been saying that when people accept that their lives are about to change they are more able to cope with what lies ahead.

Hilary started pressing out small circles of pastry, knowing that it was all well and good acknowledging the changes being forced onto her by David but she was still struggling to accept the consequences.

She looked up from the cutter in her hand, remembering what Nick had said, that awful day at his cottage: '... our response determines the consequences'.

Her response, for the time being, was to stay quiet and put her mind to thinking about a new course of direction for her own life as Johnboy had said a few weeks ago: 'Go back to teaching.' Well, come the new year, she would make enquiries. If nothing else, a job would give her independence ... independence she might well need.

The egg-shaped timer on the window-sill gave a loud shrill ring and, shaking the flour from her hands, she pulled on a pair of oven gloves and reached into the Aga for the fourth batch of mince pies she'd made that afternoon. She placed the hot tray on the draining board and wondered what David would buy her for Christmas. Probably the *Which? Guide to Divorce*. He'd want a quick economical divorce, wouldn't he?

Last year he'd bought her a daring négligé in a large box with a ribbon, and he'd been so embarrassed after the Queen's speech when everyone had insisted she open her present there and then in front of them all.

'Go on,' her mother had urged. 'Let's see what David's got for you.'

David's face had been a picture as he'd tried to deflect Louise with another glass of port. His own mother had tried to hide her shock at the transparency of the garment when, finally, the box had been opened. 'Very nice,' she had muttered, pretending to be more interested in the *Batman* film the children were watching on television.

Hilary placed the last of the hot mince pies on a cooling rack and was about to dust them with icing sugar when the doorbell rang.

It was Charlotte with Mabel. 'It's Tuesday, my day off from the shop, so how about a walk?'

'That sounds more like an ultimatum than an invitation,' Hilary said.

'You're right, it does. So get your coat and lock up.'

'But it's been raining all day, it'll be wet and—'

'It's stopped, now get a move on.'

They set off for the mere along the narrow footpath between All in the Mind and the White Cottage. Iris Braithwaite was in her back garden. She was wearing an old mac and a plastic rain-hood tied with a large bow under her chin. She was prodding at a reluctant bonfire with a long stick. 'Can't seem to get the wretched thing going,' she said, through the privet hedge. 'The leaves are too wet after all this rain.'

As Hilary and Charlotte carried on down the sheltered muddy path, a low pale sun burst through the parting clouds catching the drips of rain on the wet black branches of the trees either side of them and turning each droplet of water into a sparkling pearl. But when they reached the more exposed area overlooking the mere, where there was a large gap in the trees, an icy blast of wind swept across the water, rippling small waves as it did so.

Hilary buttoned her coat, right up to her chin. She watched Charlotte bend down to let Mabel off the lead. 'I feel like our roles have reversed,' she said unexpectedly.

Charlotte had never before credited Hilary with much intuition. Her sister had always blundered her way through any thought-provoking situation with as much mental agility and sensitivity as a charging bull. 'I know what you mean,' she said, slipping her arm through Hilary's. 'For once I do actually feel like I'm the eldest.' ·

'Ever since I can remember, I've always wanted to be the older sister. As a child I was maddened by our mother's ineffectualness and decided from an early age that if she didn't want to play the part of mother hen, then I would. And now—'

'And now you can't cope with supervising me because your well-ordered life has come to an end ... just as mine did.'

They walked down the sloping bank to the water's edge. Hilary picked up a flat stone and sent it skimming across the water. 'One ... two ... three ...' she counted, before the stone disappeared from view. She turned and faced Charlotte. 'Do you think Peter would have ever had an affair?'

Charlotte suddenly laughed. 'Oh, Hilary, Peter had been having an affair almost from the day I met him, probably before as well.'

Hilary was shocked. 'But you never said anything. Who was it? Anyone you knew?'

Charlotte bent and picked up a stone. She angled her arm low and spun the stone away from her. It disappeared into the water at once. 'It was work with Peter. His career was his all-consuming mistress.'

'Well, that doesn't count,' Hilary said off-handedly. She reached for another stone.

'Oh yes it does. When a man implies to his wife that his job means more to him than his marriage, believe me, it counts. An affair with a career is just as damaging as a sexual one. So much so, on the morning Peter died, I ... I had just asked him for a divorce.'

The stone in Hilary's hand dropped to the ground. 'Charlotte ... I don't know what to say. Why didn't you tell me? Does Mother know about this?'

Charlotte shook her head. 'No, but I told Dad a few months ago.'

'I had no idea you were so unhappy. I wish I'd known – I could have helped in some way.'

'I didn't tell anyone ... I didn't want people to know I'd failed.'

'Oh, God, that's just how I feel and Mother's the last person I'd want to know that I'd failed in my marriage.'

Charlotte went over to Hilary and hugged her. 'I can hear Mother's words now – "You girls are so careless with your husbands!"'

Hilary managed a laugh and they rejoined the path and began the circuit of the mere. In the distance they could see Mabel's furry white body moving in and out of the trees.

'What would you have done if you had discovered Peter

was having an affair – I mean, a conventional bed-hopping type of affair?'

Charlotte thought for a moment. She tried to imagine Peter in bed with another woman but found it difficult even to picture his face. Unable to come up with a suitable image, she said, 'With hindsight I'd like to think I'd have wished him a small amount of happiness in his miserable existence. But that's with hindsight and with the safety of Alex in my life.'

'But what about before Alex? Say, two years ago.'

'I probably would have gone berserk and done the same as that woman in the paper last summer.'

Hilary almost smiled. 'What – cut off all the arms and legs from your husband's expensive suits?'

'Exactly, and probably a lot worse.'

'I smashed all David's expensive glasses from his mother,' Hilary admitted.

Charlotte laughed. 'Brilliant! And how very out of character.'

'I tried something even worse,' Hilary said, quietly. She pushed her cold hands into her jacket pockets, remembering with annoyance that she'd left her gloves on the oak chest in the hall.

'Go on,' Charlotte urged. 'What did you try?'

'I ... I wanted to prove – Oh, Lord, I don't know how to say it.'

'It can't be all that bad.'

'I threw myself at another man,' she said, coming to a stop by a wooden bench that gave an uninterrupted view of the mere. She ran her fingers over the back of the seat. 'And not by chance. I planned it to happen.'

Charlotte raised her eyebrows.

'You see, you *are* shocked. I knew—'

'Calm down. Of course I'm shocked, but that's not to say I don't understand why.'

'Did you ever ... well, you know ... Were you ever unfaithful when you were so unhappy in Brussels?'

'No, I wasn't. Though who's to know what might have happened if I'd met Alex before Peter's death? But never mind me. What do you really feel about David? Do you love him or is it the tick-tock of your anniversary clock that keeps your marriage going?'

'I'm not sure of anything now. I thought I loved David and then, oh, I don't know, I just seem to be conscious of all his faults right now. Because of his affair I can't see anything good or attractive in him.'

The wind was bitingly cold as they stood still. Charlotte indicated that they should carry on walking and said, 'And what does Nick Bradshaw mean to you?'

Hilary looked up sharply. 'How do you know it was him?'

'A lucky guess. Probably it was his behaviour towards David at Derek and Cindy's party, and I'd also seen the two of you talking together earlier on in the evening.'

Hilary was shocked. 'You don't suppose anyone else will have thought the same, do you?'

'I doubt it.'

'Honestly, Charlotte, nothing's actually happened between us, I swear.' Hilary's face was earnest. 'I planned to make him seduce me, but he refused to play along. It was all rather humiliating.'

'Horrible man,' Charlotte said sympathetically. 'But why did you ... why did you turn to him?'

Hilary thought back to the night at the restaurant with David and the moment when she'd made up her mind to ring Nick. She quickly swallowed back the hurt and anger that were rising in her throat. 'I wanted reassurance, I suppose.'

'Hardly surprising, given the circumstances.'

'And now I keep asking myself the same question: Is my marriage worth saving?' She gazed into the distance across to Bosley Cloud, looming high on the horizon, then turned back to her sister. 'I've decided to confront David after Christmas.'

Charlotte put her arm round Hilary's shoulders. 'I'm so proud of you. You're handling this far better than I would have done.'

'Common sense, I suppose. You always said I was the practical one.'

As the light began to fade and a hazy twilight blurred the water's edge, they completed the circuit of the mere and returned to the clearing in the pine trees. While Charlotte put Mabel on the lead, she reflected on how much closer she and Hilary had grown in the past few months. She hoped that when Hilary's life was back on an even keel they would never lose this new-found deeper level of understanding.

'We haven't even discussed your wedding on Saturday,' Hilary said, cutting into Charlotte's thoughts. 'I'm sure I should be doing more.'

'Rubbish!' Charlotte said, recognising that the time for shared disclosures and intimacy was over. 'You've got enough on your plate. But you are coming to the rehearsal tomorrow night, aren't you? Seven o'clock. Is that okay?'

'It's fine. Becky and I'll be there.' Suddenly Hilary's face broke into a frown.

'What's wrong?' Charlotte asked, concerned.

'The children,' Hilary said in a tightly controlled voice. 'What about the children? It's all very well us having this sophisticated grown-up talk about whether or not my marriage is worth keeping, but the bottom line is that a wrong decision on my part could destroy their lives.'

'That won't happen,' Charlotte said firmly, and with more assurance than she felt. 'Now, tell me how Becky looks in her bridesmaid's dress.'

'She looks beautiful,' Hilary said, accepting Charlotte's distraction, 'but she's refusing to wear it on Saturday.' Then, looking at her watch, she said, 'Goodness, we must hurry or I'll be late for Becky coming out of school.'

As Charlotte followed her sister along the footpath she had the terrible feeling that her big day wasn't going to go exactly as she and Alex had planned. She let Hilary's words go, preferring instead to live a little longer in hope and ignorance.

Chapter Twenty-seven

'Heureux anniversaire, Martina!'

Martina smiled round at the group. 'Merci,' she said.

'Maintenant, les bougies,' Patricia instructed, glancing up from the scrap of paper in her hand with its selection of carefully thought-out phrases.

'Yes, blow them out so that we can get on and have something to eat, I'm starving,' Nick whispered in Hilary's ear.

Hilary had hoped that Nick might have missed this, their final French class of the term and small party to celebrate Martina's birthday. He hadn't turned up for the previous two lessons, since the embarrassing incident at his cottage, and now here he was standing next to her and reminding her only too well what a fool she'd made of herself.

She watched Martina cut the birthday cake which Patricia had made specially – the fondant icing was even coloured the same as the French tricolour. What a monumental creep, thought Hilary, as she stabbed a stick of celery into the Stilton and *crème fraîche* dip she'd made that afternoon after her walk with Charlotte.

Nick squeezed past her and helped himself to a stick of celery. She felt she ought to say something to him. But what? What on earth could she say to a man who, in a moment of madness, she had kissed in the hope of getting him to …?

'I hope you're not going to ignore me.'

She crunched on her celery.

'I should be very disappointed in you, Hilary, if that's to be the case.'

She crunched some more.

'We can still be friends,' he persevered.

At the front of the classroom Patricia was fiddling with a ghetto-blaster and suddenly the room was filled with Edith Piaf's husky voice singing 'Non, Je Ne Regrette Rien'. 'Just to get us in the right mood for our little *soirée*,' Patricia called out.

Nick looked at Hilary and smiled. 'Come on, Hilary, we can't pretend it didn't happen, so let's not regret it either.'

'But I do,' she murmured.

'What embarrasses you most? The fact that we kissed or that we didn't make love?'

'Please,' she said desperately, 'keep your voice down.'

'Only if you answer the question.'

Hilary tried to think straight. Just what exactly was her honest answer? There was no doubt in her mind that she had enjoyed kissing Nick, just as she'd enjoyed Johnboy's attention at the school reunion a couple of weeks ago. Thinking of that night she saw that what she'd hoped to get from Nick in a moment of madness she had, in fact, gained from Johnboy – and without making a fool of herself. In just a few short hours, her old classmate had sufficiently raised her self-esteem so that she could imagine herself coping with the future.

'You two are very cosy together, aren't you?' Patricia interrupted, handing them each a slice of birthday cake on paper napkins. 'Quite the Romeo and Juliet of the group with your regular hushed *tête-à-têtes*.'

'Always willing to make it a threesome,' Nick said lightly.

Patricia eyed him. 'A *ménage à trois*, you mean?'

'No,' he said firmly. 'Technically that would mean that Hilary and I would have to be married.'

Patricia laughed. 'Now I think David might just have something to say about that.'

'And to think I used to like that awful woman,' Hilary said quietly, as they watched Patricia move on to dole out more of Martina's tricolour birthday cake.

'Perhaps you're becoming more discerning these days.'

She looked up at Nick and met his eyes. 'You know, I do believe I am. Since I discovered David's affair I've started thinking and acting quite differently. What used to matter to me no longer does. You're the expert, is that normal?'

'Whether it's normal or not, is irrelevant, it's what—'

'I wish you'd answer my questions with a simple yes or no.'

He took a bite of birthday cake and chewed it. 'Yes,' he said at last. 'Hilary, I pronounce you quite normal.'

'Thank goodness,' she said, biting into her piece of cake. 'Ugh! Cheap margarine and too much sugar.' She looked about her for a suitable hiding place for the rest of Patricia's baking disaster.

'Here, let me finish it for you,' Nick said, taking it from her. 'I'm obviously not as fussy as you, and while I eat you can tell me why you're learning French – I've never asked you that before.'

'No,' she said, handing him her slice of cake, 'you've been too busy prying into everything else in my life.'

He smiled. 'Sharper as well as more discerning. Go on, tell me why you're here.'

She helped herself to a handful of crisps. 'Just a boring case of the annual pilgrimage to France being backed up with the ability to do more than navigate one's way around a menu.' She shook her head and sighed. 'Ironic, isn't it? At the rate things are going, a camping holiday in France *en famille* is the last thing I'll be doing next summer.'

'Who knows where we'll all be in a year's time?'

'Who knows?' she repeated, thoughtfully.

'Penny for them?'

She told him about the school reunion and what Johnboy had said to her.

'He's right, of course,' Nick said. 'This Johnboy character, he's not going to become a complication, is he?'

She shook her head. 'I shouldn't think so for one minute. So, why are you learning French?'

'Same reason as you. I love Brittany and go there each summer and last year I decided to put a stop to looking such an idiot every time I opened my mouth.'

'I don't think you could ever look an idiot.'

Nick laughed. 'Are you flirting with me?'

Hilary laughed, too, seeing for the first time that even in the depths of wretchedness there was always a degree of humour to be found.

From the other side of the room Patricia gave them both a long, hard stare.

Later that night Georgia's Jeep crept quietly along the deserted main street of the village. It stopped just outside Ted the Toup's, its engine still running. Three silent figures got out and went and huddled around the glass door of the shop. The smallest of the figures pushed open the letter-box; it made a loud grating noise.

'Ssh,' the tallest of the trio said.

The third person then inserted a polythene bag through the opening, turned the bag upside down and began to shake it.

Georgia smiled as the trio climbed back inside the Jeep. Once word got round, Ted would be lucky to sell a newspaper, never mind anything else he kept hidden under wraps at the back of his shop.

The shop was still in darkness when Ted came downstairs the next morning. He hated the winter months and having to get up in the cold to organise those militant newspaper boys and girls. They were always asking for more money or complaining that the bags were too heavy for them. Kids! Wimps, the whole lot of them. Nosy too. He'd caught that lad with the whiskers just showing through on his top lip having a good old rummage in the boxes of new gear he'd got out the back. It was expensive stuff, and he didn't need the likes of that lad's grubby hands fingering any of it.

He yawned, then pulled out a cigarette from the box in his cardigan pocket. He flicked at his lighter and walked over to the door to bring in the papers left there on the doorstep. He was looking forward to reading about that politician who was supposed to be doing it five times a night with his research assistant. No wonder the Government was making such a bloody mess of running the country, they were all too exhausted.

As he walked towards the door his shoes made a strange crunching sound. He looked down at the floor.

'Shit!' he yelled, jumping back in horror and knocking into one of the rotating racks of novels. Bonk-buster novels crashed to the floor, scattering a thousand wriggling white bodies yet further.

'Shit!' he shouted again, seeing his wig lying amongst what looked suspiciously like maggots.

A bang at the door made him jump again. It was the nosy lad with the whiskers. Ted let him in.

'Yuck,' the lad said, looking about him. 'Where've all these maggots come from?' He tried hard not to look at his employer's bald head.

'Bloody good question,' Ted said. He bent down, picked up his wig and waved it vigorously at arm's length. 'Well, don't just stand there. Get a broom and sweep up this mess.'

The lad shook his head. 'I'm a paper boy not a cleaner.'

Ted sucked so hard on his cigarette he almost bit it in two.

Within half an hour most of the village had heard from the paper boys and girls that Ted's shop was crawling with maggots. Within an hour, Iris Braithwaite had appeared and declared the shop a health hazard. And within two hours, a sharp-faced woman from the Environmental Health

Department had arrived. While Ted tried to conceal his recently bought merchandise, the woman filled in a form, slapped it on the counter and announced that unless the shop was cleaner than an operating theatre by five o'clock that day it would be officially closed.

'I've been set up,' he said, 'this is all to try and prevent me—'

'Prevent you from what, Mr Cooper?' the sharp-faced woman asked, knowing full well of the raging debate currently going on in Hulme Welford.

'Nothing,' Ted muttered. He knew disapproval when he saw it and he was looking at it right now in the face of the representative from the Environmental Health Department.

'Either I or a colleague will be back later,' she said, her hand already pulling open the door. 'Oh, and by the way,' she added, 'I think you'll find you have a maggot crawling out from under your – I mean, crawling in your hair.'

As she closed the door behind her Ted snatched off his wig and hurled it across the shop.

Chapter Twenty-eight

While Ted the Toup grappled with a mop and a bucket of Jeyes fluid, the school gym, decorated in paper chains and depictions of the Three Wise Men, erupted with enthusiastic and relieved parental applause.

Flashbulbs sparked and video cameras rolled as the school nativity play came to the end of its one and only performance of the year to a packed house, and right in the front row of a cast of a dozen or more curtsying angels, Becky, with her lopsided wings and tinsel halo, waved energetically at her mother next to Georgia. Hilary discreetly waved back. Chloe, holding an upside-down plastic Jesus and dressed in expiation blue, was sulking in the back row along with a multitude of cotton-wool-bearded shepherds. She caught sight of her mother and scowled. Georgia stuck her fingers in her mouth and let out a piercing whistle.

'A way to go!' she yelled. She nudged Hilary and whispered, 'I'm only doing that to annoy Mesdames Longton and Hampton. That, and Chloe bet me I wouldn't have the nerve. That's a week's pocket money she owes me and just look at the smile on her face now.'

When the clapping finally subsided and Mr Atkinson, the headmaster, made his way to the front of the stage and stood alongside the stable, which looked more like an exotic poolside bar than a ramshackle Judaean outbuilding, Hilary and Georgia got to their feet and crept along the row of applauding parents and associated grandparents. A few other mothers joined them. As members of the PTA, they knew from experience that the headmaster's vote of thanks would be sufficiently long-winded to give them ample time for any last-minute finishing touches required for the Christmas Fayre.

During lunch-break the PTA had decorated the classrooms in which the stalls were to be set up. The room where Hilary had her French lessons each week was to be home to 'Pin the Red Nose on Rudolf', while the surrounding classrooms were to have home-baked goods, refreshments, a bottle tombola, 'Throw the Angel's Halo Over the Crib' and the white elephant stall – where last year's unwanted Christmas presents were to be recycled.

Unable to get away from the nursery any earlier, Georgia had turned up at the last minute with her Jeep full of green foliage to decorate the classrooms, along with an armful of mistletoe. 'A wind-up for Chloe's benefit,' she'd said to Hilary as they unloaded the back of the Jeep.

While the headmaster got on with thanking his excellent and overworked staff, Georgia assembled the PTA in the largest of the classrooms, where alcoholic refreshments were to be served. 'Right,' she said briskly. 'Patricia, here's the money for each stall-holder's float, it's clearly marked, so go round all the classrooms and—'

'Yes, I'm well aware of the procedure,' Patricia said, reaching for the money-bags and snatching them out of Georgia's hands. 'I *have* done this before.'

'Look, chuck,' Georgia said, placing a hand on Patricia's arm, 'try making it easier on yourself. Okay?'

Patricia was horrified and shrugged away from Georgia's hand. 'Don't you ever, ever touch me again, you—'

Georgia laughed. 'Oh, you're beautiful when you're angry, Pattie babes!'

'Why do you do it?' Hilary asked, when they were left alone after Patricia had flounced off in a panic of potential defilement.

'I can't help myself,' Georgia replied, taking the lid off a large saucepan on a hot plate and giving the contents a stir. She popped in a few more slices of orange. 'She's such a sitting target. All that prejudice and middle-class crap all rolled up into one almighty time-bomb just waiting to go off.' She put the lid back on the mulled wine. 'Why are you looking at me like that?'

Hilary shook her head and sighed. She draped a garland of green tinsel along the front of a table covered in red crêpe paper. 'You're so sure of yourself, aren't you?'

'Arrogant, you mean?'

'No, not arrogant. I always get the feeling that you don't care what anyone thinks of you.'

'And you'd be right. Now stop jabbering on like this. Lost-His-Way Atkinson will be winding up any moment now and we've got all these cups to set out, and you know how everyone makes a bee-line for anything alcoholic after suffering one of his interminable speeches.'

Georgia was right. A flood of eye-rolling parents soon descended upon them, hands outstretched for a sedative cup of mulled wine. But the mood soon changed and with what sounded like Pinky and Perky singing 'O Come All Ye Faithful' on Patricia's ghetto-blaster, mothers who had stayed up late the night before running to earth a checked tea-towel for a shepherd's headdress, or who had knocked up a last-minute pair of wings, began to relax while their husbands, who were all playing hookey from work, stood around in groups jangling coins in their trouser pockets and comparing notes on the latest mileage allowances on their company cars.

As she took in the familiar scene Hilary felt angry that David wasn't there. At breakfast that morning he'd told her that he'd be unable to make it in time for the nativity play, something about a meeting with his accountant. Accountant, my foot, she'd thought afterwards as she'd stripped the children's beds and stuffed the sheets and duvet covers into the washing machine. Now he can't even spare an hour or so to see his own daughter on stage. Fired up with anger she had raced around the house with the vacuum cleaner, deliberately bashing into David's armchair in the sitting room, then the desk in his study. But when she'd taken the washing outside to hang on the line, her anger had miraculously vanished. Sunlight was filtering through the naked branches of the cherry trees at the end of the garden, throwing long spindly shadows across the lawn, and she found herself smiling. As she pegged the first of the sheets on the line and breathed in the pleasant smell of washing powder, she wondered at the absurdity of her situation; that even in a moment of extreme anger and bewilderment she could derive enjoyment from something as simple as sunlight streaking across the lawn. Perhaps it was true, after all, that the ordinary could always outweigh the unexpected and traumatic.

'You're looking serious, Hilary.'

'Dad, what are you doing here?' she asked, surprised to see her father on the other side of the table holding out his hand for a cup of mulled wine.

'You didn't think I'd miss Becky's big performance, did you?'

She was touched. 'Oh, how sweet of you. Is Mother with you?'

He shook his head.

'Of course not,' Hilary said, her voice matter-of-fact as she handed him his drink. 'Busy at the shop.'

'Can't stop long myself.'

'Oh?'

'Things to do in the kitchen,' he replied. 'I've got the cake to ice.'

'I haven't done mine yet either.'

'I don't mean the Christmas cake, I'm talking about Charlotte and Alex's cake.'

Hilary felt a stab of jealousy. Charlotte's wedding cake. Just as she'd set about playing Cupid last year with Charlotte and Alex, so, too, she had fully intended to take care of the catering for her sister's big day. Now that pleasure was to be denied her. She had been usurped by – of all people – her father, who up until six months ago had done little more in the kitchen than stir his own low-calorie cocoa. Now here he was preparing a finger-food buffet for an army of guests, who were going to expect a darn sight more than a few pickled onions and bowls of crisps to pick over. She knew it was nasty of her but she couldn't help but wish that Neville had stuck to his lifelong hobby of gooseberry-growing. Why the sudden change?

But it wasn't only that she'd been upstaged by her father that was causing her to feel jealous. For years she'd known and accepted that she didn't mean as much to her father as Charlotte did; there was a closeness between them that she herself had never experienced. As a young child she'd been conscious of a gap between her and her father; a gap she'd never been able to bridge. It hadn't bothered her at the time – like all children, she had simply filled her life with the busyness of growing up. The intricacies of relationships are nothing to a ten-year-old girl intent on a life given over to choir practice and ballet lessons. That Charlotte had preferred their father's company to perfecting a *grand battement* had seemed slightly bizarre to Hilary, all those years ago. Often she had come home after an arduous ballet class and found Charlotte and Neville together in the garden bent over a gooseberry bush, each convincing the other that this was the bush which would yield a prize-winning berry.

Hilary watched her father take a sip of his wine as he cast his eyes about the room. Rarely did she take the time to regard him with anything more than a passing look of interest. She did so now and, to her surprise, was taken aback by what she saw and felt. There was a reassuring benignity to his face that made her throat tighten. She felt cheated. Why had he not bestowed more of that kindliness on her? Anger and hurt merged together inside her. She felt almost as badly betrayed by her father as she did by David – the two men in her life who should have loved her most had let her down. Why?

'See you,' Neville said, as he moved away from her.

'Yes,' she replied, filled with a sudden need to rush over to him and ask what terrible thing she had done. What crime had she committed to be on the receiving end of so little love?

'Mum!' It was Becky, now out of her angel costume and wearing her school uniform. In her hands was a large jar of Smarties. Chloe was by her side and she was holding a note-pad and pen. 'We're doing "Guess How Many Smarties in the Jar",' Becky said, her eyes wide as she looked down at the sweets.

'Lovely,' Hilary said, ladling out two cups of mulled wine for a customer and trying not to think of her father. 'Don't get in anyone's way, will you?'

'Fifty pence a go,' Chloe shouted above the music. 'Each Smartie represents an oppressed woman.'

'What's that, dearie?' asked one of the old ladies from the local nursing home who, each year, were treated to this extravaganza of entertainment. She was wearing a snowball of a hat and too much make-up; in one hand she held a plastic cup and in the other a half-eaten mince pie. She should have been having tea and biscuits in Class I with the rest of her group but she'd escaped, following her nose to something stronger than Typhoo.

'Fifty pence a go,' Chloe repeated, even louder. 'Each Smartie represents an oppressed woman.'

'They don't look overdressed to me, dearie,' the old woman said, giving the jar of sweets a long, hard stare.

'Oppressed!' shouted Chloe impatiently.

The old woman thought about this. Then, chucking Chloe under the chin, she said, 'And what will Santa be bringing you this year? A nice little dolly?'

Chloe looked as though she was about to bite the woman's

hand off. 'No such thing as Father Christmas,' she said tersely. 'It's a silly myth invented by men to glorify their own self-image.'

'That'll do, Chloe,' Georgia intervened, catching the shocked expression on Becky's face. 'I'm sorry, Hilary, but I think you might have some bedtime explaining to do tonight.'

They watched Chloe and Becky move off to prey on an easier target.

'You were only joking, weren't you?' Hilary heard Becky asking Chloe.

Poor Becky, Hilary thought. This Christmas she would discover that Father Christmas was a sham ... and who knew what she would discover about her own father?

As Pinky and Perky moved on to 'I Saw Mommy Kissing Santa Claus' a harassed-looking Patricia came towards them.

'We're running out of small change,' she said accusingly, a five-pound note in her hand. 'You didn't make up the floats properly. We always have—'

'No problem,' Georgia said, reaching for the petty-cash box under the table. 'What do you need?'

'Ten- and twenty-pence pieces. If you had done it the way we—'

Georgia handed over the money, and from behind her back she pulled out a sprig of mistletoe. She dangled it in front of Patricia. 'Give us a kiss, Pattie babes,' she said, with a leery grin.

'I thought I'd warned you to leave me alone,' Patricia said, in a loud, angry voice. Heads turned.

'Ah, why don't you do us all a big favour and ease up? You're up to your panty-line in repression.'

'How dare you!' shrieked Patricia. 'And while we're about it, let me tell you, I'm sick and tired of being the butt of your foul humour. In fact, I'd go as far as saying that we're all sick of your views. People like you are quite out of place in a respectable village like this. And, what's more, we all know it's you who's been terrorising poor Mr Cooper. I saw, with my own eyes, you and your Jeep outside my house when all those things were thrown at his shop.'

'Well, if I was outside your house it couldn't have been me terrorising that disgusting man, could it?'

'It *was* you!' persisted Patricia, her voice now reaching a piercing soprano pitch. She was sounding and looking for all the world like a petulant prima donna, with one hand on her hip and the other pointing a finger at Georgia.

'How dare you speak to Ms D'Arcy like that?' thundered a familiar contralto with all the force and impact of the 'Ride of the Valkyries'.

Patricia lowered her finger and began to tremble as Iris Braithwaite marched into the room.

'I've heard quite enough from you, young lady,' Iris went on. 'And I can assure you that Ms D'Arcy is not alone in her brave fight against Mr Cooper. On the morning to which you are referring I was present. I not only saw what took place, I instigated it. There, now, what do you say to that?'

A shock wave of surprise rippled around the room – and while nobody was looking, the old lady from the nursing home helped herself to another cup of mulled wine. She took a large gulp. 'Happy Christmas,' she said merrily, then spat out a small black clove.

Chapter Twenty-nine

'Now, Becky,' Malcolm Jackson said, in his extra-specially patient voice – the one he sometimes used with the more troublesome members of the PCC. 'You've got a very important job to do, haven't you?' He smiled encouragingly at Becky, hoping that now that she was centre stage of Charlotte and Alex's wedding rehearsal she would pay attention and stop banging her feet against the pew in front of her.

Becky jumped up and joined him. Malcolm carefully manoeuvred her behind Charlotte. 'There now,' he said, 'you pretend your Auntie Charlotte's got her beautiful dress—'

'I think dresses are silly,' Becky said importantly, 'I've given them up. Auntie Charlotte, can I wear jeans on Saturday?'

Wear anything you want, thought Charlotte, just so long as you're quiet long enough for Alex and I to say *we do*. 'You'll have to check with Mummy.'

'Mummy said I'd have to check with you.'

Hilary and Charlotte exchanged looks of *now what*?

'As I was saying,' Malcolm persevered, 'I'm sure Charlotte likes dresses and the one she'll be wearing for the wedding will probably have a long bit trailing the floor behind her—'

Charlotte shook her head vehemently. She had deliberately chosen a dress without a train. She had no intention of running the risk of having anything touching the ground with Becky walking behind her.

'Well, imagine there is,' Malcolm continued, thinking that Job had got off lightly, 'because you must keep your distance,

Becky. We don't want you tripping the bride up by getting too close. Do you think you can remember that?'

'Easy-peasy!'

Charlotte suspected that this was about as likely as hell freezing over, given that her niece had the attention-span of a goldfish.

'But what about Gramps?' Becky asked. 'Shouldn't he be practising this with us?'

Malcolm looked at his watch. 'We'll try it once without Gramps, then with him.'

'You in a hurry to get home to watch *Brookside* like Mum?'

Malcolm smiled stiffly.

'It might be nice to catch the *News at Ten*, though,' Louise said, from the front pew. Neville was sitting next to her, his head drooping so low that his chin was almost touching the knot in his tie.

'Are you sure about wanting to marry into my family?' Charlotte called over to Alex, who was sitting alone on the opposite pew to Louise and Neville.

'So long as we only have the one wedding,' he answered.

'I don't understand why Auntie Charlotte's got to practise. This is her second wedding, isn't it?'

'Because she didn't get it right the first time,' suggested Louise.

'What did you do wrong, Auntie Charlotte?'

'She didn't do anything wrong,' Malcolm interrupted, hoping his wife would have the presence of mind to put the video recorder on. 'Neville, perhaps you'd like to come and join us, after all. Neville?'

'*Neville!*' Louise shouted in her husband's ear. 'You're wanted.'

'Sorry, everyone,' Neville apologised, as he got to his feet and staggered towards the group. 'Sorry, Charlotte, shan't do it on the big day.'

And as the trio at last began the walk up the aisle, to the

sound of Louise singing 'Stately as a Galleon I Sail Across the Floor', Charlotte wondered whether it wasn't too late to call the whole thing off.

It was snowing when they finally got outside, with soft downy pillows of snow lying against shadowy tombstones. Becky whooped with delight and danced excitedly about the churchyard. She picked up a handful of snow and threw it at her mother. Light and powdery, the snowball disintegrated before it reached its target. Hilary laughed at her. She turned to Charlotte. 'Do you remember New Year's Eve, all those years ago, when you danced in the snow without your shoes?'

Charlotte smiled. 'I think I was showing off.'

'Fancy trying it now?' Alex said, slipping his arm through Charlotte's.

'What, and catch pneumonia just in time for Saturday? Second thoughts, maybe that's not such a stupid idea.'

'You're marrying me in three days' time and that's an end to it,' Alex said, 'or otherwise—' He bent down and scooped up a handful of snow.

'Oh no you don't!' shrieked Charlotte. She ran off along the whitened path and out through the lychgate. Alex chased after her with Becky close behind, their feet crunching the snow.

'How about everyone coming back for a drink?' asked Hilary, thinking of the wall of silence at The Gables when she and Becky returned home.

'No,' Louise answered with a shiver. 'There's another one of those court-room dramas on the telly I want to see.' She pushed her hands into her sheepskin gloves and braced herself for the walk back up the hill.

Neville was disappointed. He would have liked to join in the fun. He kissed Hilary good night and followed in Louise's trail of footsteps.

With her parents' figures already little more than blurred

outlines in the snowy darkness Hilary crossed the main street of the village alone. Ahead of her she could hear Becky's happy voice in the muffled silence of the snow-filled sky, and within the orangy glow of light cast from the lamp-post at the top of Acacia Lane snowflakes were falling in an easy, constant rhythm. It was a perfect Christmas card setting and reminded Hilary of the scene in *The Lion, the Witch and the Wardrobe* when Mr Tumnus first appears to Lucy. How perfect it had all seemed to Lucy until she found out the truth from the sad little faun.

She hurried on and soon caught up with Charlotte and Alex. It was then that Becky's scream rang out long and shrill, jarring terrifyingly with the quietness of Acacia Lane.

They rushed over to the White Cottage where Becky stood at the open gate staring down at the ground, her eyes wide and frightened. Beneath a blanket of snow lay a body, and at one end of it a small patch of snow was turning pink.

Alex knelt on the ground and quickly started brushing away at the thick covering of snow. 'My God,' he said, ripping off his coat and covering the body, 'it's Mrs Braithwaite!'

Hilary clutched at Charlotte's arm and Becky whispered, 'Is she dead?'

'She's only mildly concussed, but we'll keep her in overnight to be on the safe side,' the nurse told Charlotte and Alex. 'We've stitched and patched her up but, like most old people who are mugged, she's as mad as hell. It's their pride as much as anything that gets hurt. I'll let you see her for a few minutes, but only one of you, mind. She's had enough excitement for one night.'

Charlotte found Iris propped up in bed with several pillows behind her. Her bandaged head was sagging to one side as if she was asleep, but when Charlotte approached, her bruised and swollen eyes immediately flickered open.

'I just came to make sure you—'

'Spare me the pleasantries, Mrs Lawrence. The man who did this to me is going to be locked up.'

'Did you see who it was?'

'Of course I did. It was Ted Cooper.'

Chapter Thirty

'Hi,' Tiffany said, as she saw Alex close the post-office door and start walking towards where she stood outside the baker's.

'No school today?' he asked, when he reached her after negotiating his way through the shovelled-up piles of snow on the pavement.

'Last day of term yesterday,' she answered. 'Barry comes home tomorrow. He said on the phone last night that the snow's been really bad in Leeds. I hope he makes it – I don't much fancy Christmas without him.'

'He'll make it,' Alex said, beginning to feel the cold – minus four had been given on the weather forecast earlier that morning, along with more snow. He stamped his boots on the pavement, shaking off the clumps of ice, while marvelling at Tiffany's ability, like most of her contemporaries, to brave the elements in little more than a skimpy black denim jacket and thin silky skirt.

'He better had, or I'll come and spend Christmas with you and Charlotte.'

'You're forgetting that Charlotte and I won't be there. We're getting married on Saturday.'

'Muffin 'ell, so you are. I wish you'd reminded me yesterday. I was late-night shopping in Manchester with Mum and Dad and could have bought you your wedding present. Now you'll have to make do with something local.' She glanced up and down the row of shops. 'What do you fancy? A pound of carrots or a bag of custard tarts?'

'Louise has got some rather nice Georgian silver candlesticks in her shop.'

'In your dreams! Either that or I'll have to go out and mug somebody.'

Alex flinched.

'What's wrong?'

'Haven't you heard about Iris Braithwaite?'

'Why, what's she done?'

Alex told Tiffany what had happened last night, how they had discovered the old lady lying unconscious in the snow and how they'd called an ambulance to take her to the hospital. 'It must have all been going on while you were coming back from Manchester.'

'Was it a burglar?'

'We're not sure yet—' but the rest of Alex's words were lost in the noise of a police car pulling up outside Ted Cooper's next to the baker's. Two uniformed officers got out and went inside.

'It's not about the maggots, is it?' Tiffany asked Alex. 'He's not prosecuting or anything daft like that, is he?'

Alex noticed the anxious look on Tiffany's face. 'I should think that's the least of his worries, right now. Mrs Braithwaite told Charlotte last night at the hospital that it was Ted who attacked her.'

'*What?*' And then it dawned on Tiffany. 'You mean revenge? He beat Mrs Braithwaite up because of the protest?'

Alex shook his head. 'I can't believe that he would do a thing like that. I know he's an old sleaze-bag, but to attack a woman he's known all these years and in a community like this ... Well, it just seems so unlikely.'

'Bloody men! You all stick together, don't you?'

'Tiffany, I'm just trying to be objective.'

'Shit you are!' She turned away angrily and pushed open the door of the bakery. From inside the shop she watched Alex walk back down the road.

'I'd like to squeeze the jam out of that one,' the younger

of the two assistants said, as she arranged a tray of doughnuts in the window display and stared after Alex.

Tiffany cleared her throat noisily. 'A French stick and a large wholemeal, when you've got a moment.'

'Got one on you this morning, have you, Tiff?'

'No, I haven't,' she replied indignantly. 'But that Ted the Toup soon will have when the police have finished with him. They're next door, right now.' She leaned towards the counter. She knew that what she was doing was malicious, but she was so angry. 'He attacked Mrs Braithwaite last night. She's in hospital, in a really bad way.'

Tiffany watched their faces with satisfaction, handed over her money and left the shop, sure in the knowledge that, within the hour, practically everyone in the village would know that Ted Cooper wasn't just a pervy but a dangerous attacker of innocent women.

On her way home, she decided she'd give Georgia a ring. Perhaps they could visit Mrs Braithwaite. As she passed Charlotte's shop she saw Nick Bradshaw's car coming along the main street, his tyres churning the slush and ice on the road. He turned slowly into Daisy Bank. Immediately all thoughts of Mrs Braithwaite were put out of her mind. She tucked the French stick and wholemeal loaf under her arm and hurried home.

She arrived at All in the Mind just as Nick was reaching into the back of his car for his briefcase. 'Hi,' she said, trying to conceal that she was out of breath.

'Been running?' he asked.

Damn! 'Jogging,' she said, with an easy laugh.

'In the snow?'

'I have to keep fit, even in winter.' What was she doing? Why was it every time she wanted to talk to Nick she ended up sounding a right geek?

He slammed the car door shut and moved towards the house. 'You look fit enough to me,' he said over his shoulder.

She smiled. 'Do you think so? If you fancy a run, you could always come—'

'Never touch the stuff,' he said.

'What?'

'Exercise.' He pushed the door open. 'And something else I never touch, my employer's daughter, especially when she's young enough to be my own daughter.' He held the door and waited for her to go ahead of him.

She held back. 'Shit before the shovel,' she said. 'After you.'

Tiffany went inside and called Georgia on the mobile from her bedroom.

'You sound upset,' Georgia said. 'What's up?'

Tiffany threw a wet screwed-up tissue across the room. She told Georgia about Iris Braithwaite, which accounted for part of her anger, but she said nothing about Nick. 'Mrs Braithwaite says it was Ted Cooper who attacked her. The police are with him now.'

'The bastard!'

'You don't suppose we went too far and pushed him—'

'Look, Tiffany, shoving maggots through somebody's letter-box doesn't mean it's open season for beating up old ladies. How bad is Iris?'

'I don't know. Alex Hamilton only just told me ... Oh, God, Georgia, what have we done?'

'Hold tight, Tiffany. I'll ring the hospital.'

By the time Georgia had dialled the number for the hospital hot tears were pricking at her eyes. She rubbed them roughly with the heel of her hand, to the sound of Tiffany's words echoing accusingly in her head. *What have we done?*

'Come on, come on,' she said angrily into the mobile phone, as she paced the few available feet of space in the caravan. 'Answer the wretched thing!'

No answer came.

She pressed the off button, followed by redial. Still no

answer. 'Bloody government cut-backs!' She cursed loudly and slammed the phone down on the table. She stared out at the snow-covered greenhouses and was suddenly struck by how very alone she was. There was no Gordon today – he and Winnie were Christmas-shopping in Macclesfield – and Chloe was at a friend's. She let out a long sigh and, resting her head against the flimsy wall of the caravan, she thought of the unimaginable horror Iris must have gone through . . . alone. She clenched her fists, knowing that it was all her fault, it was down to *her* that this terrible thing had happened. She should never have got involved. She should have left the silly old woman to her ineffectual posters and clipboard. What right had she had to go stirring things up?

And just what the hell had she thought she was doing, getting herself involved with a woman like Iris? Nobody liked her. She was a pain. A nosy, interfering woman who irritated the hell out of everyone and who had even had the nerve to start butting in on her life – baking her cakes and sticking up for her against the likes of that bloody Longton woman. Bloody cheek!

She didn't need help like that. She could manage on her own. Life was about coping, managing and getting on with it. It wasn't about tins of cakes being delivered to the doorstep.

She tried to keep hold of this anger, forcing herself to rail against the image of someone who had tried to impose an unwanted presence on her life but, despite her anger and despite her defiance, a solitary stinging tear escaped and slowly made its way down her cheek. She let it go, surprised at the unexpected warmth of it against her cold skin. Another followed, and then another.

When Nick couldn't find anyone to help him pick out a Christmas tree, he knocked on the caravan door.

He found Georgia slumped on the floor, her head tucked hard against her drawn-up knees. She was shaking and crying so violently he could get no sense out of her. He picked her up and carried her over to the bungalow where he set her down on the sofa in the sitting room and wrapped her in the throw-over from the back of a chair. He made no attempt to stop her tears but went to the kitchen to make a hot drink. When he took it through to her she had stopped sobbing but her frail body was still shuddering with uncontrollable spasms of what he took to be shock.

He held the mug of hot sweet tea against her chattering teeth and forced her to drink.

She took a sip, then looked at him through distant eyes and stammered, 'It's ... Iris. She really isn't the dragon everyone thinks she is.'

'If you say so,' he replied soothingly, pressing the mug against her mouth again and wondering whether he should call a doctor.

Cindy paused outside an empty seminar room, where earlier that morning Nick had given his class, 'Phone Home to Your Inner Self'. Peering through the glass panel she had watched a group of women lying on the floor. At first glance it could have been a fitness class from the days of In the Pink, except that these women hadn't formed a rainbow array of brightly coloured leotards and Lycra tights, they had been in their everyday clothes covered with a blanket and a pile of books under their heads – she kept meaning to ask Nick, why books? Why not a cushion? According to Nick, this supine position was a sure way to understanding your internal stress. Watching the women she had wondered how many of them lying there in front of Nick had anything remotely stressful going on in their lives. Most of them gave the impression of being completely at ease with life and here only to enjoy the attentions of their good-looking counsellor.

Nick had certainly turned out to be an asset to All in the Mind. Whether or not it had anything to do with his counselling skills Cindy wasn't entirely convinced. She suspected the popularity of his classes had more to do with the soft black curls at the nape of his neck; that and the tousled style of his dress caused most of the more mature women to want to take him in hand and mother him. The younger ones probably had sex on their minds as they lay there submissively on the floor with their legs slightly apart.

To her shame she had actually pressed her ear to the door and tried to hear what he was saying. She'd caught snatches about energy systems and auras and a lot of other nonsense. Then he'd gone on to say, 'Now imagine yourself floating ... Does that give you a sense of freedom ... or does it make you feel helpless and vulnerable?'

Remembering how his question had made her feel like a monumental con merchant, Cindy moved along the corridor and on to the next seminar room. Through the open door she caught the unmistakable sound of Derek's laughter. She raised her hand to push the door further open but hesitated when she heard a woman laughing. A million and one past scenarios leapt into Cindy's mind, along with the conclusion that a leopard really couldn't change his spots.

She listened at the door.

'Rosie, you've got me all wrong.'

'Have I, I wonder?'

'Yes, you really couldn't be more wrong.'

'Derek, you must stop focusing on the negative. Now, come here and let me help you channel—'

'I need to get back to the office – Cindy will be expecting—'

'What are you afraid of, Derek?'

'Nothing.'

'You're afraid of me. I've sensed it for some time now.'

'Nonsense!'

'Are you sure I don't unnerve you because of my strong sexuality?'

'Rosie, I'm well aware of your—'

'Derek, I know you want me, I can see it in your eyes, but it's fear that keeps you from touching me, isn't it?'

'I've never been frightened of anyone in my life.'

'I don't believe you.'

'Certainly not of a woman.'

'Then touch me.'

'Rosie!'

'Yes, Derek.'

'This has gone far enough. Shouldn't you be preparing for your next seminar? What is it?'

' "When Heavenly and Earthly Bodies Collide".'

'I don't remember that being in the diary.'

'A change of plan. Why don't you come along? You could help me with the practical side of the session.'

'I'd love to only . . . Rosie, what do you think you're doing? Get up!'

Cindy had heard enough. She stuffed a fist into her mouth, held her breath and ran as quickly and as quietly as she could to the office. She shut the door behind her and leaned against it. Tears began rolling down her cheeks as she laughed and laughed. Poor old Derek, he'd finally met his Waterloo.

She was still laughing when Derek, red-faced and sweating, came into the room.

'I'm not sure we chose exactly the right person when we took Rosie on.' He slumped over the desk, his head in his hands.

'Oh, do you really think so?' Cindy said, with only a trace of amusement in her voice. 'I thought you made an excellent choice.'

'She's a man-eater, Cindy!' He looked up at her and thumped his fist on the desk. 'You've got to help me!'

When Ted came back from the police station he couldn't believe his eyes. The front of his shop was daubed in graffiti. 'Vicious pervert' was scrawled across the window, and underneath in red letters were the words 'No scumbags in Hulme Welford'.

'Spot of bother?' the taxi driver asked, his hand outstretched.

Ted said nothing. He handed over his fare, then caught Jane and Brenda in the baker's staring at him. When he returned their gaze they both turned away. So did all their customers.

'I didn't do it!' he shouted at them. 'I didn't touch the silly old bag.'

Chapter Thirty-one

From her fireside armchair Iris saw a third plate of mince pies being ushered into the kitchen. 'I've been viciously assaulted, not starved,' she shouted through to Hilary and Neville.

Hilary appeared in the doorway with a pretty blue and white china bowl of fragrant hyacinths – another gift from a well-wisher. She put the flowers on the table in front of Iris.

'Not so close, I can't abide the smell.'

Hilary moved over to the window and placed the bowl on the sill, behind a small, prim, artificial Christmas tree that had all the charm of a toilet brush. 'Now, are you sure you're warm enough?' She began straightening the tartan rug on Iris's lap. Iris pushed her hands away.

'I'm quite warm enough, thank you. It's thirst I'm dying of, not hypothermia.'

'I'll go and see if Dad's made the tea.'

'How's it going?' Neville asked, when she joined him in the kitchen.

'Nursing a scorpion suddenly has its attractions. Honestly, Dad, she's so ungrateful. No wonder she was let out of hospital so soon, they probably couldn't cope a moment longer with her.'

'I'll take her tea through. You take a break out here and see what you can rustle up for lunch.'

'Mince pies, by the looks of things,' Hilary muttered as her father disappeared and she viewed the doily-lined offerings of

Mesdames Haslip and Bradley and the vicar's wife – a woman more known for her views on prisoners' rights than for parish pastry.

Hilary had had no intention of babysitting Iris Braithwaite when she came out of hospital that morning, but as the children had gone to friends for the day, and in the absence of anyone else being brave enough, she had volunteered. Then, surprisingly, Neville had stepped forward to collect the old lady from Macclesfield. Together they had brought her home and had put up with a constant barrage of orders and ill-temper, and now the task of pleasing her palate had fallen to Hilary. Oh, joy!

She opened the fridge and stared at the near-empty shelves: a packet of Lurpak, a couple of tomatoes – one that looked as swollen and as bruised as Iris's face – a plate of left-over cooked cabbage and a saucer of mashed potato, which had the beginnings of a fur coat. Two eggs in the door rack shone like beacons in a wasteland and Hilary picked them up and carried them carefully to the enamelled draining board. As she hunted for a small saucepan she found herself thinking of the cheerless contents of Iris's fridge – it was unseasonably empty, given that Christmas was only two days away. She had never before considered what Iris did over the festive period.

It was common knowledge that she never attended midnight mass on Christmas Eve – she had been quoted many times as saying that, over the years, the service had turned into nothing more than a drunken orgy of revellers, who on being tipped out of the Spinner found the warmed pews of St John's a welcome diversion from the bitter reproach they would expect to receive from their wives when they finally made it home.

As for Christmas Day itself, Hilary had no notion what Iris did. Friends, perhaps? Mrs Haslip or Mrs Bradley? Certainly Hilary couldn't recall any sightings in the village of anyone who could remotely be described as family coming to stay.

So what did she do? Did Malcolm take pity on her and invite her into his home for the day?

Hilary had the uneasy feeling that, perhaps, everyone, including herself, had refused to think too deeply how Iris amused herself over the festive period so as not to court disaster on themselves. A pricked conscience was a painful thing to have for Christmas.

As the eggs began to boil Hilary turned the timer upside down and watched the trickle of sand pass from one glass balloon to the other. Reluctantly she knew what steps she would have to take if she was to avoid any feelings of guilt over the next few days. It would be a squash, what with David's parents arriving tomorrow for five days.

Five days! She closed her eyes, not wanting to think of the terror in store for her. Five whole days of listening to her mother-in-law's incessant praise of her only son – David, the blue-eyed wonderboy who could do no wrong.

Ah! Did she have news for them!

She brought the flat of her hand down on the draining board with a loud crack. Plates and cutlery rattled noisily in the plastic rack.

'Steady on there, Hilary.'

She turned round to her father. She suddenly felt furious and wanted more than anything to take her anger out on someone. And here was her father, good-natured Neville, whom everyone liked and respected. So why couldn't he see how upset she was? Why couldn't he put his arm around her and make it all better for her? Wasn't that what fathers did? Hug me! she wanted to scream at him. I'm your daughter. I may not be as interesting as Charlotte but I'm still your daughter.

'How's lunch coming along?' he asked, awkwardly.

She couldn't speak.

He glanced about the kitchen for some sign of food. 'Hilary? This isn't like you, what's wrong?'

She gulped. 'No. You're right, it's not like me at all.' And that's the problem, she thought miserably, reaching into the bread bin. Everyone thinks of me as good old Hilary, the born organiser. Want anything doing? Then give it to Hilary. Sunday school, PTA secretary, Christmas Fayre. Well, I don't want to play that part any more. I'm tired of being a pillar of the community. I'm crumbling and can't anyone see that?

'Hilary, how long has that egg-timer been like that?'

'Hell!'

Neville was startled. He'd never seen his younger daughter like this before. He watched her whip the saucepan off the heat and douse the eggs under the cold tap. She then moved about the kitchen in a fury of activity. Something was wrong, very wrong, and he had the uncomfortable feeling that he was somehow partly to blame.

'Hilary—'

'Not now, Dad,' she said briskly, loading a tray with the eggs and slices of bread and butter. She was battling to stay in control.

Neville could see that her eyes were moist with the threat of tears. 'Let me take that to Iris,' he said.

'I can manage,' she answered flatly, trying to push past him.

'Give it to me,' he said, surprising himself at how stern he sounded. Perhaps he should try that tone with Louise some time?

'*Two* boiled eggs?' Iris said, when Neville set the tray in front of her. 'Good gracious, Dr Archer, you and Mrs Archer may be able to afford to live the high life, but a woman in my position can't possibly—' She turned away from him, distracted by something moving outside. Neville sensed her nervousness.

The sound of the door knocker made them both jump. Hilary went to answer it.

It was Ted Cooper, a heavy dusting of snow on his overcoat, a frozen dew-drop on the end of his nose and a small poinsettia in his hands. 'I want to see her,' he said.

'Whoever it is, I'm not at home,' called Iris.

'I don't think it's a good idea,' Hilary whispered to Ted.

Only a matter of minutes after Ted had arrived home from the police station, word had gone round that he had been eliminated from their enquiries. A few in the village had received the news with shamefaced expressions, but Iris had not been convinced of his innocence. 'I saw him with my own eyes,' she had said in the car coming away from the hospital. 'I assure you, I'm not going senile,' she'd added. 'I know what I saw.'

'Please, Mrs Parker. I want her to know it wasn't me.'

'Is it that dreadful man, Mr Cooper?' Iris called. 'Tell him to go away or I shall telephone the police.'

'Calm down, Mrs Braithwaite,' Neville placated. 'Why don't you see him for a couple of seconds? What harm could—'

'What harm?' Iris repeated. 'You stand there with the state of my disfigured face before you and you have the gall to—'

'Please, Mrs Braithwaite, nothing is going to happen to you while I am in the room.' Neville was beginning to wonder at himself. Twice now in one afternoon he had taken charge.

Iris stared hard at him. 'You're getting very high and mighty these days, Dr Archer, I must say.' She waved a dismissive hand at him. 'Very well, let Mr Cooper in by all means, but be assured, the responsibility is all yours. Be it on your own head.'

Neville went and joined Hilary and Ted Cooper in the hall.

'You'd better take your shoes off,' Hilary warned Ted. She led him through to the sitting room and watched Iris give him one of her notorious gimlet-eyed looks – black eyes or not, she was still capable of giving a good dressing-down.

Ted held out the sad little poinsettia. Iris made no attempt to take it from him and neither of them spoke.

There was something dreadfully pathetic about the scene –

a grown man in his stockinged feet with a peace-offering and a proud woman with a face like a war victim. Hilary couldn't bear it. She stepped forward and took the plant from Ted. 'Hurry up, Mr Cooper,' she urged, 'Mrs Braithwaite needs to have her lunch.'

Ted steeled himself. 'Mrs Braithwaite,' he began, at the same time pushing his hands deep inside his coat pockets. He could feel his packet of cigarettes, his lighter, too. Automatically he started fingering the packet open, then remembered where he was and jerked his hand out. Light up at the White Cottage and die!

'Yes, Mr Cooper?'

'You and me—'

'You and I, Mr Cooper. If you are going to apologise, you might just as well be grammatically correct.'

'I'm not bloody well apologising—'

Iris tutted. 'Ever wondered why one's fingers are the shape they are, Mr Cooper?'

Ted shook his head, baffled.

'It's so that one can plug one's ears when one hears such disgusting language.' She promptly stuck both her forefingers in her ears.

Ted turned to Hilary and Neville. 'Now what?'

Neville shook his head at Iris and she slowly removed her fingers. 'Merely making a stand,' she said stoically. Hilary was reminded of Becky.

Ted took a deep breath. 'I may not be much of a bloke to you, Mrs Braithwaite, but I can tell you I'd no more hit a woman to the ground than—'

'How do you know I was hit to the ground if you weren't there?' retorted a triumphant Iris.

'Jeeze! It's common knowledge. It'll be in the paper next week.'

Iris raised her fingers to her ears again.

'I didn't do it,' Ted said impatiently. 'I was at the Spinner. They all saw me there. I'm innocent.'

'Well, somebody did this to me,' Iris said, pointing to her battered face. 'Somebody who looked a lot like you.'

'It wasn't me. You told the police it was somebody with a hat on. So it couldn't have been me because I never wear a hat on account of—'

'On account of what?' Iris asked.

'On account of my wig,' he replied, embarrassed. 'I can't wear a wig and a hat.'

'Piffle!'

'It's true and I'm very sorry you're hurt, Mrs Braithwaite, and I'm sorry too about all the fuss at the shop, and ...'

'Go on.'

'And I want you to know that I've decided to get out of the clothing business. It's too much hassle.' He started shuffling towards the door. 'I've said my piece now so I'll show myself out.' He paused and then turned back to face Iris. 'By the way, you wouldn't happen to know anything about maggots would you, Mrs Braithwaite?'

'Nasty things, maggots, Mr Cooper.'

'Yes,' Ted said, scratching the skin under the front of his wig, recalling all too vividly just how nasty the little blighters were.

'That wasn't so bad, was it?' Hilary said, when Ted had slipped on his shoes and left the White Cottage.

Iris banged down her spoon on one of the boiled eggs. It made little impression. 'Hard and cold,' she replied, pushing the tray away from her. 'But, as you say, not too bad.'

Hilary was sure that beneath Iris's swollen lips there lurked a hint of a smile – a smile of victory.

As Ted plodded through the snow back to his shop, a smile hovered on his lips. Okay, so he'd given in to the old bat, but mail-order was the thing to get into anyway.

Georgia woke with a jolt, disoriented and heavy-headed. She caught sight of Nick reading a book in the chair opposite her and sat bolt upright. 'What the hell's going on?'

He closed the book and smiled at her. 'I was rather hoping you'd put me in the picture there.'

She pushed back the throw-over and got clumsily to her feet. This was her house, right? This was her sitting room, right? 'Where's Chloe?' she demanded, trying to make sense of a situation that was all wrong.

'Relax. Somebody called Cas phoned and said they were going to watch a film and she'd drop Chloe off just after six. Is that okay?'

Georgia rubbed her hands over her face, the fog of confusion beginning to lift. She could remember Cas coming for Chloe early in the morning, then Tiffany calling and sounding upset, and telling her something about Iris. Again she rubbed her face, forcing a further piece of the puzzle to appear. At last it did. Iris had been attacked ... Iris was in hospital. She swallowed hard and slowly sank back on to the sofa, remembering now her reaction to the news. She raised her eyes to Nick.

'When I found you,' he said, in response to her unasked question, 'you were on the floor in the caravan. You were crying, very cold and shaking, like you were in a state of shock.'

She looked away.

'Do you want to tell me what had upset you so much?'

'No!'

'Fair enough.'

They sat in silence and, to Georgia's disbelief, Nick opened the book he'd been reading and started casually flicking through to find his page.

'And just how long do you intend to sit there?' she said suddenly.

'Until you've decided to tell me what happened,' he answered, without even looking up at her.

She scowled, leaned back against the sofa and crossed her arms in front of her.

He raised an eyebrow. 'You look just like you did the first time I met you at Hilary's.'

'Oh, this is ridiculous!'

'I agree.' He put the book down and shifted forward in his seat, somehow managing to appear as if he were almost touching her. 'Tell me, Georgia – may I call you Georgia?'

She nodded.

'Do you always cry so violently?'

'Don't be absurd, of course I don't. I never cry.' She stood up and walked over to the window, but the sight of the caravan at the other side of the car park brought back the pain she had felt earlier. She moved away.

'Never?'

'Never what?'

'Cry.'

'Well, obviously not completely never, as today's débâcle testifies to.'

'So when was the last time you were upset?'

She ran her hand through her hair. 'What the hell is this? Derek Rogers not got enough customers to keep you busy? Talking of which, I need to get outside and get on with some work – there'll be punters wanting Christmas trees.'

'There won't be,' Nick said quietly. 'I turned the sign round at the gate. I thought it best.'

'You did what?' Georgia turned on him. 'How dare you? You make yourself well and truly at home in my house, you read my books and have the cheek—'

'Yes,' he said, rising slowly from the chair. 'How dare I call in during my lunch-hour for a Christmas tree and find you all alone curled up on the floor howling like a baby, and how dare I carry you into the warm and make you a mug of tea, and how dare I have the bare-faced cheek to sit here with you for over two hours to make damn sure you're all right. By God, they don't come much worse than me, do they?'

'I ...'

'Yes,' he said, standing over her, his face dark with fury.

'So masterful when you're angry,' she said, with just the hint of a smile.

He stared at her, his eyes blazing and she thought, for a moment, that he was going to retaliate with a further outburst. But he didn't. Instead, he reached for his coat and scarf from the back of the chair he'd been sitting in and said, 'I'll turn the sign round on my way out.'

As he pulled on his coat, she said, 'If you still want a Christmas tree you can have one for free, if you like,' her voice was conciliatory, 'seeing as I've put you to so much trouble.'

'Thank you.'

She helped him choose a tree, then watched him drive out of the snow-covered car park, the boot of his car wedged open with the last six inches of a Norway spruce poking out. She shivered in the freezing cold and looked at her watch. It was nearly three o'clock and the light was already beginning to fade. She'd lost the best part of the day and there was still so much to get done.

But first she had to find out about Iris, which she knew would mean she'd have to face up to why, today, she'd cried for the first time in three years.

Georgia found Iris alone, having eventually got through to the hospital only to be told that Mrs Braithwaite had been discharged just before lunch-time.

'Thank goodness you haven't brought any more wretched mince pies with you,' Iris said, slowly leading the way into the sitting room after Georgia had removed her boots. She pointed to a chair for Georgia and settled herself in her own armchair, which was surrounded by a collection of small tables covered with an assortment of invalid requirements – tissues, boiled sweets, a Thermos flask, a cup and saucer, a glass of water, a bottle of aspirin, two magazines and an untouched plate of mince pies. 'Dr Archer and his daughter have spent the afternoon with me,' she said, pulling a tartan blanket over her legs, 'for which I'm very grateful, but they do fuss so.'

'What on earth happened, Iris?' Georgia asked, straight to the point, but doing her best not to stare at Iris's ghastly face. She was alert, though, to the tiredness in the older woman's voice, which made her wonder for the first time just how old she was. She had to be seventy-something, which was about how old she herself felt today. 'Tiffany said something about it being Ted Cooper who attacked you.'

'Apparently I was mistaken in thinking it was that shabby little man.'

'Oh.'

'Oh, indeed.' Iris stared back at Georgia. 'And what, may I ask, is troubling you, young lady? You look red-eyed and worn out.'

'You, you tiresome, bothersome old woman, that's what's troubling me,' Georgia answered, with a small smile. 'You've caused me no end of trouble today.'

'I have, have I? Well, perhaps you'd like to help me out with these mince pies and tell me what I'm supposed to have done.' She handed Georgia the plate. 'Go ahead, they're Hilary Parker's, so perfectly edible, not like Mrs Bradley's. I wouldn't offer you hers.'

'There you go again!' Georgia exclaimed loudly, pushing the plate away. 'You see, that's what you do to me. Nobody else tries it on. You're the only one. You're the only bloody person that's got the nerve. And don't you see what that does to me?' Suddenly she was leaning forward in her seat, her head in her hands, her shoulders shaking involuntarily just as she'd cried earlier that day. 'I don't want you being nice to me,' she sobbed. 'Be horrible or leave me alone.'

'Kindly blow your nose and stop that language. I simply won't have it, not even from you.'

And as if by magic Georgia's tears immediately stopped. Looking up she saw that Iris was holding out a box of

Kleenex. She took a handful of tissues. 'I'm sorry,' she mumbled. 'It's so long since I've cried. It's all Rory's fault. When he started messing me about I was so angry and so upset I clamped a lid on anything I felt and vowed I'd never again let anyone screw me up like he did.'

'Which meant you had to stop anyone getting near you,' Iris suggested.

'Yes. And somehow, you, you silly old woman, managed to sneak under all my carefully erected barriers. How did you do it?' She started crying again. 'It's the bloody juxta-position of how you appear to everyone else and then how you treat me,' she bawled. 'Why do you do it?'

'Ever thought that perhaps I like you, Georgia?'

Georgia blew her nose. 'No you don't, you don't like anyone.'

'And are you going to add that nobody likes me?'

'Everybody's terrified of you, you know that.'

'But not you? You're not scared of me, are you?' Iris asked softly.

'Too right I'm not.'

'And perhaps that's why I like you, Georgia. Mince pie?'

Georgia threw her pile of soggy tissues on the fire and laughed. 'Iris, you're the strangest and strongest woman I know.' She took a mince pie. 'Other than myself, of course.'

'Of course.'

Georgia bit into the pastry, sending up a small cloud of icing sugar into the air. She munched hungrily. She'd had nothing to eat since breakfast. When she'd finished, she said, 'Iris, can I ask you something?'

The old lady nodded.

'I know you've been widowed for years, but did you have ... well, are there any Braithwaite juniors running amok somewhere?'

It was a while before Iris said anything. 'Sadly no,' she answered, her hands clasped together on her lap and her eyes staring dimly into the flickering fire. When at last she turned her attention back to Georgia, she said, 'I'm very tired now, would you mind . . .?'

'Of course,' Georgia said, getting quickly to her feet. 'I shouldn't have kept you talking for so long. Is there anything I can—?'

'No, nothing.'

'I'll call you tomorrow, then.'

'Thank you, that would be kind.'

Georgia had the strongest of urges to hug Iris but instead she patted the old woman's hand. She was surprised, though, when Iris took hold of hers and squeezed it gently.

Chapter Thirty-two

'Come on, David old mate,' Derek yelled above 'I Wish It Could Be Christmas Every Day'. 'It's your round so dip your hand in that dusty old wallet you keep hidden and get the beers rolling.'

Alex noticed David's long face as he approached the crowded bar. For a man who was indulging in illicit sex he looked far from happy. From the moment Charlotte had told him that David was having an affair Alex had tried to equate his future brother-in-law – a man who had never before struck him as a risk-taker – with the concept of a man who was throwing all caution to the wind.

He watched David pull out his wallet and was shocked to see his hands shake slightly. Was that the result of his duplicity? Obviously David wasn't cut out for a life of extra-marital spice.

'What's that serious expression for, Alex? Getting doubts for tomorrow?'

'No chance.' Alex turned away from David and faced his brother sitting next to him.

James cast his eyes about the public bar of the Spinner in amusement. The place was dripping with red and silver tinsel and gaudy paper chains that criss-crossed from one wall to another; from every light-fitting clusters of green baubles sparkled with glitter and dangled like swollen grapes. Over in the corner, by the entrance to the men's toilets, an old woman stood over a fruit machine, her loose false teeth sliding backwards and forwards as she stabbed with her fingers at the electronic buttons, her eyes lighting up with each spin of the drum. 'And to think we could have had your stag night in a smart little wine bar in Sloane Square,' James said, with a wry smile.

'And been bored to death.'

'You really have gone native, haven't you?'

Alex laughed. 'Come to my senses, more like it.'

'You always were an awkward bugger.'

'And still am, hopefully.'

James drained his glass of beer, then leaned back against a fake beam. 'How you found someone like Charlotte in a place like this I'll never know. But then maybe you're not the fool I thought you were.'

'So which fool does that make him?' Derek interrupted, as he handed out another round of drinks from the tray David was carrying.

Alex noticed that David still looked miserable. He watched him go over to the dart-board where Malcolm and Nick were challenging Barry and Stephen to a game.

The evening had been totally unplanned until last night when Derek had called round, saying, 'No neighbour of mine is getting married without proper respect for tradition.' His insistence had put paid to the decision that he and Charlotte had come to, which was to ignore convention and spend the evening with James and old friends, Stephen and Sally, who were coming over from Yorkshire for the wedding with their young deaf son Mark.

'Don't worry, Charlotte,' Derek had persisted. 'I've been to more last nights of freedom than there have been Conservative scandals. He'll be in safe hands with me.' Then, of course, had come the inevitable parting shot at the door. 'By the way, how do you like your kiss-o-grams, male or female?'

Over by the dart-board Alex could see Nick approaching David. He decided to join them – the last thing he wanted on his stag night was a repeat performance of Derek and Cindy's party.

*

'Muffin 'ell,' shouted Tiffany, springing forward in her seat and scattering peanuts over the floor. 'How can she say such a bloody stupid thing?' She mimicked Mia Farrow's thin, highly strung voice, ' "... That's the best thing a girl can be in this world, a beautiful little fool." '

'Quiet,' Cindy reprimanded, 'I can't hear what they're saying.'

Charlotte looked about the sitting room and smiled. She was enjoying her 'girls' night' that Hilary had arranged. 'We must do *something*,' her sister had said, when she'd heard that Derek was organising an evening out for Alex. 'The men can't have it all their own way.'

Hilary had said more or less the same thing before her wedding with Peter and had put together a night out in Manchester. Now, nine years older, they had both decided that a night in with a good video and a meal would be preferable to an exhausting night out on the tiles. Charlotte had been touched by the polite, almost tiptoey way Hilary had gone about things – normally she would have taken charge of the whole event, steamrollering everybody into turning up at the appointed time whether they wanted to or not. But not tonight. Instead, she had been most solicitous to Charlotte's request for a fuss-free evening. But her thoughtfulness had not stopped there. Hilary had remembered that Charlotte's all-time favourite film was *The Great Gatsby* and had bought the video specially. Even now Charlotte could recall how as teenagers they had gone to the cinema together and had sat in the front row both quietly drooling over Robert Redford.

'I hope this film isn't about male dominance—'

'Ssh, Tiffany!' both Hilary and Charlotte said, each knowing that Gatsby was about to make his entrance.

'When are we eating?' Tiffany asked, in a bored voice, tilting her head back and dropping a handful of nuts into her mouth. She was sick of men, especially one in particular. Nick Bradshaw, the arrogant ratbag! As if she'd ever shown any interest in him. 'I said, when are we eating?'

'Ssh!'

Bob Evans, the landlord of the Spinner, brought out the last of the steak and chips. 'Started snowing again,' he said, setting the plates on the table. He began to collect up the empty glasses. 'Another round?'

'Same again,' repeated Derek. 'I'm spitting feathers.' He dropped a dollop of Colman's on the side of his plate and offered the jar to James. 'So what tales have you got on our Alex, then?'

James looked at his brother and laughed. 'I reckon I spent nearly all my time bailing this idiot out of trouble at school.'

Derek raised an eyebrow. 'Round here he gives the impression butter wouldn't melt. Tell us more.'

'Nothing to tell,' Alex said, quickly. He had the feeling that, despite himself, his brother was beginning to enjoy the evening.

'We'll be the judge of that,' Malcolm said. 'Go on, James, I could do with a bit more background information for the service tomorrow.'

'Butter wouldn't melt, eh? As I remember it, he hated being told what to do. He was full of all that anti-Establishment bunkum and with the right provocation he could make James Dean look like a beatific Noddy high on LSD.'

Alex stuck a chip in his mouth, let it hang like a cigarette, and squinted. 'How's my belligerence rating now?'

'About as high as Mother Teresa's!' answered Stephen, with a laugh.

'Ah, of course, the best man,' Derek said, turning to him. 'You were students together, weren't you? You must have a regular cache of titbits for us. Fire away.'

'More cheesecake, anyone?' Hilary asked, standing in front of Tiffany.

'I can't see,' Tiffany said, her head moving from side to side as she tried to keep her eyes on the television.

'Changed her tune, hasn't she?' Charlotte whispered to Cindy, who nodded and helped herself to a second portion of dessert. Charlotte had never seen Cindy eat so much. Nor had she seen her drink wine before. It was strange when people started acting out of character.

'Everything all right upstairs?' she asked Sally when she came back into the room and sat cross-legged on the floor beside her.

'Fine. Mark's fast asleep. Have they got to the bit in the film where Daisy—?'

'Ssh!' hissed Tiffany.

Charlotte smiled to herself and glanced across the room at her sister. Despite all the trauma and uncertainty in Hilary's life right now, she was looking surprisingly calm and assured. Perhaps she had always underestimated Hilary. Then, in the background of her thoughts, she heard Tom Buchanan's arrogant voice, talking about people sneering at family life. She watched Hilary turn away from the screen, her eyes instantly dark with sadness. Like a swan, Charlotte thought, serene on the surface but paddling like crazy underneath.

Alex was almost disappointed in Derek. They were being tipped out of the Spinner and still nothing had happened. Where were the practical jokes? The cooking oil and feathers? The triple vodkas in the beer? The tart in nun's clothing? Perhaps Derek's behaviour had been tempered by having Barry with them for the evening – nothing like the presence of a child, even a grown-up one, to bring out the maturity in an adult.

'I'll be off home,' Malcolm said, peering out into the darkness at the snow-covered road. 'See you all tomorrow. Mind how you go.'

Shouldering each other to stay upright, they watched

Malcolm trudge through the snow, which was coming down so fast that his footsteps were almost immediately covered up.

'I've got an idea,' Derek said suddenly.

'Dad?' warned Barry.

Derek grinned. 'Follow me.'

'What are we doing here?' David asked, when at last they'd staggered to a stop in the churchyard. He swayed slightly as though the wind had caught him.

'We're going to build a pair of snowmen,' Derek said, 'like the figures on Alex's wedding cake tomorrow.'

They laughed, then James said, 'I've got a better idea.' He was sitting on top of a tombstone dangling his legs like a small child. There was no mistaking how drunk he was. The mistake was that none of the others realised that they were equally inebriated.

Chapter Thirty-three

Hilary looked at her daughter's implacable face and knew that it was the turd-in-the-potty syndrome all over again.

When Becky was sixteen months old she had, much to Hilary's delight and motherly pride, sat on Philip's old Thomas the Tank Engine potty and performed splendidly. Then, to a round of applause, Becky had stood up, seen what was behind her and had promptly burst into tears. She was horrified with what had come out of her tiny perfect body. From that moment, toilets and potties were no-go areas and served only to remind Becky that something ghastly had once happened to her. Until the age of two and a half she had clung tenaciously to her Pampers, her mind made up that she would never undergo a repeat performance of such abject humiliation. Hilary had tried all manner of chocolate-button bribery, together with persuasive arguments along the lines of, 'But everyone does it, Becky, even the Queen.' Such comments were sometimes met with quiet contempt but usually a full-blown Oscar-winning tantrum would be the response. Either way Becky would display a grim determination that she was not going to give in, or be taken in for that matter.

Hilary was face to face with that expression now. It was Christmas Eve, the morning of Charlotte and Alex's wedding and Becky, still in her pyjamas, was holding her bridesmaid's dress in one hand and a pair of kitchen scissors in the other.

'As a member of the Sisterhood I'd rather die than wear this dress.'

Becky's words were slow and well rehearsed and sounded more than a little absurd spoken by a seven-year-old. But Hilary knew her daughter well enough to understand that her words had the equivalent of a Herculean task force behind them. It was certain that Becky had no idea what Chloe was teaching her, but the whole thing was bound to appeal, given the club-membership perks on offer – immediate supremacy over her brother and the licence to rebel at will.

Hilary watched Becky flex open the kitchen scissors and decided that it was now or never to take control. She pounced on the dress, but Becky held on tightly, and the terrible but inevitable sound of ripping filled the gap between them. They stared in astonished silence at each other – Hilary because she didn't want to let herself believe her ears, and Becky because she was just beginning to wonder how much more courage she would need to remain Chloe's friend.

'So what do you suggest we do now, Becky?' Hilary asked, frighteningly calm.

Becky remained silent.

'Any ideas?' Hilary pushed on.

Still neither of them lowered their eyes, each lacking the courage to see just how much damage they had caused.

Becky opened her mouth to speak. She wanted to say sorry but she couldn't. Instead she could feel herself about to cry, like when she'd been told off at school last week for flooding the toilets. She had only meant to see what would happen when you unravelled a roll of toilet paper and stuffed it down the loo. How was she supposed to know that water would pour all over the floor? Mrs Wilson had been furious and had made her stand up in class the next morning and apologise to everyone. Mum didn't know about that ... but she did know about the dress. Then inspiration hit her. 'You shouldn't have tried to snatch it from me,' she said, in a clear loud voice. 'It's your fault I can't wear the dress. You'll have to tell Auntie Charlotte.'

Hilary stared in disbelief. Surely she had misheard. But no. There was Becky pushing the dress away and walking over to her unmade bed. She threw herself on top of the rumpled duvet and lay on her front, elbowing Peter Rabbit and Jemima Puddleduck out of the way as she opened and shut the scissors in her hands, snipping the air as though keeping in time to a piece of music.

The performance was breathtaking.

When and how had she gone so badly wrong? Hilary thought desperately. Then, as the satin fabric slipped through her fingers and dropped to the floor, she thought, To hell with that! Why did she always assume it was *she* who had gone wrong?

'I'm not sure I even want to be Auntie Charlotte's brides-maid any more,' Becky said, tossing away the scissors and turning over onto her back. She kicked both legs in the air above her head and did a neat roly-poly. She faced her mother once more. 'Chloe says marriage is like a verruca, the more you pick it the worse it gets, and then one day it just disappears.'

Hilary breathed in deeply. 'Perhaps,' she said slowly, 'you'd like to go over the road and share your pearls of wisdom with your aunt. Then maybe you'd like to tell her what a spoiled brat of a niece she has.'

Becky pouted. Spoiled brat? Her mother had never called her that before. Precious. Special. Clever. Brilliant. Beautiful. Lovely. Perfect. That's what she'd always called her. Indignation made her jump off the bed. 'I'm not a spoiled brat!' she screeched.

'Oh yes you are!'

It was Philip. He came into the bedroom and stood by his mother.

'How long have you been standing there, Big Ears?' Becky shouted.

'Long enough to know you've got a vending machine of a gob.'

Becky scowled and moved back to the bed. She picked up Peter Rabbit and held him to her.

'Right,' said Hilary, finding she was gaining strength from Philip standing next to her. 'You've got a couple of hours to sort yourself out, madam. You've created the problem as to what you're going to wear for my sister's wedding, so you can resolve it.' She turned to go, but then added, 'And a word of warning. If you make yourself look ridiculous everybody will laugh at you.'

When she was alone Becky rushed to the door and slammed it shut. She picked up the silky dress from the floor and looked at it reproachfully. Tears began to trickle down her cheeks and she stuffed her face into the cool fabric. It wasn't fair.

She sat on the bed and hunched herself up against the pillows. She thought about running away. That would show them. She got off the bed and went over to the window. It was misted up with condensation and a small pool of water had gathered in the mildewy corner of the frame. She wrote her name on the glass then drew a Christmas tree with a large star on the top. She placed her eye to the star and peered through it. It was snowing again. Perhaps running away wasn't such a good idea ... but she could hide for a while, couldn't she?

She quickly got dressed and wondered where nobody would think of looking for her.

Chapter Thirty-four

Alex was up first. After he'd showered and shaved he made a large cafetière of strong coffee. He took it through to the small sitting room where James and Stephen were still on the floor in sleeping bags. They looked like two gigantic comatose caterpillars.

He drew the curtains and stared out at the garden. It reminded him of a Brueghel landscape. The trunks and branches of the trees, darkened by the effect of so much snow, were set against a pewter sky. Laurel bushes and rhododendrons, almost buried in deep snowdrifts, drooped beneath the weight of last night's blizzard, and in the distance a crow landed on a branch and created its own mini snow-storm.

Alex turned his attention to the two sleeping bodies at his feet and rattled a spoon against an empty coffee mug. There was no response. He bent down on one knee, held the mug next to his brother's ear and rattled the spoon again.

'Go easy with that bell, won't you?'

'Not a bell, James, just an empty mug which I'm about to fill with coffee for you.'

Stephen slowly surfaced. 'Somebody mention coffee?' he asked with a yawn. Then with a sudden burst of movement he stretched out his arms above his head and punched James in the eye.

Sally stopped tying Mark's shoe-laces. 'Am I imagining

things, Charlotte, or did I just hear a scream from next door?'

Charlotte put her flowers down on the table and smiled. 'A scream followed by something quite rude is what I heard.'

'It didn't sound like Stephen?'

'Alex neither.'

'James, then,' Sally said, continuing with her son's shoe-laces. 'He's not at all like Alex, is he?'

The sound of crashing furniture and more outbursts of angry words made them turn towards the wall that backed onto 1a Ivy Cottage.

'Here,' Charlotte said, grabbing a glass and handing one to Sally. 'Let's have a proper listen.'

'Having fun, aren't they?' Sally said, as they jammed themselves up against the wall.

'What are you doing, Mummy?' asked a bemused Mark, who was unaware of the commotion next door.

Sally put down her glass and faced Mark so he could read her lips. 'We're listening to Daddy and Uncle Lex next door, they're having a fight.'

'A fight?' Mark looked worried.

'Not a real fight,' Charlotte said, kneeling in front of Mark, 'they're just being silly. Men are like that.'

She stood up, suddenly serious. 'Sally, you don't think it's all going to go disastrously wrong today, do you?'

Sally gave a loud laugh. 'Not disastrously wrong.' She put her glass against the wall again. 'But I have the sneaky feeling it could well be the funniest day of your life.'

As the bells rang out and the wedding guests arrived they were met by the sight of a six-foot fully erect penis against the west wall of St John's. It was quite complete in all its icy construction even down to a frozen ejaculatory spurt of semen.

'Busy last night, were you?' Malcolm greeted Alex's entourage when they made their appearance. They stared shamefaced at the sight of their handiwork – it looked bigger in daylight.

'Boys will be boys,' James said, sheepishly, from behind a pair of borrowed sunglasses.

'Hangover, or a bad case of snow blindness?' Malcolm enquired, looking at him. He also noticed that Alex was wearing a bandage on his left hand. Stephen, though, looked as if he'd come through the night unscathed. He led the way towards the front of the church. The gathering congregation were in buoyant mood, laughing over what they'd just seen outside. It struck Malcolm as odd, however, that they all looked so red in the face. Blushing? Surely not.

'I should watch yourselves,' Malcolm said, reaching out to Alex as he skidded slightly off balance. 'The floor seems a tad slippery today. Must be all this snow people are bringing in on their shoes.'

They paused at the front reserved pew just as James slid to a halt. He reached out to a long mahogany candle holder at the end of the pew and snapped it clean in two. It crashed on top of his head, knocking his sunglasses to the floor.

Malcolm flinched. 'Heck of a black eye you've got there. How—'

'Don't ask,' growled James, scrabbling on the floor for his sunglasses.

Malcolm picked up the broken candle holder. 'Right,' he said, 'seeing as you're the usher, James, I need you to come back to the porch with me.'

'Do I have to move? This aisle's like a bloody ice rink.'

Malcolm laughed. 'Come on. You can hang on to me if you like.'

'Bloody odd show you've got here,' grumbled James as he followed behind. 'Most unorthodox.'

'I assure you we're straightforward Anglican.'

'What the—!' This time there was nothing for James to reach out for. Malcolm helped him to his feet. 'I'm all right,' he said bad-humouredly. Red-faced, he dusted down his suit and inched his way towards what he hoped was the safety of the porch. 'If I'd known it was going to be like this I'd have brought snow chains,' he muttered.

Neville eased his gleaming Volvo carefully out of Charlotte's driveway. Everywhere was inches deep in snow with a treacherous layer of ice beneath, and he drove painfully slowly down Acacia Lane. At the end of the road he turned into Daisy Bank and glanced up to look in his rear-view mirror. He caught a glimpse of Charlotte in the back of the car. She looked beautiful.

'I wouldn't have minded walking,' said Becky, who was sitting next to Charlotte.

In the front passenger seat Hilary turned round. 'So that you could have worn wellington boots up the aisle, no doubt, just to finish off your attractive attire.'

'Becky looks fine,' Charlotte said, in an effort to keep the peace.

Becky took a sideways peek at her aunt. 'Do you really think so?'

'Yes,' Charlotte said, looking at Becky's wrinkled black leggings and oversized check shirt. She hadn't liked the dress Hilary had chosen in the first place.

'And is my hair okay?'

'Really suits you,' Charlotte answered truthfully. Becky had done her own hair and had tied it up into two stubby bunches either side of her head – she looked like a little devil complete with horns.

'You don't mind me not wearing—'

'I told you, you look great.'

Becky almost felt guilty about the ripped dress now. After she'd got dressed earlier in the morning she had come up with the perfect hiding-place. The only trouble was that no one had come to look for her and she'd got bored all on her own and had then gone home, only to find that nobody had missed her anyway. She'd stayed in her bedroom, then, and spent ages trying to decide what to wear and fiddling about with her hair. She was glad Auntie Charlotte liked it.

Neville slowly manoeuvred the car alongside the pavement on the north side of the church. A sudden tooting of a horn from behind made him slam his foot down hard on the brake pedal. But instead of the brake he hit the accelerator and lurched the car into the Volvo in front. 'Oh my God! Oh my God!' he panicked. 'What have I done?' His face was white with shock. He looked round to check his passengers.

'Calm down, Dad,' said Charlotte, picking up her posy of red and white carnations. 'We're all fine.'

'Hilary?'

Hilary turned to her father, and with a strange smile on her lips, said, 'That's David's car in front.'

Another toot from behind made them open the doors and start to get out. They were greeted by Barry coming towards them. 'You okay?'

'We're all fine,' Charlotte said calmly.

Barry went round to the front of the car and stopped to pick up a piece of smashed headlamp in the snow. 'I told Dad not to hit the horn.'

Tiffany came over, followed by Cindy, her face wreathed in concern. Derek, who was oblivious to what he had caused, sauntered towards them and let out a long whistle. 'Charlotte, have I ever told you how ravishing you—'

'Derek, this is certainly not the time or the place to be trying your luck.'

'Cindy, as if I would.' He faced Charlotte and grinned. 'Bit cheeky of you to go for white, don't you think?'

Charlotte laughed and pulled the fur-lined hood that formed part of the Cossack-style dress over her head. 'I'm freezing, can we get a move on?'

'Allow me,' said Derek, offering his arm.

'That's my job,' Neville said, and with his composure fully restored he pushed Derek's arm aside and, with all the grandeur he could muster, steered Charlotte towards the lychgate.

As the small party made its way up the path – their eyes to the ground as they picked their way through the snow – Charlotte let out a sudden laugh. She had just caught sight of the large penis. Her poor father stood still, his face white with shock again.

Derek stared appreciatively. 'Now that's what I call—'

'What is it, Mummy?' interrupted Becky.

'It's a ...' Hilary looked around for help.

'Could be a bottle of champagne,' Barry suggested.

'Yes,' said Tiffany, smirking, 'it's just been opened, you can see the bubbles coming out of the end.'

'That's enough, you two,' said Cindy.

'Well, I think you're wrong,' Becky said, her voice matter-of-fact. 'It looks like an enormous willy to me.' She ran on ahead and waited for them in the porch.

Malcolm greeted Charlotte; he looked hot and flustered. 'Here at last,' he said, relieved. 'A word of warning, make sure you—'

But his words were lost as Mr Phelps, eager to get on, caught sight of Charlotte and started up with Mendelssohn's Bridal March.

'Oh, never mind,' muttered Malcolm, and he started to walk tentatively up the aisle. To Charlotte's surprise he almost fell over. Drunk? It would explain his red face. She watched him reach out to the back of the pew and saw that in front of him one of the decorative candle holders lay in pieces on the floor.

'I think we'd better sit down,' Hilary said to Cindy, 'or we'll spoil Charlotte's big entrance. Let's hope David and Philip have saved us a pew.' She turned to Becky. 'Now, you know what to do, don't you?'

'Go on,' urged Neville, 'leave her to us.'

Derek led the way and straight away found the going slippery. Miraculously they managed to reach the safety of a pew and, thinking that he was home and dry, Derek sat down and slid clean off the wooden seat, his knees firmly planted on a hassock.

'Say one for me while you're down there,' giggled Tiffany.

'I'm not bloody praying!' he hissed. 'Help me up, won't you? God, but it's hot in here, I'm sweating cobs.'

As Barry and Tiffany helped their father, Charlotte and Neville, followed by Becky, made their entrance. Someone from the congregation yelled out, 'Steady as you go, it's as slippery as hell out there.'

'And about as hot,' joined in somebody else.

By the time Charlotte stood beside Alex she was stiff with concentration and her face felt like cement with the effort of trying not to laugh. 'Okay?' he whispered.

She pushed back the hood of her dress. 'I feel like Maria Vetsera in this.'

'Just so long as I don't have to agree to a suicide pact. It's turning into a bit of a farce, isn't it?'

Charlotte looked at his bandaged hand and then at James on the other side of Stephen. 'What have you all been—'

'If you don't mind,' Malcolm interrupted, tiredly. He ran a finger round the inside of his collar, then wiped at the sweat that was beading on his forehead. 'It's Christmas tomorrow and I've still got my shopping to do, so can we get on?'

'Yes, Malcolm,' laughed Charlotte. She lifted her eyes up to the ceiling bosses and thanked God that Sally had been right – this was fast becoming the funniest day in her life.

As Malcolm started the ceremony she looked at Alex out of the corner of her eye and gave his hand a squeeze.

He winced and withdrew his bandaged hand.

Chapter Thirty-five

'Goodness! I suppose you really are quite married? It was all such a fiasco it's hard to know.'

Alex handed his mother a glass of sweet sherry. 'I think it was when the boiler blew that I really felt things were getting a bit out of hand.'

'Out of hand,' his father repeated, eschewing the sherry and helping himself to a tumbler of Famous Grouse. 'It was wonderful. The whole thing was tremendous. Never seen anything like it. Not many wedding guests leave behind them a trail of devastation like we just have. I counted at least two twisted ankles, a platoon of firemen, not to mention a rather flaccid John Thomas.'

'I thought Malcolm was drunk when I saw him,' laughed Charlotte, 'he looked so flushed and then when I saw him nearly fall over—'

'It was the heat from the boiler,' Alex said, 'it was getting to us all.'

'And to your handiwork outside,' Charlotte said, with a grin. 'The boiler backs onto the west wall.'

'Doesn't explain why the floor was like a black run, though, does it?' Alex's father said. 'By the way, how did your brother get that shiner?'

'Yes, tell us what the three of you were getting up to this morning. Sally and I heard you through the wall, but couldn't for the life of us work out what was going on.'

'It was Stephen.'

'Not maliciously so,' said Stephen, coming over and

stooping slightly to avoid one of the beams in Louise and Neville's sitting room, to where they'd all escaped for the reception, leaving poor Malcolm to sort out the mess at St John's.

'It was you who punched James in the eye then knocked the coffee all over my hand.'

Stephen shrugged his shoulders. 'Just as well I'm a doctor, then.'

'Thought I was going to need a doctor at the start of that service,' joined in Derek. He was carrying a plate piled high with cold meat and salad. 'My bum slipped off the pew that fast. What the hell do the good ladies of the parish use to polish those pews? T-Cut?' He bit into a large pickled onion and chomped noisily.

'Don't go blaming me for your inability to sit down properly,' Iris Braithwaite called from an armchair by the log fire where she was comfortably settled in her fur coat with a pot of tea by her side. A wide-brimmed hat perched on her head gave her an elegant and superior air and went a long way to disguising her disfigured face. 'I can assure you Mrs Haslip and I have not polished those pews in over three months. Have you any idea of the price of beeswax, Mr Rogers? Perhaps if you contributed more to the running costs of St John's we—'

'Got your drift, Mrs B. I'll think on it,' Derek replied, poking out a piece of onion from between his front teeth. 'It did look like fate was determined to keep you two apart,' he said to Charlotte. 'Maybe the Big Fella up in heaven doesn't approve of your earthly match. I reckon it was a wrathful thunderbolt that made the boiler blow up.'

'Ignore him, Charlotte,' Barry said, over his father's shoulder.

Charlotte noticed the badge pinned to the lapel of Barry's suit: 'Without Jesus at Christmas You're a Dead Turkey.' She smiled at him and he winked at her. How he had changed. Just over a year away at university and he'd lost all his nervousness and was now completely at ease with himself and, Charlotte suspected, at ease with his father.

'I hope you're aware, Dad,' Barry said, 'that Malcolm thinks it was you who sabotaged the church and the service.'

'Now why on earth would Malcolm think I had anything to do with it? I mean, Charlotte's like a sister to me. Why would I want to spoil her big day?'

Alex laughed, and Charlotte said, 'Seriously, though, it was you, wasn't it, who turned up the heating too high, changed the hymn numbers and did heaven knows what to the floor to make it so dangerous?'

Derek shook his head. 'Hand on heart. Not guilty. The only crime I'll admit to is my share of the artwork outside St John's.' He gave Charlotte a nudge. 'Modelled on me, of course.'

'Don't you believe it.'

'Ah, Cindy,' Derek said, draping his arm loosely round her shoulder.

'Seen Tiffany?' she asked.

'She herded the children upstairs ten minutes ago to watch a video,' Barry answered.

'That's right,' Louise said, coming among them with a tray of chicken nuggets and chips. 'I'm on my way up there now with this little lot.'

'I didn't know you had a telly upstairs, Mother.'

'Lots you don't know about me, Charlotte. When your father's fallen asleep I need something to amuse me, so I bought myself a clever television with a natty little built-in video player. I saw one of those interesting Tarantino movies the other night. One has to get one's pleasure somehow.'

'You'll have to excuse my mother,' Charlotte said to Alex's parents, when Louise had disappeared. 'She has a strange sense of humour.' She was conscious that Peter's parents had always acted like 'Horrified of Aldershot' whenever the two families had got together. She wondered how last night had gone: her parents had offered to have Angela and Toby

Hamilton to stay with them. She hoped her mother had behaved.

'She's an interesting and colourful woman,' Toby said, crinkling his eyes approvingly.

'You make her sound like a Jackson Pollock painting.'

'Language, Mrs Lawrence ... I mean, Mrs Hamilton,' Iris called once again from the fireplace.

'So, then,' Angela said, slowly and deliberately, looking first at Charlotte then at Alex. 'Grandchildren.'

'Banging on the wrong door there, I shouldn't wonder,' Derek said, waving a cold sausage in Alex's direction.

'Derek!'

'Yes, Cindy?'

'I'd like a glass of wine.'

'But you don't drink wine,' he said, incredulously.

'I do now.'

Derek sloped off.

'Now, about these grandchildren,' Angela tried again.

Alex rolled his eyes.

'And we're banking on you, Charlotte, to get Alex back into a proper job. Children need a father who's bringing in a regular salary.'

'Attaboy, Dad,' agreed James, who was over by the window talking to Hilary.

'You always could sniff out an argument, couldn't you?' Alex answered, good-humouredly.

James came over. 'Am I right in thinking, then, that Charlotte is pregnant and this is in fact a shotgun wedding?'

'No,' said Charlotte, her voice slightly raised. 'I am not pregnant.'

'Conceived out of wedlock but at least born within it,' chipped in Iris.

'No, Mrs Braithwaite,' Charlotte said, horrified, and in a loud voice she said as clearly as she could, 'I said I am *not* pregnant.'

'There there, Charlotte,' Derek said, reappearing with a

glass of wine for Cindy and putting his arm round Charlotte. 'Don't take on so. If Alex can't cut the mustard I know a man who can.'

Cindy took a sausage roll from Derek's plate, stuffed it into his mouth, then dragged him over to talk to Hilary who was now standing all alone.

It had started snowing again when everyone gathered outside in the dark to see Charlotte and Alex off.

Becky stood in front of her mother and next to Mark. They had spent most of the afternoon together and, despite all Chloe's warnings about boys being stupid and growing up into selfish men, she had found herself enjoying the company of this quiet thoughtful boy. He had told her he was deaf and that if she spoke slowly he'd be able to read her lips and understand what she was saying. He'd even told her she was very good at it. It was then that she'd decided to tell him what she'd done. He had laughed and told her he thought she was very funny.

She was bursting now to tell somebody else.

She looked at her Auntie Charlotte through the open window of the car and, seeing her so happy, she stepped forward and said, 'You didn't mind about everything at the church, did you?'

Charlotte smiled back at her. 'I wouldn't have missed it for the world.'

'Good.'

Charlotte hesitated and then laughed. 'For a moment there, Becky, I had the craziest of feelings that maybe you had something to do with it.' She then stopped laughing. 'Becky, you didn't, did you?'

Becky beamed. 'It *was* me,' she said proudly. 'I went over to the church this morning because I was so cross with Mummy. I hid there, but then nobody came to look for me and I got bored and ...'

Everybody around the car, including Hilary, was staring

at Becky but, blissfully unaware, she carried on, '. . . and I went into that funny little room at the back and found some cans of polish. I started spraying one of the pews, then the floor . . . I thought it looked so dirty. Then I got cold and so I fiddled with the boiler . . . I've seen Mummy do it when she does the flowers . . . It was funny when it exploded, wasn't it?'

Nobody spoke, but when Charlotte saw the expression on David's face, she whispered to Alex, 'Start the engine before we get caught up in another explosion.'

Becky's confessional timing was perfect. As Charlotte and Alex drove slowly away, another car appeared. It was Nanna and Grandpa Parker. They had arrived too late for the wedding, but in time for Christmas.

Chapter Thirty-six

The Parker Seniors followed the Parker Juniors back to Acacia Lane. Barbara and Jeffrey were listening to the closing moments of the afternoon play on Radio Four – a nineties inner-city interpretation of *The Little Match Girl* – and Hilary, David, Philip and Becky were listening hard to nothing in particular. Nobody seemed inclined to speak. Hilary wanted to but was terrified of laughing.

She tried to excuse herself on the grounds of too much wine and champagne that afternoon, but she knew that wasn't the real reason behind the bubble of mirth rising within her. Every time she recalled Charlotte and Alex standing at the altar and Malcolm pronouncing them man and wife she thought of the explosion that had come only seconds later from the boiler room next to the vestry. And trust old Derek to have his mobile phone with him so that they could call for the fire brigade.

The funny thing was that she didn't feel at all cross with Becky. By rights she should be punished and if David had his way she would be, but Hilary had no intention of taking her daughter to task. She couldn't remember a time when she had laughed more.

She felt her face breaking into a smile even now, and turned to look out of the window as they pulled up at The Gables. The children leapt out of the car at once, as if they were glad to escape the threatening silence, and started scooping up handfuls of snow. Inside The Gables the timer device had automatically switched on the lights, including the pretty fairy lights on the Christmas tree in the sitting room and the house beckoned welcomingly.

It wasn't by any means the smartest or most attractive property in the village but Hilary had loved the beautifully proportioned Edwardian house from the moment they had viewed it and had wanted David to make an offer to the owners there and then. Six months later they had moved in – Philip had been five at the time and in his first term at school, and Becky had been a wobbly toddler just finding her feet.

'You love this house, don't you, Hilary?' David said, unexpectedly at her side.

She froze. What was he saying? That he was leaving her and they'd have to sell it? Was that it?

'What do you mean?' she said, turning slowly to face him. She was shocked to see how tired he seemed. There were lines around his eyes, shadows even. And had he lost weight? She couldn't remember the last time she had sat this close to him and looked at his face, *really* looked at it.

To her annoyance she found herself feeling sorry for him, but this was one emotion she didn't want and immediately she stamped on it. 'What do you mean?' she repeated, her voice hardened with resolve.

'I just meant . . .' He, too, now stared up at the house. 'Oh, nothing,' he said, and got out of the car to help his parents with their luggage.

'Oh, nothing to hell and back!' Hilary muttered as she unlocked the front door and walked through to the kitchen. Hadn't Cindy warned her that she might lose the house? She covered her face with her hands and leaned against the Aga. She felt miserable. And furious. Furious that her future lay so hopelessly in the hands of a man who no longer loved her.

She reached for the kettle, knowing that at any moment Barbara would come waddling into the house bringing with her half a dozen suitcases and enough edible 'contributions' to stock an entire corner shop. She turned on the tap and felt the familiar feelings of isolation and alienation she experienced whenever David's parents stayed with them. David was their only son and between them they never missed a chance to take the credit for having treated the world to such a splendid chap.

When Hilary had first met David's parents she had assumed that their comments towards their son and about him were heavily loaded with sarcasm – in those days she knew no other kind of parental affection, having been fed all her life a continuous diet of sarcasm by her mother. But then it had slowly dawned on Hilary that Barbara and Jeffrey were in earnest: in their eyes they had quite literally produced a Christ-like super-being.

She put the kettle on the Aga and noticed Becky's cut-out nativity scene tucked behind an open packet of shortbread and a tissue box. She smiled. There they were, the Parker clan – Barbara kneeling at the manger with Jeffrey standing dutifully behind, the pair of them gazing down at the world's Saviour in among the straw.

Well, by the end of this Christmas dear old Barbara and Jeffrey were in for one hell of a shock. They'd produced a Judas, not a Jesus. And just how would they come to terms with that?

Heavy footsteps told Hilary that Barbara was heading this way.

'Hilary, there you are. I've brought you some Darjeeling, I know how much you like it. And never mind that it's almost twice the cost of PG Tips.'

'Thank you, Barbara,' Hilary said, bracing herself for the rest of her mother-in-law's offerings from the large box she was carrying into the kitchen. She hated Darjeeling. It was Earl Grey she liked. She had told Barbara that a million and one times, but the simple message had never once penetrated those ghastly grey poodle-perm curls. She watched her lower the heavy box to the floor, her wide-skirted bottom sticking up in the air revealing a large area of dough-like flesh bulging over the top of a pair of brown pop-sox.

'Dates. I've brought you some stuffed dates. Just how David likes them.'

'Lovely.' Hilary took them and plonked them on the worktop.

'A pot of damson jam. Home-made, of course.'

'Naturally.'

'Mince pies. Reduced. I simply couldn't let them go in the supermarket this morning.'

'Super.' They'll go nicely with the four dozen in the freezer and the two dozen in the pantry.

'Lime marmalade. David's always had that on his toast ever since he was a boy. I know how fond he is of it.'

'Wonderful.' These days he has orange.

'Coffee. Real coffee beans. I thought I'd treat David. That decaff you give him is all very well, but it's got no taste.'

'How thoughtful.' Yes, why don't you go ahead and just poison him for me? Save us all a lot of trouble.

'Turkish Delight. Do you remember the Christmas when David ate so much he made himself—?'

'Yes, Barbara. I remember cleaning the bathroom afterwards.'

'Poor boy. He never did know when to say no.'

Oh, how true. 'Well, Barbara, how about I put all this away while you go upstairs and sort yourself out? You must be exhausted from your journey.' Come on, Hilary, show her whose house this is!

'A cup of tea while I'm in the bath would be most agreeable.'

'Good idea. You go ahead and I'll send David up with a—'

'No, no, no. The poor boy's exhausted. Let him have a glass of whisky in the drawing room with Jeffrey. He must be so upset after Neville crashing into his car like that. How careless of your father. Don't forget the ice, will you?'

'Ice?'

'In their whisky.'

'Sure you wouldn't like one?'

Barbara let off a laugh that sounded as cheery as a fire bell. 'Hilary, I sometimes wonder about you. You know perfectly well that whisky's a man's drink.' Her foot already on the lower step of the stairs, she called back, 'Just the one sugar in my tea.'

'Man's drink indeed,' Hilary said, lifting the kettle off the Aga and filling the teapot. But, then, Barbara had always been obsessed with gender, especially one's femininity – this from a woman who had tufts of whiskers growing from a large mole on her cheek!

Hilary crept past the family bathroom where she could hear Barbara finally running the bathwater away – she'd been in there for over an hour, having consumed two cups of tea and a plate of Hobnobs.

Hilary held her breath until she was in her own bathroom and the door was firmly locked. She exhaled deeply, put the plug in the bath and ran the water.

She lay in it, cosseted by the knowledge that she was safe for at least the next twenty minutes. She had given David – the poor exhausted boy – strict instructions to keep an eye on the crown of lamb in the Aga and to put the new potatoes on in exactly twelve minutes' time. When she'd asked him to do this simple menial task she had been given the usual baleful-eye treatment by her father-in-law and had half expected him to say, 'She'd never have got away with that with me' – Hilary always awarded Jeffrey a broad Yorkshire accent when she imagined him speaking, it seemed so apt for his chauvinistic character, whereas in fact he was as clear-vowelled as any southerner she knew. What he had actually said as Hilary had handed him his second whisky was, 'Indispensable, David, that's what you are. You spoil Hilary, you really do. She's a lucky girl.'

Hilary sank deep into the water, her frilly shower hat

clamped tightly on her head. 'Indispensable. Well, we'll soon see, won't we?'

At the end of the bath, among the baskets of toiletries and bottles of shampoo, Captain Scarlet and Mr Blobby stared back at her – they had been decamped from the family bathroom to make room for Barbara's armoury of Bronnley products. Captain Scarlet was down on one knee, his head twisted round so that he was staring over his shoulder at Hilary. Mr Blobby, with both his arms raised in the air, had lost the dot from one of his eyes and he looked as if he was winking salaciously at her. Hilary didn't like the way they were both eyeing her and slapped her knees together.

Stupid thing! she told herself with a smile. They're only bottles of bubble bath – anyone would think they were Derek or Nick sitting there.

She hadn't seen much of Nick recently and she wondered what he would be doing for Christmas and why she had just thought of him. She closed her eyes and for the sheer fun of it tried to imagine him kissing her again. Disappointed, she found she couldn't. His face eluded her, as did his lips. How unfair that she couldn't even fantasise adultery, whereas David was busy doing the real thing.

She glanced at her watch, in front of Mr Blobby's left foot. In two minutes' time poor exhausted David would have to stagger along to the kitchen. She reached for the bar of soap and began washing herself. She scrubbed her neck, shoulders and breasts hurriedly and uncaringly, her eyes staring straight ahead, unable even to view her own body for fear of coming to the dreadful conclusion that, perhaps, here lay the reason for David's rejection.

She tried to think of something different as she carried on washing. Charlotte and Alex. Had they arrived at their honeymoon destination yet? Everyone had tried to prise out of Alex where he was taking Charlotte, but he had parried their questions effortlessly. Louise had joked that he was taking her back to Brussels. How typical of their mother to make a joke in such poor taste.

There was a loud rap at the door.

'Hilary, you're needed in the kitchen.' It was Barbara.

'I told David what needed doing,' Hilary answered.

'We can't find the salt for the potatoes.'

'I never put salt in . . .' Oh, what was the point? She tugged on the plug chain and reached for a towel. 'Coming.'

Later that night, when supper had passed without incident and the children had gone to bed in a state of Christmas Eve fever, Hilary left David and his parents reminiscing on his days of glory as the most perfect child ever. She put on her warmest coat, donned a hat, scarf and gloves and escaped into the snow for midnight mass.

At the top of Daisy Bank she could see the village hall. Unusually for Christmas Eve it was brightly lit and she could make out people moving about inside. As she drew nearer she noticed a piece of paper stuck to the door. She went over and read it: 'St John's out of action – midnight mass here.'

Hilary stepped inside. Rows of chairs were set out with a small central aisle. Most seats were occupied and everyone was chattering and laughing. It was more like a party than a church service.

'Over here, Hilary.'

Hilary was surprised to see Georgia waving to her from a row of seats near the back. Next to her was Chloe – she was the only child there as far as Hilary could make out.

'Hello,' Hilary said, when she'd eventually squeezed along the row of knees.

Georgia kissed her on the cheek. 'And before you pop a shot at me, this is the one and only time I ever come to church because, as everyone knows, it doesn't really count. What's up? You look exhausted.'

'In-laws. They've arrived.'

'No worries. You'll lose them when you divorce David.'

Hilary looked shocked.

'Oops. Being too blunt, am I? Tell me what you think Santa's bringing you instead.'

Hilary turned her sapphire and diamond engagement ring round on her finger. The stones caught a beam of light from a fluorescent tube overhead and sparkled brightly. 'I suppose I'd rather like Santa to bring me a ready-made solution,' she said thoughtfully.

Georgia squeezed her hand. 'I hate to put a dampener on things but he can only bring you what you've asked him for.'

They heard a loud tut from further along the row. It was Patricia, leaning forward and staring in disgust at Georgia's hand covering Hilary's. They looked at one another and laughed loudly. Enjoying the unfamiliar sensation of knowing she was misbehaving, Hilary pulled a face and mimicked Patricia's admonishment. 'Tut-tut,' she clicked with her tongue. She then wondered if this was how Becky often felt.

It was strange, but when she really thought about the shenanigans Becky had got up to earlier that day she had to admit to a curious sense of pride in her daughter. When she had been Becky's age she had never done anything naughtier than sneak the raisins from the Whitworth's packet in the larder. Small-time compared to Becky's exploits. Single-handedly, in one day, she had caused more mayhem at St John's than your average person would in a lifetime. Extra-ordinary. But how exciting and liberating to know that you alone had been responsible for so much. Oh, to be that rebellious, to have that freedom of self. Lucky Becky! And what if she herself was to be so cavalier? What would she do and to whom would she do it? Quick as a flash, Jeffrey and Barbara came into Hilary's mind. Odd that they should receive her first strike. Or was it? Wasn't it all their fault that David was the way he was – the sins of the father and all that?

She was just smiling to herself when the hall was plunged into darkness.

'Sorry!'

The lights immediately came back on. 'Sorry,' the voice repeated, 'caught it with my shoulder.'

Hilary looked up to see Derek by the light switches. He was holding the door open for his family. They came and sat behind Hilary and Georgia. Derek kissed Hilary and shook hands with Georgia. 'It was Bas's idea we came,' he said, by way of explanation. 'Cindy was all for an early night, but I said if my lad Bas wants us to go to midnight mass then the rumpy-pumpy will just have to go on hold.'

'A little louder, Dad.' Tiffany smirked. 'I don't think they heard at the front.'

Derek winked at his daughter, then put his arm round Cindy's shoulders.

How like Becky Derek was, Hilary reflected, as she turned to face the altar. Quite simply, the pair of them didn't give a damn.

'Good evening, everyone,' Malcolm greeted his congregation. He looked a lot less flustered than he had earlier, Hilary decided, as he stood behind his makeshift altar of two covered trestle tables. 'As you all know we had one or two surprises at St John's this afternoon, which is why we're assembled here.'

'What d'yer mean, surprises?' heckled Derek. 'We were fannying around doing more triple axels than Torvill and Dean.'

'Quite,' continued Malcolm, 'but I'd like us all to take this opportunity to pray for St John's to be back in action as soon as possible ... and for the person responsible for the chaos to stay out of my way until I've had a chance to cool down.'

Hilary lowered her head, hoping to goodness that nobody from the wedding reception had had an opportunity to talk to Malcolm. She felt Derek nudging her from behind. 'You praying extra hard, Hilary?' he whispered.

The first carol was 'Hark! the Herald Angels Sing', and as

the congregation let rip with merry gusto Hilary thought of Charlotte. It was her sister's favourite carol. Suddenly she felt sad. She wanted Charlotte here with her. It was quite likely that the next time she saw Charlotte her life would be very different. It was then that she knew with absolute certainty exactly what she wanted from Santa.

She wanted the courage to tell David that she'd had enough.

Chapter Thirty-seven

'Louise, happy Christmas!'

'You too, Barbara.'

The two women faced each other with all the warmth and enthusiasm of a pair of sumo wrestlers. Louise stepped over the threshold of The Gables and thought how fortunate she was that she and Neville had no cause to go to Peterborough and that Barbara's visits to Cheshire were limited to a minimum.

'Hilary's in the kitchen and I'm afraid to report that the turkey went in far too late.' Barbara's voice was low and confidential as if she was breaking the news that a loved one was at death's door with only minutes to live.

Here we go, Louise said to herself, rule-the-roost Babs telling tales again. But what poor, stupid Babs couldn't get into her tea-cosy of a head was that she didn't give a damn how inefficiently Hilary ran her life and The Gables. As far as Louise was concerned, Hilary could cavort naked in the kitchen partnering the turkey for a tango with a Christmas pudding shoved up its—

'David's absolutely shattered,' Barbara said, with a little wobble of her head. She took Louise's coat, then Neville's. 'I wonder whether you could have a word with Hilary,' she burbled from the depths of the under-stairs cupboard. 'Not exactly what you'd call spick and span in here,' she added.

'What do you want us to say to Hilary?' Louise asked, reaching out her hands as if to close the cupboard door on Barbara. Neville smiled and walked away.

Barbara finally emerged, a sticky cobweb clinging to a grey curl. Louise decided not to tell her it was there.

'I think Hilary expects too much from David,' Barbara said, smoothing out the creases in her new Christmas frock. She produced a neatly folded handkerchief from her sleeve and blew her nose. 'So much dust in there.' She blasted noisily a second time into the small square of embroidered linen.

'In what way, exactly?' Louise was intrigued.

'I'm sure you must have noticed how tired David's looking,' Barbara stepped closer to Louise and added, 'to say nothing of the atmosphere.'

Perhaps only since you arrived, Louise thought. 'To be honest I think it's Hilary who's worn out. Ever thought that your son might be expecting too much of his wife?' Louise had no grounds for suggesting such a thing, but why should dreary old Babs have it all her own way?

Barbara gave a dismissive laugh. 'Louise, dear. I've been here barely twenty-four hours, but grant me sufficient intelligence to detect which way the wind is blowing. Your Hilary is constantly asking David to do a never-ending number of jobs around the house. Little jobs that Hilary's quite capable of doing herself. Call me old-fashioned, but the kitchen really is the woman's domain.' She gave off another irritating laugh.

Louise wanted to grab the nearest object to hand.

'I think you've spoiled your girls,' Barbara went on. 'You taught them to expect too much.' She smiled, as though her opinion would be welcomed as an enormous act of kindness. 'Let's join the others for a glass of Christmas sherry. We've brought some of our favourite. Especially dry.'

'I'll have a gin and tonic,' Louise said, through clenched teeth. 'Especially strong, please.' Bloody queen bee, she scowled as she followed Barbara in her fluffy mules through to the kitchen. Why couldn't she just sting herself and have done with it?

'Mother,' said Hilary with a potato peeler in her hand and

a harassed expression on her face. 'Happy Christmas.'

Louise embraced her and whispered in her ear, 'How long's the witch staying this time?'

'Five days,' Hilary whispered back.

'You poor devil,' Louise said, her arms uncharacteristically still round her daughter's shoulders. She then stepped back and in a louder voice, said, 'Goodness, all these guests staying and no one to help with the vegetables. Here, let me give you a hand.'

Both Hilary and Neville stared at Louise in surprise. Louise never offered to help in the kitchen, or anywhere else for that matter. 'Where's David and the children?' Neville asked, by way of conversation.

'Dear David's upstairs with Becky and Philip,' answered Barbara. 'He's loading a new game on to the computer. I think that's the correct expression, isn't it?' She looked around the kitchen as if waiting for a burst of applause. 'Ah, there you are, Jeffrey,' she said, as her husband appeared in the doorway with a tray of filled sherry glasses. He was dressed in a smart double-breasted grey suit and his shoes gleamed as if they'd been treated to a lick of black gloss paint. Neville fiddled with the top button of his old tweed jacket and rubbed one of his Hush Puppies on the back of his trouser leg.

'I thought it was about time for a sherry,' Jeffrey announced.

Barbara beamed. 'Call me old-fashioned but I do think a man should pour out the drinks, don't you? It's like carving the turkey. It's proper etiquette for the man of the house to carve.'

'Well, let's hope David won't be too exhausted to carry out that onerous task later on this afternoon,' Louise said, attacking a potato with a small knife. 'Though doubtless Jeffrey or Neville could step into the breach if one of us poor idiotic females couldn't manage it. Personally I love nothing better than carving up an old bird, especially a dumb old bird.'

Hilary joined her mother at the sink. Normally it was she who was on the end of her mother's tongue – it was good to hear somebody else coming in for a good lashing.

'I rather think Louise has been sleeping in the cutlery drawer again,' Barbara said with a patronising little laugh. She ran her hand over her sculptured hair and found the cobweb. She pulled a face.

Go on, Mother, Hilary silently urged, say something else. In the past she had always seen herself in the role of a peacemaker. Now to her surprise she found herself wanting to encourage her mother to fight on, but not only that: she found herself wishing that she could be more like her maverick mother. She cut a potato in half and plopped it into the saucepan on the draining board, thinking that only yesterday she had been wishing she was more like her daughter. She had never before thought that Becky was anything like Louise, but it was as plain as the nose on her face that Becky was exactly like Louise. And didn't Charlotte have that same rebellious streak of not wanting to conform? So why had she always been such a Goody Two Shoes? Why had she missed out on the genes of nonconformity? Or had they always been there but she had suppressed them?

With the sound of polite conversation in the background about the quality of the amontillado they were drinking, Hilary reached in front of her mother for another potato.

'Silly old witch,' Louise muttered. 'Does David really mean that much to you that you can put up with her?'

'No,' Hilary said, without thinking.

Her mother looked at her.

Hilary stared at the potato in her hand.

'Hilary?'

She looked up and met her mother's questioning gaze. 'I didn't mean—' she started to say, then she thought of her decision made during midnight mass and what lay ahead of her. 'I meant exactly what I just said,' she said. Her voice quiet but firm.

'I see,' was all Louise said. She turned the tap on and rinsed her hands. 'I suppose you'll eventually get around to telling me what's going on here.'

Barry was wearing another of his badges. Derek wondered how many more his son had. Today's was 'Stuff the Turkey, Not Jesus!' He smiled and looked down at his plate. An enormous half-eaten turkey leg stared back at him along with a lone sprout. He didn't know about the turkey but he felt pretty stuffed himself. He leaned back in his chair, picked up his glass of Hunter Valley red and took a large mouthful. Contentment flowed through him. He was one hell of a happy man.

He noticed that Cindy was staring at him. He noticed, too, the smile on her face as she twirled her wine glass round between her fingers. Strange that she should have suddenly taken to drinking wine ... odd, also, the way she was looking at him. Self-conscious, he turned his attention to Tiffany on his right.

There she was, gorgeous, angry Tiffany. His little girl, all but grown-up now. He thought of all those years of confrontation with her. How the hell they'd survived he didn't have a clue, especially Cindy who had borne the brunt of Tiffany's toddler to teenager tantrums. He looked over to his wife and found she was still staring at him, and there was that smile again.

Bloody hell! Was she flirting with him?

He reached for the bottle of wine, refilled his glass and tried to remember when he'd last felt this good. To hell with that! When was the last time he'd felt this turned on at the family dinner table?

He tried to think of something else and turned to his left where Bas was sitting. He was chatting across the table to Tiffany and was telling her about some medical-school prank that had involved a jar of eyeballs. What a bloody neat son he was.

And what a bloody fantastic family they were.

He risked a quick look at his wife again and found she was *still* staring at him. 'A toast,' he said, raising his glass and crossing his legs.

They turned and looked at him.

'To my bloody neat family,' he said. 'I feel like the luckiest man alive.'

'Are you drunk?' Tiffany laughed.

'And what if I am?'

'Dad's right,' Barry said, 'we are pretty neat.' He and Tiffany raised their glasses against their father's.

'Cindy?' Derek waited for her to lift her glass. It was suddenly important to him to hear his wife's agreement, as though it would be the seal of approval to all he felt and had achieved over the past years, and more recently the creation of All in the Mind. But as he waited for her response, it occurred to him that what was also important to him was not just his own happiness ... but Cindy's. Had he made Cindy happy?

Never before had Cindy felt herself to be the entire focus of her family. And right now she was. Tiffany, Barry, even Derek, they were all looking at her. She knew, too, what they wanted to hear from her. Ironic, that for what seemed for ever they had each pulled in different directions, each straining against the other.

'I've got something to say,' she said, sensing her family's disappointment. 'Barry, would you go and get me that large brown envelope with the red ribbon I showed you last night? It's at the bottom of the Christmas tree.'

'This what you want?' Barry asked, when he came back into the dining room.

Cindy nodded. 'Thank you.' She took the envelope and pulled at the satin ribbon. 'I'm afraid you'll think this totally self-indulgent. It's a Christmas present to me, from me.' She met her husband's eyes as the ribbon slipped away from the envelope.

'I don't have a problem with that,' Derek said, watching Cindy's fingers playing with the ribbon.

It reminded him of a strip-tease.

'You told me not so long ago that we've all got to find a niche in this life. Well, I've decided that you don't really need me here, Derek, so before it's too late I'm going to—'

'Mum, you're not ... you can't—'

Cindy looked at her daughter. 'What, Tiffany?'

Tiffany turned to her father. 'Dad, don't let her do this. Do something. Say something.'

Derek was silent. All the joy and contentment he'd experienced only moments ago drained out of him. Dejected, he stared down at his dinner plate. He pushed it away. The idea was unthinkable.

Barry reached over to his mother. He touched her hand lightly and smiled. 'I think you'd better finish what you were going to say, Mum, and put them both out of their misery.'

Cindy smiled, embarrassed. 'I've got Barry to thank really,' she said, pulling a brochure out of the envelope in her hands. 'He's convinced me that I should go back to school, so I'm joining what's known as an access course for a year and then I'm going to have a go at studying ... What is it?' she asked, seeing the look first on Tiffany's face and then on Derek's. 'Don't you think I can do it?'

Tiffany laughed. 'Muffin 'ell! 'Course you can do it, Mum.'

Derek slowly got to his feet. He went to Cindy and kissed her.

'What's that for?' she asked, genuinely surprised.

He swallowed hard. 'No reason,' he answered, his hand resting on her shoulder.

'Liar!' shouted Tiffany with a smile. 'You thought Mum was—'

Barry reached across the table and waved a cracker under his sister's nose. 'Pull a cracker with me and shut up, will you, Tiffany?'

'Anything I can do?' Iris asked for the third time from the quiet comfort of the sitting room.

'You've done quite enough already,' Georgia called, from the chaos of the steam-filled kitchen. 'More than enough, in fact,' she muttered under her breath, as she drained off the fat from the meat juices in the roasting tin. Inviting Iris to spend Christmas Day with her and Chloe had turned out to be nothing more than a monumental battle of wills rather than a festive act of good cheer to all men.

The day after she had made a fool of herself in front of Iris she had phoned Hilary, who'd said she was just about to call on Iris to suggest she spend Christmas at The Gables. 'No,' Georgia had said. 'You've got enough on your plate with the dreaded in-laws coming, she can come to me.' Hilary's relief had been almost palpable but when the idea had been put to Iris she had refused point-blank even to consider the invitation.

'I couldn't possibly spend Christmas Day away from the White Cottage.'

By this stage Georgia was determined that if it was the last thing she ever did, it would be to get Iris away from that depressing little sitting room for Christmas Day. By their third phone call Georgia lost her temper with the old woman and shouted down the line, 'I shall never speak to you again if you don't do this one simple thing for me.'

'What a pity,' Iris had responded, 'but so be it. Unless . . .'

'Unless what?' Georgia had asked, recognising a classic negotiating opening.

'Why don't you make more of an occasion of the day? Why not invite Nick Bradshaw as well?'

'No way!' she'd roared, when she'd regained the power of speech.

'I shall see you some other time then. Goodbye.'

'Don't you dare hang up on me, you meddling snake in the grass!'

A long silence had ensued between them until Iris had said craftily, 'So what time will you be expecting me? Perhaps Mr Bradshaw would be kind enough to give me a lift?'

Georgia had conceded the battle on the basis that the war would be won with Nick turning down such a ridiculous invitation. But she had been wrong. Nick had accepted and offered immediately to act as chauffeur for Iris and now here he was back in her house once again and in the sitting room charming the thermal underwear off Iris and quoting Simone Weil to Chloe. God rest ye merry, gentlemen, indeed!

'I've set the table,' Nick announced, standing in the kitchen doorway. 'What else can I do?'

'You can pour some of that wine you brought, and quick, before I pass out.'

He filled two glasses and handed her one. 'Happy Christmas,' he said, chinking his glass against hers, 'and thanks.'

'Oh, no, you don't!' she said, taking a gulp of wine. 'Don't start on all that sincerity stuff about Christmas not being Christmas unless you're amongst friends and family. You're here because it was the only way I could get Madam in there to accept my invitation. Okay?'

'I'm flattered.'

'Yeah, well, don't let it go to your head. Now pass me that dish by your elbow – these sprouts are ready.'

As she stood by the sink and drained the vegetables, one hand holding the saucepan and the other holding the lid firmly against the pan, she felt Nick come up behind her. He kissed her neck lightly just below her ear. She was so taken aback at his sheer nerve that she almost dropped the saucepan. She put it on the draining board and then turned and faced him. 'What's that for?'

'I should think that's obvious.' He handed her the dish for the sprouts.

She stared at it for a moment and then at him. 'So why wait until my hands were full before kissing me?'

He smiled. 'It was the only way I could be sure of you not hitting me.'

Georgia laughed loudly.

'Everything under control out there?' enquired Iris.

'Oh, yes,' answered Georgia, smiling, 'everything's completely under control.'

Lunch was noisy and fun, with Chloe in high spirits insisting on pulling crackers with everybody in turn – crackers that, late last night after coming back from midnight mass, Georgia had doctored by slipping some extra novelties inside the green and gold cylinders of card and crêpe paper. And now Nick at the opposite end of the table was wearing a false nose and Poirot-style moustache, with Chloe on his left sporting a pair of Mr Spock ears, while Iris was laughing and playing with a pair of clockwork false teeth, winding them up and then sending them chattering across the table. 'Perfectly disgusting,' she chortled, reaching out for them to set them off again.

'Come on, Mum,' Chloe said, 'it's your turn now to pull your cracker with me.' She grinned. 'And I know what's inside it.'

'You do, do you? Well, here goes.'

They both tugged hard, but it was Georgia who fell back against her chair the victor. 'What's this?' she asked, when a small silver brooch decorated with tiny sparkling marcasites tumbled out of the cracker and onto the table. She was expecting a plastic bleeding finger with a nail through it, not this exquisite piece of jewellery.

'Let me see,' Chloe said. 'Cool! It's great.'

'It certainly is,' Nick agreed, leaning over to have a closer look. 'Looks expensive as well.'

'But I only put silly things inside the crackers, not anything like—' She looked up and stared round the table, her eyes finally resting on Nick.

He shook his head. 'As much as I'd like to take the credit, it's got nothing to do with me.'

Iris cleared her throat. 'It was me,' she said. 'I put it there.'

'You! But when?'

'Don't look so surprised. I had plenty of time when you and Mr Bradshaw were busy in the kitchen.' She smiled and looked across the table. 'And Chloe was a willing accomplice by keeping a look-out for me.'

'But why?'

Iris swallowed. 'It's a present, and before you start with any of your nonsense I insist that you accept it. It belonged to my mother and I'd very much like you to have the pleasure of wearing—'

'Give over and give me a hug, you silly sentimental old woman.'

With eyes wet with tears they held onto each other tightly. Nick smiled to himself. He knew little about the strange relationship between Georgia and Iris but he could see only too well that they touched each other in a way that forced themselves to acknowledge some part deep within them that they had previously kept from anyone else. He winked at Chloe, hoping that one day she, too, would know that sometimes a risk was worth taking, especially where relationships were concerned.

'Nanna Parker?'

'Yes, Becky dear.'

'Why have you got that black thing with hairs growing out of it on your cheek?'

'Because she's a witch,' muttered Louise, helping herself to a dollop of brandy butter.

'I beg your pardon?'

'I asked why you had that black—'

'Not you, dear,' Barbara said, without looking at her granddaughter. 'Louise, what did you say?'

'I was just saying what a pretty dish this is,' Louise said, making a play of examining the bowl of brandy butter. 'Alfred Meakin, excellent condition.'

Barbara viewed Louise suspiciously with her pale grey eyes. 'I could have sworn I heard you—'

'So why have you, Nanna Parker? You'd look nicer without it.'

Barbara straightened the purple paper hat which she had swapped for David's so that he could have one to match the red tie she'd given him. 'Even if I put myself through the painful experience of having the mole removed,' she said, her voice matter-of-fact, 'I'd still be the same lovely old Nanna Parker, wouldn't I? Outward beauty is nothing compared to inner beauty.'

Louise snorted into her wine.

'I wonder how poor old Mrs Braithwaite is today,' Hilary ventured, desperate to avoid any bloodshed at the table. 'I had invited her to join us for the day but—'

'Yes, David mentioned that to me last night,' Barbara interrupted, seizing her opportunity. 'And I told him how wonderfully thoughtful he was to open his home to a lonely old neighbour on Christmas Day.'

'Apparently the police have caught the man who attacked her,' Louise said to Hilary, ignoring Barbara at the other end of the table. 'He was after Royal Doulton figurines, which is ironic because he wouldn't have found anything like that in Iris's house.'

'I knew a woman who had her entire collection stolen. The burglar came right into—'

'Any more takers for Christmas pudding?' asked Hilary, who couldn't bear the thought of Barbara clacking on a minute longer.

Everyone shook their heads. 'In that case perhaps you'd like to make some coffee, David, to go with our mince pies and cheese?'

'Hilary! There you go again.' Barbara looked triumphantly at Louise. 'You see what I mean? She just never leaves him alone.' Barbara reached out to her son. He looked on as though in numb sufferance; a sad and lonely figure at the head of the table surrounded by bits of spent crackers. Barbara patted his hand. 'You sit there, my love. Hilary and I'll make the coffee.'

'Can we get down now, please?'

'Yes, Philip,' Hilary said quickly. If something awful was about to happen amongst the adults she didn't care for her children to witness her mother wrestling Barbara to the floor.

'Tell you what, I'll make the coffee,' Neville said, helpfully, when the children had gone.

'Barbara always makes the coffee in our house,' Jeffrey asserted as Neville slipped out to the kitchen. 'Damn fine coffee maker she is too.'

'You make her sound like a percolator,' Louise said, acidly.

Barbara made a warning rattling noise in her throat. 'Tell me, Hilary, was that the recipe I gave you last year for the Christmas pudding?'

'No, it's Delia's—'

'I thought not,' Barbara said smugly, pulling the string on the light-up Santa brooch she was wearing.

'Okay, Babs. I've had enough. Are you going to spend the whole of Christmas criticising my daughter's cooking, or is there any hope of you keeping that rictus mouth of yours shut?'

Everyone gaped.

'You have always shown us, Louise dear, what a way with words you have. But you have to admit that leaving the bag of giblets in the plastic bag inside the turkey is certainly a novel way to serve the lunch. I wonder how David has survived Hilary's cooking all these years.'

'Perhaps he won't have to much longer,' Hilary said quietly.

'And what's that supposed to mean?' demanded Jeffrey.

Hilary, who had always been a little scared of her father-in-law, met his hostile gaze. She then looked at David at the opposite end of the table. He stared back at her unseeingly. His indifference was the final straw. She screwed her napkin into a tight ball and threw it at his face.

'Barbara and Jeffrey, there's something you should know,' she began in a determined voice. 'Your son is a cheat, a liar, and he's been having an affair for goodness knows how long. There, what do you say to that?'

Chapter Thirty-eight

Barbara kept her pale insipid eyes on Hilary, never once letting them drop or turn towards her son. She got to her feet slowly, as though she were about to deliver an after-dinner speech.

'If you had been a better wife he wouldn't have needed to look elsewhere. If you had appreciated what a wonderful and special—'

But Barbara's words were lost in the sound of crashing crockery and glass as David, in one single movement of his arm, swept his place setting onto the floor. He looked up at everyone around the table. 'I've lost everything!' he shouted.

'That's what happens when you play with fire,' Hilary screamed back at him, on her feet now and shaking with the awful truth hammering inside her that there was no going back. This was it.

Barbara moved towards David. She put her hand on his shoulder and stared defiantly at Louise. 'You see what you've brought upon your family.'

'Oh, shut up, you old trout,' Louise fired back.

'Shut up, the lot of you,' David roared.

'Well said—'

'Be quiet, Dad, and let me speak.' David looked at Hilary. 'I don't know where you've got this idea that I'm having—'

'You are!' she shouted. 'I know you are. Don't sit there denying it. After what I've been through at least have the decency to own up to what you've been doing.'

He got to his feet and moved towards her but she backed away, tears streaming down her cheeks.

'Hilary, I don't understand—'

'And what about all those nights when you said you were working late or at some Rotary meeting? You weren't there. I know you weren't.'

David's face darkened and he turned from her. 'I can explain—'

'I bet you can. But it's too late because I've had enough. I want a ...' She clenched her fists and willed herself to say the dreaded words. 'I'm leaving you.' There! She had done it. She sobbed even louder and stumbled out of the room crashing into her father, who had been hiding outside in the hall. She grabbed her car keys and slammed the front door after her.

It was dark when she returned. Two hours of driving around on her own in the snow had left her feeling numb with exhaustion. She let herself in. The house was in darkness and behind her there was no sign of her parents' Volvo on the drive or of Barbara and Jeffrey's Rover. She stepped into the hall and reached for the light switch. She started.

David was on the bottom step of the stairs, slouched against the wall with an empty wine bottle next to him. He looked dreadful and as he blinked and tried to shield his eyes from the light he said, 'Hilary, please listen to me. I've got something to tell you.' He moved the empty bottle for her to sit next to him.

She stayed where she was. 'Where is everyone?'

'At your parents', I thought it best.'

'It's a bit late for your consideration,' she said flatly. She turned away from the sight of him and hung her keys on the hook by the telephone.

He stood up and came towards her. 'Hilary, I'm not having a bloody affair.' He took her by the shoulders and turned her round to face him. 'We're in a worse sodding mess than that!'

He sounded drunk and she recoiled from him. 'Mess?' she said angrily. 'What kind of mess?'

He stroked her hair gently, as though suddenly distracted. 'I've been seeing a new firm of accountants these past few months. The business is ... Oh, God, Hilary, I'm so sorry.' He lowered his eyes and moved back towards the stairs and leaned heavily against the banisters.

'David, what is it? Tell me.'

'I've lost it all.' He shrugged his shoulders, then covered his face with his hands, unable to speak.

She stared at him. Was he so drunk that he was saying the first thing that came into his head?

'I'm so sorry, Hilary,' he whispered, coming back to her. He held her hands. 'It's all been such a nightmare ... and the worst part was I couldn't tell you.'

Dear God, he was serious.

'I didn't want you to think I was a failure, that I couldn't ... I just didn't want you to find out, ever.'

'... *Hilary must never find out* ...' She felt sick. What had she done? 'Catherine!' she blurted out, clutching at the last remnants of what she'd thought was the truth. 'You've been seeing her. I know you have.'

He looked confused. 'My secretary? Or my new accountant? They're both called Catherine.'

Hilary swallowed. 'In your sleep ... you've been talking about Catherine ...' Her voice trailed away.

They stood in silence. Then David said, 'We might have to sell the house.'

She looked up at him, remembering his words in the car only yesterday – '*You love this house, don't you?*' 'And Philip ... his school fees?'

He shook his head. 'Hilary, I'm so sorry. It's the recession. I thought I could ride it out, I ...'

In disbelief she shook her head and then slumped down onto the bottom step of the stairs. 'How? How's all this happened? Surely this doesn't happen to people like us?'

He sat next to her. 'Hundreds of small businesses are going to the wall. Rents are so high these days. I thought I could sell the business to a chain. That's what I've been trying to set up with Catherine these past few months. But then they discovered things weren't as good as I'd tried to make out. They lowered their offer by half just this week. They've told me to take it or leave it.'

Hilary raised her eyes. 'But you could stay on as manager, couldn't you?'

He shook his head. 'They want me out.'

'Oh, David. Isn't there anything else we can do?'

'If I refuse this offer, word will get out and I'll be lucky to get even as much from anybody else.'

'Well, then, there's nothing else for it, I'll have to get a job,' she said briskly. 'I'll go back to teaching. I always said I would.'

He stared at her, but she lowered her eyes, unable to bear the suffering in his face.

The phone rang and made them both jump. Hilary went to answer it, glad of the diversion.

'Charlotte! ... Where are you? ... Lake Coniston ... Snowed in, I'm not surprised ... We're all fine ... Well, not really, David's just told me ... No, not an affair, after all ... It's the business, he's lost it ... I've no idea. Yes, well, it does explain things. Yes, I'll give him your love. 'Bye.' She put the receiver down.

'My God,' David said, 'did you really think I was having an affair?'

She walked through to the kitchen and he followed her. 'Hilary, did you?' His words were clearer now, as though he had sobered up.

She chewed her lip and nodded. 'It's always been my worst nightmare, David, that you might leave me ... I ... I just jumped to the conclusion that—'

'But how the hell did you manage to carry on as if nothing was happening?'

'I could ask you the same thing. How did you hide all your problems from me?'

'And Charlotte, did she think—?'

Hilary nodded again.

David rubbed his chin with his hand. 'I thought she was distant, that somehow she didn't approve of me.'

Hilary began to cry. 'Oh, David, I'm so sorry ... I feel dreadful that I thought the worst of you, when all the time you were going through hell and ...'

He smiled. It was the first time in months that she could remember him smiling.

'It'll be all right, won't it?' she said, as she tentatively reached out to his hands. She wasn't sure just what she was really asking him, but she knew that losing the business was nothing compared to what she had thought she was going to lose.

Chapter Thirty-nine

Star Struck was busy with people wanting to escape Boxing Day turkey remains. Tony Farrand himself was resplendent in one of his sparkly seventies game-show-host suits. He greeted Hilary and David at the door in his usual flamboyant manner and stuck out his tongue at Becky and Philip.

'I love Christmas,' he said, as he showed them to a table. He held a chair for Hilary. 'One day of being polite with the miserable old relatives and everybody's here wanting to lap up my scintillating company. What can I get you to drink? Something lavish and expensive – champagne?'

'Yes,' said David, 'why not?'

'But, David,' Hilary said, when Tony went off to fetch a bottle, 'we mustn't, we can't afford—'

'Today we'll eat and drink exactly what we want—'

'And tomorrow?'

He smiled. 'We'll see.'

'Are we going to be really poor?' Becky asked, tipping over the salt pot and making a white trail. She dipped her finger in the salt and then licked it. She looked up when nobody answered her question.

'I don't know,' Hilary replied awkwardly. She didn't know what to say. It was all so bewildering. One minute she had thought David was having an affair and the next he was about to join the ranks of the unemployed.

Last night, after David had explained everything to her, she had telephoned her parents. Her father had been wonderful and had insisted that Barbara and Jeffrey stay the night with them. 'You and David need to be alone,' he'd said. 'The children can stay as well.' But Neville's suggestion had been met with a firm refusal from Barbara. They had set off for Peterborough immediately, saying that neither of them was prepared to stay under the same roof with a woman who had been so intolerably rude. When Hilary had apologised to David for her mother's behaviour he had laughed and said that it was about time somebody had taken his mother in hand.

'We'll be a lot better off than some,' David said, meeting Hilary's gaze.

'Chloe's poor, isn't she, Mummy?'

Hilary thought of Georgia's tiny bungalow and the coldness of the caravan that she and Chloe had lived in and how she herself had viewed it all with an air of 'I couldn't possibly live like this'. But then she thought of the closeness between Georgia and her daughter. 'No,' she said at last, 'no, Chloe isn't poor.'

'You're very quiet,' David said to Philip, who was next to him, his head hidden behind the menu. 'What are you going to eat?'

'I'm not hungry,' Philip answered, his head still lowered.

David leaned into his son. 'You don't have to be that stoic,' he said. 'You can eat exactly what you want tonight.'

Philip looked up. 'Will I have to change schools?'

David frowned and Hilary's heart went out to him. 'Let's not talk about that,' he said.

'Only I'd like to.'

Hilary and David both stared at Philip. 'Why?' they said together.

'No big deal.' He shrugged. 'I just don't like it very much.'

'But you're doing so well,' Hilary said, 'your report was excellent at the end of term and Mr Wells himself told me—'

'I keep being picked on.' Philip's words were almost lost in the noise of a large party at a nearby table suddenly cheering.

'You mean you're being bullied?'

Philip looked up at his father. 'Yes,' he said, his voice still quiet, his face a picture of misery.

'Why didn't you tell us?' Hilary asked, every ounce of her wanting to protect her child. 'You should have told us. We could have helped.'

Philip shrugged again. 'You can't go running home to your parents every time something goes wrong at school.'

Hilary was appalled. All this time she'd been so pre-occupied with her own life that she'd been totally unaware of Philip's problems.

'Mum's right, you should have come to us,' David said, putting his arm round his son. 'But if you're anything like me,' he looked across the table at Hilary, 'or your mother, for that matter, you kept it to yourself because you thought you could sort it out on your own.'

Philip smiled awkwardly. 'So can I leave and go to the High where all my friends are?'

'We'll see.'

'I'll take that as a yes. Thanks, Dad.' His problems over, Philip picked up his menu and said, 'I'll have a pizza with everything on it and a large Coke.'

'I need the loo,' said Becky, who had now written her name in salt on the table in front of her.

'You'd better go with her, Philip,' laughed David.

As Philip shepherded his sister towards the toilets Tony Farrand arrived with their bottle of champagne. When he left, another waiter squeezed past their table with more customers.

Hilary felt a hand on her shoulder. 'Hello, Hilary.' It was Georgia with Chloe. 'Did Santa bring you what you wanted?' she asked, glancing at David.

'He brought a total surprise,' Hilary said. 'How about you?'

'The same, I guess,' she answered with a sly smile on her face. She turned away.

Hilary followed her gaze and saw Nick over by the door pulling off his overcoat and scarf and hanging them up. He came towards them.

'Hello,' he said, seeing Hilary and David. 'Happy Boxing Day.' He turned to Georgia. 'Have they kept our table for us?'

'Yes. You go on ahead with Chloe.' Georgia bent down and whispered in Hilary's ear, 'See you in the loos.'

'That all sounded rather cryptic,' David said, when they were alone.

Hilary laughed and, not giving any explanation, she said, 'I need the loo too. I'll have a pizza like Philip's.'

On her way to the toilets she crossed over with Becky and Philip and a couple of seconds after the door closed behind her it opened and in walked Georgia.

'Come on then, spill the beans.'

Hilary told her everything.

'Bloody hell and the stupid idiot couldn't bring himself to tell you because of his huge ego. It's the same old story, again and again.'

Hilary frowned. 'Don't be so hard on him.'

'I'm sorry. I didn't mean it quite like that. It's just that these poor fools are moulded into being super-beings and can't ever be seen to fail. I blame the parents.'

Hilary thought of David's parents. Georgia was right. She'd never thought of the pressure David must always have been under. All his life Barbara and Jeffrey had built him up to practically god-like status. She wondered now whether David in a strange way would feel relieved that he was no longer Mr Perfect, that no more would he have to stand precariously aloft the pedestal of his mother's making. She suddenly remembered what Nick had said to him the night of the bonfire when he'd asked him if he was frightened of not making the grade in some way. Poor David, no wonder he'd been so aggressive towards Nick. And no wonder there had been that scene at Derek and Cindy's.

'Aren't you going to ask me about Nick?' asked Georgia, looking at Hilary in the mirror.

Hilary smiled at the coincidence of their thoughts and delved into her handbag for her lipstick. 'Go on, then,' she said, through stretched lips. 'What have you been up to?'

'You were right about him being a good kisser. He's bloody good.'

Hilary laughed. 'Hypocrite!'

Georgia smiled. 'And, believe me, this is no meeting of the minds, this is purely physical. When I'm finished with him I'll send him on his way.'

'Will you, I wonder.'

'Oh, no, not you as well. Look, I'm having enough trouble in that department with Iris.'

'So how was Christmas with Iris?'

'Unbelievable! I've never known anyone to cheat so blatantly at Scrabble.'

'I get the feeling she's taken a liking to you,' Hilary said, with a smile. 'I think it's rather sweet.'

'And since when has there been anything wrong in a simple case of mutual respect?'

'I think there's more to it than that.'

'You do, do you?' Georgia replied, looking in the mirror and straightening one of her ear-rings. 'And so what if she's decided I'm the daughter she never had? I don't have a problem with that. In fact, like you just said, it's rather sweet. Now get a move on, I've got a mug out there offering to buy me supper.'

When Hilary returned to David he was alone. He said, 'Tony's taken the children off with Chloe to watch the pizzas being tossed about the kitchen.' He handed her a flute of champagne. 'Do you remember the last time we came here and Philip was asking me how I loved you?'

'Yes. He was talking about different ways of loving, wasn't he?' She reached for a breadstick and broke it in two. She offered David half.

'I can't remember which way round it was,' David continued, 'whether it was *agape* or *eros*, but – and I know I'm not very good at this romantic stuff – but I love you unconditionally, Hilary.' He clinked his glass against hers. 'And I'm sorry for mucking up our lives and spoiling everything.'

She leaned across the table and pressed a finger to his lips. 'Nonsense, I think we were ready for a change anyway.' Then she kissed him, happy in the sure knowledge that whatever the future held, it could never be anything like the hell they'd both just put themselves through.

'You sound like you're already rolling up your sleeves to sort this mess out.'

She squeezed his hand. 'It's easy when you know what you're up against. It's the not knowing that turns your world upside down.'

*

'Boxing Day,' wrote Iris in her diary, sitting by the fire, 'spent quietly and alone listening to the radio. Tomorrow, though, Georgia and Chloe are coming for tea. Must remember to order an extra pint of milk and bake a cake.'

She closed the diary then flipped it open again and re-read her entry for Christmas Day: 'Quite a departure from the norm. Spent the day with Georgia and Chloe and that nice man, Mr Bradshaw. I can't recall a happier time. A change certainly does one good!'

If you have enjoyed *Time for a Change*
don't miss

A Sense of Belonging

Set deep in the Cheshire countryside, Cholmford Hall Mews, a converted 18th-century barn, offers more than an exclusive location in which to live. For Jessica Lloyd, it is the perfect bolthole for recovering from a love affair long past its sell-by date; for Kate Morris it represents a fresh start where her love for recently divorced Alec can flourish; for Amanda Fergusson, whose marriage to Tony is one of straightforward convenience, it is a chance to get the most out of her situation; and for Josh Crawford, his new home offers a place of sanctuary to help him come to terms with his uncertain future. In their different ways, all the newcomers to Cholmford Hall Mews are searching for something – love, peace of mind, a sense of belonging – but will they find rather more than they bargained for?

Price: £6.99
ISBN: 0 75282 607 7

A Breath of Fresh Air

Charlotte Lawrence is consumed by guilt – after months of agonizing she finally asked her workaholic husband for a divorce. That very same day, Peter was killed in a tragic accident. Charlotte's only wish is to return home to the idyllic Cheshire village of her childhood. Ivy Cottage and Hulme Welford are all Charlotte remembered – and her interfering sister Hilary hasn't changed either, organising everything from milk on the doorstep to Alex, the sitting tenant. Hilary is determined that Charlotte should find love anew. And what better place to start than with the eligible bachelor next door?

Price: £6.99
ISBN: 0 75282 713 8

Airs & Graces

Ellen has been living alone in her picturesque, if damp, cottage since her husband left. She married once for love, but is now determined that the second time around it will be for money. And who better than her attractive divorce lawyer, Duncan, who is single and enticingly wealthy? Then into Ellen's life comes Jo-Jo, a young homeless girl several months pregnant, and Matthew, an artist. And as Ellen plans for a future with Duncan, both Jo-Jo and Matthew know that you can't plan love.

Price £6.99

ISBN: 0 75282 646 8

All Orion/Phoenix titles are available at your local bookshop or from the following address:

Littlehampton Book Services
Cash Sales Department L
14 Eldon Way, Lineside Industrial Estate
Littlehampton
West Sussex BN17 7HE

telephone 01903 721596, *facsimile* 01903 730914

Payment can either be made by credit card (Visa and Mastercard accepted) or by sending a cheque or postal order made payable to *Littlehampton Book Services*.

DO NOT SEND CASH OR CURRENCY.

Please add the following to cover postage and packing

UK and BFPO:
£1.50 for the first book, and 50p for each additional book to a maximum of £3.50

Overseas and Eire:
£2.50 for the first book plus £1.00 for the second book and 50p for each additional book ordered

----

BLOCK CAPITALS PLEASE

name of cardholder ....

address of cardholder ....

....

....

....

postcode ....

delivery address
(if different from cardholder)

....

....

....

....

postcode ....

☐ I enclose my remittance for £...............................

☐ please debit my Mastercard/Visa (delete as appropriate)

card number ☐☐☐☐☐☐☐☐☐☐☐☐☐☐☐☐

expiry date ☐☐☐☐

signature ....

prices and availability are subject to change without notice